Mystical Greenwood

Book I of the trilogy *One with Nature*
Trilogy

Andrew McDowell

To Larry

Andrew McDowell

Mystical Greenwood

Book I of the trilogy *One with Nature Trilogy*

Andrew McDowell

Mockingbird Lane Press

Mystical Greenwood
Copyright © 2018 Andrew McDowell

This is a work of fiction. While some names, characters, places, and incidents are the product of the author's imagination, some are accurate, but are used to further the story. The publisher does not have any control over and does not assume any responsibility for author or third-party websites or their content.

Mockingbird Lane Press—Maynard, Arkansas

ISBN: 978-1-64136-282-5

Library of Congress Number in publication data

0 9 8 7 6 5 4 3 2 1

www.mockingbirdlanepress.com

Cover art: Jamie Johnson

To Mmes. Hopkins, Gibson, and Becker, who recognized my budding passion and encouraged me to pursue it.

Acknowledgements

Many thanks to Dad and Uncle Chris for being my first readers, John DeDakis for his insightful critique, and Lee Chapman for the wonderful music he composed for this novel's feature songs. Special thanks to Mockingbird Lane Press for believing in my book, Regina Riney for her invaluable editing, and Jamie Johnson for her excellent cover art.

Thank you to my fellow writers from St. Mary's College and the Maryland Writers' Association for showing me I'm not alone in my efforts. To my family thank you for always being there with your love and support.

Prologue

*S*ee how peaceful it is here. Don't think. Just listen, feel, and observe. Those had been her words as they walked deeper into the greenwood.

Now that they had arrived at their destination, to his surprise it proved far easier than he might've anticipated. A strange, warm feeling overcame him. It seemed familiar to him somehow, but he couldn't really explain why. Taking steady breaths, in that moment, all his earlier thoughts faded away.

The greenwood abounded with broad oaks, tall pines, and old ash trees. Golden sunlight trickled through many branches. Their leaves rustled in a gentle breeze. A woodpecker's tapping and other birds' voices filled the air. Water could be heard flowing down the nearby stream nearby. Wildflowers adorned the forest floor. High above the treetops, white clouds passed across a blue sky.

He blinked a few times. "You were right. Thank you."

"I knew you would be touched by the ways of the woodland," she smiled. "Imagine: a squirrel may be burying an acorn someplace for later. Perhaps a family of deer is resting in the shade, as we are."

He remembered why they came. "Where is she?"

"She shall be here, my young friend. I promise. You should also witness Nature's glory at dusk. The heavens present an array of colors. Only yesterday evening, while listening to the owls and the crickets, I beheld a rich pink, streaked with deep violet! Later, beautiful stars…"

I

She paused once she saw his posture stoop. He gazed at his feet.

"Are you all right?" she asked.

"Oh, aye I'm fine, thank you," he replied, rubbing his hand through his hair.

"Are you sure? You know you can tell me."

"Well, it's just I—I remembered a dream I had; an – awful dream."

"Tell me about it. You'll feel better later."

Nodding, he recounted his dream about another forest in midsummer, long after night fell. In the dream, a hooded figure emerged between the trees, swathed in a sweeping dark cloak. He grasped a black staff in one of his gloved hands. It was crowned by the iron model of three lizard-like claws clutching a smooth blood-red stone. He halted and raised this same staff as high as his arm permitted. That stone gleamed, as if a potent fire burned inside it.

Suddenly, the immediate area burst into flames. The fire grew wider, devouring every tree and plant in its path. Terrified animals fled for their lives. Most did not escape. This shadowy figure however never caught fire. Though his eyes now blazed red, his face remained hidden beneath his hood. He thrust his staff into the earth, whereupon its jewel emitted a beam of scarlet light. It collided with a similar emerald-colored beam, which came out of the darkness. A thunderous explosion penetrated the air. Everything went white.

"And I awoke, sweating," he concluded. He noticed she appeared troubled, having placed her hand to her chest and slightly bending her neck.

"What's wrong?" he inquired, leaning in closer.

Lowering her hand, she lifted her eyes. "When did you

have this dream?"

"Two nights I think after I first met you and..."

A stomping noise came from behind them. They both slowly turned. His skin tingled.

"...her."

Chapter 1

Dermot stepped into the sun, holding a wooden bucket. He shut his eyes instantly, raising his free hand above them. For no light existed inside the forge save from the fire and heated iron. Once his eyes had partially attuned themselves, he was ready to continue on.

"Don't take too long!" called Pádraig, his father.

"I won't, Da!" Dermot said without looking back. The lad made his way to the well in Emerin's square with the bucket swinging back and forth in his hand. He wore a light woolen shirt with a vest, woolen trousers, laced-up napped leather boots, and a sooty leather apron.

Not yet sixteen years of age, Dermot was almost his father's height, with bright green eyes, rich brown hair, a boyish face, and a rounded nose and ears. Nine years as his father's apprentice had awarded him strong shoulders and steady hands. Pádraig, the village smith, earned his trade crafting and repairing not only horseshoes and common tools, but also armor and swords for the local chieftain and his soldiers.

As he lowered the bucket into the well's black abyss, Dermot recalled several tales that he'd heard about Denú in past years during the annual festivals in years past, of her vast forests, rocky rolling hills, great mountains, and rugged shores overlooking the Llyrean Sea. Yet Emerin was all he knew of his homeland. It was a small village in Harlíeo, a county within the realm's northern province of Núinna. Like almost every other villager, he had never set

foot beyond its boundaries.

I cannot wait for the Midsummer festival, he thought. It will be here soon.

He sighed when the bucket finally reached the water. He was wiping his sweaty forehead when he froze. Having heard the familiar cry of a bird of prey, he presumed the chieftain was out hunting again. Gazing toward the hills in the distance, he saw only the chieftain's bastion. Positioned on the highest of the local hills, it had been erected out of stone blocks, coated in whitewash. Atop every tower fluttered a large blue banner. Dermot knew they each depicted a white stag, the chieftain's emblem.

It must've come from a wild bird, he thought. Yet, it sounded unusually loud.

Bringing the now-filled bucket up, Dermot observed the fields, where most villagers had been toiling since morning. Crops had long since replaced the furrows of springtide, excepting those fields left fallow this season. Knowing that his mother and brother were out there somewhere, he was grateful not to be with them, to have to endure the sun, rain, and his mother's tongue all day long.

Her voice echoed in his mind from childhood. *Do your work, boy! You will learn your place! Do as you're told!*

He shook his head, not wishing to think of her any further. His task done, he prepared to leave. That same cry resonated even louder. Dermot noticed several villagers nearby pause and gasp, some with their hands over their mouths, all gazing skyward. When he leaned his own head back, what he saw made him grow stiff. His heart almost skipped a beat as the dark shape soaring

overhead at last came into full view.

"Mercy of the heavens!" he gasped. "Can this really be happening?"

There, soaring amongst the clouds, was a giant creature the likes of which Dermot had never seen, truly magnificent to behold. The head, forelimbs, and wings resembled an eagle, except for the pointy ears. The hindquarters and tail however were akin to a feline. What a piercing yellow were those large eyes! The front feet and beak were yellow too. This creature boasted sharp black claws, a black-tipped beak, and a wingspan greater than three fully-fledged warhorses.

The creature, evidently very powerful, swooped close to the cottages. Dermot ducked, dropping the bucket and shielding himself with his arms. Villagers screamed, running in different directions. Horses, if they didn't run, instead reared upon their hind legs, all neighing. Other livestock, from hogs to chickens, to cattle, goats, and sheep, likewise scurried about, creating even more noise and confusion.

After the creature's enormous shadow passed overhead, Dermot cautiously lowered his arms. He stood up, watching the majestic animal ascend again but harm nobody. Thick, reddish-brown fur and feathers coated the body, gleaming in the golden sunshine. The wingtips were black, streaked with white. The throat and belly were entirely white. This animal kept all four limbs tucked tight underneath, protecting the belly. With another descent toward the fields, the forelimbs extended out, the talons outspread and ready for grasping.

By this time, Pádraig, a tall, well-built man, had emerged from his forge with a small hammer in his hand.

"Dermot!" he cried upon seeing the creature for himself. "Get back inside!"

But Dermot didn't budge. He hadn't even heard his father. His eyes tracked the creature's every move. He was oblivious to everything around him, even forgetting about the bucket.

About to seize a running cow, the predator was forced to give up the hunt and ascend. Arrows flew out of nowhere. Dermot realized archers were firing them from the manor's battlements. Attempting to evade them, the creature twirled down near where the youth stood.

Dermot still didn't move, even as a steed came running past at full speed. Pádraig tried to reach his son. Terrified villagers and loose animals unfortunately kept getting in his path.

"Dermot, no!" Padraig yelled.

The giant creature neared Dermot and began to turn upward again. The boy raised his arms and shut his eyes. He felt something immense and furry strike him, around which he compulsively wrapped his arms.

The next thing he knew, he found himself clinging for dear life onto the creature's giant furry limb, high above the village and fields.

"Help me!" he screamed, "Please someone help!"

Alas, no one did. No one could. His legs swayed about as the creature curved through the air, squawking uncomfortably at his presence. Even though he gripped as tight as he could, his hands were sweating and he knew he couldn't hold on for much longer. Whenever the creature made another sudden turn, he screeched, "Ahh!"

I cannot believe this is happening to me, he thought.

To his horror, he soon realized the manor's bowmen

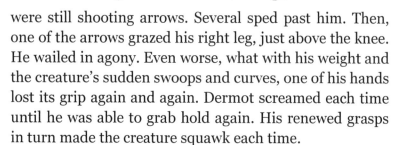

were still shooting arrows. Several sped past him. Then, one of the arrows grazed his right leg, just above the knee. He wailed in agony. Even worse, what with his weight and the creature's sudden swoops and curves, one of his hands lost its grip again and again. Dermot screamed each time until he was able to grab hold again. His renewed grasps in turn made the creature squawk each time.

Looking up, his eyes met those of the creature. Although his breaths were rasped, Dermot found his voice. "Listen, I don't want to be up here anymore than you do, all right? So please, let me down! Please!"

The winged predator dived. Dermot shut his eyes.

Reopening his eyes after a moment, he realized the creature was gliding above the fields, close enough for him to let go and drop down. He couldn't believe it. Hearing another squawk, Dermot looked up, and realized the animal was staring back at him. Somehow, he knew this creature understood him.

"All right, all right, I'm ready!"

The creature squawked again. Dermot released his grip. He hit the ground hard, tumbling until at last, still in a state of shock, he stopped. He looked at his leg. A river of fresh blood flowed from his injury through the hole in his trousers. He pressed his hands down on it, staining them red.

Dermot struggled to stand upright. He kept one hand pressed on his injury. He gazed at the magnificent animal again, his mouth agape.

Then, hearing human voices roar, combined with the sound of running horses, he caught sight of a large group of soldiers led by the chieftain himself, charging from the manor with swords and spears. More arrows took flight as

this majestic animal flew toward the nearby Forest of Úaene.

"No!" Dermot shouted. Out of an impulse he couldn't comprehend, he gave chase. He limped all the way, keeping one hand on his leg. With more blood lost and his body sore, he grew short of breath. Still, he pressed onward. He was so focused on the creature he paid no attention to where he was headed.

Dermot saw the great animal plunge, disappearing beneath Úaene's treetops. One moment he gazed skyward, the next his foot came down in midair and he found himself tumbling downhill, crashing into a row of colossal pine tree at the bottom of the incline.

In shock, he rolled onto his back with his mouth wide open. He was angry with himself. How could he have been so foolish? As he lay moaning, he beheld a dark silhouette leaning over him. He attempted to speak, but no words escaped his lips. The figure knelt down, whispering in a deep, feminine voice, "Hush."

Her hand moved slowly over Dermot's face. The tone of her voice soothed him, and he grew calmer. Blackness claimed him.

**

The faint yet brief touch of something furry made Dermot's cheek twitch. A strong smell of herbs hung in the air. Both his eyes watered when he tried to open them.

Groaning, he managed to keep his eyes open. He saw giant oaks looming over him, not the pine he remembered crashing into.

Wriggling like a worm, he discovered he lay not on

the ground but a bed out in the open. Moreover, he was barefoot, shirtless, his apron missing, and his trousers rolled above his knees.

Feeling uneasy, he lifted his arm. To his surprise, he felt the distinguishable grain of rough, wooden planks. Moving his head, he realized he was lying next to a cottage. Its curved walls were close-jointed, and oaken like the two old trees between which the cottage had been built. A squirrel watched him from halfway up the trunk of one of those trees. Dermot now understood where that furry touch came from.

His stomach convulsed as his breaths grew raspy. His head throbbed. *Why is there a cottage out here in Úaene? How deep within the forest am I? Who lives here?*

He turned his head, only to discover something his imagination had not envisaged: a woman wearing a leafy green robe and white apron, tending a garden populated by scores of vibrant-colored flowers, fruits, vegetables, as well as other plants unfamiliar to him. He couldn't see her face, as she had her back to him. Her long hair was a light blonde, almost white, implying she was of an elderly age. It dropped past her shoulders, and had little leaves and flower petals caught in it. She bore a large red blossom above one ear.

Dermot struggled to sit upright. Managing to raise his head, he gawped. He realized not only was his chest covered with small cuts and scrapes, but his left leg had been badly bruised. As for his right leg, he found some sort of cloth bandage already wrapped around the wound, with something inside it. He must have been washed too, for his skin was remarkably cleaner than it had been earlier. Unfortunately, his body hurt so much he flopped

back down with a groan.

"Please," she whispered in that same gentle voice he'd heard earlier. "You need rest."

He was too petrified to speak. She separated the roots from a plant appearing to have long since been pulled out of the earth. This particular plant had tiny, bell-shaped purple flowers, broad leaves, and the roots reminded him of those belonging to the turnips in his mother's garden. Looking towards this woman's garden, he didn't see that particular plant growing at all.

She crushed those roots well using a mortar and pestle. For the first time, Dermot noticed a circular stone-enclosed hearth and above it, a small copper kettle hung from a wooden tripod. The lady removed the kettle and poured hot water onto the roots, mixing them well. All the while she spoke softly. He could not figure out what her exact words were.

After mixing the herbs, she waved her hand gently over them. Dermot thought for a minute he saw a bright blue light emanting from her palm. It soon disappeared however, making him wonder if his mind was still so foggy it might be playing tricks on him.

Chapter 2

The lady brought the roots and cloth straps back to Dermot. Seeing her face for the first time, he found himself taken by her natural beauty. She had brilliant green eyes and a petite nose. Most remarkable of all, her skin was pale, smooth, and clean as a young maiden's, despite the apparent age in her hair. Feelings of deep wisdom, care, and understanding were conveyed within her eyes, which could only have come from many years of life. A thin silver headband crowned her brow. Even the aroma of fresh wildflowers followed her.

"Wha—where—where am I?" he asked. The lady's wide smile was so warm he felt mostly at ease. Still, he could not shake off the worry and fear inside him.

"Someplace safe," she said.

"Ho – how did I get here?"

"I brought you here from where you fell. You've been unconscious for nearly an hour. It was fortunate your leg was grazed and not struck directly. But you still lost a great deal of blood."

Dermot couldn't believe it. Had he really been out for that long? He shivered, gasping for air. "Why—why wasn't I killed? I—I was..."

The lady placed her hand gently on his shoulder. "Please, child, be still, so these herbs may perform their magic."

He kept his eyes on her as she carefully tied the pieces of cloth with the roots between them. She squeezed the

bandages tighter, letting out water, before wrapping them around his left leg. He cringed at the heat radiating up his calf and thigh. Regardless, he was still too weak to resist.

"Shush," she whispered, her hand touching his cheek.

"Wha—what're you doing to me?" Dermot asked.

"This is a poultice prepared with blackwort, or knitbone, for your bruises. I cleansed the cuts you suffered from your fall with a skin wash made from the rosin rose. The arrow wound I cleansed too and dressed forthwith with a poultice of the thousand-leaf flower, which halted the bleeding."

"So—you're a healer?"

"I am proficient in wortcunning, the ancient art of herbal lore."

"Wortcunning," Dermot said. "By what name are you known?"

"To those closest to me, I am Saershe."

"Saershe," he said. "My name's Dermot. It's nice to meet you."

"It's a pleasure to meet you too, Dermot."

"Did—did you—wash me too?"

"With fresh water from the stream, yes. Cleanliness is vital for proper healing."

"Oh," Dermot said. "Well, thank you, madam."

"You're quite welcome. And you needn't call me madam. Saershe will do."

"Sorry, madam, I mean, Saershe. Forgive me."

She smiled. "It's all right, my young friend."

"Wha—what was that creature? Did you see...?"

"I did see," she said calmly. "What you saw today was a gryphon from the east."

He lifted his head. "What? Are you sure?"

"Yes. What do you know of them?"

"Only what I've heard in tales and legends. They are reputed to be a powerful, majestic breed. Few folks are capable of even approaching them. Their feathers and claws are said to be imbued with magical properties. You know, like a unicorn's horn or dragon fire. But, they haven't been seen in Denú for years! Why would one appear now, and here, of all places in the kingdom?"

"They are indeed powerful, and majestic," she said. "There was a time when gryphons thrived in these parts, coming down from the Denuan Spine. These days, to encounter one in Denú is a true miracle. They never leave the mountains anymore, more's the pity. The gryphon you saw today is one of the few remaining of her noble tribe."

"Her?" he said. "Ho—how do you know that gryphon was a she?"

"Female gryphons are far superior in size and prowess compared to their male counterparts. You will find it a trait common among many wild animals, for females must be so, in order that they may protect their children."

"Wait, you—have you seen them before? What're they like? Please tell me! How old do they grow? How big? How powerful are they?"

"Please, Dermot," Saershe said, resting her hand on his shoulder. "You mustn't excite yourself, not in the condition you're in."

Dermot let his head drop. "Of course, forgive me."

"It's all right. Now come, let's get you up."

She slid her hand beneath his neck. He found her touch gentle and soothing. With her assistance, he managed to sit upright, uttering another groan. He still

felt quite weak, not to mention in agonizing pain.

"Here, drink this. You must be thirsty," Saershe said, handing him a ceramic cup that sat on a small table near the bed. Dermot stared at the water within it then back to her. When she nodded, he raised the cup to his lips and drank nonstop. Never had cool water tasted so good to him, so refreshing. Some of it trickled onto his cheeks and throat.

He placed the cup on the table and wiped his face, taking a deep breath. He asked, "Forgive me, but how is it I've never even seen you before? I mean, I've played in this wood many times as a child. Yet I had no idea you lived here, so close to Emerin."

"I prefer the peace and harmony of the forest," Saershe said. "The trees and the wild plants and animals content me. Do you not cherish the greenwood?"

He didn't have an answer.

She's a strange lady, he thought to himself. He caught sight of a large, dark green stone dangling from a thin, silver chain around her neck. She wore a silver bracelet with an engraved pattern of entwined knots around her right wrist. A plain gold ring adorned her left forefinger.

"You may not have seen me, but when I saw your face, I knew I'd seen you many times before, the last of which was years ago," Saershe said.

He bit his lip. "You—you have?"

"I never forget a face. I've seen you at play many times in this forest, both alone and with other lads from the village. You climbed trees, and you chased after butterflies and fireflies. Often you stayed out so late your parents and others came searching for you on many a dusk."

Dermot glanced away, blinking rapidly. He felt rather disturbed she had watched him as a child, and recalled as much so vividly. It made him twinge uncomfortably. At the same time, she had conjured up memories of his own that he hadn't thought about for many years.

When he was younger, he'd been a troublemaker and rebel. He received one scolding after another from his tyrannical mother, and taunts by his brother, who enjoyed every one of them. Dermot had never meant any harm in his mischief, but only his father seemed to understand, even if he didn't always necessarily approve.

"Are you all right?" Saershe asked.

"Aye, I'm fine, thank you. So, um. Saershe, do you live out here alone?"

"Nay," uttered a voice.

A youth about Dermot's age, perhaps a year older, appeared at Saershe's side. He was somewhat taller and thinner than Dermot, with golden blond hair and watery blue eyes.

"I thought I asked you to wait inside," Saershe said to the boy.

"Forgive me, Grandma," an air of curiosity in his voice. "I had to come see if our guest is faring any better."

"In that case, Dermot, permit me to introduce my grandson, Ruairí," Saershe said.

"It's a pleasure to meet you, Dermot." Ruairí, got down on his knees to look more directly into his face. His attire essentially matched Dermot's, but lacked an apron.

"And you," Dermot said.

"Grandma says you're a smith's apprentice. What's it like, working with iron?"

"Please, Ruairí," Saershe said. "He's had a trying

afternoon."

Dermot was surprised Ruairí would ask such a question, but even more unsettled Saershe knew of his apprenticeship. So he asked her how she knew.

"When I found you, you were covered in soot, and you were wearing an apron as well," she said. "Those signs, and your age, indicated as much to me."

"Oh," nodded Dermot feebly. "I see."

"You will find, my young friend, that keen and close observation enable one to unearth a great many truths about others, as well as their surroundings," Saershe said.

"Forgive me, Dermot," Ruairí said. "I didn't mean to swamp you."

"It's all right, Ruairí," Dermot said. "Well, my father is proud of his work. But me, well I—it's not that I'm dissatisfied with it. I'm just not sure it's what I was truly meant for."

"And what is it you believe you were meant for?" Saershe asked.

"I—I honestly don't know," he was forced to admit. "I've wished for it to be something significant; something worthwhile. I spent all my childhood pretending I was away on adventures. I wanted to see the land, not spend my whole life in Emerin. I kept on dreaming even after my friends no longer played. Perhaps I hoped going on adventures might help me find my purpose. But my mother's never understood, nor my brother. Ma cares nothing for what I've felt or wanted. She never has. And my brother, oh that..."

Dermot averted his face. His stomach grew heavy.

"I've never opened myself up so freely to anyone, he thought. Well, I have, but certainly not like this Oh dear,

why did I say so much? This is not good.

"I believe in doing what you love, Dermot," Saershe said. "One's true calling resides with their truest passion, Dermot. Never lose sight of, or relinquish, your dreams and wishes, or relinguish them, but you ought to learn to appreciate your mother's feelings too. Then she can respect yours. If you do, you may find they're not what you assumed."

She slowly stood, keeping her eyes on Dermot. She said, "Forget not your deep roots."

Before he could respond, Saershe walked around the cottage corner. All he could do was watch until she disappeared from sight.

"I want to travel the land myself one day," Ruairí said once she was gone. "I hope to visit all the great woodlands of Denú, and explore them as I have Úaene."

"Have you lived here all your life, Ruairí?" Dermot asked, rubbing the back of his neck.

"Yes, ever since I can remember. From the time I was little, Grandma brought me out with her into the midst of Úaene. Together we studied and mingled with trees, plants, and animals. I brought home wildflowers, insects, bird nests, feathers, and eggshells. I still do, for I still accompany Grandma. 'There is always something new to discover within Nature,' she has often told me. She would know of course, having herself visited all the great forests of Denú."

Dermot's head jerked up. "She—she has?"

"Indeed, many times throughout her life. She cherishes each moment she has spent in the company of every tree and wild animal she's met. Even here, whether she took me to new parts of the forest or revisited old

ones, to her they were all familiar to her."

Ruairí's words amazed Dermot.

Saershe soon returned with his shirt, apron, and boots, all of which had been cleaned. Ruairí stood when he saw her.

"Here you are, Dermot," Saershe said, placing his clothes beside the bed.

Dermot stared at the clean garments, sighing. "What a day."

"Indeed. Now listen, Dermot. Your legs may ache for a few days more. I advise you to be careful not to do anything too strenuous during that time. I recommend you remove the poultices after a few days. The thousand-leaf could be harmful to your skin if worn for longer."

"Thank you, Saershe, but I better head home now," Dermot said in a shaky voice. "Da must be worried. And I'll be in enough trouble with Ma as it is."

Though he tried to stand, the pain in his legs combined with his weakness forced him to sit back down, groaning bitterly. Saershe gently placed her hand on his shoulder when he was about to attempt to stand a second time.

"You shall be home soon," she said. "But for now, you must rest again."

"Wha...?"

Saershe waved her hand in front of his face, whispering words he did not understand. He became dizzy. So dizzy, what little bodily strength he had evaporated like morning dew. He would have fallen, had Saershe not caught him. With Ruairí's help, she lay him back down on the bed. He wanted to resist, but he was too weak to move. He opened his mouth to ask Saershe what

she was doing, but his voice had disappeared too. He was certain they were about to do something terrible. If only he could beg for mercy, he would.

Dermot could resist no longer. He fell fast asleep.

Chapter 3

Opening his eyes, Dermot discovered he lay not upon the bed but thick grass. He muttered Saershe's name, then Ruairí's. Only the voices of the birds responded. He pushed himself upright with a groan.

Gazing around, he realized he was surrounded by trees, tall and old, with bark gnarled and straight, winding branches, and leaves of various shapes in multiple shades of green. But Saershe, Ruairí, and their cottage were nowhere in sight. Furthermore, he was fully clothed again, apron and all.

"How'd I get here?" he asked aloud. He moved his hands slowly across his shirt and trousers. Underneath, he could distinctly feel the injuries to his chest and the poultices wrapped around his legs. He could see one through the hole in his trousers.

He glimpsed down to his right side, where, to his surprise, there lay a hiking stave with a leather wristband lay. He wondered if it Saershe left it for him.

Regardless, he struggled to stand. However, he noticed his pain was not as excruciating as earlier, and he felt less weak. Once on his feet, leaning against the stave, he wrapped its band around his wrist. He searched around, seeing no trace of Saershe or Ruairí. Despite hearing a bird chirping overhead, he didn't look up.

I'll never forget her, or the gryphon. Forgetting them is impossible. He still couldn't believe he had seen such a creature. The mystery lingered as to why a gryphon would

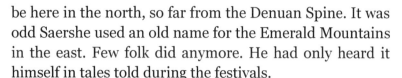

be here in the north, so far from the Denuan Spine. It was odd Saershe used an old name for the Emerald Mountains in the east. Few folk did anymore. He had only heard it himself in tales told during the festivals.

New thoughts dawned on him. How will I explain all this once I make it home? What am I going to say? Oh dear, I'm going to be drowned with questions by the villagers and the chieftain's men. What about Saershe and Ruairi? What will happen to them?

Of course he couldn't lead anyone to their cottage, but they might search the forest and find them anyway. His eyes fell on the hiking stave. He knew what he felt in his bones he must do, though he couldn't completely explain why. Even if it meant the journey home would be more strenuous, he decided, so be it.

Raising the stave, he painfully hurled it into the air. To his surprise, it dived straight down among the bushes like rain without a wind. A moment later, he walked the other way, his posture slumped.

He almost tripped, but he managed to save himself by retaining his balance with his arms.

Bracing one hand against an old oak's trunk, he realized he had no idea where he was headed, or which way he needed to go. He could not even guess how long he'd ambled amidst these trees. He placed his other hand to his chest.

He remembered something Saershe had said about keen observation. Then, he heard a pack of dogs barking, followed by the sound of running steeds. He spun and stood upright to see the sheriff, accompanied by soldiers on horseback along with members of the watch, who were on foot. They carried an array of weapons, including

swords, longbows, spears, clubs, battle-axes, and shields. They all wore thick leather jerkins, but only the soldiers had on tunics of iron mail underneath. Every jerkin bore the chieftain's emblem.

"Oh dear," Dermot said. "I'm done for."

He knew the sheriff of old, and was not at all pleased to see him. He found himself circled by these men. The sheriff, astride a black horse, trotted up. He wore a dark blue cloak and a sword sheathed in a scabbard of fine leather.

I can remember when Da and I made that sword, Dermot thought. The sheriff taunted him regardless. Only his father kept him from talking back to the man.

"Well, well, well," the sheriff sneered. "Look who we have here. Back from the dead, I see."

Dermot didn't speak. He glared at the sheriff, his lips turned down. *It's been nine years since I was a rebellious troublemaker,* he thought, *and the sheriff still sees me for who I was then.*

"Dermot," the sheriff said, "the beast captured you earlier today. You were given up for lost, and yet here we find you, alive and well. Your parents will be relieved."

She didn't capture me. I wouldn't say well *either.*

"Tell us where the beast went, and your family will be well rewarded."

"I don't know where the creature is," Dermot said.

"You don't know?"

"No. I don't know. Need I say so again?"

The sheriff straightened his back. His eyes narrowed and his mouth stiffened.

Dermot knew the man was offended, but he didn't regret his words. He kept his chin high.

"Well then, perhaps your memory needs a little refreshing."

The sheriff spoke again. "Well then, perhaps your memory needs a little refreshing."

He motioned with two fingers. Two of his men on foot came up behind Dermot and grabbed his arms. He fought to shake them off, having regained some of his vigor during his walk.

"What're you doing?" he cried, feeling the blood rush to his face. "Unhand me, you brutes!"

They ignored him. A third man came up and swung a small, heavy club hard into his chest. Grunting, Dermot lost the effort. They dragged him away by his arms.

Leaving the forest behind, they trudged uphill. Dermot thought he recognized the spot where he fell as they passed it. Soon they reached the top.

How deep in the woods was I? I still don't know where precisely Saershe dwells. At first, it all felt too extraordinary. Then, he remembered he had never ventured far beyond the forest's border as a child. There was so much more of Úaene he had never seen.

I suppose – it isn't impossible.

Dermot raised his head. Nobody was out in the fields, now that the hour had grown late. Beyond the fields was the common, where sheep and other livestock grazed. He observed the village's place of worship, where their local sagart led them in prayers and rituals, situated beside the burial ground with its great yew and magnificent chestnut tree. The lad recalled sometimes climbing and stealing nuts as a child when they were in season. The sheriff had told him self-amusingly that he could watch while others picked the nuts, for he could view that tree from the lock-

up's window.

Between the manor and burial ground, stray livestock had been confined to the pound. The payment for reclaiming them was often steep. Dermot gazed on the green, an area on a smaller hill where festivals, including the impending Midsummer celebration, were hosted. He and his friends used to play ball there, stage mock battles using sticks as swords, pretending they were great warriors of old.

As they passed through the village, Dermot felt the eyes of the villagers on him, though none dared approach the soldiers. He could even hear some of the villagers whispering to one another. "Look. Is that...? It can't be. Oh, my goodness! Is that Dermot? Is that Pádraig's son? Dermot is alive? He's alive! I don't believe it. It cannot be. No, that's impossible."

They brought him to the lock-up, a small stone structure with a heavy wooden door and one tiny window with iron bars. Dermot again tried to break free of the watchmen's grasp. His face was flushed. For all his strength, they hurled him inside. He fell on his hip, causing him to cry out. They slammed the door as he scrambled toward it. Its iron hinges creaked, followed by a single, shrill click.

"It's been a while since you were in here last, hasn't it, laddie?" the sheriff said. "Maybe it will do you good, and refresh your memory."

"I've done nothing wrong! You can't do this! Let me out of here! Let me out!" Dermot said, banging the door several times. He eventually stopped, for his outburst tired him.

Once the men's footsteps faded away, there was

silence. At that moment, Dermot understood he could do no more. He crawled to the opposite side of the door and leaned back against the circular stone wall.

He remembered being thrown in here a number of times in the past, like when he talked back to a soldier whilst playing ball. He didn't mean to upset him. The ball only rolled too far the wrong way. He tried to apologize, but it was to no avail. That soldier told Dermot he would never be worth anything, and called him a filthy brat. Dermot felt then, as now, he did what he had to do.

How many years it has been since then, he thought.

Dermot pondered over the day's events again. He could not understand it. Why did the gryphon let him go? She hadn't been distracted, or forced to. There was something about her, something in her eyes that conveyed compassion, and mercy. He felt guilty for not thanking her, strange as it sounded. Saershe had healed him, asking for no favor or reward, even if she did take him and leave him to be found by the sheriff. Yet he didn't hate her for it. He could make no sense of it all. He pressed his palms against his temples.

His contemplating faded, replaced by fear, and a concern for Saershe, Ruairí, and even the gryphon. What if they were discovered? Could they already have been? Would they be all right? He knew the gryphon wouldn't. The soldiers would slay her on sight if they got the chance. He dreaded the thought of it.

Sighing, he shook his head. He tried to sing a song he liked, *Beyond the Forest,* to pass the time and distract his mind. Unfortunately he remembered but a few words, which he kept on repeating as a result: *Beyond the forest this path goes...ever so deep...for when a gentle breeze*

blows...the great mighty trees...

He gave up trying to sing it. He fell quiet after simply humming it. He moved to the window, where he saw children hurrying home. The sun was setting. No curious villagers came near him, and he thought that strange. He figured they probably decided he was just an ordinary troublemaker caught for theft.

Well, better that than they had come peering, he thought.

He slunk back into the corner, closing his eyes and sighing again. He reopened them when he heard the door's iron hinges creaking again.

He was surprised. He was being released already? It had been less than an hour.

"All right, come out o' there, you scalawag," grumbled a scruffy voice he recognized as belonging to the sergeant of the watch. He was the sheriff'sdirect subordinate and almost as equally hateful.

Although hesitant, Dermot stretched his arms and back, groaning. He stayed crouched until he stepped out. A large, strong hand grabbed his arm. He then stood upright. Peering over his elbow, his throat dried out.

Pádraig didn't speak. He stared at his son with a combination of disappointment and relief. Then he hugged him tight. He whispered in Dermot's ear. "I'm so glad you're safe."

The sergeant, a beefy man with a thick beard, clasped a shillelagh, a heavy knotted club, made of thorn wood. A large double-edged dagger hung from his belt as did a sheathed sword. Four watchmen stood behind him. Each grasped a shillelagh almost their height.

He was the sheriff's direct subordinate.

"Try keeping a more vigilant eye o'er your firstborn in the future Pádraig," the sergeant said. "The sheriff may wish to question him further."

"Thank you," Pádraig said. "Now if you'll pardon us, we will go home."

"Da, please!" begged Dermot. "Let me explain!"

"Save your breath, son," Pádraig said. "Your mother has been worried to death."

The smith led him away by the arm, his grip firm. Villagers stared at Dermot like before, but none approached him. Some children tried, but were held back by their elders. It all brought Dermot more discomfort. He hung his head most of the way. He almost shut his eyes as he heard their whispering again: "Look! It *is* him! It's Dermot. He's alive! It's a miracle!"

Soon they reached home. Home for them was a cottage like any other within the village, apart from Pádraig's extended forge. Rounded walls were built from a durable wooden frame and filled in using a mixture of mud and straw that had been dried in the sun's heat. Smoke billowed out a hole in the thatched roof. A large signboard bearing the faded images of a hammer and anvil hung on creaky hinges above the forge's doorway.

Father and son entered the hearth chamber. Lifting his head, Dermot nearly jumped in surprise when his mother threw her arms around him.

"Dermot!" she cried. "Thank the heavens you're safe! We were certain we'd never see you again, what with all the talk going 'round the village, and that beast! Your father was out with the search..."

"Granuaile, please, give him some air," Pádraig said.

"Of course," she said, composing herself. She wiped

her long, dark brown hair out of her face.

Dermot, free of his mother's grasp, took a step back. He looked into her eyes. "What talk?"

"Everyone was sure you'd been eaten by the beast that kidnapped you!"

I wasn't kidnapped! Dermot turned around, pressing his hand to his shoulder.

"The chieftain's soldiers have been combing Úaene Forest," she said. "It is rumored the beast might be one of the gryphons from the east, which haven't been seen in Denú for years. Either way, the chieftain has sworn to take the beast's head."

Dermot could feel his heart thrashing.

"Many village men have been recruited for the search party," Pádraig added. "All are equipped with longbows, quivers, and hiking staves, eager to prove their strength and honor as men."

Dermot remembered the stave he had found, now wondering if maybe Saershe hadn't left it after all. He faced his father. "Are *we* in the search party, Da?"

"Your mother and I made the case you still need more time to recover from your ordeal," Pádraig said. "We insisted you'd fare far better at home than in the lock-up. Our sagart agreed. Once you've had your rest, I explained to them I would need your help in forging more weapons for this search.

"It was not an easy task to convince them, I assure you. But, word is Lord Emerin wasn't too pleased with the sheriff for locking you up. Everyone's talking about it. They're now even more astounded you're still alive."

"I know," Dermot grumbled.

"Now, Dermot, where've you been?" Granuaile asked,

crossing her arms. "How did you escape that beast? And why are you so clean?"

Chapter 4

Dermot's muscles became tense. "I—I washed myself in the stream. I—I then—I wandered about the forest for a long time 'til I was found. I can't honestly explain why or how I..."

"Wait," Pádraig interrupted. He stepped between them, turning to his wife. "My dear, we've all had a trying day, our son most of all. What he needs right now is rest. Please, let's not ask him any more questions for now."

Granuaile's face reddened. She crossed her arms. "Very well, but I do wish the boy wouldn't be rude about it, like I'm told he was toward the sheriff."

Dermot turned to her, raising his chin higher. "Are you defending him, Ma, after what he did to me? He threw me into the lock-up. I told him the truth!"

"I don't approve of his throwing you in the lock-up, son, not at all. But you could've spoken to him without being rude and avoided all this. He *is* the sheriff, charged with maintaining order in this village."

"*He* was the rude one! Why should he keep treating me this way? I'm fifteen now, not six! What of the rest of us? Aren't we humans as much as he?"

Pádraig was surprised.

Granuaile pressed her lips together. "I'm disappointed in you, Dermot. I thought you'd outgrown such behavior after nine years. It seems I was wrong."

Horrified, Dermot stomped out of the chamber into

the foyer. To his right was the gate to the stable where the family kept a cow, a pair of hogs, and a few chickens. The stable and Pádraig's forge adjoined the cottage on opposite sides. Dermot's face flinched from the filth and stench. Next he smelled food cooking from within the hearth chamber. He had only raised his hand to his forehead when he felt he was not alone. Lowering his hand and raising his head, he saw his brother, Brian.

Brian was younger by two years. He had the same hair and eyes as his elder brother, but a slightly different nose and wider mouth which made his face more boyish.

"What do you want?" Dermot asked, scratching the back of his neck.

"How was the lock-up? Did crowds come peering to see if it was really you?"

Dermot rolled his eyes then blinked before turning away. "No, Brian."

"Really?" Brian asked. "How strange. Well, I suppose you knew to keep away from the window. People couldn't hurl insults and mud at you like they always have."

"I don't want to talk right now," Dermot said, rubbing his forehead. "Go away."

"What's the matter?" Brian asked. He stepped closer, his mouth forming a nasty smile. "What're you hiding?"

"Please. Leave me alone," Dermot snapped, leaning his head back. *Not again!*

"Come on, brother," Brian said. "Admit it. You're a troublemaker still, aren't you? You always were, you always will be, and what's more, you know it!"

"Leave me alone!" He wheeled around, slapping Brian's cheek.

Brian groaned, pressing both hands to his face. He

glared when his eyes met his brother's and he slapped him. Dermot in turn fought back.

Granuaile and Pádraig arrived. They grabbed their angry sons, pulling them apart before the fight could grow beyond slapping. Nevertheless, each boy attempted to give the other another blow. Granuaile, holding Brian firmly, slapped Dermot's face. He yelped, pressing his hand against his cheek. Brian turned aside to hide a smirk.

"What was that for, Ma?" Dermot asked, trying hard not to whimper.

"Please!" Pádraig shouted. "Everyone, stop!"

Once they'd all gone quiet, the smith said, "Now, let's try and resolve this matter *peacefully*."

He followed his children and wife into the hearth chamber. Granuaile faced Dermot, her brown eyes still flaring. "What have you to say for yourself, Dermot? First you talk back to the sheriff, now you start brawling with your brother! Do you still not know your place, boy?"

"I didn't start this!" Dermot said.

"Yes, you did. You hit me first, Brian said, jabbing his finger at Dermot."

"You're the one who kept taunting me! I begged you to leave me..."

"Enough! Both of you!" bellowed Granuaile, clenching her fists.

A moment of sheer silence ensued. Pádraig's face fell.

Granuaile faced Brian. "I expected better from you. Brawling like that with your own brother! You are better than that."

"Forgive me, Ma," Brian apologized. "I'm sorry."

Dermot frowned. Brian meant not a word of it, and he

always enjoyed respect and mercy from his mother, something Dermot never had.

"You shouldn't have hit Brian, Dermot," Pádraig said. "There is a time to fight, for standing up for oneself, but petty insults are never worth fighting over, for *both* of you."

Dermot shook his father's hands off and backed away from the rest of his family, causing them all to stare at him. His father asked him what was wrong. Dermot simply insisted, "I—I don't want to talk right now. Please, can I go up to the loft and rest?"

"Of course," Pádraig said. "We'll talk later."

"Thank you, Da."

Dermot climbed the ladder, his leg still hurting. Once up, he maneuvered his way through heavy sacks.

The loft served as a storage area, as well as where he and Brian slept. Had it been dark out, without candlelight it would be pitch-black. The sleeping area itself encompassed little space. A roughly-carved table sat between two straw mattresses. At the opposite end of those beds, rested a wooden chest. A small dressing-screen stood in the adjacent corner, barely noticeable in the dimness.

Reaching the beds, Dermot plopped onto the mattress adjacent to the pathway. Not only did he feel broken inside, but his mind was lost in a thick fog of feelings and thoughts, some which felt as if they had long been asleep. The greatest was his childhood desire for adventure, to leave Emerin behind and see the kingdom.

Nevertheless, he hadn't forgotten his father's words to him nine years ago, the day his mischief-making ended. Dermot could still remember overhearing from the loft his

father suggesting the idea of apprenticing him, whereas his mother expressed her belief that he would never accomplish anything. Then, he came into the hearth chamber and sat down before his father, trying to hide his grief and anger toward his mother.

"*Dermot, we depend upon one another to work so we may keep food on the table, a durable roof o'er our heads, clothing and fires to provide warmth during wintertime. If we do not aid each other, we shall not survive. Can you appreciate that?*

"*Family is more important than anything in this world. Remember, Dermot, I love you. So does your mother. We shall always be there for you in times of adversity, always, but you cannot go on like this. You can't live your life as if you were in a Denuan folktale. What if we have to search the forest for you at dusk again and you're not found before dark? Your place is here. We need you. If you don't help us as we've helped you, by providing for you, you will have not only let us down, but you will have let yourself down. You'll never be able to achieve anything in life, which is the last thing your mother and I want for you.*

"*Of course you should stand up for yourself, me lad, but there's a time to act and a time not to. If you cannot distinguish them, you'll find yourself in repeated, unwelcome predicaments.*"

Dermot heard his father's words echo in his head as if it were yesterday. He had tried to take them to heart for the past nine years, and felt foolish for not heeding the last part of his advice. He also felt once again that longing to go, to see the land. He couldn't quench it, even if he wanted to. The two needs were ripping him apart inside.

It was following that talk when his father offered to teach him his trade. Dermot recalled how touched he was at his father letting him decide. Seldom did he ever feel he could make such a choice in life. He had accepted out of great respect for his father, and of course a desire to never set foot in the fields. Dermot buried his eyes in his hand as he thought about it, only to hear a throat clear itself. He raised his head and saw Brian.

"What do you want?" Dermot asked.

"Supper's almost ready," Brian said impassively. "Ma sent me to tell you."

"All right," Dermot nodded grumpily. "I'm coming."

Brian clambered back down. Dermot soon descended, as if he were reliving that fateful day from long ago. Brian had been sent to fetch him then as now.

Dermot entered. A small fire enclosed by large rocks burned in the hearth at the chamber's center. Granuaile was finishing preparations for supper in an iron cauldron hanging above it. A lumpy straw-filled bed used by her and Pádraig stood off in one corner, with a couple large wooden chests positioned at its foot and a dressing-screen beside them. Tools and implements hung on the wall, not far from the wooden cover of the food storage pit. An axe leaned beneath them. Brian and Pádraig were seated on opposite sides of the large wooden table. Dermot sat down beside his brother.

The family ate supper without conversation. They made sure their livestock was watered and properly bedded for the night afterward.

Brian went up to the loft early, carrying an unlit candle. Dermot soon scaled the ladder himself. He was able to maneuver through the dark with relative ease. The

light from his brother's now-lit candle guided him. When he reached the beds, Brian stepped out into the light, dressed in his nightclothes.

"Hello," Dermot said.

"Hello," Brian replied.

Dermot averted his eyes. "Seen any rats lately?"

"No. Da can never find them," Brian said, sitting on his bed. "They're always hiding in the darkest corners, nibbling more tiny holes into our sacks. Besides, they're not the only animals up here, you know. Just the other day, Da drove out sparrows nesting in the rafters."

"Hunted," Dermot said, thinking about the gryphon.

"What did you say?"

"Nothing," Dermot said. He briefly noticed his brother staring at him suspiciously.

Brian coughed twice.

"Are you all right? You sound ill."

"I'm fine, brother." Brian coughed a third time.

"Are you sure?"

"Yes. Now *you* leave me alone!"

"Fine." Dermot turned away.

Brian lay down and rolled on his side.

Dermot went behind the dressing-screen and began removing his shirt, pausing halfway. Seeing his dressed injuries again, and remembering the poultices, he realized if his parents saw them, they or the authorities would interrogate him until they forced out of him the truth of Saershe and Ruairí's existence out of him. In a flash, he whirled, thinking he heard a noise. He peeked around the screen. Brian was still fast asleep. Dermott let out a mild sigh.

Then, he found himself questioning why he was

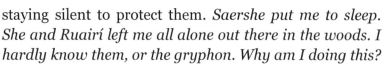

staying silent to protect them. *Saershe put me to sleep. She and Ruairí left me all alone out there in the woods. I hardly know them, or the gryphon. Why am I doing this? Do they even deserve protection?*

The answer came to him soon enough. *They were kind to me. They helped me. I must return the favor.*

Guilt gripped Dermot. In his heart, he knew it was the right thing to do, even if he couldn't explain why to himself. He was careful, trying not to make any loud noises as he undressed himself, pausing once or twice when he heard his brother groan or stir.

Fortunately, Brian never awoke. Dermot lay on his bed. As for his torn trousers, he decided to tell his mother he had ripped them in the forest but luckily didn't cut himself.

I need to make sense of all this. I must find her. I must see Saershe and Ruairí again, he decided, feeling a tingle in his fingers.

Only then did he remember he had no idea where within the forest Saershe and Ruairí were. He scrunched his eyelids together. *What am I to do?*

Chapter 5

Villagers gathered together in Emerin's square, among them Dermot's family. Dermot however, watched from the cottage doorway. His parents explained at breakfast that a village meeting had been called before he and Brian had come down.

"So that's why they were ringing the bells so early, Brian said groggily.

Pádraig suggested Dermot could speak to the sagart or the saínchí, the chieftain's storyteller. He declined.

"That's not at all like you," Granuaile said, narrowing her eyes. "You always enjoy talking with him and listening to the legends of Denú."

"Please, I don't want anyone besieging me with more questions," he said. "Can I not go to this assemblage?"

Fortunately, Pádraig thought it best he remain home, and Granuaile didn't argue against the decision. For as Dermot learned, his father had already sent away a couple curious villagers who came to their door yesterday evening while he was in the loft.

"The sooner we all move on from this ordeal, the better off we'll all be," Granuaile said.

Still, Dermot had to help his family feed and water the livestock before they left. He did his best not to strain himself due to his injuries, remembering what Saershe told him.

Dermot thanked his father as they all washed their

hands and faces around a large basin, but asked him what they would say to the sheriff or anyone else who inquired after him. Pádraig assured him they would insist he was still in shock and needed time at home. He prayed the sheriff wouldn't insist he had enough time.

Dermot at first hoped he could use the opportunity to sneak back into Úaene, for he was determined to find a way back, having spent the whole previous day under his parents' constant eye. His mother at least took his torn trousers after they'd all washed themselves and planned to resew them, not questioning him further.

Alas, with the sheriff and armed men present, Dermot realized he couldn't slip past them without being spotted. Though he wanted to return to the forest, he had no desire to be caught again either, least of all by the sheriff.

The heralds beat their drums and blew their ox horns. The sheriff held up his hand. Once their music stopped, he faced the assemblage, with the sagart by his side no doubt to bless them in their search.

The sheriff spoke, "The search for the beast…"

Not wishing to hear another word, Dermot grunted and stomped back inside. He eventually found himself pacing about the forge.

It's hopeless, he thought. He froze when he caught sight of a sword lying on a small table beside a couple horseshoes. He drew closer. His hand quivered as it grasped the sword's black handle. Like most Denuan blades, it featured a crescent-shaped hilt and pommel, and a blade milled to a diamond-shape with a fuller down the middle. Marveling at the weapon, he walked in to the forge's open center and swung it multiple times, his face a concoction of concentration and enthusiasm.

Once, his carelessness caused a mess. No one had been hurt, nor any damage caused, but his father told him afterwards these were no toys, advice that Dermot tried hard to follow. Still, once in a while, seldom though it had become, he couldn't help himself.

When Dermot sensed another's presence, he scurried back to that same table, tossing the blade back onto it. It clanged, making him tighten his shoulders. When he turned, trembling, he found no one there, not even outside the forge. Taking a deep breath, he looked at the other swords displayed about the forge. They were all clean and shiny, unlike the soot-covered tools and walls. His father loved to display his work in his forge, even if it was only for himself, a reminder always of the effort endowed to them. Swords were his truest talent.

Dermot distracted his mind by thinking of the early days of his apprenticeship. He presently recalled a conversation he had had with his father, not long after he first joined him inside the forge as his official apprentice. It was a conversation that in some ways reminded him of his fantasies.

"*The fire element speaks to us through its color, Dermot, to let us know when our medium is ready. We just need to read the different colors properly.*"

"*Da, you make it sound like a living being.*"

"*Fire is a living, breathing being, me lad. We smiths need it as we need the air and water. That is how we smiths are thereupon empowered to turn mere iron into these instruments.*"

"*Your swords are amazing.*"

"*You like them do you? Well, let me tell you, there sometimes is a time in the life of us smiths where our work may reach a level we may call it art."*

"Are your swords art, Da?"

"Dermot, I consider all the swords I craft art. But I have yet to forge one which I may truly gaze upon as a masterwork."

"But you will someday, won't you?"

"I pray so, and that such a blade shall be used by a warrior in a great battle, earning the prestige of its own name, so I can say 'twas my hand that forged it."

Dermot left the forge and entered the hearth chamber. His head slumped forward. Then he lifted it in thought. *Maybe I'm being too cautious. Perhaps I can sneak out o' here later, and start searching. I could take a sword—no, no, Da would notice. He always notices his individual swords. No sword then, but I had better...*

His hands and legs stiffened the second he heard a voice say his name. He reeled to see his father standing by the doorway.

Confound it, they're back, he thought. He did his best to keep calm. "What is it, Da?"

"They will scour the forest again soon," Pádraig said. "It seems the chieftain is certain that the creature was a gryphon. Now, if you're ready to work me lad, we have much we need attending to."

"Of course." Dermot felt empty inside, though he was grateful to be recovering remarkably well. "What of Ma and Brian? Will they be going out into the fields?"

"Under heavier guard like yesterday, aye."

Dermot nodded. He followed his father into the forge, still wondering how he was going to reach the forest now that the sheriff and soldiers were all there. He prayed Saershe and Ruairí were safe. He feared for the gryphon

too. If they found her, she would be slain. The thought ran through him worse than that arrow grazing his leg.

**

Sweat drenched father and son. Black soot coated them both from head to foot, as it coated the forge's walls. With no windows, the forge was extremely dark, lit only by the fire and heated iron. One entrance led outside, a second opposite the first into the cottage.

"Check the color again, Dermot," Pádraig said. "See if it's ready."

"Aye." They had worked long into the afternoon now, and he was tired. Putting down the bellows with which he had blown onto the fire, he used his tongs to remove a hot iron sheet from inside the furnace. His eyes widened. It cast such a fiery glow!

"It's not red," he said. "Somewhere between orange and yellow, I daresay."

"You daresay? You must be certain, me boy. Never act without certainty."

Dermot paused. "I'm certain."

Pádraig eyed him still, but eventually said. "Excellent. It's time then."

Dermot knew what to do. He brought the sheet of iron over to the anvil, where his father hammered it into the desired shape. The boy clasped in his tongs another sheet of iron already hammered, similar in size but with a glow more whitish in color. Dermot immersed this sheet into a bucket on the floor, filled to the brim. The water crackled on contact, producing a small rising cloud of steam from which Dermot diverted his face until it dissolved, along with its thick, throttling scent. The youth smelled the fire's grit and smoke yet again.

Argh, this stifling heat, he complained to himself. Exhausted, he ignored his father's constant humming. He couldn't concentrate on his work, for he could think only of what happened and the pain in his leg. It still hurt, but not as much as before. He also found, much to his surprise, he was healing faster than he imagined he would.

Dermot pulled out the sheet from the bucket and placed it on a side table. Returning to his father's side, he immersed the second sheet into the same bucket. Like before, the water crackled and steamed. He raised his arm and wiped his forehead with a sigh.

"Keep working, me lad," Pádraig said. "Rush not. Remember, patience and diligence always."

"Aye, Da," Dermot mumbled, familiar with those words. His father had said them often over the years.

A moment later, they paused to wash their faces with water in a small basin. Pádraig rubbed it through his long chestnut colored hair and goatee.

"Forgive me, son, but is something wrong?" he asked as he finished. "Your heart isn't in your work today. You're not even humming like usual. Is it the gryphon, or what the sheriff did to you yesterday?"

Dermot froze, but then shook his head. "No, no, it's none of that, Da. I—I just seem to have a little pain in my leg, that's all. It's nothing to bother about. It'll pass."

"Well then, may I ask you something else?"

"What is it?" Dermot asked, rubbing his face.

"Why is there still hostility between you and your brother after all these years?"

"What do you mean?"

"I mean what happened yesterday evening, and when you two came down for breakfast this morning. The sole time you made eye contact then, I saw hatred in your eyesas well as his. You and Brian seldom speak to one another anymore, except whenever you quarrel."

"We just don't get along."

Pádraig crunched his eyebrows. "Look at me. Do you know what I see here, me boy?"

"What?" Dermot's voice betrayed his desire for no answer at all. He looked into his father's dark brown eyes.

"A wound from long ago that's still open, and festering. It would be much better if you try to let it heal, else it will worsen 'til it cannot be healed."

Dermot paused, glancing at his chest and limbs. Did he know? How could he?

"Da," he huffed, "you know I've always valued your advice, but I don't believe Brian would even let it heal. He'd never trust me, not with his life."

"How do you know?" Pádraig remained calm. "Maybe you haven't given him a chance yet. Show Brian he can trust you. Then you can trust him in turn. I'm confident you can."

Dermot remembered Saershe's words about his mother, and his father's letting him decide whether to be his apprentice or no. Wishing to switch the subject, he asked, "Is the chieftain determined to slay the gryphon?"

"I thought you'd know the stories of those creatures' prowess and strength, Dermot. We were reminded on the first day of the search such a feat is considered a badge of valor and courage to Denuan nobility, like slaying a dragon. The men were won over thus, along with their

mutual desire for the village to be safe for the Midsummer festival."

"I know, I know. But they might as well scour the skies. That gryphon may well be long gone by now, having flown after dark for all we know."

"I wouldn't say that in front of the sheriff if I were you, Dermot."

"And why does he wish to hunt the poor animal down like this? I mean, no one was harmed yesterday, certainly not his lordship or the sheriff. It doesn't feel right."

Pádraig paused from his work. "Where'd all this talk come from?"

Dermot froze. Eventually he said, "It's—it's nothing. Would you mind if I step outside for a moment? I need some fresh air."

Smiling, Pádraig consented, "So long as you stay near the forge this time."

"You mean in case I get snatched again?" Dermot asked, attempting to sound humorous.

Pádraig shook his head, smiling again. Dermot almost laughed, but promised he would stay near.

Outside, Dermot instantly shielded his eyes from the bright sunshine until they adjusted to it. As he lowered his hand, he suddenly had that impulse to sneak off again, only to hear a dog bark. He turned and beheld a retriever dog standing nearby. He was struck by the canine's proud stature and thick golden fur. Never had he seen such a beautiful dog.

"Hello there." Dermot smiled as the dog, to his delight, trotted up to him. Dermot petted the ears and head, blackening the canine's fur with soot.

"Oh dear, I'm sorry. Allow me," Dermot said. He

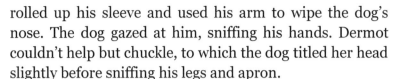

rolled up his sleeve and used his arm to wipe the dog's nose. The dog gazed at him, sniffing his hands. Dermot couldn't help but chuckle, to which the dog titled her head slightly before sniffing his legs and apron.

This blissful moment was interrupted by the unmistakable sound of tramping hooves. The sheriff was mounted on a powerful black steed. He rode up, looking down at both Dermot and the retriever, the latter of whom whimpered.

"Yseult!" scolded the sheriff. "You are supposed to be by your master's side! Come!"

Yseult circled, toddling behind the horse. Dermot stood up. He couldn't believe it. Was she the chieftain's dog? She seemed too nice to be. He had assumed she was another villager's dog.

The sheriff turned to him. "Well, you seem to be faring much better today, young laddie."

"Thank you," Dermot remarked, crossing his arms. "Are you here to question me?"

By this time, Pádraig had emerged from the forge. "What's all this here?"

"Nothing, Da," Dermot said. "Everything's fine."

"There'll be no need for further questions, Dermot," the sheriff said. "Today's search has ended. Tomorrow morning, another announcement shall be made to the village. Be sure to attend."

Pádraig promised they would. The sheriff turned and rode off with Yseult following him.

"She was a nice dog," Dermot said after they were some distance away.

"Come, son," Pádraig said. "We've got plenty of work to accomplish."

Dermot followed his father. He stopped in the doorway and turned to look back, but he saw the dog no more. Instead, what he saw, to his surprise were villagers and soldiers alike, back from the search party. They walked slowly, their heads and arms hanging down, drenched in sweat. Many were being carried with their arms over others' shoulders. From the looks on their faces, they all appeared to be in a daze.

Chapter 6

Dermot wondered what had happened to them, if maybe they had encountered the gryphon, or even Saershe. Then he heard the unmistakable chirrup of a grasshopper. He gazed down and saw the tiny creature in the grass near his boot. Before long, the grasshopper hopped away.

"Dermot!" Pádraig called.

"I'm coming!" Dermot hurried into the forge.

Brian and Granuaile returned home later that evening, when Pádraig was chopping firewood. After washing down the livestock and cleaning the stable, the family ate supper quietly, apart from Granuaile's irritation at Dermot's not remaining still while eating.

Dermot, remembering his wounds' dressings, went up before his brother. He was headed for the ladder when his mother intercepted him. She hugged him tight before he could say a word. Feeling awkward, he put his own arms around her.

"Wha—what's this for?" he stuttered, feeling a little pain but doing his best to hide it.

"Because I love you, Dermot," she said, her voice sounding rather impassive. "I always have, from the time you were knee high to a grasshopper. And no matter what, I always will."

"Th—thank you, Ma," Dermot felt his stomach sink.

"I thought I'd lost you once. I don't wish to lose you

again." Pulling his head down, Granuaile kissed his forehead. Dermot broke free of her grasp and quickly walked away, scratching his neck. Seldom did she ever show such affection compared to her devotion to strict discipline, so it proved difficult for Dermot to take in.

He took a candle and sulking, clambered up to the loft. Dermot changed and sat on his bed. Pulling his nightshirt back, he gazed down at the cuts on his chest. Then he let go and rubbed his hand against his forehead and eyes. He was beginning to wonder if he would ever make it back to the forest, even if the chieftain did cease searching for the gryphon. The thought drained him of hope but simultaneously heightened his burning desire to know the truth about Saershe, her grandson, and even the gryphon if he could.

Only now, he truly believed he would not be able to sneak away and return without his parents noticing. The sheriff would lock him up again, this time with justifiable reason. Brian's teasing would never cease. His mother would likewise admonish him forever. He couldn't sneak out after dark, when all were asleep. It would be far too risky. Taking a torch would alert the watch for sure. While he may have once remained out at dusk, the thought of being lost in the night terrified him.

For a moment Dermot paused, thinking he heard the sound of a running steed.

For what possible reason would anyone be out riding after dark? Well, maybe I'm wrong. Or it could be a soldier.

Brian appeared, startling him.

"Oh, hello," Dermot said.

"What's the matter with you, big brother?" Brian

asked. "Ma feels you've changed since returning home from the forest yesterday, that you've reverted back to your old self."

"I know it's nothing you would care about. Honestly, is it truly terrible to desire something more out of life? Haven't you once wished to find out what lies beyond this village?"

"I have all I will need in life right here," Brian said proudly. "I do good work with Ma out in the fields. She single-handedly ensures a good harvest every season for this village. I'm perfectly content, brother. You should be ah—ah..."

Brian sneezed. Once more, Dermot asked Brian if he was certain he was not ill.

"Leave me be," Brian said, a slight hint of anger in his tone as he climbed into bed.

Dermot blew out the candle. He lay there for a time, listening to the nonstop chirping of the crickets with the occasional owl's hoot. Ultimately, he did succumb to tranquil slumber.

Late in the night, Dermot woke with a start, bolting upright. Gasping for air, he could feel his heart racing.

"What is it?" Brian asked, havving been awakened. "What's the matter?"

Dermot reclined on his bed, calming down only a little. He whispered, "Nothing, just a bad dream."

Brian grumbled and resumed his sleep at once. Dermot, on the other hand, lay awake for a while longer, eyes half-open. He eventually did shut them, but squirmed about for the rest of the night, not forgetting that awful dream.

**

The entire village gathered once more in the square after breakfast early in the morning a couple days later. This time Dermot came with his family. Villagers stared at him, but his parents made sure they left him alone. All they needed to do was to give any villager a look or hold their hand out to keep them away.

At the sounds of horns and drums, the sheriff stood before the crowd and announced, "Despite a whole day yesterday of searching Úaene, no trace of the gryphon has yet been found. Furthermore, a number of incidents have occurred within the forest. Members of the search went missing, only to be found later, many having lost staves and other implements. None were harmed thankfully, but all lost any memory of what transpired or how they got where they were."

The villagers whispered among each other about the forest. Dermot remembered what he had seen yesterday afternoon, and understood why all those people appeared dazed. He felt certain Saershe somehow was involved.

"Furthermore," concluded the sheriff, "the gryphon being a creature with wings, and likely to have flown away in the night, it has been decreed by his lordship the search is to cease hence, but to be certain, and for your safety, no one is allowed near Úaene for the next couple weeks. Keep your children at home, so we might still avoid losing any lives. The Midsummer Night festivities will go ahead as planned, but under guard as a precaution. Thank you all."

As the villagers dispersed, some were still talking amongst themselves over the events of the last two days. Dermot could hear them express frustration at not killing

the gryphon. Others were afraid the creature was still here, and might return, and still others questioned why the search was being called off so quickly, and what of the festivities and guards. He cared not for any gossip. He shook his head, his mind rioting.

His father turned to him. "You seem rather glum still, Dermot. Is anything wrong?"

"Nothing, I'm fine," Dermot was quick to answer.

Pádraig raised his eyebrows. "Honestly, me boy, whatever is weighing down upon you, won't you talk about it? You'll find it will be a great relief for you if you do."

"I..." he faltered.

"He just wants to see the land again," Brian interrupted. "He always has."

Dermot gave him a nasty glance. Granuaile looked as if she suspected as much all along. Pádraig however frowned at his younger son. "That was extremely rude, Brian. Never be a telltale, not on anyone, especially your brother. Do you understand?"

Brian's chin trembled. His gaze turned blank. "Forgive me, Da. I—ah—ah..."

He let out a loud sneeze. Granuaile placed her hand on his forehead.

"Goodness me," she said. "Brian, you're burning up! Let's go. No arguments."

Granuaile hurried him home, with Dermot and Pádraig trailing behind. She rushed Brian up the ladder with Pádraig following her. Dermot remained below, trotting into the hearth chamber. He viewed his right leg. He had not removed the poultice. He reached down to touch his knee, but drew his hand back because his

parents returned.

"Is Brian going to be all right?" he asked, rubbing the back of his neck.

"I sent him to bed," Granuaile said without making eye contact. Instead she walked past him and searched about the hearth chamber. Her face became pinched. "We're out of herbal remedies, confound it!"

"Then we must procure fresh medicine from the chieftain's physician," Pádraig said.

"But who will watch o'er the boys?" Granuaile asked, her hands gripping her head.

"Dermot can watch Brian, and care for himself," Pádraig said, surprising his wife and son.

"Darling," Granuaile dropped her arms. "I don't..."

"My dear," Pádraig said, "our elder son is nearly of age, and he's done well o'er these nine years, yesterday notwithstanding. I'm sure he's earned our trust. I have faith in him."

Dermot was touched. His mother, however, pressed her lips together, but nodded. "Fine. But you better be right. The sheriff ordered..."

"I'm sure of it. Now, Dermot, we don't know how long we'll be," Pádraig said. "Make sure Brian drinks plenty o' water, all right?"

Dermot promised he would. As soon as his parents left, he scaled the ladder, and made his way toward his brother, who frowned. Brian lay on his bed, sneezing harder than earlier. Dermot got down on his knees and placed his hand against Brian's forehead.

"My goodness," he said. "Ma's right. You are burning up."

"Just a summer cold," Brian said, shaking his head.

"It'll pass. Now leave me be."

"Brian, you need help, quick."

"Ma and Da are going to get help," Brian said.

"All right, well, let me get you some water." Dermot went toward the ladder, but he slipped and fell on his side.

"Argh!" he yelped. He ran his hand inside his shirt.

"Hey!" Brian said. "You're covered with scratches! Is there something under your leg?"

"What are you talking about?"

"I can see it under your trousers. There's something, it looks like a bandage."

"I'm done for," Dermot mumbled.

"What do you mean?"

"All right, all right!" Dermot shouted. He lifted his shirt and then rolled up his trousers, revealing the poultices.

Brian stared at the wounds. Then he finally asked, "Is that why you were acting so strange these past few mornings?"

"Yes. That's why I said I'd get dressed after you went down. That's also why I went to bed early every night since I went in the woods."

"What happened to you out there?"

"After my encounter with the gryphon, an affable healer tended my injuries. Her name was Saershe. She lives in Úaene Forest with her grandson, Ruairí."

In a split second, Dermot realized he had divulged a secret to the last person he would ever want to share such a secret with. He felt like a fool for choosing to take this risk. Then he recalled what his father said about letting old wounds heal, and giving Brian a chance. Breathing

deep, he explained everything that occurred up to when their father brought him home.

"So, you knew what happened and kept silent," Brian glowered. "You didn't even tell Da. Why?"

"No one can know, brother. Not now," Dermot said. He knew Brian would delight in watching him beg not to open his mouth.

Brian sneezed again.

An idea struck Dermot like lightning to a tree during a storm. He knew it would be risky, but with his parents at the manor, he might not get another chance. He slid his arm behind Brian's shoulder and lifted him up.

"Dermot, what're you doing?" Brian asked, sneezing. "Ma and Da…"

"I'm going back to find her. You're coming with me."

Brian shook him off. "Me? What're you talking about We can't go anywhere! Why should…" his cough was more ragged than before.

"Do you want to feel better or not?" Dermot asked.

"Well, yes," Brian said, "But…"

"Then let's go. We won't take too long."

"We can't go anywhere! The sheriff said…"

"Look, brother," Dermot said. "Da told me yesterday I need to make amends with you. I believe you could say the same after that fight and Da's own words to you. So here's what I propose. We go together, and if we get caught, or if I'm lying, I'll take full blame. I'll tell Ma and Da, the sheriff, I coerced you."

"Are you serious?"

"As serious as I'll ever be. Now do we have a deal?"

After a moment, Brian sneezed again. "I can't believe I'm saying this, but yes."

"All right, let's get going."

Dermot helped Brian down the ladder and outside. They tiptoed to the corner of the cottage. The moment Dermot peered around it he bounced back, keeping his arm tight around his brother's shoulders. His breathing hastened.

"Dermot, we..." began Brian, his body going rigid.

"Shush," Dermot whispered with force, putting his other hand over Brian's mouth. Cautiously, he peaked around the corner again. Brian looked the other way.

Chapter 7

Just as Brian was about to sneeze, Dermot put a finger under his nose, stopping him. Dermot breathed, and peeped around the corner again. The village carpenter and his apprentice were chopping a tree trunk with large axes. At the neighboring cottage, a young maiden tended a small vegetable garden. A stooped, older woman sat near her, spinning fresh wool. She raised her head. Dermot gasped and jumped back again.

"Thank goodness," he whispered, feeling fluttery in his chest. "That was close."

"I don't think this is a good idea!" Brian said, biting his lip. "What'll Ma say if we..."

"Shush, brother! Keep your voice down!"

The last thing he needed right now was Brian doubting himself. They returned to their cottage. Peering around the other corner he saw two men repairing another cottage's thatched roof. One stood on a gigantic ladder. The other surveyed from the ground, standing near a huge cart overflowing with straw. When the one on the ladder turned his head in their direction, the brothers jerked back behind the wall.

"Which way can we go without stumbling into anyone?" Dermot said.

"How're we going to find this lady of yours?" Brian asked. His face was bathed in sweat.

Dermot grew agitated. "She does exist, Brian. I don't

know the exact way back, but I've got a good idea. The sheriff found me not far from where she located me. She can't be too far."

"What if you're wrong?"

Dermot instantly regretted his words. In truth, he did doubt he would find her, but he didn't want to believe it.

"Oh, no," Brian said. "I don't believe this. You drag me out while I'm..."

Dermot shushed him again and peeped around the corner. The men were finishing their task. He waited until they led the cart away, and took a deep breath.

"Now's our chance," Dermot said. He led Brian behind the forge, peeping past the wall. When he saw no one fetching water from the well or fishing in the stream, he hurried Brian along behind one wall to another.

On their knees, they paused behind the well, then jumped up and dashed behind the stable adjoining the inn. They made it across the stream thanks to the large rocks barely jutting above the water's surface.

Dermot kept his arm wrapped tight around Brian as they scuttled behind those trees nearest the village. They advanced onward, staying near the forest's edge. A moment later, they reached the incline where Dermot fell.

"This is where she found me," Dermot said.

Gradually they progressed downhill. Dermot kept his eyes on his trembling feet. Arriving at the border, they hiked deeper and deeper into the forest, surrounded by the chirping of birds. Dermot wondered if he could find the spot where he left that stave.

"Is this necessary?" Brian asked.

Dermot stopped. "What are you talking about?"

"I'm talking about you keeping your arm 'round me.

Can't you let me go now?"

"How can I know you won't wait for an opportunity to run back home?"

"I thought you said we needed to make amends, Dermot. How can we if you don't trust me?"

The expression on Brian's face gave Dermot no clue to what he was thinking. He asked, "Will you promise me, then, that you won't run home, or turn me in to the sheriff or our parents if we make it back unnoticed?"

Brian didn't answer. He looked down. Dermot knew not what to make of it. He wondered whether Brian felt should he agree to keep a secret from their mother, or perhaps if their father's recent orders to never be a telltale were on his mind.

Then he recalled his father's words about trust again. To his surprise, and Brian's too, he removed his arm.

Brian, though stunned, said, "Well, all right, since I'm in trouble now too."

"Good, now can we please stop arguing, little brother? We're wasting time."

"No argument there. I hope we'll get home in time," Brian said. "We can't search the forest all day for this lady of yours, or someone will realize we've gone. Ma..."

"Her name is Saershe," Dermot said.

"All right, Saershe. How do you propose to find her cottage?" Brian asked. "You don't you even know which way to go!"

He knew Brian was right, but he couldn't admit that, not now. He had no idea, just a feeling he would find the path. The idea Brian would ridicule him made him feel stupid. When he faced his brother, there was no sign of contempt in Brian's countenance, only a strange

understanding.

"Dermot," Brian said, putting up his hands. "I know you want to find this woman. But are you even sure she wants you to find her?"

Dermot was surprised. The possibility never crossed his mind. He gazed downward.

"See, brother? For all you know, her cottage may not be yah—ah—ah..." He sneezed so hard he sank to his knees.

Dermot got down beside him, feeling a tense sensation in his stomach. "Brian, what is it? What's wrong?"

"I—I need to lie down, I..." He let out another sneeze.

Dermot placed his hand on Brian's head. His fever was worse. Brian slunk to his side, too weak to move.

"Mercy of the heavens." Dermot wanted to smack himself in the head. "What in the high king's name was I thinking? I shouldn't have taken you out o' bed like this! Ma's going to kill me!"

Brian was sniffling and coughing, so he couldn't answer. Dermot immediately took Brian up in his arms. It was then Dermot beheld a white stag a short distance away whose head was crowned with a pair of magnificent antlers. The stag gazed at him before dashing away. A strange sensation flooded his body. It was a feeling he didn't understand, but he carried Brian along the stag's path. He could hear birds chirping cheerily overhead.

Dermot stopped, exhaustion overtaking him. A familiar voice suddenly called his name, bringing him hope. He looked around. When he heard the same voice cry out, "Up here!" he was giddy with relief as he gazed up into the thick branches of a giant oak.

"Ruairí!" Dermot smiled.

Ruairí clambered down from the branches where he had been resting, and came beside Dermot, a satchel slung over his shoulder. He looked at Brian. The younger brother stared back.

"My brother needs aid, fast," Dermot said. "Is your grandmother's cottage far?"

"No. Follow me." Ruairí remained calm.

Dermot did so, walking fast while trying to keep hold of Brian, until at last they arrived.

"Look, Brian!" Dermot said. "There it is! We made it!"

From this view, Dermot fully grasped the great size of the oak trees between which the cottage had been built. The cottage definitely had to be one floor, but it was large nonetheless.

Carefully, they plodded down a gentle incline. They arrived at a section of the stream where giant rocks protruded the placid surface. Dermot followed Ruairí across the water by way of those rocks, taking each step as cautiously as he could. He almost stumbed once, and got one boot wet, but he didn't fall. Brian paid no attention, for he couldn't tear his eyes away from Saershe's cottage.

They crept around behind the place. Sure enough, there she was, swathed in green and her apron, tending to her garden. The boys walked right up to her. Brian trembled.

"Dermot came back, Grandma, like you said he would," Ruairí said.

"Ah. Welcome back, my friend," she greeted in her usual warm, welcoming voice.

Dermot didn't know how to respond. He was a little surprised she actually predicted his return.

She stood, eyeing Brian closely. "And who might this be?"

"My brother, Brian," Dermot said. "He's got a real bad fever. Can you treat him?"

"Of course," she agreed, extending her hand. "Please, sit."

He gently laid Brian down on a wooden bench in place of the bed he remembered laying on.

Brian kept his arms crossed, rubbing them with his fingers. Dermot wondered why he didn't complain, concluding he must have been petrified with fear.

"Brian, this is Saershe," he said. "The woman I told you about. You've already met Ruairí, her grandson."

"Welcome," smiled Saershe.

"It's a pleasure to meet you, Brian," Ruairí said.

Brian nodded, sneezing.

Peering into Saershe's garden, Dermot recognized some of the flowers he noticed the last time he was here. An elder tree stood near the garden, bedecked with small white blossoms. She plucked sprigs from a plant coming in clusters of five tiny white flowers.

Dermot could hear her mumbling again. He wondered what exactly she said, pondering if it might be some kind of blessing or incantation, or if she even spoke in the common language at all.

Could Saershe have actually spoken in the old language of Denú? Dermot sucked in a swift breath. He had heard of it, but it was considered lost. If any still spoke it, they had to be but a rare few.

It was all coming together in his mind. Incantations, the old language, healing plants, could it be she knew magic? Could Saershe indeed be a real sorceress? Dermot

never believed he would meet someone who knew the ancient arts. He decided it best not to question her. It didn't feel right, at least not the right time. He turned his face away.

Saershe wrapped the sprigs in a white cloth strapping tied to a string, which she subsequently dipped into a full copper teapot. She hung it above the oven, a small circular hole enclosed by low stone walls. As soon as it boiled, the elderly woman removed the pot and poured tea into a yellowish-green ceramic cup.

"Here. Drink this," she said, handing Brian the cup.

He sniffed the tea, making a face. "It smells real strong."

"Drink it up now, please, and swiftly lest it go cold," Saershe said.

Brian, with an apprehensive look on his face, drank the tea. He coughed afterwards, grasping his chest.

"Are you all right?" Dermot asked.

"Something's stirring inside me stomach," Brian complained groggily.

"The medicine is taking effect," Saershe said. "Fret not. It will settle shortly. Tea concocted from the thousand-leaf flower is good against fevers."

"Thousand-leaf," repeated Dermot. "That's the herb you treated me with."

The memory brought the gryphon to mind.

"Indeed," she replied. "It's invaluable for its ability to halt the flow of blood, hence its other name—the soldier's woundwort. But like the rosin rose it's dangerous for animals to eat."

"I must say, I've never seen a great many of these plants and flowers you have in your garden, Saershe,"

Dermot said.

"They come from all different parts of Denú, my friend," Saershe said. "But of course, I neither sow nor cultivate without permission from those that have already taken root. The rosin rose can spread perilously if not checked."

"What do you mean permission?"

"Trees, plants, all green beings, have spirits the same as you, me, and any other animal. Those already rooted here, I must ask their consent when I plant new seeds. I listen to them, their voices, their souls, so I may sow the sacred seeds they shall welcome, that new life may grow."

Dermot was at a loss for words. His belief that Saershe knew magic grew greater still.

"Now I think you should rest, Brian," Saershe said, waving her hand in front of him.

Dermot stood up so Brian could lie down. Once he shut his eyes, it took him no time to fall sound asleep. Dermot was not surprised, but a little nervous, knowing what Saershe did the last time.

"How are you feeling today, Dermot?" Saershe asked, eyeing him.

"Oh, much better, thanks to you. I—I'm looking forward to the Midsummer revelry."

"Midsummer happens to be my favorite time of year. Tell me, Dermot, as you've told your brother about us, have you perchance mentioned me and my grandson to anyone else?"

He trembled, "No, no, no one, I swear."

"You needn't be afraid, Dermot," Saershe said. "I shan't harm you. Please, sit. Let me examine your injuries."

Dermot was afraid. Brian's words earlier made him wonder why she was so hospitable, not to mention how or why she expected him to return, given that she'd made an effort to keep him from finding her the last time.

Chapter 8

Hesitantly, Dermot sat on the ground beside Brian. He took off his shirt and rolled up his trousers. Saershe knelt down in front of him and removed the poultices carefully, one at a time.

"How is it you found Ruairí, Dermot?" Saershe asked while eyeing her grandson.

Dermot looked at Ruairí too, thinking he seemed nervous. Nevertheless, he related how he and Brian had been searching for her, and came across Ruairí in a tree. After Dermot mentioned how surprised he had been to see him up there, Ruairí asked, "Didn't you climb trees when you were little? I recall Grandma mentioning so whenever you stayed out in the forest late at night."

"Aye, that's true," said Dermot. "But it was so long ago, years actually."

"Don't you ever catch yourself wanting want to climb trees once again?" Ruairí asked.

Dermot fell silent. Instantly, he felt a desire to do so, to recapture a moment from his youth. Just as quickly, he wondered if he only felt it because of what Ruairí said. He decided, "Probably not. I'd be no good. It's been too long."

"You never know, my friend," Ruairí said. "You could surprise yourself."

Dermot shook his head. Ruairí continued, "Grandma always encouraged me to climb trees when I was a little boy. She still does, so that I may see as birds and other tree-dwellers do. For observing the greenwood from the groundlings' view is merely one of many ways to observe one's surroundings."

"I see," Dermot said, gazing at his body. His injuries were still noticeable, but fading.

"And the trees themselves, they always fascinate me. To those who are willing to listen, the trees, even the animals, they speak back," Ruairí said.

"What?" Dermot asked, jerking his head up.

"Well, I must say, Dermot, you are healing remarkably well," Saershe said, interrupting them. "Your leg will have scarring of course, but you are already walking fine again."

"That's good to hear," Dermot said. His injuries made him think of the gryphon again. He looked down now that Saershe had removed them. His legs had, to his relief, indeed healed remarkably well.

Saershe looked up at him. "Is everything all right, Dermot? You don't sound pleased."

"Well, it's—it's..." Dermot, though hesitant, simply couldn't resist opening up to her, more so when he recalled once more his father's recent advice. He described to her how the gryphon swept him up, yet somehow understood him, and let him go without giving him a scratch.

"I've been worried about her ever since," he said. "I ran after her. I don't know why—I—I just wish I knew if she's all right. Does that even make any sense?"

"It does." Saershe nodded, smiling. After a moment, she said, "You would like to see her again, wouldn't you?"

Sure, I guess, Dermot thought. He felt better now that he had talked. From the look in Saershe's eye, he could

tell she knew. He felt himself blush.

Saershe, however, exchanged glances with her grandson. There was a long pause before she spoke again. "If you wish, I can take you to a spot in the forest where you can see her."

Dermot's ears perked. "You—you can? Are you serious? But—but how..."

"I can, *after* I redress your injuries."

He turned to Ruairí, who nodded, smiling. Dermot couldn't believe any of it.

"Don't worry. I'll keep a watch o'er your brother," Ruairí said. "You should go."

"So—we wouldn't take too long then?" Dermot asked.

"No, not at all, I assure you," Saershe said.

"I—I don't believe any of this," Dermot stammered.

Sometime later, he and Saershe were deep within the forest. They trekked amongst weeds and high grass, regularly stepping over thick protruding tree roots. She wore a nicer, cleaner robe of the same leafy green color with a darker green surcoat in place of her apron. She seemed to be right at home amidst the trees. Dermot kept swatting insects out of his face, regularly ducking underneath low branches. From what he observed, Saershe appeared to be listening and watching for something.

Dermot finally plucked up the courage to ask, "Saershe, where are we going?"

"A certain spot within the greenwood I'm certain you will find most enchanting," she replied. "It's not far from a small stream. While we wait for our mutual friend, you can truly see why I revere the forest."

"What do you mean?"

"See how peaceful it is here?" She looked back at him and smiled. "Don't think. Just listen, feel, and observe."

"I still don't follow, Saershe. The gryphon..."

"Don't worry about her, or anything else. Just relax. Observe the forest and the trees together, with the wild animals. You may thus discover, and be touched by, the sacred ways of Nature and her sacred beauty, more than ever with Midsummer upon us."

Dermot didn't respond. As they continued on, he thought he felt something else within him for a fleeting moment. He couldn't figure out what, but deep in his bones it somehow seemed right to go with her, to try what she suggested. Still, he wondered why.

**

Dermot's knees wobbled. A few paces away from him and Saershe stood none other than the gryphon, viewing them with a piercing gaze. She was much larger than he recalled. Her head almost reached the tree branches. Memories of their first encounter flooded back into his mind as if he were reliving it. Saershe bowed her head to the gryphon, who in turn bowed hers. Both of them eyed him. He didn't know what to say or even think.

"Show that you respect her, and she will let you approach," Saershe said. "Don't be frightened."

Dermot stiffly bowed his head. After a fleeting moment, the gryphon returned the gesture. Dermot turned to Saershe again. She nodded, smiling. He moved cautiously toward the gryphon, raising his hand to touch her. She snapped her beak, squawking. He stepped back, almost stumbling. His arm trembled, but he didn't lower it.

Saershe told him to let the gryphon come to him now. He remained as still as a stone. Slowly the creature did so, sniffing him. He gently let his fingers touch her black-tipped beak before gently moving his hand across her cheek, and then her large neck when she raised her head.

She squawked feebly, blinking. For his part, Dermot was so overcome by petting her he smiled, forgetting all about being afraid.

"Her name is Maeve," Saershe said. "She comes from a long, noble line of gryphons. She's been my dear friend for many years."

Maeve squawked, *Thank you. It's good to see you again.*

For a moment, Dermot felt his heart miss a beat, for he was not wholly sure what just happened. It was almost as if he felt what she did, and thus heard her speak somehow.

Maeve moved her head closer. Her beak gently nudged Dermot's face. Albeit apprehensive at first, he smiled. "Oh, thank you, Maeve. I'm Dermot."

Maeve squawked again. All three were startled by a voice—Brian's voice—calling Dermot's name twice.

Ruairí's followed. "Wait! Please! You don't understand! Come back!"

"I'm coming for you, brother!" Brian shouted.

Dermot's heart raced. Maeve stretched out her wings as if she might rear up on her hind legs. Saershe remained calm, walking up to Maeve, who had taken a step back.

Brian appeared. He froze in disbelief at seeing the gryphon, unable to move a muscle. Ruairí emerged soon after. Maeve, soothed by Saershe's hand, lay down.

"Forgive me, Grandma," Ruairí said. "I tried to stop

him. I couldn't."

"What happened precisely?" she asked.

Brian opened his mouth, but Ruairí spoke before the younger boy had a chance. "When Brian awoke, I offered him fruit, cheese, and more tea, and asked if he'd like to see my sketches. When he couldn't find Dermot or you, Grandma, he demanded to know where you both were. Before I could say anything, he ran off."

Brian managed to take a step backward. He pointed at Maeve, stuttering. "Th—that's…"

"The gryphon, yes," Saershe said. She introduced Maeve and Brian to each other.

"You—you *know* her?" Brian asked.

"Indeed," Saershe said. "But I haven't seen her since she was young, many ages ago."

"Have you been hiding her from the chieftain's search party all this time?" Brian asked.

Saershe stared at him. "Tell me, my young friend, is it right to turn away an innocent in need? What would you do if someone, anyone, came to you, seeking shelter and aid? Suppose she was your mother, your father, or a dear friend. Is she any different from any other creature? Does she deserve any less? She's been hunted by a man seeking prestige, like many heartless, greedy men preceding him. Maeve was desperate, even more so given her delicate condition."

Dermot and Brian widened their eyes. Their jaws dropped.

"You—you mean…?" Dermot stuttered. "Sh—she…"

"Yes, Dermot," Saershe nodded, looking to the gryphon. "Maeve is with child."

Silence swept over them both. Their eyes converged

on Maeve, who folded her forelimbs. The look in her own eyes somehow confirmed the truth for Dermot. He felt his muscles weaken.

"She must deliver her child to ensure the survival of her noble line, and all her kind," Saershe said. "All offspring, born and unborn, are the hope for their tribes' survival. Maeve's may also be the greatest hope for restoring glory to the Denuan gryphons. If either of you wondered why she hunted your village's livestock, therein is the same reason for which she cannot become the prize of a hunt: she is living for herself *and* her child."

"And you, Dermot," Brian turned to his brother. "Did—did you know all along?"

Dermot scratched the back of his neck. "No, brother. I wanted to know if she was all right. Saershe told me she could let me see her. So we came out here..."

"And you never thought to tell me?" Brian asked. "You told me I could trust you. You left me back there, all alone, and you never thought about that either? You..."

"I had no intention of abandoning you, honest. I was going to return."

"And what about all the time we've spent here?" Brian asked. "Weren't you still worried we might return home too late? We've spent too much time out here already! Oh, I see! This was your plan all along, wasn't it?"

"No! I swear." Dermot was sinking inside.

"Please, both of you," Saershe said. "Keep calm. Shouting will resolve nothing."

Brian frowned and crossed his arms. "And what about those strange occurrences during the search over the past few days; the lost memories and all? Are you responsible for that, Saershe?"

Saershe raised her chin. Her face, though calm as ever, conveyed a sense of power, strength, and will Dermot had never seen before in her. It was spellbinding too.

"I am a guardian of the forests," she said, "Of the trees and the wild animals. It is my avowed duty to defend them all. I will do what I feel I must to protect each and every one of them, including Maeve and her child. It is my responsibility to ensure their safety from you. How else can I make sure you shan't breathe a word to anyone, even your parents out of the guilt of remaining silent, as it might reach the self-serving chieftain's ears?"

Fear swept across Brian's face. Dermot could feel such a fear within himself. He had never heard Saershe speak with such sternness before.

Saershe flicked a quick glance at Dermot and asked. "You do not wish to forget?"

He shook his head. "I don't see myself going back. Nay, I can't go back. I can't. Is it even right to forget what has happened? Can you understand that?"

Saershe smiled empathetically. "I do, for I would rather not do that to you. Despite having known you for but a few days, I have grown rather fond of you, Dermot. I see something deep within you, something good which I sense your brother shares."

Ruairí's eyes widened.

"What's that supposed to mean?" Brian asked.

Dermot, on the other hand didn't speak, for Saershe's words sent him into deep thought. He himself had grown fond of Saershe. He admired her, respected her. He had even come to think of Ruairí as a good friend.

"Since you left behind the hiking stave Ruairí left for

you the day we first met," Saershe continued. "Perhaps it is possible I can indeed trust you, and Brian, as you trust him. You wouldn't have brought him here otherwise."

So that stave did *come from them!* Dermot was stunned. He didn't notice Brian staring at him, surprised by what Saershe said about trusting him.

Saershe eyed them. "Are you both men of your word?"

Dermot and Brian took another glance at Maeve. A longing was still manifest in her eyes, a silent plea for mercy. The brothers exchanged glances with one another. Dermot hoped his father's advice to Brian would bear some weight.

When they came to their decision, Dermot turned to Saershe.

Chapter 9

Quietly passing through the trees, the two brothers were still somewhat in a daze. Dermot trotted at a slower pace to begin with, for he was deep in thought. He did catch up with Brian once he noticed him ahead. Brian was still coughing from his last cup of thousand-leaf tea.

They stopped once they came to the edge. Presently, Dermot and Brian heard numerous voices laughing and singing. They scuttled behind bushes. They heard the squeaky noise of wooden wheels turning. Slowly the two of them raised their heads.

"Heavens, how could I have forgotten?!" Dermot said.

"The sheriff did say the Midsummer festival would be held as usual," Brian said.

They saw a tremendous succession of wagons and carts not far away, headed toward the green. People and goods crammed each. A great number of the villagers hurried out to meet them. The brothers remained still and watched.

Whenever a festival came to the village, it would always be held on the green, near an old solitary knotted thorn tree which grew there, one tree Dermot remembered never climbing during his childhood. The tree seemed an anomaly, but was never cut down.

Festivals were a time where none of the villagers were expected to work, almost like a day of prayer. Everyone could indulge in pleasure and recreation, something

rarely enjoyed or experienced in their lives.

For Dermot, these were always times where he could hear tales from not only the saínchí and sagart, but minstrels and those storytellers who roved from village to village. He could listen to those fascinating legends of great deeds, heroes, warriors, and magic that had always enriched his imagination.

"This is our perfect chance to sneak back into Emerin—and into the cottage without being noticed," Dermot said. "Come on, let's go."

"We're in for it now, Dermot. Ma will use her switch on us both. There's no telling what the sheriff will do."

"Maybe nothing, Brian." Dermot tried his best to remain hopeful.

"I wouldn't be so sure. What if Ma and Da have already come home? They'd be out searching for us, and would've told the watch. We're both going to get a lashing. Da won't protect you this time."

Dermot froze. In all this time he hadn't considered his father's reaction should he find out. He would never look at him the same again. Dermot shook his head. He had to keep calm. He knew, as much as he hated it, he had to keep his promise to take the blame if caught. He didn't want Brian taunting him again, especially after what occurred in the forest. Then again, there was a glimmer of hope that if he did so, Brian might be moved by his honesty.

"Look, have we been seen by anyone yet?" Dermot asked. "No. That should be cause for hope. Saershe promised we would make it back unseen."

"Through the forest, remember," Brian said. "The watch might still catch us in the village."

Both tiptoed as fast as they could, remaining behind the forest's border. After pausing for a brief moment, they finally made a dash into the village. Nevertheless they always stopped and looked around every corner they came to.

"How much longer will this be?"Brian asked.

"Not much. Look!" Dermot said, pointing. Beyond the corner was their cottage. "See? We made it. Come on."

They walked straight toward the door, and were a few steps away from it when their mother's angry voice said both their names. They stopped, shutting their eyes.

"Won't take too long, huh?" Brian muttered.

"Keep quiet!" Dermot whispered.

The boys turned around to face their parents, who walked up to them. Granuaile's face boiled. "What in the high king's name are you two doing out here?"

"W-well," Brian said.

"I—Brian was feeling a little better," Dermot said. "I thought I'd take him out so he could get some fresh air. I thought it would do him good. It was a short stroll around the village. That's all."

"And did you consider what we might've felt, if we arrived while you were out to find neither of you at home? Especially with Brian's illness, and the cottage and our livestock unattended?" his mother shouted.

"Granuaile, please," Pádraig said, placing his hand on her shoulder. "They haven't even left the village, nor strayed far from the cottage, *have they*?"

He looked at the boys with those last two words, which came from him in a sterner tone.

"No, Da," Brian was quick to say. "We kept the cottage in our sight. We weren't going to be out for long."

Dermot could feel his toes curling, but he kept himself from moving. He couldn't believe Brian had lied. He never lied, certainly not to their mother.

"Well, you certainly seem to be faring much better, Brian," the smith observed. "I'm glad to see the two of you getting along. Still, your mother is right. You shouldn't have left the cottage."

"Indeed," Granuaile said. She walked up to Brian and placed her hand on his forehead, surprised. "Your fever is broken! What a miracle, considering the chieftain's physician was indisposed."

"What? Why?" Brian wanted to know.

"He was busy tending the chieftain," she said. "His Lordship is unwell. Your father and I were compelled to wait all this time. We never got to see him."

The brothers stared at each other.

"We would've waited longer, if the sheriff hadn't sent us away," Pádraig added.

"He sent you away?" Dermot asked. "Why?"

"He insisted the physician could not be torn away from his lordship," Granuaile said. "He was kind enough though to provide us with some recommended remedies, strange as that itself was."

Brian perked up. "Mercy of the heavens, is the chieftain's illness that serious, Da?"

"I don't know," Pádraig said. "The sheriff would say no more, although he did apologize to us for his treatment of you, Dermot. But personally, I am thankful you're recovering, Brian."

"I guess we've been touched by a healing hand," Dermot said. "What about the festival? Will it still be on, with the chieftain being ill?"

"We met them on our way home," Pádraig said. "Preparations shall commence tomorrow morning at the earliest, if his lordship's is well enough to approve that is. If he does, every able-bodied person is expected to help, as always."

"Of course," Brian said. Dermot said the same almost instantly.

"Well then, let's go inside and I'll prepare our supper," Granuaile said. "As for you, Dermot, consider yourself lucky you won't get a lashing. See you take this as a lesson."

He placed his hand against his back. "I will, Ma."

Granuaile and Pádraig went in first. The brothers, on the other hand, stood there a moment, speechless. Then, they raced into the cottage, Dermot getting there first.

Dusk arrived. The family ate their supper of mutton and potatoes once their chores with the livestock were done. Dermot thought back to that moment right before his second meeting with Maeve. Saershe somehow opened him to the greenwood in a way he had never thought or felt of Úaene before. All troubles in him had faded in that brief moment. Then there was Maeve herself. There was something about her he could not understand.

Dermot left the table and sat before the fire. Brian kept his eyes on him.

"Aren't you going to finish your supper, me boy?" Pádraig asked.

"I'm not too hungry right now," Dermot said, without turning his head.

"Eat your supper now," Granuaile said. "Food doesn't always come easy for us."

Dermot didn't want to argue, not tonight. Without a

word, he came back to the table and continued eating, Granuaile rolled her eyes, while Brian continued to watch his brother as he finished his food. Dermot rubbed his eyes with both hands.

After eating, Brian himself sat facing the fire. Dermot got up and made for the doorway, insisting he wanted a little air. Outside, he listened to the crickets. Once in a while he saw a firefly glimmer in the dark. In the distance, he could see tents and carts all scattered about the village green, thanks to the fire from several torches. He could barely make out the thorn tree though.

Dermot decided he had had enough of the night air, and went back inside. He stuck his head in the hearth chamber doorway, informing his parents he was going to bed. Brian said the same, standing up.

"Good night, lads," Granuaile said. "Be awake bright and early tomorrow. We've got a lot of work to do. You will work too, Brian, if you're feeling better."

"Of course, Ma," Brian and Dermot promised.

Both of them scaled the ladder into the loft. Dermot held a candle he took from the hearth room earlier. He set it down on the wooden table between the beds once he and Brian reached them. By the time they put on their nightshirts, Brian said, "I still can't believe we snuck back into the village unnoticed. Nor can I believe neither Ma nor Da suspected us."

"I am too."

"Is something troubling you, brother?" Brian asked. "You may be good at creating tales, but you never could hide your emotions, not from me."

Dermot suspected Brian might really feel concerned this time. He gazed blankly at a large wooden chest

opposite their beds, in which were kept his and Brian's clothes. Most clothes he and Brian wore had been handed down to them by their father, but every now and then their mother wove them new ones, if she could. She also sewed patches of mismatching colors onto those that had worn considerably.

"No," Dermot replied, shaking his head. After a momentary silence, Dermot said, "Brian."

"What?"

"Why did you not rat me out?"

Brian frowned. "I wanted to. Don't think because I kept silent means I trust you. I only knew Ma would still punish me for letting you take me."

Dermot didn't fully believe him, but said nothing of suspicions. Instead, he said, "Come on, Brian. Da would believe we were inside the whole time, hence why we weren't seen 'til then. We left the cottage right when they returned. By the way, what did you make of Saershe?"

"I honestly don't know what to think anymore, Dermot. All I know is you're taken with that sorceress."

"So you think she knows magic too?"

"Well, after what we've seen today, especially with Maeve, I wouldn't be surprised if she does."

Dermot turned his head away. "There's more to them than we know, I'm sure. Her words actually remind me of something, of legends I think I heard once during Midsummer festivals past regarding certain forest-dwelling sorcerers. Oh, what were they called?"

"Well, if we're both going to be silent about this, then I suggest you not slip again."

Dermot looked back, frowning. "What're you talking about? I never mentioned once to our parents what's

happened today."

"You mentioned *a healing hand*, remember?"

Dermot knew Brian was correct, and it pained him terribly, even if he had been lucky. Of course he still couldn't help wondering if his brother was on his side. Part of him felt Brian only remained silent by force. He could not decide.

Brian blew out the candle.

Dermot didn't sleep well that night.

Chapter 10

It was at last the day of the Midsummer festival. Dermot, Brian, and their parents departed for the green late that morning. Many villagers wore crowns of flowers, keeping with tradition. The chieftain approved the festival the night the entertainers came, which surprised Dermot when his parents told him. They assumed the chieftain must have recovered, but he wasn't satisfied. He even felt his mother had doubt in her eyes, but he didn't speak to her about it.

Everyone worked hard for days preparing, and it paid off. Food and drink were plentiful. Entertainers of all kinds amused the crowds.

Eventide came. Guards and watchmen patrolled all over the festival, ensuring order was maintained as the bonfire was lit at the heart of the green.

The sagart addressed them in a ceremonial white robe, expressing a prayer with a dagger and chalice in his hands. "Blessed be the abundance of Midsummer, when life is full and strong. Blessed be the sun, for the sun gives this world life, as with this world the sun has meaning. Blessed be our souls and those long past."

The prayers led to community dancing. The family participated, singing of the summer and crops and rain in a line with clapping hands. Minstrels, whose instruments counted a lute, harp, flute, and drums, played music as they sang. Their instruments included a lute, harp, flute,

and drums. The merriment continued with other songs such as *Men of the North*, whose lively rhythm contrasted the deeper, soothing flow of *Beyond the Forest*. The minstrel playing the lute sang, as did some villagers who danced with total passion:

When the call is heard across the land,
With great heart ye go forth,
O'er mountains high or valleys low,
Ye be the men of the north!

Come many lads and fathers all.
Thy courage will prevail.
Around the flame on winter's nights,
They henceforth tell the tale.

Return again to the hearth and home.
Where all will know your worth!
The best to hold on high above,
The bravest, bravest, the bravest:
The men of the north!

Everyone clapped once the song concluded. Some villagers continued to dance to other songs too.

Dermot and his family moved on. Granuaile, wearing her finest shawl, went to assess goods being sold by the merchants. While she examined cloth, her husband and sons walked away, the brothers huffing in chorus. Neither of them cared to shop for goods.

Dermot hung his head. Pádraig eyed him, asking, "Is something wrong, Dermot? I'd have thought you'd be excited right now, with the festival and all."

"Oh, I'm all right, Da," Dermot said. "It's nothing."

"Are you sure?"

Dermot nodded.

"Very well," Pádraig said. "You do seem to be garnering lots of secrets these days. I maintain it would be better if you find someone to talk to about them. You know what I mean."

"Thank you, Da." Dermot almost flinched when his father said the word *secrets*.

Pádraig chose to help himself to a pint of ale and converse with other craftsman near the tables, for they had called out to him heartily, waving their hands.

"Will you boys be all right on your own?" he asked.

"We will, Da," Dermot said.

"But where will we meet later?" Brian asked.

"We can meet by the thorn tree."

"Good choice, Dermot," smiled the smith.

"Pádraig!" one of the other village men called again. "Are you coming?"

"I'll be right there!" he called, turning back to the boys. "Let's all meet there at dark."

"All right, Da," Dermot said.

Brian agreed. With that, the smith walked off and joined his friends. They greeted him with smiles, hearty laughs, and friendly slaps on his back. He shook their hands, repeatedly saying it was good to see them.

"It's not nothing, is it, big brother?" Brian said once they were alone.

"No, it isn't." Dermot shook his head. He looked into the sky. Normally by this time the moon would be visible. Tonight, it was nowhere to be seen. Sadly, his thoughts of Saershe, Ruairí, and most especially Maeve and her

unborn child, returned into his mind, alongside a suspicious feeling that something was wrong.

A few of the villagers had spoken to Dermot about his alleged kidnapping while he and his family were helping setting things up, but the sagart urged them to leave him be. His father had consoled him the other day, as preparations neared completion.

"Don't worry about them, Dermot. Perhaps it's time we all moved on, including you. I believe they will. Let's begin with this Midsummer festival, and have a wonderful time."

Still, even now as then, Dermot could not help but worry for his new friends.

"You sure you don't want to talk to me about it?" Brian asked him presently.

"Maybe in a jiffy," Dermot said. "I've got to watch after you as it is."

Brian smirked, shaking his head.

As they walked, the boys observed children younger than themselves beguiled by jugglers, jesters, and above all a the dancing bear. Dermot and Brian faintly giggled. They came across older boys wrestling, with people cheering them on. To that, Dermot simply shook his head and strode on.

"That man's standing on his hands!" one girl exclaimed to her mother, bouncing up and down. The brothers smiled when they passed by her. Then, they shuffled backward in surprise as they turned back around.

"Good evening, lads," the sheriff said. "You two aren't out here all by yourselves, are you?"

"We'll be meeting our parents later at a specific spot," Dermot said. He just wished he could somehow get away.

The sheriff didn't smile. "Well then, be sure you do."

"We will," Dermot said, raising his chin.

"Good," the sheriff said. "I trust your parents passed on my regrets for my recent behavior. I would have apologized myself in person, but what with the search and his lordship's illness, I have been besieged with duties."

Brian spoke up. "I hope his lordship is faring better, sir. Our parents mentioned he was unwell the other day. Nothing serious, I trust."

"How kind of you, young Brian," the sheriff replied. "He'll recover, I assure you. His ailment only worsened out of grief. His favorite dog disappeared during the hunt, you see."

"His favorite dog?" repeated Dermot. "You—wouldn't happen to mean Yseult, would you?"

"Ah! You remember her," the sheriff said.

Dermot tightened his fists. "Yes, I do."

"Yseult?" Brian asked.

The sheriff's eyes squinted. Dermot felt a slight pain in his stomach. Brian on the other hand appeared curious, staring at his brother.

The sheriff continued, "We never found her, alas. I'm afraid our chieftain has lost all hope. He's convinced the beast ate her, like we thought she did you, Dermot."

"But I wasn't killed."

Brian, a slight panic in his voice, said, "Well, Dermot survived. Maybe the poor dog has too."

"Perhaps, but let it not trouble ye tonight, lads. Revel in the merriment, while you still can. It shan't be long before darkness falls."

"Thank you, sir," Brian said.

Dermot didn't speak.

The brothers walked away. Once Dermot felt certain they were away from the sheriff, he whispered to Brian. "Didn't that strike you as odd?"

"What do you mean? The sheriff apologizing to you?" Brian asked. "I admit..."

"No, no. I mean, well, you're not aware of any search party for the missing dog, are you?"

"No. But since she vanished while they were searching for Maeve, they must have been searching for the dog at the same time."

"So why isn't there any search still ongoing? I mean, if Yseult is the chieftain's favorite..."

"Speaking of which, how'd you know about this dog, Yseult?" Brian interrupted. "And how'd the sheriff know you know?"

Dermot related how he met her the day before returning to Saershe's cottage, and the sheriff leading her away. Brian nodded, replying, "Well, perhaps they are looking but haven't told us."

"Maybe, but I would've thought someone would have mentioned or heard something. The chieftain would've surely offered a reward for his favorite dog's return. That would've brought in a lot more people into search, and a better chance to find her. I tell you, something doesn't feel right, and not merely with Yseult."

"What do you mean?" Brian asked, rolling his eyes.

"I mean, how is it, if the chieftain is as ill as our parents said, he was able to approve a festival that same night? And why would the sheriff be so open to discussing his illness with us? And what did he mean 'revel in the merriment, *while we can?*' It..."

"Dermot," Brian interrupted. "Please. Can't we try

and enjoy ourselves tonight? We've had enough trouble as it is already. Come on. It's time to put all this behind us."

Brian walked ahead. Dermot followed, but with his head down. He had no desire to argue further, but he felt more troubled, and it was eating away at him, as he was sure could be seen in his face. He couldn't move on, nor did he want to.

"Say, there's the sagart and saínchí," Brian said, standing in sight of the old thorn tree. "Why not talk to them? That should ease your mind."

Dermot nodded, and they walked up to them. The sagart was a tall proud man with a proud face, his long dark hair and beard showing strands of gray. The saínchí stood beside him, wrapped in a blue cloak. A third man Dermot didn't know was with them, wearing a similar blue cloak, but attired like any other villager. He had a broad nose and the thickest beard of the three men.

"Good evening, sirs," Brian said. "I hope we're not intruding."

"Not at all," the sagart said. "How fares you young lads on this Midsummer's Night?"

Dermot professed they were well, and thanked him. The sagart reminded him to collect charred embers from the bonfire to spread around homes and the fields, to bring good fortune and a good harvest. Villagers did so every Midsummer.

"This is the young lad I told you about," the saínchí said to the third man, "The one who was taken by the gryphon."

Dermot felt himself go cold. He could hear his brother's heavy rasping. From the corner of his eye, he saw Brian rolling own.

"Are you really?" this man asked. "Forgive me, but I'm one of the travelling saínchí. I've heard much talk tonight about this creature."

"Please," the sagart said. "Do not trouble him. If you wish to speak privately to me alone..."

"Thank you, sir, but I'm fine. Tis true. But it was brief. M—I mean, the gryphon has not been seen since. It actually was astonishing to see such a creature."

"Indeed it was," the traveler said. "Gryphons are the subject of many a great tale and legend. There is one well-known legend pertaining to this majestic breed in particular. Have you heard it? Tis an epic tale of sorcery, Denú's deep magical forces, and brave warriors."

He now had Dermot's full attention. The boy said, "Do tell, good sir. I have been trying to recall a tale of sorcerers who protected this kingdom's forests."

"I know of whom you speak," the traveler said.

"As do I," the village saínchí said. "There once existed a coven of sorcerers, men and women, known as the Dríacht, who indeed wandered Denú's great woodlands. They were adept in magic, healing, music, and poetry. Tis reputed their abilities and great wisdom sprung from Nature herself, whom they revered most deeply, and with whom they shared a strong spiritual connection. They were able to sense the emotions of trees, wild plants and creatures, and even somehow speak to them. They could approach any being, even magical ones, without fear of harm. They were known as guardians of the forests."

Dermot and Brian looked at one another. Dermot remembered Saershe's proclaiming herself as such. There was also her friendship with Maeve, a creature of magic. Dermot gazed at his boots. Could Saershe be one of them?

What about Ruairí? If so, everything made sense. It all fit together perfectly.

The sagart continued. "The Dríacht, for a time, became skilled warriors instead of the peace-loving sorcerers they always were. In this role, they were noted for wearing tunics green as midsummer's leaves. The oak tree was their crest, as it had been long before they took up the sword.

"In battle, they rode gryphons rather than warhorses. They and their gryphon allies stood as Nature's arm and shield. We sagarts do our best to lead this land in prayer and ritual as they did, but alas we have not their secret ways."

"What happened to them?" Dermot asked.

The traveler's face turned grave, as did the other men. He finally said, "There was one who sought to eradicate the Dríacht, wipe out their legacy, and the gryphons—toothe same villain because of whom they became warriors."

The brothers simultaneously asked, "Who?"

The traveler took in a deep breath, and blinked. A single name escaped his lips—*Taranis*.

Chapter 11

Never had Dermot heard this name before, not in any story. His eyes narrowed. Then, he and Brian asked in chorus, "Who?"

"Taranis," repeated the traveler. "He was a very powerful wizard, and the sworn nemesis of the Dríachht. He was renowned for his heartlessness toward other living beings, and for his ruthless ambition to dominate the kingdom and disrupt the balance and harmony of Nature. He was once a member of the Dríacht himself. But he left the coven, devoting his life instead to the study of darker arts. He gathered followers, and even succeeded in winning over many of Denú's dragons. Soon, he devastated much of the landscape, thereby declaring war against the Dríacht and Denú. 'Twas by then Taranis had given himself the title, 'The Dark Prince'."

The brothers briefly looked at one another.

"Aye," the sagart said. "Once he turned his cloak, Taranis retreated into the shadows. To those who encountered him, he was henceforth no more than a faceless, shrouded figure. It is purported he had a special talent o'er men's minds, preying on their emotions and dreams."

Dermot shivered. He instantly remembered the dark figure from his nightmare. How could he have forgotten? It also reminded him of Saershe's reaction after he had shared the details of his dream with her.

"The Dark Prince's determination," the traveler continued, "against the steadfast forebearance of Nature and those who stood as her shield, initiated an epic clash between good and evil, to determine the fate of all that is wild and green, and the kingdom itself. The outcome was a bittersweet victory for the Dríacht."

"So Taranis was defeated," Brian said.

"Aye," confirmed the saínchí. "But not before Denuan earth and the western seas became red with the blood of the fallen. The Dríacht's remaining members retreated into secrecy afterward, nevermore to openly practice their magic or council this realm. Ever since, rumors have swirled that they may, in small numbers, endure still, roaming the forests and mountains as they had done for countless generations, keeping an ever watchful and caring eye o'er Nature."

"And Taranis?" Dermot asked, the saínchí, intrigued. "What became of him?"

"He fled to the Ashland, that barren valley enclosed by the Black Mountains in the south, formerly known as the Valley of Fire. But not before swearing an oath: that once he replenished his strength, he would not fail again to wipe out his adversaries and their bloodlines."

"You mean he swore to return?" Dermot asked.

"Did he?" Brian asked.

The traveler shook his head. "Like the Dríacht, Taranis was never seen again in Denú. But as some believe the Dríacht may still exist, there are those who say he shall return to exact his revenge. You see, the Dark Prince is reputed to have made this oath in blood. Still, that was many years ago. Despite those persistent rumors, with the passing of years most folk believe that Taranis,

like the Dríacht, simply faded into legend."

"Well, that's quite a story," Brian said. "Thank you for sharing it with us."

Dermot nodded hesitantly.

"You're most welcome," the saínchí replied. "Do you fancy another story?"

"Nay, I don't think so," Brian said. He turned to Dermot. "What about you?"

Dermot did not respond, for he was lost in thought. Brian and the men observed him curiously.

"Brother?" Brian poked him in the ribs. "Brother!"

Dermot looked up at them, stammering, "No, no, thank you, I..."

He turned and darted away.

"Dermot!" Brian called. "Where're you going?"

Dermot didn't answer. Hanging his head, he gave no regard to anybody or anything he passed. He just wanted to get away from it all.

**

Granuaile finished examining and purchasing goods. She found her husband among several friends, enjoying an endless stream of ale. They clapped along while several others were dancing. She walked over to him, putting her hand on his shoulder.

"Come, my darling," she said, her brow furrowed.

"Oh come, my dear, and enjoy yourself!" Pádraig said, tugging gently on her dress.

"Please, my dear, come with *me*."

"Oh, very well," he finally relented. After bidding his friends farewell, they did the same in return.

"Have you had too much to drink?" Granuaile asked sternly, leading her husband away.

"Not at all, my dear wife," Pádraig kissed her cheek. "You know I watch me drinking."

"Yes, I do know. Now where're the boys?"

"Oh, we agreed to meet by the thorn tree at dark. They may be waiting there for us now."

"Well, let's go. They'd better be."

They made their way through the masses, repeatedly uttering, "Pardon," or "Pardon me," and "Please, let us pass," especially whenever people were clustered close together. They also briefly acknowledged anybody they knew well if they crossed paths with them.

However, when they reached the thorn tree, to their dismay, neither Dermot nor Brian was there waiting.

Granuaile looked around, but didn't see them.

"Well where could they have gotten to?" she asked. "Where did you last see them?"

"Right before I joined my friends."

A frown marked her forehead. "Those boys are in big trouble."

"They have to be around somewhere, my dear," Pádraig said. "Perhaps they're still enjoying themselves, watching entertainers, and simply lost track of time."

"You think so?"

"Well, someone must've seen them someplace. Let's ask around. We can retrace their steps."

"All right, you wait here in case they show up. I'll go 'round and see if I can find them."

**

Not until he had reached the green's edge away from the festival did Dermot finally stop. Meanwhile, thick clouds blotted out the sun, which had almost slipped below the horizon.

"Dermot!" Brian shouted.

Dermot turned to see his brother run up to him, out of breath.

"What's the matter with you?" Dermot asked.

"Never mind me, what's the matter with *you*? Why did you run off on me like that? I almost lost sight of you, trying to catch up."

"I didn't hear you."

"I figured as much, what with the sounds of the festival and the crowd. But, you shouldn't have run off."

"Oh, I—I'm sorry, Brian."

"Never mind. Will you please tell me what's wrong?"

Dermot hesitated, to which Brian frowned. "Don't you hide anything else from me, not after all we've been through. What is it?"

"It's—well." Dermot faltered. "I, well, I had this nightmare the other night, the night before I took you to Saershe. You remember? When I woke up? Well, in it, a dark, shrouded figure somehow kindled a wildfire that destroyed an entire forest. The tale of Taranis, and the way they described his appearance was described, it reminded me of that nightmare. I..."

"You think these events are somehow all connected?"

"I can't say for sure, yet I feel so strongly they are. In fact, right before I met Maeve again in the forest, Saershe, she uh..."

"What?"

"She seemed to know something about my nightmare.

What precisely, I cannot say."

"Didn't you ask her?"

"I never got around to it, Brian. Maeve appeared before I could ask. I—I got caught up in the moment. It just slipped my mind."

"So you suspect Saershe knows of this dark wizard. You think she's one of the Dríacht."

Dermot furrowed his brow. "Don't you?"

"It seems that way. She did call herself a guardian of the forests. But that proves nothing. Aren't you wondering, if it is true, why did she not tell us?"

"Well, perhaps she was trying to protect us."

"Or herself," Brian said, crossing his arms.

Dermot was shocked. "How can you say that of her, after what she's done for us?"

"Well, how is it can you trust her so? Do you forget she left you alone one time in the forest? You *idolize* her! And you're obsessed with Maeve after meeting her twice."

"I do not idolize Saershe! And Maeve let me live that first day. She has a good heart."

"Even if she could've killed the chieftain's missing dog?" Brian asked.

"I can't believe I'm listening to this. Saershe helped us. Aren't you even grateful I brought you to her, and she healed you like me?"

"Of course I am."

"Then why are you still complaining?"

"Because we had to lie to our parents, and you idolize Saershe."

"I already told you I don't."

"Oh really?" Brian sneered, crossing his arms. "You don't respect her more than Ma?"

"What does Ma have to do with all this? I don't see what you're getting at."

"I mean you prefer Saershe to your own mother! You've known Ma your whole life. She brought you up, yet you met Saershe only a couple days ago."

Dermot's jaw dropped. Seldom did Brian ever lose his temper like he did himself did. Then he leaned in closer, his nostrils flaring. "I've heard enough of your tongue, little brother. Maybe I was wrong to take you there, to try and trust you. I should've foreseen this from you."

Brian didn't move back, but his lips formed a scowl. "I tried to trust *you*. I see now I never can, brother. You lied to me about why we were out there! You care nothing for our home, for no one here!"

"Certainly not you!"

"Good!"

"Good!"

At that point, they impulsively turned their backs on one another, walking a few paces' distance but then they stopped and remained where they stood. However, they did not turn around.

I tried, Da, Dermot thought as if he were speaking to him now. *Brian did not take it. I didn't lie to him.*

Then, in his heart, he knew what he might ask him. *Did you really try, Dermot?*

Dermot stopped. He knew what his father would say next, because in his heart he knew his own answer. Brian couldn't take this chance, because he himself failed again to give it. He should have waited, and told him he was going with Saershe to see the gryphon. But what would Brian have said to that? He wondered what his brother was thinking right now. He looked up into the sky again,

which had turned dark. He was rather disappointed to still see no stars or moon. Then, he heard a faint sound.

"Brian," Dermot finally managed to utter.

"What?"

"Did—did you hear something?"

"Hear what?"

"That," Dermot said again.

By happenstance, both glanced at the forest.

Chapter 12

Granuaile made her way through the crowd. She asked men, and women, anyone she could, but none of them were able to help her, or they were too busy to notice her. She passed boys wrestling and playing. She asked them also, and even young girls, if they had seen either of her sons. None had.

She grew worried. It was as if they'd vanished. She returned to her husband, still standing by the thorn tree.

"You didn't find them?" he asked.

She shook her head and frowned. "Dermot better not have snuck off again and left Brian all alone."

"Come now," Pádraig said. "Dermot wouldn't do such a thing. He may have been a troublemaker in his youth, but he's matured since then."

"Has he? Given recent events, the sheriff himself told us he's having doubts."

"He's always had doubts. Dermot wasn't to blame for any of that, my dear," Pádraig said calmly.

"Well, then how do you explain his recent behavior, Pádraig? I've watched him, and he seems more secretive than ever."

"That I cannot say, but he's my son and yours, and he has a good heart. Besides, don't you think Brian would've come looking for us if he had?"

"Nevertheless, we should inform the watch or at least a guard. I would hate to involve them, but I see no other

choice."

"Very well," he agreed.

They made their way through the crowd. They could see one guard not far away, and were approaching him when Granuaile stopped her husband.

"What is it?" he asked.

"Over there!" she pointed. They saw two figures standing far from the green, barely visible in the dim outreaches of the firelight.

"You sure that's them?" he asked.

"I feel so."

"But what would they possibly be doing all the way out there? You think they lost their way?"

"I don't know. But if it is them, we better fetch them before they get into more trouble."

"I agree, my darling."

**

Preceded by the sound of leaves rustling and branches swishing, a hot dry wind came roaring through the forest. It was so strong it creaked and cracked the trees, thrashing leaves and pine needles and branches off. It blew past the brothers and throughout the festival, startling everyone, and knocking most off their feet. Fires from the torches were extinguished all at once, leaving the anxious assemblage in complete darkness. It made the brothers and many others groan.

Lightning flashed, every bolt preceding a sharp clash of thunder, some violently louder than others. People convulsed each time. Regardless, no raindrops fell from the sky. A great wave of fear swept over the people. Not

even the youngest child stirred. Their only sounds were quick, heavy breaths and faint whispering.

Never in his life had Dermot felt as frightened as he did at this moment. The memory of his dream came back to him in a rush.

As he was thinking about his nightmare, Dermot caught a faint image in the corner of his eye. He tried to convince himself his mind was deceiving him. In a flash, his mind and body froze like water in midwinter.

"Brian," Dermot whispered, "do you see that?"

"What?" Brian asked, speaking less softly than his brother.

"Over there, in the midst of the trees."

An indistinct figure swathed in black, like the one from Dermot's nightmare, strode leisurely out of the forest. Dermot couldn't move a muscle. Neither he nor Brian spoke.

The hood of the shadowy figure's black cloak clouded his face, almost as if there were no face at all. Dermot's lower jaw fell in horror as he observed the object this figure clasped firmly in one of his hands: a tall, dark staff topped by three iron claws clutching a large, smooth blood-red stone. It was almost hard to see this figure against the night's ever-strengthening shadows. Frequent flashes of lighting, however, did reveal him clearly. Dermot tried to tell himself what he dreamt was a dream, nothing more. Thoughts of Saershe and the tale he recently heard made it difficult.

This figure moved towards the spot where Dermot and Brian stood. He was still a good distance away from them when he finally stopped. Brian slowly opened his mouth. Before he could utter one sound, the dark figure

lifted his staff high. He raised his other arm, extending out his fingers. In forethought, Dermot braced himself. The jewel glowed fiercely, but that was it. Dermot was puzzled. He didn't know what to expect now, which frightened him even more.

At present, the shadowy figure lifted its head as if to gaze up into the heavens. Still bewildered, Dermot looked up. Brian and the other villagers did the same. A blanket of dense and dark clouds veiled the skies, out of which a murky silhouette emerged. All had gone so uncannily silent that Dermot could hear a pair of enormous wings flapping soft and slow.

"You think that might be Maeve?" Brian asked, pointing to the shilhouette.

"No, this creature's too large to be her. It's more like a—a..."

"Like what, Dermot?" Brian asked, his lip trembling.

"Oh mercy of the heavens, please tell me I'm wrong!"

"What do you mean?"

Everyone stared at the shadowy outline. Two enormous, glaring orange eyes came into view. More gasps billowed from the villagers. Most shuffled back a few paces, even Pádraig and Granuaile.

Cries of "Dragon!" and "Run!" rang out. Dermot himself was actually first to shout out the former. Everyone scattered, screaming. Even from the castle's battlements, soldiers were scurrying about. Despite the efforts of the sheriff, sagart, watchmen, and the chieftain's soldiers to preserve order, it was no use. For a horde frightened beyond reason can never be detained, no matter how much exertion is applied. Only the brothers and the dark character remained still.

The hooded figure thrust his staff downward, striking the earth. Though the ground was not hard as rock, Dermot still felt a mild tremor beneath his feet. Shocked beyond reason, he watched as an immense stream of fire gushed down on the green.

Everything set up for the festival was engulfed in flames. Many villagers were incinerated too, the fire drowning their screams.

"Come on!" Brian shouted. "We've got to find Ma and Da!"

Before Dermot could answer, Brian ran off with Dermot close on his heels.

**

As Granuaile had been compelled to freeze then jump to avoid a runaway horse, she lost sight of her husband. She called out his name when the hem of her dress caught fire from debris. She stumbled, screaming. Much to her relief, he reappeared, rushing to her side.

He put the flames out and helped her back up. "Come on, we've got to get back to the cottage!"

"Pádraig we've got to find our sons! They're somewhere out there still!"

"We don't have time!"

"Dermot!!!" Granuaile screamed. "Brian!!!"

Pádraig had to drag her away by force.

Once they reached their cottage, they set about freeing their livestock so they wouldn't be trapped. Fleeing, they broadsided Granuaile, knocking her off her feet. She struck the earth once the last of the family livestock had sprinted past. She lay there, whimpering.

Pádraig rushed to her side, hurriedly helping her back up. She continued to whimper, so he took her in his arms. They turned to witness their cottage being devoured by a beam of fire unleashed from the dragon's nostrils.

Husband and wife became instantly still, watching the fire slowly consume their home. Granuaile in particular looked as if she might shed tears. She buried her face in her husband's neck.

Their focus was so fixed on their burning cottage they were caught unawares. Pádraig and Granuaile were struck from behind and they fell to the ground with a thud. Shortly thereafter, they were slowly dragged away by their ankles.

**

Dermot and Brian scurried about the village. They evaded debris, fire, and fallen bodies. The sight of the latter most especially brought about intense fear for them, but they kept running. Dermot kept looking, but he saw no sign of his parents.

They dropped down on their knees and shielded their faces, for the dragon sent another stream of fire out its nostrils, straight in their direction. When they stood again they beheld Emerin ablaze.

Orange and yellow flames of orange and yellow seeped into every home, slowly consuming everything, while also roaring with hate and triumph. Heat and grit from the fire and ash brushed harshly against the boys' faces.

The dragon was closer to the ground than it had been previously. From what Dermot was able to make out, this

dragon had sharp claws, a forked tongue, heavy tail, and wings resembling a bat's. Thick, rough dark red scales coated the entire muscular body. Then there were those fiery orange eyes. They had an evil gleam within them.

The dragon twisted his body in midair, roaring so loud everyone still alive instinctively covered their ears, including the brothers. Both lowered their hands when the roar ceased.

"Look," Brian said.

Dermot's eyes moved in the direction of the manor, which was discernible by the fire of hundreds of torches posted about the outer wall. Squinting, they could barely make out dozens of archers along the battlements, firing volley after volley of arrows at the dragon. Growling with the utmost fury, the beast breathed another fiery gush straight at the castle. The manor went up in flames, instantly killing many soldiers.

"Come on!" Dermot said. "We've got to get out of here, and fast!"

The dragon swooped over the village again. He swung his tail down low, demolishing a number of cottages. The impact sent debris flying outward. Dermot promptly shielded Brian using his own body.

It ended as quickly as it began. They stood, and to their surprise, were largely unscathed. Then in horror, they saw their sagart and saínchí among several singed bodies lying before them, smeared with blood, dirt, and debris.

"No," Dermot said. Though overwhelmed with grief and tears, he managed to grab Brian's arm, dragging him forward. "Come on!"

"Our parents are still here somewhere!" He tried to

break free of Dermot's grasp. "Please, we must find them!"

"We don't have time! Now, come on!"

Brian resisted, but Dermot exerted force and grabbed him by both arms. Brian whimpered, but that didn't stop Dermot. They continued on, until they ran into the traveling saínchí.

"Come with me!" the saínchí said.

"What're you talking about?" Dermot asked.

"Listen to me, laddies! If we make for Úaene, we might have a chance!"

"Why should we go with you?" Brian asked.

"Aside from not burning, Saershe sent me here to protect you."

Dermot couldn't believe his ears. "You know her?"

"Yes! Now come on! Follow me!"

Reluctantly, they went after the man. The three hurried on, but then stopped. They sighted the dragon diving near the line of trees in front of them. Without warning, a large bolt of lightning struck the earth close to where they stood.

The three of them were knocked off their feet. The dragon swung his tail down again. Trees were ripped out of the earth, roots and all, and sent hurling into the air.

"Watch out!" Dermot yelled.

Brian screamed. The brothers curled up. A gigantic tree barely missed them, crashing into the earth. Brush fell upon them but didn't hurt them.

When more debris fell, the brothers lowered their arms. Dermot urged Brian up, but they had only stood when the dragon uprooted more trees. Before the lads could drop, it was not debris but the gust conjured by the

dragon's tail that sent them off their feet. They landed on their backs with a small thud, groaning. Albeit battered, they lifted their arms to defend themselves from the brush.

Then, the debris ceased falling. Nevertheless, their hearts continued racing. Consumed by exhaustion and heat, it was no wonder they were taken by blackness.

Shadows loomed over the brothers. Both of them were dragged away.

Chapter 13

When Dermot regained his wits, it was no longer dark. He was lying on his belly. Opening his eyes, his vision was blurry. He blinked a couple times, groaning due to a slight headache. As if by impulse, he jerked his head left and right. With his vision at last restored, he beheld a sight he did not envisage.

The forest was no longer green as he remembered, instead resembled late autumn, perhaps on the verge of midwinter. As far as one could see, trees had lost their leaves. Strangely, even the pines were bare. Branches bore a chilling resemblance to outspread human arms and hands. Every leaf, every pine needle, lay on the ground. All were shriveled and brown, not the scarlet and golden hues of autumn. A faint but dense mist hovered above the earth. A blanket of thick, gray clouds blotted out the heavens. Storm clouds, by their looks, but no storm ever arose. Not even a single wild animal could be sighted anyplace.

"It looks so—dead," Dermot said, staring emptily. He didn't want it to be real. It couldn't be.

A heart-twisting grief overwhelmed him, even more so by his memory of Nature's beauty that Saershe had introduced him to right before his second meeting with Maeve.

He struggled to move his aching body, during which time he discovered thick ropes securely tied tight around

his wrists. In his rising panic, he turned to see his brother lying alongside him, motionless, and likewise bound.

"Brian?" he whispered.

No response came. Brian didn't even move.

"Brian?" Dermot whispered more fervently.

When he still didn't move, Dermot reached over and poked him with his knuckles.

Brian stirred. "Stop that."

"Thank goodness." Dermot took a deep breath, pulling back his hands.

Brian opened his eyes halfway. He muttered, "D— Dermot? Is that you?"

"Yes, little brother. Are you all right?"

Brian groaned. "I've got a splitting headache."

"I do too."

Brian noticed the ropes binding them. "Wha—what's happened? Who—who's tied us? Where's the man who helped...?"

"I don't know. I..."

"What is it?" Brian asked.

"Look," Dermot whispered. Casting their eyes up, they beheld an imposing figure clad in dark armor. In one hand he held a giant sword and in the other a huge, oblong black shield lacking an emblem, matching his tunic. His back was turned toward the brothers.

"Mercy of the heavens!" Brian said. "What're we going to do now?"

"Shush, brother."

Turning his head in the opposite direction, Dermot spied a large yew tree less than a stone's throw away. His face cheered somewhat, bewildering his brother.

"What is it?" Brian asked.

III

"Come on," whispered Dermot. He crawled toward the tree, for he still felt too groggy and weak to stand. Brian instinctively crawled beside him. They both groaned.

"What're you doing?" Brian asked.

"Be patient. I'm almost there."

Pressing the rope binding his wrists against the trunk, Dermot commenced to rub it rather violently. He muttered, "Come on! Come on!"

Finally the ropes began to part.

"It's working!" Brian said.

"Once I'm free, I'll untie you," Dermot said. "I'm almost there!"

Alas, their elation was short-lived. A sword blade came down, its tip touching Dermot's throat. Both brothers froze, and then slowly turned to look up. Looming over them, stood four figures garbed in corresponding suits of black tunics and armor. Dermot and Brian had not even heard them move, and yet here they stood, each of them holding a dark sword.

Dermot muttered, "Confound it. I should've known it would've been too easy."

Brian appeared far too terrified to speak.

The one holding his sword to Dermot's throat cackled. Like the others, he wore a helmet with a visor. Dermot shuddered, for the voice sounded familiar, yet strangely distant.

That armored man said, "Aye, you should have."

Dermot's eyes broadened.

"Sergeant?" he said as the other three men joined their comrade.

"That man is no more," the sergeant said, his voice

still bearing its familiar sternness. "I am a mairág, one of the legions of the Mairágh, laddie as are these men."

"You're a what?" Brian asked.

The sergeant slowly moved the tip of his blade slightly up Dermot's throat, making him tremble.

Then, a fifth dark-armored figure appeared.

"What is the meaning of this?" he said.

Dermot recognized the sheriff's voice. Now we're really in trouble, he thought.

"Everything's under control, sir," the sergeant said. "We made sure the old man was dead. These rascals thought they could escape, foolish as they are."

"I see," the sheriff said. He turned to the sergeant, directing him with two fingers. "You go join the search and see if any others may have escaped the dragon's breath or our master. You and you, go with him, now!"

The saínchí's dead? O-others? Who's their master? Dermot wondered if their master might be the chieftain, and if so, whether or not this was all some monstrous joke. Remembering the dragon's rampage, the burning of the village and castle, he felt that unlikely, that something else was at play. Then he remembered that shadowy figure. Could it be him? Dermot had had many encounters with both these men when he was younger, but never felt as frightened of them as he did now.

The sergeant grumbled as he sheathed his blade and raced off with two others. The sheriff turned to the one who remained. "You and I shall take these two rascals to our master. This one in particular ought to finally learn what *true* punishment is."

"I agree, sir."

Dermot and Brian gaped as the two men sheathed

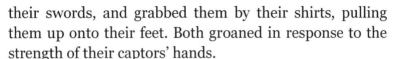
their swords, and grabbed them by their shirts, pulling them up onto their feet. Both groaned in response to the strength of their captors' hands.

The brothers were dragged through the dead trees. For how long and how far Dermot knew not, but a horrifying sight awaited them when they arrived at their destination. More villagers were either lying on their chests or on their knees, arms behind their backs. Standing proud in a perfect circle were at least thirty men equipped and garbed as the sergeant and sheriff were. Each carried a sword and large dagger. Most boasted other weapons too, ranging from flails to longbows, crossbows, maces, and battle-axes. Those holding longbows likewise wore quivers full of black arrows slung over their shoulders.

The captive villagers stared at the brothers. They themselves were small in number, perhaps no more than twenty, not even a fifth of Emerin's population. Two large wooden carts with chests and bundles stood close by.

Two voices called out the brothers' names, voices Dermot knew all too well. Their eyes fell on their parents, who were lying beside several other villagers, their faces aghast with fear and surprise at seeing their sons.

Dermot's legs wobbled.

"Ma!" Brian shouted.

"Da!" Dermot cried, "Are you all right?"

"Silence!!!" the sheriff said, making the prisoners cringe. He quickly grabbed his dagger and held the blade to Dermot's throat.

"Let me make this perfectly clear. If either of you speak unless spoken to again, I will slit your throats. Do you understand me?"

Neither brother spoke, but both nodded hastily. The sheriff sheathed his dagger.

Dermot's lower jaw slackened, but not for long. He noticed, standing at the center of the circle of armored men was the dark figure from his dream, the same figure he and Brian witnessed emerge from behind the trees preceding the raid.

The figure pulled down his hood slowly. Terror gripped Dermot. Seeing his face, he preferred the man faceless. His long hair and beard were black like his attire, but bore streaks of gray. He had pointed ears, and a hooked nose with arching nostrils. A long scar ran across the left side of his face. He parted his pale lips, exposing a set of white teeth, the canines oddly long and sharp, much more like those of a wolf than a man. Then there were his eyes, the blackest of eyes, so black in fact they seemed much larger than those of any other person.

Two other mairágs approached the wizard. These two had in their grip, to everyone's shock, none other than the chieftain himself. A tall man with a proud face, his extravagant garments and polished armor were all gone. He wore naught but a simple, dirty, ragged nightgown. His face, hands, and bare feet were repeatedly bruised, smeared in mud and what Dermot realized to be dried blood. His long hair and beard were a mess too.

Never in all his life had Dermot seen the chieftain in such a state. The other prisoners stared in disbelief.

In spite of his downtrodden appearance, by the expression written on his face he disdainfully tried to maintain a dominating persona. The wizard made a motion with his staff. One of the Mairágh beside the chieftain forced him onto his knees. The chieftain

groaned, at which the dark wizard said, "How does it feel to have been brought so low, my Lord Emerin?"

"I trusted you," the chieftain said. "When I thought the gryphon long gone, you came and assured me the beast was still there. You promised me your magic would succeed after all my men failed. You deceived me."

He hired him? Dermot couldn't believe his ears. The feeling was universal amongst the other hostages, who glanced at one another with widened eyes. Dermot gawped at Brian in horror at knowing this truth. Dermot, for his part, felt stupid again.

I should've known, he thought to himself.

"I spoke true when I said the gryphon hadn't gone," the wizard smirked. "But I promised to find her. Never did I say a word that I would turn the creature over to you. Of course, you never asked me to."

"You treacherous monster!" the chieftain yelled. "You burned down my house and my village! You and my sheriff have seduced my men into serving you!"

The mairág standing over the chieftain struck him in the back, making him moan.

The sheriff was working for the wizard? Dermot never liked the sheriff, but he'd never expected treachery of this sort from him. He remembered the sheriff telling him earlier to enjoy himself, while it lasted. Had he not suspected something wasn't right? He could see horror in the other villagers' faces, including his parents.

"Oh, it was not hard to *change their minds,*" the wizard sniggered. "The sheriff was more willing than you. Once you see the truth as they all do now, you shall understand."

As he spoke, the dark wizard stepped forward until

the chieftain's head almost touched his knees. Dermot could barely make out his face.

"Look into my eyes," hissed the wizard.

The chieftain flinched, turning his face away.

"Look at me!" the wizard ordered more forcefully.

Chapter 14

The chieftain's head turned painfully slow, as if it was pushed by an unseen force too powerful for his own will. He gazed into the wizard's eyes, which began to glow a fiery red. The warlock thrust his staff down into the earth. A deafening sound forced the captives to try to cover their ears. A brilliant red light appeared from the staff's crystal.

The warlock uttered an incantation:

Shadows so dark
Escape no free will
Shadows so dark
Spreading to every heart

He repeated those words many times over. He raised his arms up like wings. All the villagers cowered. Dermot himself was unsure as to what might transpire next. He didn't have to wait long to find out.

Thick black smog seeped out of the wizard's palms and swirled, gradually growing larger. The spiraling smog encircled him like gigantic serpents. The chieftain held his arms out in an eager, accepting manner.

The wizard stretched out his fingers, and the smog moved through the air away from him and swirled around the chieftain's head, going into his nose, mouth, and ears. At that, the wizard stopped chanting.

The sight brought about shudders and whimpers from the prisoners. However, the dark wizard and his minions remained steadfast as ever.

Fortunately the shadows faded as quickly as they had manifested. The chieftain was silent. His eyes glowed red too, and his lips relaxed. The wizard's eyes had by now returned to their natural color. The two armored men holding the chieftain unhanded him and moved away. Their master stepped forth, a smirk on his face.

The chieftain rose slowly to his feet, keeping his back stiff and straight. His face in some way had developed into something even more demonic.

"How may I serve you, my most excellent prince?" the chieftain asked.

Dermot and Brian stared at each other then back at the chieftain. Dermot's shock was mutual among the other prisoners. He understood the chieftain's behavior somehow had to be related to what the wizard said about "changing" minds.

"As one of the Mairágh," the warlock said, "You shall be empowered by dark magic, to serve my command alone. You shall willingly give your life for my cause."

"I am truly honored, my most noble prince and dark wizard. To all of this, I solemnly swear."

The chieftain bowed his head, horrifying the villagers even more. It was then that the wizard stepped back and eight mairágs came forward, carrying various pieces of armor, along with a black tunic, a sword, shield, dagger, longbow, and quiver with arrows. They crowded around the chieftain like hungry dogs.

No one could see the chieftain fully, but Dermot heard the ripping of his nightgown, along with every other

distinct sound that followed.

The chieftain was soon dressed from toe to head in the armor of a mairág. He himself put on a pair of gauntlets, a helmet, and armed himself with the weapons they brought him. Once he was handed his own sword, the mairágs eased back. He brandished the weapon in front of him, stating calmly, "To the fall of the high-king, and to your rise, my liege!"

"That'll do," the warlock ordered, holding his hand up. "Step back. You shall await further orders, and only speak when spoken to first. Am I clear?"

"Your whim is my will, Dark Prince," the chieftain said, saluting him with his weapon and bowing his head. "I serve you alone."

Dark Prince? Dermot remembered the evil wizard that the minstrel had spoken of. *Could it be?* He felt a lump form in his throat. He looked to Brian, whose face bore utter shock and wonder.

Once the chieftain stepped out of the circle, he sheathed his sword. Two mairágs holding Dermot and Brian dragged them forward. They hurled them to the ground where they landed face down into a small pile of shriveled leaves.

"What is this?" the wizard asked.

Before the sheriff could respond, the dark wizard spoke again. "Have you found any of those who escaped the fire?"

"Not yet, sire. We're still looking," the sheriff said.

"That's unacceptable," the wizard hissed, who looked at the brothers again.

"We will find them, sire, I swear."

"You will, or you will pay. Now why have you brought

these boys before me?"

"These are the two scoundrels I spoke to you about, my noble prince."

"Ah yes, of course," the wizard said with a nasty smile, "Greetings, Dermot and Brian."

Again, the brothers uttered not a sound.

"Permit me to introduce myself," the warlock said. "I am Taranis, heir to the Denuan throne and practitioner of black magic. Many Denuans know me simply as the Dark Prince."

Dermot tried hard not to think of Saershe, Ruairí, or Maeve. No matter how often he told himself in his mind to not think about them, the images and their voices kept returning. He wished he could hide away in shadow. But he was also bewildered. What did Taranis mean he was heir to the throne? How could that be?

Taranis observed Dermot, intrigued by his flinching and sweating. "I think you're trying to dismiss thoughts from your mind. What memories torment you so?"

Dermot knew he had to lie and lie quick, so he said the first thing he thought of: "The—the destruction of my village!"

"Nay, me boy," Taranis said. "I know when someone is lying to me. There is something more, isn't there?"

Dermot kept his eyes shut and face bent to his chest, out of Taranis's eyes. With that, Taranis stepped backward and hid his face beneath his hood once more. Dermot slowly raised his head, and observed with grief the wooded area once more.

"Well, well" Taranis said. "You are dismayed at the present state of Úaene Forest. So rare it is today to find one in this kingdom so desiring of goodwill unto all that is wild and green."

"No thanks to you, you monster," Dermot said.

"I wish you hadn't said that!" Brian said.

"Such a sensible boy!" taunted Taranis. "Don't be hesitant to speak your mind. One shouldn't withhold who and what he truly is. It makes cowards of men."

Dermot turned away, regretting opening his mouth.

"Well, well, me lad," Taranis said. "I suspect your feelings regarding the realm of wildlife aren't what you desperately desire to hide from me either. No matter. Whatever your secret may be, my quest for the truth shan't be toilsome."

Seizing Dermot by the throat, Taranis lifted him up with one arm. He dragged Dermot's face close to his own, their noses almost touching. Choking, Dermot recoiled. Taranis glared directly into his eyes. Brian hid his face, while Dermot tried not to dwell on what could ensue, but it was no use.

Excruciating pain invaded Dermot's body as Taranis's eyes glowed bright red once again. Dermot's memories of his experiences in the forest, his encounters with Saershe, Ruairí, and Maeve, all flooded back into his mind faster than water. Only this time, there was a great feeling of darkness that hadn't existed when he had experienced those moments.

Taranis's face beamed malevolently. He let Dermot go. The boy landed on his chest and arms.

Dermot saw Brian's mouth open. He hoped his brother would say something, but he didn't.

For Dermot, his agony did not dwindle. Somehow, he knew the truth. The wizard had used his dark magic to probe Dermot's mind and heart, and in doing so felt what

he felt. Taranis had been able to see what Dermot once saw, hear what he once heard, and know what he and his brother knew. Dermot couldn't bear to lift his head.

Taranis momentarily seemed surprised, but nodded, then laughed.

Lord Emerin asked, "Shall I, milord?"

"Not yet," he said. "Wait a moment."

"Yes, my lord."

"Well, I humbly thank you, Dermot," Taranis said, "and your brother, too. How fortunate it was that you were not among those who were given to my fire-breathing friend for his supper. I never foresaw a pair of common boys would know their whereabouts. Now, it is with great dismay that I must inform you that neither of you are of any use to me any longer, or else I possibly might have been persuaded to prolong your eventual fate. I cannot deny that it is a terrible waste to extinguish such potency. But, alas it is necessary, and can't be prolonged."

The wizard beckoned the chieftain with the snap of his fingers. Lord Emerin bowed to him, gripping his sword tightly.

"What are my orders, my most noble prince?" he eagerly asked.

"You may dispose of these two young fools," ordered Taranis without casting a glance on him. "This will be far better a kingdom without them."

"It will be my pleasure, your highness." The mairág eagerly bowed his head, gripping the handle of his sword. Before he could draw it, Granuaile and Pádraig cried aloud together. "No! No! Please! Don't hurt them! Please!"

Taranis turned to the couple, who fell silent. He

extended his arm out to his minion, and raised his hand. With that, the mairág obediently lowered his blade back into his scabbard, clenching his fist.

Taranis maneuvered his way toward the smith and his wife until he stood above them.

"Ah, you two must be the brothers' parents," he cackled, "How lovely."

"Please, sir!" Granuaile said. "Whoever you are, whatever you want, please don't kill my sons! Have mercy! Please!"

"I beg you, sir, please don't!" Pádraig added. "Take my life instead! Please, just let my sons and my wife live!"

Granuaile and the brothers were stunned into silence.

Taranis smiled. "Your love for them is quite touching. Personally, I am astonished you didn't keep a better watch over them. Right under your noses, they convened with my adversary. They promised to help protect the gryphon by keeping silent, even from you."

Granuaile and Pádraig turned their eyes toward their sons. She asked them if he was telling the truth, whereas the smith was at a loss for words.

Dermot didn't speak. His chin slumped onto his chest. Brian whimpered.

All around, bewildered villagers stared. Not one among them made a sound. Most of them turned to look at one of the other villagers beside them, and then the other.

"How tender," Taranis sniggered. "Even families can harbor deep, dark secrets, masking them with an imprudent sentiment. You know, my friends, in all my years, I have always found our innermost emotions inflict torments a hundredfold more torturous in comparison to

any amount of physical suffering."

Taranis looked at the chieftain, who in turn stood at attention.

"As you were," the wizard said.

"Yes, milord," the chieftain bowed his head. Without a word, he unsheathed his sword slowly.

"No!" objected Pádraig and Granuaile in chorus.

Taranis and his minion ignored them. The chieftain stood over the boys. He positioned the tip of his blade over the back of Dermot's neck. The sharp point brought a stinging prick to the boy, but not a drop of blood was shed.

Dermot so desired to call to his father, but his throat had gone dry. He could feel his heart pounding faster as he breathed hard. He shut his eyes. He had no desire to appear weak at this moment.

"Please, sir!" Granuaile pleaded. "I beg of you!"

"Worry not, my dear woman," Taranis said, finally looking toward her. "Once your beloved husband is one of mine, I shall have him dispose of you personally."

"I'll never serve you!" Pádraig said.

Taranis smirked, grabbing the smith by his hands. "That is what your chieftain's soldiers said. Now, they all serve me and my cause."

The chieftain no sooner raised his weapon when a voice shouted, "Torin!"

All mairágs turned in the direction from where the voice came, as did their master, sinking their heels deeper into the earth. Those of the wizard's minions who hadn't yet drawn their weapons did so now.

All the prisoners likewise turned their eyes. Only Dermot felt a little light-hearted. He knew that voice.

Chapter 15

Swathed in an elegant, leafy green robe, a darker green cloak and matching surcoat, Saershe emerged from behind a cluster of dead ash trees. She held an oaken staff slightly resembling an old gnarled tree, with a light green crystal top embedded in its little branches. The stone in her cloak's silver brooch was also dark green. Once again, behind those brilliant green eyes of hers shimmered a strong feeling of power and will, which gave Dermot hope.

A chilling silence swept over the prisoners. Many of them gazed in awe, Granuaile and Pádraig included. Dermot and Brian on the other hand half-smiled.

"Ah," scowled Taranis, "The Lady of Green Trees herself. I wondered when you would show your face to me."

"Torin," scolded Saershe. "It was brazen of you to return to this kingdom."

"Torin?" Brian whispered to Dermot. "I thought he said his name was Taranis."

Dermot shushed him. He didn't want them to get into any more trouble than they already were.

"I never break a promise, Saershe," remarked Taranis. "You of all Denuans should know that. And need I remind you I am no longer known by that name?"

Saershe shook her head. "You haven't changed. You never did learn the most valuable of our lessons. Nature, life and love are this world's greatest treasures, the deep

roots of the flowers of harmony and goodness. We ourselves are part of Nature, for without her, there is no life."

"Mark my words," warned Taranis. "Once my forces are fully restored, I shall snuff out the old coven like a candle's flame. You and a few I will spare 'til the end, after you witness my final victory. All Denú will be subject to my will, to be done with as I please."

"She is not yours to control," said Saershe, remaining calm as ever, "Nor any of us."

"Nor am I yours to control." Taranis pursed his lips. "I've heard enough of your lectures! Now you'll be first to feel my wrath!"

Taranis steadily raised his arm and swung it as if slicing the air with a sword. Each mairág who carried a longbow pulled an arrow from his quiver, and aimed straight at Saershe.

"No!" screamed Brian and Dermot simultaneously as the arrows were set free.

Saershe, a smile on her face, stood still. As the arrows sailed within inches of her, she spread her arms and floated up into the air. Her robes and long hair fluttered on a sudden breeze that carried away some of her leaves and flower petals.

The brothers became still, not taking their eyes off her. Certainly for Dermot, she seemed more a divine than mortal being, floating above them. If he had ever even harbored any doubt she was a sorceress, he had none now.

Not one arrow hit its intended target. In seconds that area of the forest erupted in flames. The prisoners panicked, but their captors remained steadfast and kept

them trapped.

Dermot noticed every time arrows flew, Taranis murmured beneath his breath, while his eyes and those arrowheads shone red. Saershe however managed to evade them all. She never once appeared to lose her calm.

"Slay her!" the wizard bellowed. His eyes blazed a fiery red again.

The archers fired more waves of arrows. Every so often, one came close to striking her, but Saershe eluded each one. Even within this carnage, Dermot was spellbound by her still.

The arrows set dead trees and piles of shriveled leaves afire. Saershe gently wove both vertically and horizontally through tree branches. She landed back on her feet, and elevated her arms. She rotated them faster and faster, speaking in the old language.

A great gust of wind was summoned, carrying up mounds of leaves, twigs, stones, and dirt along with it. Taranis floated into the air himself in order to avoid being swept up into it. Dermot, Brian, and the prisoners shielded themselves with their arms. The mairágs were swept off of their feet, including those nearest the brothers. A number of them smashed into dead trees, each which cracked and fell. Amidst all this, a number of the hostages surged up from the ground and tried to run.

"Stop them, you fools!" Taranis ordered his minions. Meanwhile, he soared as smoothly as Saershe. Whereas she appeared ethereal, he was ever more horrific than before.

Dermot watched in horror as mairágs slaughtered as many of the villagers as they could. They took no prisoners.

Dermot felt a presence behind him. Assuming it to be another mairág, he slowly turned to look over his shoulder, and gasped.

"Ruairí!" he whispered.

Brian jerked his head around, and like Dermot gasped, then smiled. Ruairí, wearing a sea blue cloak, had been hiding behind a nearby tree. He placed his right forefinger atop his mouth, so both brothers sealed their lips. Dermot nodded. He did his best to stay calm, difficult as it was for him.

After a moment of relief, all three boys' attention was drawn to the sheriff and a few other mairágs. They were staring straight back at them.

"Well, well," he clenched his sword. "Take them!"

Before the mairágs could take a single step, a new blast of wind swept them off their feet, but it didn't affect the lads. The mairágs crashed against a dead tree, which cracked and fell to the ground.

The lads meanwhile remained where they were, staring until their attention was drawn back to the battle.

Once the wind died down, Taranis landed on the ground himself and stood opposite Saershe. The wizard thrust his staff forward and sent more beams of red light at her. This time, she held her hands straight out. Green beams shot out of her palms and clashed against the red ones. These beams crackled like lightning.

Spying an opportunity, Ruairí crept forth and produced a knife from his belt. Dermot attempted to speak, but Ruairí shushed him. He cut the ropes binding their wrists.

"Thank you," Dermot whispered.

"Can you two get up?" Ruairí asked.

They nodded.

A caw familiar to all three permeated the air. All activity halted, even the duel between the sorceress and dark wizard. Everyone's eyes veered above the treetops, prisoners trying to flee, and mairágs in pursuit.

"Maeve!" exclaimed Saershe. "What are you doing here? Leave now!"

Maeve ignored her, spreading her mighty wings and talons. Caught off guard, none of the Mairágh had time to raise their weapons to strike or their shields to defend themselves. Cawing loudly, Maeve sent several of them falling to the ground using her forelimbs and wings. The rest slipped and tumbled. One fell close to Pádraig and Granuaile, who were still among those close to the battle.

A dagger on the Mairágh's belt slipped out during the fall, landing next to the smith. He squatted down in order to grab it, and turned to his wife. She took it and cut the ropes.

"You blundering fools!" thundered Taranis. "Seize that gryphon!"

Maeve thereupon flew into the sky, cracking branches with her powerful wings. Mairágs shot more arrows at her. Maeve evaded them for she had passed the treetops until another wave of arrows was fired and Taranis, speaking in the old language, imbued them with black magic. The arrow tips were glowing purple, flying fast, when...

"NO!" Dermot winced.

Several of the arrows struck Maeve's wings. Laughing in triumph, Taranis conjured fire, sending gushes of orange and yellow flames from his hands towards her.

Saershe whirled her arms again, incanting a new

charm. A giant wave of water rose from the stream nearby and flew through the air. It broke into a number of sisters and splashed mairágs, pushing them off of their feet as well as extinguishing flaming trees and earth.

"Hurry up, let's move!" Ruairí said.

Dermot asked, "But what about your grandmother and Maeve?"

"We'll catch up with them," said Ruairí. "Now let's go!"

"No!" Brian stopped and looked back. "Ma and Da..."

"Come on!" Dermot said, dragging his brother away.

They ran a short distance through the trees. To their surprise, they heard their parents' voices and turned to see them coming with other villagers. Pádraig held the dagger tightly in his hand. Granuaile hugged Brian. Her husband hugged Dermot. The boys assured them they were all right. The smith and his wife both stared at Ruairí.

"Who are you?" Granuaile asked.

"I'm Ruairí, grandson of..."

"Da," interrupted Dermot, raising his hands. "Please, let me explain."

Granuaile frowned. "Explaining won't excuse all the trouble you two are in."

Pádraig shook his head. "We can discuss all this later, darling. Right now..."

"You there!" hollered a voice.

They wheeled to see the sheriff pointing his sword at them. Accompanied by two mairágs, he charged at the group.

"Go," Pádraig said sternly.

"Da," Dermot hesitated.

"Don't argue with me. Run. Protect your mother and brother."

"Pádraig," Granuaile said.

"Don't you argue with me too, now go!"

Padraig raised the dagger, but the sheriff was quicker and knocked it out of his hand in one swipe. Granuaile heard her husband scream and shouted his name. All four stopped and watched.

The sheriff aimed to strike Pádraig, but he quickly evaded the blade. Some of the other imprisoned villagers grabbed handfuls of earth and threw them at the sheriff.

The other two meanwhile charged toward Granuaile and the boys. She tried to catch up with her sons, but she tripped on the hem of her dress and fell. Brian instinctively turned and ran toward her, shouting, "Ma!"

Dermot spun around to go after him. Pádraig wheeled and saw the other two mairágs approach his family the moment Brian called to his mother. He turned away from the sheriff.

By then, more mairágs came to his aid. The second grabbed Granuaile as Brian neared her. Dermot seized his brother in his arms. The third mairág raised his sword at the brothers, but Pádraig grabbed the mairág's arm.

"Da," Dermot said.

"Go! Now!" he ordered his sons, while struggling with the mairág. "Boys, go!"

They had little choice but to flee, as other mairágs raced after them. They heard their parents struggle and scream. Their screams were joined by others from the crowd. And then there was silence.

With heavy hearts, they stopped and looked back in the direction of their parents, even though they couldn't

see them anymore. A terrible pain flooded Dermot. By the look he saw in his brother's eyes he knew beyond a doubt Brian felt the same.

"We must keep moving," Dermot said with a heavy heart. "Come one."

Brian didn't argue. They ran to catch up with Ruairí. Dermot wanted to get away from it all.

Chapter 16

As fast as they could, they scurried through the trees, dodging low branches and leaping over fallen logs and large rocks. The raging fire spread behind them. Ruairí urged the brothers onward. Dermot was too miserable to argue. A while later they finally stopped to catch their breath.

"Did we lose them?" Dermot asked, pressing his hands pressing hard against his legs.

"For now," Ruairí said. "But not for long, I fear."

"I have to know," Brian said. He attempted to run back, but Dermot grabbed him and yelled, "No!"

"Keep your voice down!" Ruairí said. "You want them to find us?"

"We can't go back, Brian," Dermot said.

Brian broke down in tears. Dermot himself couldn't contain his own feelings. Tears streamed down his cheeks too. They stopped when he heard a noise.

"Shush," Dermot said. "Do you hear that?"

"Aye," Ruairí said. "It sounds like wings."

"Could it be the dragon?" Brian said, sniffling.

"Let's climb this oak and see if we can find out," Ruairí said.

"Are you sure that's a good idea?" Brian asked, furrowing his brow.

Ruairí didn't answer. The tree hadn't been severely burned yet, so Ruairí placed his foot squarely on a large

root and reached toward one of the branches. With a little difficulty he managed to push himself upward. Dermot followed, losing his foothold at first, but not his balance. He almost chuckled, reminding himself he hadn't climbed in a while. On the second try, he managed to pull himself up with relative ease, much to his amazement. Brian, who had never climbed a tree in his life, remained where he was, gazing around. Dermot looked down at him in mid-ascension and told his brother not to move. Brian promised he wouldn't.

"How's it feel to be up in a tree again, Dermot?" Ruairí asked, sounding more inquisitive than encouraging as they pushed small branches away from their faces.

"Not quite as I imagined," Dermot said.

"But you got off the ground easily."

"Well, true, I—look over there!"

Looking up, they saw a dragon flying overhead. Taranis himself was riding the creature. Although they were far below, the boys heard him bellow, "You think you can defeat me, Saershe? I'll find you, and the rest of your kind, no matter where you hide! And I shall slay all of you!"

"Come on, let's go," urged Dermot, though part of him longed to relish being up in a tree once more. He and Ruairí climbed down then jumped to the ground.

"What'd you see?" Brian asked.

"Oh no," Dermot said. "Look!"

They turned to see the wildfire spreading rapidly throughout Úaene. Without warning a river of dragon fire came down, incinerating many trees. All around, the boys could hear the sounds of screams, suddenly silenced.

"We've got to keep moving," Dermot said. "Come on!"

They ran. Eventually, they crossed the woodland's border right before the fire was able to ensnare them. They sank to their knees, wheezing and helplessly watching the fire devour the trees. When Dermot turned, he beheld to his horror all that remained of Emerin. He stood up and took a step forward.

Not a single cottage had survived intact. It was no use searching for whatever charred wreckage had once been their home. Wisps of black smoke still rose from the debris, as well as from the ruins of the manor, where the battlements had been severely damaged, and piles of stone lay. What they did not see were any lifeless bodies, human or livestock.

Dermot remembered once hearing long ago that a dragon's breath was so powerful a person would be completely turned to ashes, flesh and bone and all.

He fell to his knees, followed by Brian. Both wept for their lost home and loss of their parents. The heavens let loose tears too. All three boys became soaking wet, yet none gave any thought to it.

Ruairí knelt down beside the brothers. Brian wiped his runny nose. Dermot griped his chest, feeling guilt as well as grief. Guilt that he couldn't have done anything to prevent this destruction. He thought not only of his parents, but the other screams he'd heard, followed by that terrible silence. He knew each scream that was silenced came from someone who had been born and grew up on the same patch of land as he.

"Brothers," Ruairí whispered, putting a hand on each of their shoulders. Brian shook him off and turned away. Dermot did nothing.

As the wind and rain died down, they turned around,

realizing the fire was out. Much of Úaene was left a graveyard of bare trunks. Some were singed, but most were blackened. For Dermot, it was a dreadful sight to see the woodland in such a state, worse than before.

When they heard the sound of heavy wings coming from above, they leaped to their feet and whirled around, gazing skywards. There emerged from the gray clouds not one but two gryphons. The second appeared to be supporting Maeve in flight, while carrying bundles in her beak and talons.

Dermot knew right away who the second gryphon was. Then, to his horror, he realized Maeve was covered in blood, particularly her wings. She was flying rather awkwardly, scattering blood drops and feathers, and might have fallen if not for the other gryphon using her body to support her.

The boys backed away as the gryphons descended into the area. The second gryphon let the bundles drop gently. Glowing amidst green light, Saershe instantly transfigured back into herself. She and the boys turned to Maeve, who trotted rather slowly. From what Dermot saw, her limbs were badly bruised.

Then, unexpectedly, Brian charged in anger at Maeve, screaming. Dermot failed to grab him. Ruairí, however, succeeded in doing so. Dermot then helped him to restrain Brian.

Brian sobbed so loud it smacked of a roar as much as a wail. Saershe remained still, whereas the gryphon arched her wings and reared on her hind legs cawing defensively. She didn't strike him. She kept cawing. *Stop this! Don't be a fool!*

"Brian, please!" Ruairí said. "Control yourself! This

won't solve anything."

"This is your fault! All of it!" Brian railed at the gryphon. "None of this would've happened if you hadn't come here! They're all dead because of you! *My parents* are dead because of *you!*"

Dermot's stomach grew heavy. He nevertheless kept a tight grip on his little brother.

"Enough!" Saershe said.

They stopped struggling and gaped at her, then diverted their focus toward Maeve. She wobbled before dropping down, squawking feebly. *Help!*

Saershe rushed to her, followed by the boys. She thoroughly examined the gryphon's injuries. The boys watched with Dermot standing between Ruairí and Brian.

"How is she?" Dermot asked, wiping wet hair out of his face. "Will she be all right?"

Saershe didn't reply. She turned to her grandson, pointing to the bundles.

"Yes, Grandma," he replied, going to the bundles and looking through them.

"You shall feel better soon," Saershe said in a soft voice, gently rubbing Maeve's neck.

Maeve made an effort to relax, gathering her inner strength.

Ruairí returned carrying a small satchel. He retrieved a ceramic bottle and several large pieces of white cloth, both of which he handed to his grandmother, whispering "The rosin rose."

Saershe opened the bottle, carefully pouring liquid onto the cloth. Dermot knew what would occur next. Saershe dabbed each of Maeve's injuries. She received from Ruairí sprigs of blackwort and the thousand-leaf

flower, and pieces of white cloth. It took time to dress the bruised limbs and bleeding wounds, but Saershe was patient, and calm. Maeve squawked rather uncomfortably, but Saershe shushed her.

Dermot couldn't help but be overwhelmed by a wave of empathy, and deep understanding for Maeve.

She's being treated the same way I was, he thought. He heard Saershe mumble again, as she slowly waved her hand across the injuries. For a moment Dermot thought her palm somehow glowed blue. He remembered having seen it glow once before, or so he thought.

"There," Saershe said. "Now, I advise you not to fly 'til your wings are properly healed."

Maeve grunted. Saershe whispered something in her ear. Dermot couldn't hear what it was. Still, he wondered.

Saershe turned to Brian. "Tell me, do you honestly think the same fate wouldn't have befallen another village or town if Maeve journeyed there instead? Even if she hadn't sought me here, another forest could have suffered the same fate as Úaene. Another village or town could have been burned to ashes. Either way, Taranis would have laid Emerin to ruin sooner or later. No blame can be placed on Maeve. Is it not natural for any mother to protect her child?"

Brian's face fell. Dermot knew she was right, but he kept silent. He thought about his own mother and father, giving themselves up for him and Brian. Hanging his head, his thoughts pained him terribly.

Maeve squawked at Brian, nudging him. *I forgive you. Don't blame yourself, child. I know you loved your parents.*

Brian wept. He asked Saershe, "Couldn't you have

done anything to stop the raid?"

"She did," Ruairí said.

Maeve squawked. *Yes.*

"Taranis acted far swifter than I anticipated," Saershe said. "Normally he prefers to lure his enemies to him. He caught me off guard this time. Significant damage had already been done when we fought. I had to defend the forest and all the creatures as well as fight for your fellow villagers. I tried, but in their terror and confusion I could not help them to safety."

"And you sent that traveling saínchí to rescue us?" Dermot asked.

"I did," she said. "My fellow guardians and I have allies who possess not our gifts, but who aid us greatly in defending this realm. I have mourned his death, and I do still, but he knew the risks and was willing to do what needed to be done. For his courage, I honor and remember him."

Dermot faced her. Now that his mind was not preoccupied with the present situation, he asked, "Uh, Saershe, we—earlier today, before the attack, Brian and I heard a story from him and our own saínchí and sagart about a war Taranis waged against the gryphons and a magical coven..."

"You mean the Dríacht," Saershe said, standing up. "If you're asking me if I'm one of them, the answer is yes, I am one of the Dríacht, a dríadór. Denuan lore knows me as the Lady of Green Trees."

Silence ensued. Though Dermot suspected she was a sorceress all along, especially after Taranis mentioned his intent of snuffing out "the old coven," the revelation was still stunning.

Brian turned to Ruairí, who said as if on instinct, "I'm apprenticed to become a dríadór. I've known it to be my destiny since I was little."

"Speaking of which," Saershe said, glaring at her grandson, "I specifically instructed you to watch o'er Maeve. You disobeyed my orders."

"Forgive me, Grandma, but I had to do something."

Maeve exhaled softly. *Please, don't blame him, Saershe. He...*

"I know you meant well, Ruairí," Saershe said. "But you must always be mindful of your decisions and their consequences. I vowed to your parents I would protect you."

"I know, Grandma. But you also promised them that you would raise me to become a great dríadór, worthy of our ancestors' name. How can I ever be so if I don't do what I feel in my heart is right? I seek justice for our family as much as you do, and I must play my part."

"Your family?" Dermot said, his forehead wrinkling. "What are you talking about?"

Saershe and Ruairí stared at him. Dermot instantly wished he hadn't opened his mouth. He knew he had gone too far.

"Did I ever tell you why my grandmother raised me?" Ruairí asked.

Dermot and Brian shook their heads.

Ruairí put his arms behind his back. "Taranis took many innocent lives after he first rose to power, including my parents."

Dermot was stunned. Ruairí continued, revealing he was just a baby when they died. Maeve walked up to him and nudged his cheek with her beak.

"I'm so sorry, Ruairí," Dermot said, thinking of his own parents.

"Me too," Brian added.

A small smile formed on Ruairí's mouth. "Thank you, my friends. I think and dream about them often. All I know of them is in the stories Grandma's told me."

They all turned to the sorceress. She smiled, "Ruairí is my daughter's son. Her name was Haf. She was a lovely woman, and a promising sorceress. Our family's roots lie in the western province of Crandáir. I brought Ruairí to Úaene after his parents' deaths, to raise him in a secluded, peaceful environment until he was ready to fulfill his duty, and destiny, as a dríadór."

Dermot nodded feebly.

"Where's Taranis now?" Brian asked. "We heard him not a moment ago."

"He was beaten here," Saershe said. "But he isn't vanquished yet. I daresay he will dispatch his mairágs soon. I cannot say when, but he will return."

"So what're we going to do?" Dermot asked.

Chapter 17

Lifting her chin, Saershe said, "We must get Maeve out of danger, and protect her unborn offspring. The Dríacht must be reunited once more if a stand is to be made against the Dark Prince and his Mairágh."

"What about us?" Brian asked, looking to Dermot, and then Saershe. "Are we to...?"

Dermot understood straightaway what his brother meant.

"Brian," Saershe said, "Emerin has been lost. Do you believe you could survive on your own out here? There is only one certainty if you stay here: the Mairágh shall find and kill you. I don't know how many more are out there, but no matter their numbers, Taranis will send more. The Mairágh are relentless, and swift. And the dragons of the south are most ruthless.

"We are in this together. Many more lives are at risk. They can still be saved, if the Dríacht come together once more. Come with us, brothers, and I shall teach you all you shall ever need to know for survival in the wild. You shall in turn become familiar with Nature and her sacred ways, and be prepared to defend yourselves and others from Taranis."

Brian looked to Dermot, but he turned away. A feeling of heaviness overtook his body, for he was deep in thought. *All my life I've dreamed of adventure, of roving the land and discovering new places and people. But now that I'm leaving, I'mf far too nervous about it. I've lived my whole life here. This has been my home, and it's gone. Part of me doesn't wish to leave. I don't know what to think any longer. I...*

Still, Dermot felt he had no choice. He turned to Saershe, who, like everyone else, was gazing at him. He solemnly nodded, although his heart was not fully in it. Brian's shoulders drooped. Nevertheless he nodded too.

"Very well then," Saershe said.

"Where do we start?" Brian asked. "I mean, how many dríadórs are still around?"

"There are a few of us left," she said. "Among them is a dear friend of mine, known as the Dragon's Bane. His name is Iorwerth."

Dermot nodded. *Another dríadór...*

"But, how can we find him?" Brian asked. "He could be anywhere in Denú, right?"

Saershe guided their attention in the opposite direction from which they had come. They beheld another vast forest in midsummer's bloom, like Úaene had been, beyond the scorched fields.

"The town of Harlíeo is located beyond Oísein Forest yonder," she said. "An old friend of mine who lives there must be informed the Dríacht will come together once again. We must determine the best place in the kingdom to seek out and meet Iorwerth."

"Is he an ally like the traveler?" Dermot asked. "Your friend in Harlíeo, I mean? Or is he a dríadór?"

"He's not a dríadór," she replied. "But he is a good man whom we can trust."

"But how are we going to hide Maeve?" Brian asked. "I mean, we can't exactly travel around with a gryphon in

tow without attracting attention. If some outlaw or wayward innocent should..."

Before he could say another word, Saershe faced the gryphon. She raised her arms, staff still in hand, and uttered an incantation in the old language:

A thick fog I cast o'er thee,
Shrouding thee from the eyes
Of human strangers we may pass
Till the night hath descended

Dermot could still see her after Saershe stopped, and by Brian's and Ruairí's facial expressions, and Saershe's calm demeanor, they did too. Saershe asked the brothers, "How else do you think I was able to hide her from your chieftain's men?"

Dermot nodded. Only they, her friends, could see her.

"Oh, uh, Saershe," said Brian, his tone apprehensive. "Could...?"

"Very well," she understood, nodding. "If you both need a moment, brothers, you may of course have it. All I ask is that you don't take too long. The Mairágh will come for us, and if we make good time we can lose them within the midst of Oísein."

"Thank you," Brian said. Dermot remained silent.

The brothers faced the remains of their village one last time. Their heads drooped like thirsty flowers underneath a hot sun. Dermot's eyes swelled with tears. He missed his father, and even his mother despite their constant quarrels. Brian cried.

Dermot then stood and faced Saershe, Maeve, and Ruairí, his eyes red but soft. He said quietly. "Thank you both, for saving me and my brother."

Brian stood too, his shoulders slumped.

"Are you ready?" Saershe asked.

Though he didn't think he ever would be, Dermot weakly nodded his head.

"You believe we can do this?" he asked Saershe.

She smiled at him. "You can never do something, my friend, if you already believe you can't."

Dermot made another slight nod, sniffling. Ruairí pulled out from another bundle two more traveling cloaks. Both were the same leafy green color of Saershe's robe, with circular iron brooches like Ruairí's. He offered them to the brothers, who took them without question.

"Wait," Brian said, "we should check the food pits in the ruined cottages and see if we can stock up on food. I mean, if there's any left."

Saershe agreed. They spent the next half hour in the ruins, looking for trapdoors leading to the food pits. Some had already been opened and ransacked. Luckily, Dermot found one pit that was still well-stocked and alerted the others. They took dried meat and vegetables, as much as Saershe determined they could carry.

"Now, we have no time to lose," Saershe said, handing each of the boys a satchel and water-skin. "We must get going right away. Stay alert."

It took them a few hours, but they made to Oísein. On into the afternoon they wandered amid a maze of trees, bushes and ferns. The trail grew arduous as the ground became rugged. They hiked up, over, and down mounds of earth. Never did they remain in a straight line for long. Dermot noticed that Saershe constantly observed the trees and other plant life around them. His memory

harkened back to the day she had taken him to meet Maeve.

Dermot nearly tripped over a massive fir tree root. He managed to maintain his balance by keeping his arms stretched out like boughs.

"Careful," Saershe cautioned. "You wouldn't want to step onto, or into, something."

"Thank you," Dermot mumbled. His eyes drifted as a rabbit hopped out from behind that same tree and vanished into the underbrush.

Brian meanwhile ducked beneath a great ash tree, grunting. "It's too bad a trail hasn't been cleared. Traveling would go much smoother for us, and Maeve."

They gryphon squawked. *I can manage, thank you.*

"The trees shan't prosper unless they branch out," Saershe said. "They are as they were meant to be, my friend. We should thus be joyful."

"I don't find these bugs joyful," Brian said, frantically waving his arms, driving gnats away. "They're maddening!"

"Dermot," Saershe said, calm as ever. "Did you not once tell me you felt you were meant for something more in life?"

"Aye," Dermot nodded. "I want to believe so."

"I believe that's true for all species," Saershe said. "Why would any being or an entire species exist without a reason? Hence, nothing within Nature is random. Every plant, every animal, they are our teachers in lifeways if we but listen to them. Wild spirits are highly sacred, as are the realms they inhabit, for they can't survive without them. Honor and respect them as such, from the small to the great. With further observation and interaction, you

shall come to realize how all Nature is woven together like the threads of a spider's web, existing in a delicate harmony which gives rise to her sacred beauty."

Dermot remembered how Saershe deduced his apprenticeship by observing his attire. Alas, that didn't sway his grief. He perused the greenwood. Lushness abounded high and low, as plentifully as in Úaene prior to last night's events. Still, his surroundings brought him no comfort, only more pain. He muttered, "Like us."

"What'd you say?" Brian asked.

"Nothing," Dermot said, shaking his head. "It's—it's nothing."

Brian frowned.

"I heard you, Dermot," Saershe said without turning her head. "Must I remind you again containing your feelings will make you feel even worse?"

Dermot remained silent a moment, but nodded. "I can't help thinking—Úaene was home for so many wild plants and animals. They've lost everything, like we did— if any are still alive. I never really knew them, but still…"

Brian's head slumped.

"Few of Úaene's residents survived the dragon fire," Saershe said. "Those I was able to save have come here. I shall attend them while we pass through. I have mourned those lost, and the green beings too. I still do. There were so many I knew when they were bequeathed life."

Dermot sensed the sadness in her voice, thinking again of his parents. He saw Ruairí, apparently in deep thought.

"What are you thinking, Ruairí?" Dermot asked.

"Reminiscing," he said. "All those times I spent in Úaene, collecting plants, bugs, bird's nests, and eggshells

will never be the same again. You don't realize how much something in your life means to you 'til you've lost it forever."

Dermot looked away. "True, you don't. So much has changed in my life. I'm not sure how I can endure much more."

"Boys," Saershe said, "change is part of life. Without change, the seed never grows into a tree or flower. The caterpillar couldn't grow into a moth or butterfly, or the tadpole into a frog. No matter how painful it can be, change will always come, and it can never be avoided. I shall continue to mourn my friends, but their memory is what shall keep me moving forth."

"I still have Grandma," Ruairí said, to Dermot, trying to be helpful. "That keeps me going. You and Brian have each other."

Dermot and Brian exchanged glances. From the look in his brother's eyes, Dermot knew he was no less confused and discomforted than him. Ruairí was correct of course, but that did not wash away all the mistrust and fights that had defined their relationship for so long. Dermot knew that mistrust had not yet faded.

"How far is it to Harlíeo?" Brian asked. "Will it take us long to get there?"

"It will be a few days' walk," Saershe said. "But not too long, I assure you."

"What if we should get lost?" Brian asked.

"We won't," Ruairí said.

Brian wasn't persuaded. "How can you be so certain?" he asked.

Saershe turned to face him and the others. "You must learn patience, and fortitude," she said. "Complaining solves nothing, and never will. It only sprouts greater anxiety. Remember, my friends, I'm a dríadór, a guardian of the forests. I have walked among them for many years. Experience has taught me to detect the distinguishing, subtle traits within these trees, such as the curving branches of that oak yonder, or the swirling pattern in this yew's bark. I know the woodland creatures well, as they know me. I listen to them. They advise me as they always have, and as I have always served them."

"It sounds like you know every single tree and animal, where they dwell, where each bird nests, in both Úaene and Oísein," Dermot said, intrigued.

Saershe smiled. Somehow, Dermot knew he had been right.

"Keep faith, Brian, please," Saershe said. "We are on the right path."

Maeve squawked again. *You would certainly never find the right path without her.*

Ruairí touched Brian's shoulder. "Don't worry. Things may turn out all right in the end. You never can predict what might happen next. But, as Grandma says, it will for a reason."

"Your mood never dampens, does it?" Dermot chuckled.

Ruairí blushed. Brian actually smiled as they each stepped over an old log coated in thick, bright green moss.

"What do you suggest we do, Saershe?" Brian asked.

"Try observing your surroundings," she replied. "Let all your senses be open to the wonders Nature has to offer, especially now during midsummer, when the days are long and the leaves green. Heighten your awareness of all the life and essence around you. Be aware of the forest

and the trees, of every root and leafy branch, all the creatures and waters. You shall find yourselves worrying not as much about your troubles."

Chapter 18

Dermot remembered at once Saershe's words to him right before meeting Maeve for the second time, followed by what he had felt, seen, and heard that day in the forest. He gazed once again at the wide tapestry of trees, ferns, and bushes, and listened to the various bird calls and rustling leaves. He felt the sunlight and cool air touch his flesh, and inhaled the fresh aroma of the trees, grass, and flowers.

Somehow, his troubles dwindled from a dense fog into a frail mist. He worried less and less about where they were or what they had endured.

A squirrel caught his attention, chasing another up a tree trunk, which lead him to spot a third squirrel resting atop a nearby fir tree, eating seeds from a pine cone. A rabbit rested beside the tree's thick root. The first two squirrels leapt and dashed from branch to branch across other trees. Dermot's mouth curved into a half-smile.

"I see what you mean, Saershe," he said.

"Me too," Brian said.

"Magic springs forth from Nature, my friends, flowing through the trees, wild plants and animals, through earth, the wind, water, and flame," she stated. "Nature's sacred beauty may be realized if her wonderfully diverse children are free to live and flourish in harmony, intrinsic goals they all share. Taranis's dark ambitions for Denú threaten that delicate balance, and therefore all life, and every free

spirit, not just ours."

No one spoke for a long while. They trudged through high grass and flowers, stepping over logs and tree roots, swatting insects away, and ducking under low branches every so often. Brian, gazing at his boots, sulked the entire way. Maeve groaned when she grazed her wings against a tree, but she never made any attempt to fly. Dermot, in contrast, kept quiet. He could sense the gryphon's pain, as well as her far greater concern for her unborn child.

In due course, they came alongside the stream bank.

Ruairi stopped and pointed, "Look."

Dermot paused, staring past Ruairi's finger. Clusters of little flowers had taken root along the stream's edge. They were whitish to light purple, like blackwort, but a different shape. Each stood roughly two feet tall. Their squarish stems resembled hairs bending backward.

"Come," Ruairí beckoned to the brothers. "Sniff these blossoms."

They squatted down and complied. Saershe remained standing.

They smell—crisp," Dermot said, taking a deep breath.

"Very refreshening, too," Brian said. Like Dermot he had his nose buried in the fragrant blooms.

"This is wild mint," Ruairí said. "This particular plant thrives in shady locations such as stream banks. Like the thousand-leaf flower, wild mint is excellent for treating fevers."

Ruairí reached into his satchel. He pulled out a thin journal fastened by deep red leather, a rough piece of charcoal, and a couple white cloth ribbons similar to those Saershe had used to bandage Dermot, except these

ribbons were smaller.

Ruairí flipped the journal's pages, finally finding a blank one. He sketched the flowers using the charcoal. Dermot was fascinated by the sketch's fine detail, but after Ruairí asked both him and Brian to not look over his shoulder, they apologized and complied.

It took some time, but when Ruairí completed the picture, he closed his journal and carefully placed it back into the satchel. He looked at the flowers muttering, "Do I have your permission?"

"Who're you talking to?" Dermot asked.

Ruairí didn't answer.

Dermot then heard a swishing sound. He understood immediately for he remembered Saershe's words about plants and animals possessing spirits, and about seeking permission when planting new seeds in her garden.

Ruairí plucked a few of the smaller blossoms. Once he was done, to Dermot's amazement, there was no sign that he had plucked even one flower.

Whispering thanks, and blessing the area, Ruairí told the brothers, "Grandma taught me when I was little to never ever collect from any site that's not abundant, nor to disturb another animal's home. 'Always respect other living beings,' she says."

"Rightly so," Saershe said.

Ruairí opened his water skin and poured water onto the earth where the flowers were rooted. An offering back, he explained. His grandmother taught him to always give back when receiving from the forest and wildlife. Not doing so would be unfair and selfish. To this, Saershe mentioned the importance of being thorough and charitable as a dríadór.

Dermot looked up to Saershe, who smiled. Dermot, breathing slow and easy, looked back at the stream. He spotted a small turtle paddling along the surface, sending ripples that passed over their own reflections in the water. He saw another turtle resting serenely on a thick branch lying in the middle of the stream. He began to understand Saershe's and Ruairí's view of life, and their reverence for Nature. He wondered if perhaps being a rover might not be as bad as he thought.

"Come," Saershe said. "We should be going."

Just as the boys were preparing to rise, a presence distracted them. They peered beyond the brushwood at a young red fox. Without warning, the creature ran away. They heard also the voice of a passing bird, which Saershe said was a swallow.

"That fox was afraid; the swallow, too," Dermot said.

"How do you know?" Ruairí asked.

"I—I'm not sure. I—felt it."

"I did it too," Brian added. "But I—I cannot explain it."

Ruairí stared at them, as did his grandmother.

Dermot stopped. "Listen! I think I heard something!"

After a moment of keen listening, Ruairí whispered, "I hear it too. It sounds like running horses. They're coming from over there!"

They gazed in the direction he pointed. The distinctive wail of a dog, echoed through the trees.

"My goodness," Saershe said. Without another word, she made her way toward the sound, with Maeve alongside.

Ruairí headed after them. Dermot was about to do the same when Brian grabbed him.

"You don't know what's out there. Are you sure we should follow?" he asked.

Dermot shook off his brother's arm and followed Ruairí. Brian threw his arms up and scurried behind.

They stopped when they heard the dog moan again.

"We must be getting closer!" Ruairí said.

They slowly crept forward, and stopped in their tracks, their jaws dropping as they stared.

A young female retriever lay before them. Her golden fur was soiled, with not a trace of luster. She appeared as if she hadn't eaten or slept for days.

Ruairí stared in horror at the sight before him.

Saershe moved toward her, but the dog's head jerked back. She fixed her eyes on Maeve, whimpering. *Who are you? Y—you're...*

"Shush," Saershe whispered. "Do not be afraid. We're your friends."

After a moment, the dog relaxed slightly, but she was too weak to move. Maeve bowed her head to her.

"Ruairí, bring me the water-skin," Saershe said as she helped the dog to stand.

She pulled a clean towel and brush from her satchel. After Ruairí soaked the cloth, Saershe washed the dog's body and ears. The dog shook herself as soon as Saershe stopped. Fortunately no one else got wet.

Saershe examined the dog's body as she brushed the fur down. "Thank goodness there aren't any serious injuries. We must take her back to the stream now. She must have a nice, long drink, and we can collect fresh water for the days ahead."

"But what's this dog doing out here in the first place?" Brian asked.

Dermot had been gazing into the retriever's eyes the entire time. His throat went dry. Finally he said, "I don't believe it!"

"What is it?" Ruairí asked.

"I've seen her before!" Dermot trembled with excitement. "Her name's Yseult!"

Yseult barked feebly twice.

Brian couldn't believe his ears. "Who...?"

"Brian, don't you remember?" Dermot explained to the others how he had first met her outside his father's forge, and the sheriff mentioning her disappearance the night of the festival.

"Of course, I remember now," Brian said.

Yseult moaned again. Her stomach growled. *Do you have any food?*

"Get down!" Ruairí whispered.

They dropped to their knees around the dog as they listened to footsteps maneuvering through the thick underbrush.

"Who could it be?" Brian whispered.

Dermot shushed him as the footsteps came closer. They all gazed ahead.

Three characters came into view, carrying longbows and knives. One held a coil of rope. Each of the three men was unkempt in appearance, with shabby clothes and untidy hair and beards. In each of their faces, Dermot saw only greed and hatred.

"That canine must be around here somewhere," the one with the rope said.

"What about those horses?" another asked. "Where were they going?"

"Maybe it has something to do with the fire the other

night," put in the third.

"That's no business of ours," the first professed. "Those dark-armored men want the dog dead, though I don't know why, after we kept her starved so long. But it's no matter. We won't get the other half of our payment 'til we've disposed of her."

"Then why haven't they contacted us, like they said they would?" questioned the third. "It's like they fled, and left us to be hung. I think we've been duped. We should leave now."

Dermot couldn't believe what he was hearing. His heart thumped heavily in his chest.

Yseult moaned again, but Dermot grabbed her muzzle. It was no use. The bandits wheeled. The first said, "Listen! There it is again! It's close."

"It's coming from over there!" the second pointed.

"What if it's a wolf?" the third asked, fear in his voice.

The second character moved closer regardless. To everyone's surprise, Saershe revealed herself, waving her staff in front of the men before they had a chance to react. Without warning, they fell to the ground, sound asleep.

At that, Dermot and the other boys stood up. Saershe rested her staff against a tree, closing her eyes as she raised her arms and hummed. Green light glowed around her. Slowly, the sorceress grew a bushy tail as her hands and feet became limbs and her robes a coat of silvery-gray hair. When the light faded, she had taken on the form of a large mare.

Ruairí came up to her as she knelt down in her new form. He asked the bedazzled brothers to help him. With effort, at Ruairí's direction they lifted the first of the men onto Saershe's back.

She dashed off, and quickly returned without him. One by one, she carried the other two away. Once she returned after all three men were gone, she glowed in green light again and reverted to her true form. She told the lads that with the next dawn, those men would remember nothing. Now Dermot understood how she had moved him from her home the day they first met to the area where the sheriff found him.

"Come," Saershe said. "Let's return to the stream bank."

Saershe guided Yseult along, for the poor dog was still too weak and tired. Once they arrived, Yseult lapped up water as though she was dying of thirst. Maeve joined the dog and drank her fill as well, as did the boys. Saershe washed Yseult again, while the boys splashed water on their faces. The sorceress was the last to drink.

After satisfying their thirst, Saershe and the boys gazed skyward. The heavens were a much deeper blue than before. Only then did Dermot realize how cool the air had grown. Fewer bird calls filled the forest, unlike the chirping of crickets.

He rubbed the side of his head. Once more, the recollections of the past few weeks flocked back into his mind. He tried hard not to think about them, but to no avail. He turned to Yseult, thinking to himself, *Lonely, without deep roots...*

Yseult made a weak noise. Dermot took this as a gesture, through which she conveyed a feeling of inward grief. *I don't wish to think about it, not now. Please, I just want something good to eat.*

I don't blame you, Dermot thought. He turned away with a slight shudder, not totally sure what happened. It

was as if the dog had spoken through feeling, like Maeve had, and he had responded on instinct. He turned to look back at her. Yseult merely winked, and he turned away again. He didn't know at first that Saershe had been watching him. Finally feeling her gaze, he looked up at her. She smiled, but he could not. He didn't know what to feel.

Chapter 19

Pádraig and Granuaile, despite what their sons believed, were far from death's embrace. Still deep within the ruins of Úaene, both their thoughts and worries, since that dreadful night, were for their children. For themselves, presently they dared not speak, or even whisper, for fear of incurring their captors' wrath.

The smith was still in disbelief that he and his wife weren't killed. They had been knocked senseless, and awoken once more bound at the wrists with but a few of the other villagers had also been recaptured.

They presently sat together, guarded by six of these dark-armored men. Each of them held either an battle-axe or a sword. Granuaile kept close to her husband, holding his hand. He kissed her forehead, seeing in her eyes not fear but a fierce, burning determination to not give up, something that didn't surprise him.

"Sir!" shouted a voice Pádraig recognized as that of the sergeant of the watch. He, along with two other mairágs emerged from the thickets. They approached the sheriff who stood a short distance from the prisoners.

"Any sign of the others?" the sheriff asked.

"Not yet, sir," the sergeant replied. "But we're still looking. They cannot have flown far."

"Find them!"

"What of those brothers? Shouldn't we hunt them, down, sir?" another asked.

"They're with the Lady of Green Trees now. We would

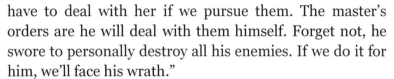

have to deal with her if we pursue them. The master's orders are he will deal with them himself. Forget not, he swore to personally destroy all his enemies. If we do it for him, we'll face his wrath."

Pádraig was elated. His sons were alive! They were with that sorceress now, so he was certain they were all right. However, worry soon replaced his joy. The dark wizard, according to these mairágs, counted his sons amongst his mortal enemies. Their lives were in peril, perhaps a far greater peril than his and his wife's. He glowered at the sheriff.

Traitor! He betrayed us all, not just his lordship, Pádraig thought. He tightened his grip on his wife's hand, but she grumbled so he loosened it, apologizing. That was when he heard the distinctive sound of running footsteps. The mairágs drew their weapons, but lowered them on seeing it was one of their own.

"What is the meaning of this?" the sheriff demanded.

"Soldiers from Harlíeo," the newly-arrived mairág said. "They're close."

"They must've seen the smoke rising from the fire," the sergeant said.

The sheriff asked, "How many are there?"

The mairág, who wasn't the sergeant responded, "At least eighteen, but not much more. So it's not enough to outnumber us."

"But there could be more," the sheriff grumbled. "And more will come. We have to move. Get the prisoners up."

"Yes, sir," the sergeant said. He stomped towards the captives. A number of them huddled even closer together, shuddering at his approach.

"All right you lot! On your feet!" he commanded.

They all obeyed, albeit rather slowly. Some of the other mairágs pulled a few of them up by their arm. The sergeant raised his blade at a small child, the first to make a peep. That child trembled, and the woman nearest to him begged the sergeant to show mercy.

The sergeant instead turned his blade to her, saying, "The next person to cry for help loses their life. Not one of you speaks unless spoken to. All of you keep quiet as we move you through the forest. Get moving."

Slowly they made their way forward, following the sergeant, surrounded by guards. Pádraig looked at his wife. He leaned down and gave her a small kiss on her cheek. She looked at him. He gave her a small wink.

"What're you two talking about?" a guard asked.

"I said not a word," Pádraig said. "I swear."

"Don't lean near her," the guard ordered. "Now keep moving."

The sound of a horse's neigh penetrated the air. The sergeant raised his hand and they halted. The neigh came again. An armored man on horseback emerged. He was not one of the Mairágh, for his armor was not dark, and he wore a red tunic with a yellow hand emblazoned on the front. He mildly twisted his hands, which gripped the reins.

One of the evil mairágs unsheathed a dagger and hurled it at him. It struck his arm. His horse, a large roan, bolted. The armored man screamed as he fell off, his armor clanging when he hit the earth with a groan. Before his horse could flee, another guard drew another dagger, and struck the steed.

The poor creature reared up on his hind legs, a trickle of blood tracing the muscles down his leg, causing the

hostages to flinch in sympathy.

"This way!" a loud voice urged in the distance. More horses thundered toward them. The roan broke free and limped away despite his wound.

"Stop them!" the sheriff the yelled.

"Let's go!" the sergeant ordered. "Get the prisoners out of here!"

The guard nearest Pádraig approached him. As the guard came close, Pádraig whirled and shoved him with all his might. The guard staggered. But before he fell, Pádraig quickly grabbed his sword, pulling it fron its sheath. He stabbed the mairág as soon as he hit the ground. As another mairág came at him, he swung the weapon. Although he was not a swordsman, he kept the mairág off himat bay in spite of his bound wrists.

When the mairág knocked the sword from his hands, an entire troop of armored horsemen emerged as the guards faced them.

Granuaile hastened to her husband's side slamming into the guard while he was distracted. She shouted to the others. "Come on! Now is our chance!"

As the guard tumbled to the ground, Pádraig reached over and grabbed his dagger as the hostages bolted.

They ran until they were exhausted. Pádraig carried the sword in one hand and the dagger in the other. With the knife, he slashed at the ropes binding his wife's hands.

"Where did you learn to do that?" Granuaile asked.

"You know me, my dear," he said, "I wasn't born a smith."

She nodded.

The other survivors, many of whom sat down, looked at Pádraig and his wife with new respect. He continued to

release them from their bonds, taking a little extra time to pat a trembling child on the shoulder or to utter a soothing word to a crying one.

"Listen, we won't last long out here," Granuaile said to the group. "We need to make a plan, and fast."

"What about the soldiers?" one of the women asked. "Should we seek them out for safe passage to Harlíeo?"

"We must avoid our captors at all costs," Granuaile said. "We must make our way together if we're going to survive."

"She's right," Padraig said.

"Listen!" Granuaile whispered. "Did you hear something?"

"Hear what?" Pádraig asked, only to have his wife shush him.

Not a sound came from the hostages as they strained to hear whatever caught Granuaile's attention.

"Hallo!" called a voice. Everybody gasped.

"Who—who said that?" Granuaile asked.

Pádraig looked around. He stopped and pointed, "Over there! Look!"

Other villagers emerged from the thickets: men, women, even children. With joy in his heart, Pádraig's spirits rose. They were not the only survivors.

His wife put her fingers over her parted lips as did several of the other women. They ran to meet the new arrivals. Hugs and subdued laughter were exchanged.

"I cannot believe it!" Pádraig said. "How is this possible? Where have you been?"

"We fled into the forest during the raid," one of the men said. "Where've you been?"

"You won't believe us," Pádraig said.

Granuaile put her hand on Padraig's arm and turned to everyone else. "We'll have time to talk later. Right now we must keep moving. Those monsters may have lost our trail, but they're still out there. If we go now, hopefully we can make it. Have any of you seen our sons, perchance?"

One of the women asked her what she was talking about. Granuaile was compelled to relate with a heavy heart about that they had seen and endured.

The new arrivals shook their heads regarding Dermot and Brian. Granuaile lowered her eyes as Pádraig put his hand on her shoulder. "You mustn't give up, my darling."

"I haven't."

"I'm hungry," wailed a wafer thin boy.

"I'm hungry too," said another. The women did their best to console them.

Granuaile folded her arms. "We must first try to find something to eat and a source of fresh water, fast."

"If only we had longbows we could hunt," one of the men said.

"If there's any game to find," one woman said. "I haven't seen one deer or squirrel, or heard a bird all day."

"Nevertheless, we have to make good with whatever we can find," Granuaile said. "And we cannot stop looking or we *are* done for!"

Pádraig rubbed a hand over his face. "Perhaps there are still a few edible herbs left somewhere."

One of the newly-arrived women, holding a little girl by her hand, and a boy in her other arm, spoke up. "We ourselves have been foraging for hours, and found nothing. I don't know how much longer the children can go on."

"Indeed," a man beside her said. "We have to face the

truth, all of us. We're lost. How'll we ever find our way out of here?"

"That doesn't mean we must give up," Pádraig said. "Once we give up, we'll never find our way out. Hard as it is to do, we should be thankful we're still alive."

No one argued with him, although many of their faces expressed a loss of hope. Granuaile ignored them. She turned to her husband, ignoring their sentiment. "We have to find our sons, Pádraig. You heard, as I did. That evil wizard wants them dead."

"I know, my dear."

"But what I want to know is why would he want them dead? Then out of all of us?" one of the women amongst the new arrivals asked.

"Wait," said another woman who had been with the original hostages. "Didn't he say that Dermot and Brian knew something about the gryphon?"

"You're right," Pádraig said. "When Dermot came home after we thought the gryphon killed him, he was remarkably clean, apart from the lock-up's dirt. He'd been working with me all morning."

"Could it have had something to do with the sorceress?" asked yet another woman. "The—what was it the evil wizard called her?"

"The Lady of Green Trees!" a child piped up.

"Aye, that's her," Pádraig said. "Dermot and Brian are with her. And there was that boy too."

"What boy do you mean?" a man asked.

"Ruairí he called himself, I believe. The wizard said my sons had been aiding his enemy, protecting the gryphon. The sorceress must have been hiding the gryphon all this time. Dermot and Brian knew all along!"

"But how could Brian have been involved, dear?" Granuaile asked. "Dermot was the one who'd been in the forest. He never trusted Brian."

Pádraig pondered for a bit. "Wait, wait, Brian was terribly sick that day, but when we returned from the manor, he wasn't ill anymore! We thought it a miracle. I never bothered to wonder why!"

Granuaile's eyes widened. "You don't think Dermot could've taken Brian to that sorceress, do you, darling?"

"It would explain Brian's improved health, and why they were outside. Dermot mentioned something about a healing hand, I think. That must be what he meant. And that lad, we met, Ruairí, whoever he is, must be somehow involved too."

Granuaile frowned, "Which means our sons both lied to us. The wizard was right. They're in trouble now."

"Darling..."

"Look!" sputtered one of the men. "Over there!"

Their eyes followed the direction of his finger, staring in horror. No one moved. Once woman opened her mouth as if to scream, but nothing came out.

Chapter 20

The morning sun arose higher as Dermot and his comrades hiked within Oísein. Saershe had taken yet another solitary stroll within the lads' eyesight, as she had every day since Yseult joined them. Saershe met with and tended the forest-dwellers of the Oísein and those among Úaene's survivors. They were comprised of all sorts of creatures.

Dermot watched with the utmost intrigue from afar. He listened and observed the greenwood as before, wondering how he felt Yseult's and Maeve's feelings like thoughts in his heart and mind, just like Maeve. He understood how much Yseult missed home and the manor's other dogs from the manor. He understood all too well. He was happy now that Yseult had regained enough strength to walk with them on her own.

Yseult it turned out required frequent grooming, at least once a week. Saershe decreed they would take turns. Dermot was reminded of having to constantly bathe family livestock.

They walked late into the afternoon, constantly skiring trees. The terrain itself was uneven at times. They had to assist Maeve down inclines, for which the gryphon thanked them despite her inner vigor never waning.

Yseult looked up at them, begging for food. When they didn't produce any, she stopped frequently to sniff the earth and tree trunks, but continued whining.

They found themselves dodging low-hanging branches. Ruairí ducked his head beneath a small one from an ash tree. Dermot shoved the same bough out of his way. When he let it go, it swung back, hitting Brian in the face. Brian yelped, pressing his hand to his nose and jaw. Ruairí and Dermot spun around, not sure for a second what happened.

"Sorry," Dermot said.

Brian glared at his brother as they continued onward.

"I hope we reach Harlíeo soon," Brian said later. "Crisscrossing all these trees isn't exactly my idea of fun."

"You'll get used to it," Ruairí said, stepping over a moss-covered log.

"I am, sort of," Dermot said.

"Besides, our provisions are running low," Brian went on. "We may be able to find food out here in the woodland, but not clothing."

Yseult whined pitifully again. *I haven't had a delicious meal in a long while.*

"Remember what I told you," Saershe said. "Complaining solves nothing. Please have faith. We will refurnish our provisions in good time."

Saershe spoke as much to Yseult as Brian. She raised her hand and they all stopped. Ahead, settled in a small glade, a spring sprouted from a pile of huge rocks. Clear water trickled into a shallow pool, which was home to tall reeds, a couple small fish, newts, and frogs. Insects hovered above the pool's placid surface.

Splendid young trees grew amongst the older ones, including three large willows encircling the spring. Golden sunlight poured through the canopy of leafy winding branches, casting such a lovely glow. The

surrounding grassy forest floor was covered in wildflowers, ferns, and mushrooms.

Dermot stood spellbound. Yseult sniffed around. Ruairí got down on his knees. Closing his eyes, he pressed his nose to the earth, sniffing first the thick grass, then the air, after he straightened his back. With a smile, he rose to his feet.

"This spring is known as Willow's Root," Saershe said.

"You've been here before?" Brian asked.

Saershe nodded.

Dermot meanwhile gazed into the treetops. He pointed out to the others a blue, white-bellied bird perched in one of the willows.

"A swallow," Ruairí said. "And that trill sounds like a blackbird."

The swallow spread his wings and flew away, vanishing into the forest's midst. Next, the group heard a soft splash. They turned to the pool where they saw a frog, half-submerged near two fish, surrounded by tiny lily pads and tall reeds. That frog remained very still.

"We shall rest here for now," Saershe said.

All three lads sat down once their knees gave way. Brian let his head fall back, his mouth agape. Observing the forest, the tension in Dermot's shoulders faded like morning dew. Maeve, on the other hand, struggled to lie down. She folded her limbs painfully.

"How long will it be 'til Maeve can fly again, Saershe?" Dermot asked, gazing at the gryphon.

"A few more days," she replied.

"Can't you use some spell to heal her?" Brian asked.

"She already has," Ruairí replied.

"Indeed," said Saershe. "Your brother's injuries, and your fever, Brian, were not inflicted by magical means like Maeve's wounds, so hers require more time. Furthermore, being a magical creature herself, she's healing well with my treatments.

"You must always remember: magic is a resort only to take only if no other is open to you. Never think magic can resolve every problem in life, for it never will. As for Nature's forces, the course they follow is not something to be tampered with lightly. True power stems from wisdom, acuity, patience, and fortitude. Be brave in difficulties. At all times, remember thyself."

Dermot nodded. He and his brother watched Yseult lie down nearby.

"I'm still wondering why Taranis's men hired those ruffians to kill Yseult," Brian said.

"There must be a reason." Dermot rubbed a hand through his dirty, tangled hair. "But I cannot imagine what it is. Wait, I recall the sheriff said during the festival that she'd gone missing."

"Me, too," Brian said.

Saershe, without a word, approached the dog. "Are you ready to open up, my dear?"

Yseult raised her head, making a faint grumble. *All right, there's no use hiding it.*

Saershe nodded, knelt down and looked into the dog's eyes, while fingertips stroked the dog's cheek. Dermot noticed her green eyes glowed even greener.

A moment later, Saershe looked up, her eyes no longer glowing. "Taranis captured Yseult while your chieftain was hunting Maeve. He saw she was his favorite dog, so took her in order to make her master sick with

worry and grief. Taranis arrived at the manor late in the night, claiming to be a student of lore and magic. He told your chieftain Maeve was still here, insisting she had likely killed his beloved dog, and that he himself could find her if the chieftain pulled back his soldiers, pretending to call off the search.

"All these lies were to make Lord Emerin and your village completely vulnerable to assault. Yseult was there, in the forest, Taranis's prisoner, as he laid out his plans to his men. The outlaws were paid to take her away into Oísein and kill her, so he could frame Maeve. But, as you already know, she escaped. The outlaws got careless. Taranis then proceeded to attack Emerin."

Dermot remembered something about the night before he returned to Saershe. He had heard someone riding after dark. He now wondered if it might have been Taranis.

They relaxed in the quiet glade until a young bird's frantic peeps broke the hush. The group turned toward a nearby apple tree. A baby sparrowhawk jumped up and down by the tree's roots, flapping her wings rapidly. They scurried to the bird's side. When they got close, he saw them and bounced back, flapping even harder. Yseult made a move toward him, but it took only a stern look and hand wave from Saershe that kept the dog at bay. Dermot recognized the hunger in Yseult, who moaned despite her pride.

I have been trained to hunt and retrieve. That is who I am. I must smell everything.

"What happened here?" Dermot wondered out loud, looking back at the bird.

"This bird's too young to fly," Ruairí said. "So how..."

They all looked up, sighting a nest in the thick bough above, almost hidden from view.

"She must've fallen out," Dermot said.

Ruairí knelt down in front of the bird. She hopped backward, peeping faster.

"Shush," Ruairí reassured it in a gentle whisper. "It's all right. You needn't fear me. I won't harm you. I merely wish to help. You can trust me, little one."

Ruairí gazed into the young bird's eyes. Whistling softly, he cupped his hands together. Dermot thought he could almost hear a rhythm in his whistling, like another bird's song. Gradually, the baby hawk grew serene. In no time at all, she leaped into Ruairí's hands.

"Wow! How did he do that?" Brian whispered, his eyes widening.

"Shush," Dermot said.

The bird chirped snuggled in Ruairí's hands. Dermot gazed long at the infant, who gazed back at him.

Ruairí reached, but unfortunately, he wasn't tall enough to return the bird to the nest. He attempted to stand on the tree's thickest root, but nearly lost his balance. Brian and Dermot put their hands on his waist, supporting him and bringing him back to the ground. The infant peeped in fear, but fortunately Ruairí didn't dropped it.

"Shush," Ruairí's thumb stroked her head. He turned to the brothers. "There must be an easier way."

"Can you do something, Saershe?" Brian asked.

She shook her head. "You need to learn to rely on yourselves for such tasks, without magic. You *can* do it. Think, me lad. Observe your surroundings. Be patient. A solution will present itself."

Dermot gazed about the forest. He admitted to himself he still worried about being able to reach Harlíeo and eventually find Iorwerth. They couldn't delay much longer.

Still, when looking into the young bird's eyes, he knew he could never forgive himself if he left without helping it. He continued to ponder.

"I have an idea," Ruairí said. He looked at Brian. So did Dermot.

"What?" Brian asked. "Why're you looking at me?"

"Brian," Ruairí said. "You hold the bird. Dermot and I will lift you to the nest."

"Me? Why?"

"You're the youngest, and the lightest," Ruairí said.

"He's right," Dermot said. His words did not ease his brother' trepidation.

"Please, Brian," Ruairí's tone softened. "Do it for the bird."

The three boys looked down at the infant, who peeked into Dermot's eyes, and then Brian's.

Brian nodded, saying they were right. He looked as if he might cry. The two older boys smiled.

"All right," Dermot said. "Cup your hands."

Brian did so, his hands wobbling. Ruairí extended his hands so they were but a hair's thickness apart from Brian's, thus enabling the bird to move into them. The infant skipped back, palpably alarmed by Brian's hands.

"Come," Brian whispered softly to the bird after a moment of silence. "Don't be nervous, little one."

His words, to Dermot's amazement, worked like magic. The bird peeped and hopped into Brian's hands, startling the youngster. He nervously stepped up in front

of the tree. Dermot and Ruairí squatted and grabbed hold of his legs.

"Don't lose your grip, Dermot," Ruairí said, "Now!"

They lifted Brian, groaning as they strove to prevent themselves from toppling over. Brian cupped his hands even tighter together when the baby hawk squawked fearfully. He wobbled, but fortunately didn't drop the bird. Brian whispered to the sparrowhawk to remain calm, despite the quiver in his own voice. Dermot wondered if Brian might actually be talking to himself.

Brian stretched his arms as high as he could. His hands barely made it to the nest's brim, whereupon he reopened them. The bird leapt from his hands, peeping cheerfully.

"We did it!" Brian said.

"Thank goodness," Dermot's arms felt as if they might pull out of their sockets.

He and Ruairí lowered Brian back to the ground, and he breathed a heavy sigh. They smiled as they listened to the bird chirp happily from her nest. Dermot happened to glance down and spotted a couple feathers near the tree's root. He bent down and picked one up, showing it to the others.

"Beautiful," Dermot held it up and turned it in his fingers.

"A sparrowhawk's feather," Ruairí said. "It might've come from her mother."

"Well done," Saershe smiled. "You see not all of life's tasks and problems require magic to be resolved. Always serve and defend those who cannot defend themselves."

"But this wasn't Taranis and the Mairágh we had to deal with," Brian pointed out.

"Nevertheless," Saershe said, "it is these small deeds of charity that show you to be capable of caring for others beyond yourself, proving that goodness and love have not been lost in our kingdom. The power of one person, one act, or one choice, can make all the difference for so many. These are the moments worth cherishing, to remind us that mercy and charity are the marks of true valor."

"Well, we'd better get moving," Brian said.

Ruairí asked Dermot for the feather. He gave it to him, and Ruairí put it in his bundle. The group was just leaving, when Maeve paused, groaning feebly. Everyone stopped.

"Maeve?" Saershe asked. "Is something the matter?"

Maeve unexpectedly sank to her knees then fell onto her side. She groaned again, sounding rather queasy. Saershe got down beside her. The boys drew closer, watching.

Saershe froze, managing to utter, "Oh my goodness."

"What? What is it?" Dermot asked. "Is she all right?"

Saershe looked up. "It's time."

Chapter 21

Dermot could not believe his ears. His eyes widened and his jaw fell, as did Brian's and Ruairí's. Dermot could feel his knees shake. He was about to find his voice and say, "Already?" but before he could Ruairí was quick to ask her what she needed them to do.

"Please, all of you get around her," she said. "I need you to hold her down. Hurry!"

All three of them complied without hesitation, moving around and getting on their knees. They braced their hands against Maeve's wings and limbs.

"Come on, old friend," Saershe said firmly but kindly. "You can do it. I know you can."

She reiterated those words as Maeve howled in pain. Her neck, her wings, and limbs were writhing in all directions. The boys fought to keep her down, for she was indeed a creature of considerable strength. Dermot, in fact, almost lost his grip at one point in spite of having the steadiest hands, and would have fallen backward, but fortunately did not.

Yseult barked. Dermot sensed encouragement to Maeve from the retriever. *You can do it!*

"Please!" Brian insisted to Yseult. "You're not helping, girl!"

"There's no need to be rude," Dermot said, surprised by his comment. "But please, Yseult not so loud! Do you want someone to hear us?"

She moaned. *I'm sorry.*

I understand. It's all right. He knew her feelings were hurt, and he felt he had to let her know he was not angry. Nevertheless, guilt struck him. *I'm sorry too, Yseult.*

Maeve still groaned.

"You can do it, Maeve. I know you can," Saershe said. "You're almost there. Just keep pushing!"

At last, Maeve breathed more smoothly. Saershe held up a magnificent egg unlike any Dermot had ever seen. It was the largest he had ever seen, about the length of his forearm. It's shape closely resembled that of a hen's egg, only a little flatter. The egg's most peculiar trait was its remarkably smooth shell, more resembling a polished gemstone. It was silvery gray in color, akin to clouds on a midwinter's dawn, with streaks of a darker gray.

Before Maeve could stand and claim her egg, Saershe had already removed and relocated other items from her bundle to those of the lads. She placed the egg within hers. It fit in nicely.

Maeve squawked. *No! No! Please, Saershe! That's my child!*

"This will be much safer," Saershe said. "I know it isn't what you want. But please, my friend, trust me."

Her words did not sway Maeve's concern. The gryphon grumbled, begrudgingly accepting Saershe's decision.

Dermot understood Maeve's feelings right away. She was a mother. To her, as much as she trusted and loved Saershe, the most secure place for her youngling was in her care. He noticed Brian's face fall, and realized his brother must have been thinking of their mother at this moment, just as he knew he had never thought of her in

that way as a child, even though she had given him a home and kept him fed, warm, and healthy. Shame gripped his chest.

"I wonder when the egg will hatch," Dermot said, trying to distract his mind.

"Tonight," Saershe said.

"Tonight?" Dermot and Brian said at the same time.

Saershe nodded.

Dermot couldn't believe his ears. "Whoa. That's fast. I mean, well, the hens back home laid eggs that always hatched about three weeks afterward."

"A gryphon is part eagle," Saershe explained. "Eagles, like all birds, do lay eggs. But, a gryphon is also part feline. Felines deliver their young live, a trait distinguishable of the furry, but not the feathered, in Denú. As gryphons share features from both these distinctive breeds, it is likewise for the course of their younglings' births."

Dermot nodded. He turned back to look in Maeve's eyes while stroking her neck. There was something about them which made the lad wonder if his mother felt as Maeve did now when he and his brother were born. He was distracted by Yseult, who growled.

"What is it, girl?" Dermot asked. "What's the matter? Did you hear something?"

Yseult growled again, capturing the entire group's attention. *They're back!*

With that, Saershe arose, calm but firm, telling the boys to stay down, keep quiet, and watch over Maeve and Yseult. She stepped in front of them, partially hiding behind an oak's thick trunk. While Ruairí protectively held his arm over Maeve and Brian wrapped his own

around Yseult, Dermot, who was closest to Saershe, kept his eyes on her. In spite of knowing what she was capable of, he feared for her.

When Dermot heard the sound of several horses running, his heart raced. He almost got up, but Saershe's head made a slight turn, so he remained where he was. It was then he heard a familiar voice shout aloud, "That bark came from someplace nearby!"

It was one of the ruffians they had seen after they found Yseult. The faint but distinct whinnying of a horse pervaded the air.

"What is it, Saershe?" Dermot whispered.

"Soldiers from Harlíeo," she said.

Yseult raised her head, eyes widened. Saershe told her to stay quiet, once again without looking back, amazing Dermot. Yseult lowered her head, and Dermot rubbed her ears. She looked straight into his eyes. Dermot experienced again that peculiar, warm feeling within, as if she spoke. *Thank you.*

There came a voice shouting, "You! Halt right there!" and the horses ran, but not in the direction where the group lay in hiding. Eventually, the sound faded.

"What was that all about?" Brian wondered.

"The soldiers must have been pursuing those outlaws," Ruairí said. "Why I cannot say."

"Come on," Saershe said. "Let us use this opportunity to tread forth, and avoid any entanglements with ignorant strangers; may the wit of the fox guide us."

They moved in a different direction, as cautious and quiet as they could. Dermot kept looking over his shoulder, thinking he would catch a glimpse of those soldiers Saershe had spoken of, wondering still who it was they were really pursuing. He saw no one. He also noticed Maeve kept looking back at the bundle in which Saershe had placed her egg. He gazed at the gryphon with sympathetic, sad eyes.

A moment later, Saershe raised her hand. They all stopped, and looked ahead. There, amidst the thick leafy green, they beheld a streak of vibrant blue. The lads and Yseult ran forward, Saershe and Maeve walking behind. The lads stopped once they came into the gleaming golden sunlight. Instinctively they shut their eyes tight and raised their arms. After a moment, they lowered them and were able to look. They had reached the greenwood's edge. For a moment, Dermot could hardly believe they'd actually made it.

Beyond a small lake, they could see a town in the shadow of a small hill, surrounded by a large wall erected out of whitewashed stone blocks. They could see atop the hill a castle far larger than the manor in Emerin had been. On the path leading to the foregate, there were a great many merchants and farmers making their way into town, several of whom were leading carts packed with food, grain, and other assorted goods.

"Harlíeo," Saershe said. She, along with Maeve, had reached the others.

"So what do we do now, Grandma?" Ruairí asked.

"I shall escort Maeve around town, and beyond into Fianúa Forest, yonder," pointed the sorceress. "There we will be waiting for you."

The brothers stared. Dermot asked. "You mean you're not coming with us?"

"You don't expect we can escort a gryphon, a creature of such size and renown, into a town without attracting

interest, do you, Dermot?" Saershe asked. "Even if she's disguised, she couldn't very well avoid all contact with buildings and people."

"What about us, Saershe?" Brian asked.

"I shall cast a fí-fá over you lads. It will make each of you appear as men instead of boys. Only those of us here, our friend in Harlíeo, and the wildlife will be able to see your true selves," she asserted. "Once you enter Fianúa, the fi-fá will fade."

Dermot recalled not only the enchantment she cast over Maeve every day so strangers couldn't see her, but another she cast every night when they made camp.

Their first night within Oísein, he remembered Saershe walked a short distance from the camp, and circled the area where they camped at a calm pace, her arms outstretched. Dermot had noticed how everything behind the nearest trees, ferns, and brushwood, darkened. Ruairí explained to him it was to protect them in their sleep from prying eyes, that both were the same camouflaging spell known by that name.

"Who is it we're searching for in Harlíeo, Grandma?" Ruairí asked.

"His name is Lonán. He's the town potter," Saershe said. She took off her pendant off and gave it to her grandson. "Show him this, and he shall know who you are."

"Of course, Grandma."

"But what if something should happen of us, Saershe?" Brian asked. "How are we supposed to find you and Maeve afterward?"

"Do your best to avoid speaking to anybody you meet on Harlíeo's streets," Saershe said. "Be cautious. Reveal

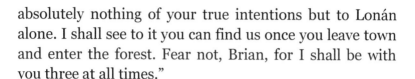

absolutely nothing of your true intentions but to Lonán alone. I shall see to it you can find us once you leave town and enter the forest. Fear not, Brian, for I shall be with you three at all times."

Her words evidently didn't convinced him, for he gave Saershe an irritated look.

"I've got a bad feeling about this," he whispered to the older lads.

"Oh, quit complaining," Dermot snapped, trying to ease his own nerves.

Brian huffed. Ruairí said nothing.

Saershe asked the youths to stand in a line before her. Once they were in place, she took a step back and raised her arms like the wings of a bird. She crossed her arms three times in a slow pace, uttering an incantation in the old language:

A cloak of shadow and camouflage
Twice ten years of age I cast on thee
In the eyes of both man and woman,
Of youth, maiden, and the little child,
But not our truest friends, wild and man,
'Til we again meet within wooded groves

Saershe lowered her arms. The lads gazed at one another. They looked exactly the same.

"I hope I'll be in Fianúa in time for the hatching," Dermot said.

Maeve squawked. *Thank you. I hope so, too.*

"Well then you lads had best get going," Saershe replied. She reached deep into the bundle slung over her shoulder, and pulled out a bulging purse, giving it to her

grandson. The jingling sound made it obvious it was bursting with money.

"Use this coin to obtain fresh provisions," she told Ruairí. "Only what we need."

"Where'd you get that money?" Brian wanted to know.

"I didn't always live in the forest," she said, intriguing even her grandson.

"You'll have to tell us about that sometime." Dermot crossed his arms.

"Sometime, my young friend," she said. "But right now, we have more important things to worry about. You lads had best be going. Take Yseult with you."

"All right, Grandma."

Neither of the brothers said a word, for they knew not what to say.

Saershe's urging, the boys turned around and walked forward. They stopped momentarily at the edge of the lake and peered down into the water, almost stepping back in surprise. Indeed, in their reflections, they appeared as if they were twenty years older. Dermot rubbed his hand across his chin, because in his reflection, he had a goatee like this father's.

Remarkable, Dermot thought to himself. I wonder if we sound different.

"We cannot linger," Brian said. "Let's get moving."

"I agree," Ruairí said.

Dermot took one last look at the greenwood. He understood from this moment on there would be no turning back, if indeed such an option had ever existed. He had hoped to catch a glimpse of Saershe and Maeve, but he saw neither.

"Dermot!" Brian shouted.

"I'm coming!" he said, catching up them.

They hiked along the road to the town's foregate. They stealthily joined the procession of farmers and merchants. No one seemed to notice them.

Located at opposite ends of the gate were two tall men fully armed and armored. They clutched sharpened halberds, with shields hung behind their backs, and swords at their sides. They wore red tunics displaying a yellow hand. The guards stood still as stone as the friends approached Harlíeo.

Chapter 22

*C*arefully, but nervously, they avoided eye contact with the guards as the lads passed underneath the great oaken portcullis. As he entered Harlíeo, Dermot wondered if he should be feeling a sense of peace due to being in a familiar setting now, but he did not. Instead he felt like an outsider, more nervous than ever. He longed for the forest.

A few dwellings in town were cottages like those in Emerin. The rest however, towered above them. Unlike the cottages, their roofs consisted of wooden planks instead of straw. Several were also shops, with items on display which they observed as they passed. Signboards hung over the doorways of many.

The town square was full of bustle and hustle from merchants and farmers, selling goods of all kinds. Yseult's eye was on the food. Guards patrolled and watched it like the festival back home had been.

At the town's inn, people sat at wooden tables outside talking and drinking. A signboard hung above the door, displaying the words name, *The Risen Sun*, together with the painted image of three rays of gold sunshine against a sky-blue backdrop.

Dermot couldn't help but feel the townspeople were watching them, even if they probably weren't. He remembered Saershe's words and did his best to avoid making eye contact with them. He was thinking about

Lonán, but had no idea what to expect. He knew this man was an ally like the traveler, but he was a tradesman with a permanent resident. He felt uneasy about meeting him in a town like this one.

Ruairí led the way, suggesting they should acquire provisions first, to which the brothers agreed. They purchased clothing and boots from the tailor and cobbler (Dermot noted Emerin had neither), then fresh food from the market place. Brian attempted to look at other goods, but Ruairí pulled him away. Making their way through the marketplace, they noticed several people turning toward the foregate to behold soldiers coming into the town, leading none other than the ruffians from the forest bound with ropes.

"You were right," Dermot whispered in Ruairí's ear.

Ruairí nodded. "Now let's go find Lonán. Yseult, no, ignore the food. Come away from there. Come on, girl."

Yseult came away, moaning. *They looked so delicious. I just wanted...*

"Hello, me dearies," interrupted a stooped, old woman leaning on a stick. "Whereabouts are you headed?"

None of them spoke, for they were all startled. Dermot did his best to compose himself.

"Come dearies, ye can speak to me," she cackled.

"Leave them alone woman," another voice said.

They turned to see a young man, older than Dermot and Ruairí by a few years, leading a small horse attached to a cart filled with chopped firewood. The woman hissed and walked limped away.

"I'm sorry," he said. "Don't mind her. She's quite harmless, really."

"Thank you," Dermot said.

The young man began to walk away, but Ruairí stopped him by putting his hand on his shoulder. "Pardon me."

"Can I help you?" the young man asked.

"Pardon me, good sir, but could you direct us to the potter's shop?" he asked.

He smiled. "Certainly, sir. Call me Éibhir. I'm headed there meself. Come this way."

"A pleasure to meet you," Ruairí said. "Thank you."

They walked for a short while, eventually arriving at one of the houses on a different street in Harlíeo, stopping at one of them. Clay pots of many various sizes, shapes, and hues were displayed out in front on many shelves. The boys stood there while Éibhir unloaded pieces of wood, placing them under one of his arms. Ruairí offered to help. The brothers did the same.

"Thank you," Éibhir said with a smile.

"Will Y—our dog, be allowed inside, or must one of us wait outside with her?" Dermot asked, accepting two large pieces of firewood.

"Oh, Ol' Lonán loves dogs," Éibhir said, "so long as they break nothing."

"Well that's comforting," Brian said.

Dermot elbowed Brian's arm. The younger boy frowned at his brother, who didn't look back at him. They followed Éibhir into the shop, except Ruairí, who offered to guard the cart until they returned, as it was not yet fully unloaded. Yseult stayed with him.

Looking up before entering, Dermot caught sight of a blackbird perched on the roof. He remembered Saershe's words about being with them at all times. For a moment

he felt more at ease, though not so much about meeting Lonán.

More pots were on display inside the shop. An old man sat at a potter's wheel, shaping fresh clay. From his appearance he was certainly old, possibly as old as the hills, or so Dermot thought. His skin was visibly rough, almost like leather, covered in light and dark spots, more so on his arms than his face. His moustache and thinning hair were white. He wore rough, torn clothing that smelt of clay, which itself covered his hands and apron. Finally, his countenance included mild, serene eyes. He stopped and looked up to see those who had entered his shop.

"Greetings," he welcomed in a kind voice. He noticed the young man, "Ah, Éibhir!"

"Greetings, Master Lonán. I've brought you the wood you ordered from my master, Lonán," Éibhir said.

Dermot guessed this young man had to be apprenticed to a carpenter.

"Thank you," Lonán said, standing up. "Give me a moment, and I'll help bring it in."

"These men offered to assist too," Éibhir said, looking toward the brothers.

Lonán stared each of them with a puzzled look on his face. He nodded and walked over to a basin filled with water to wash off his hands. Dermot watched as the old man dried them with a towel and removed his apron before joining the others. Together they all went outside.

First Lonán pointed to a corner inside his shop where he wanted the wood to be placed. When they finished, they walked back outside to the cart for more. Lonán cast a long glance at Ruairí, but said nothing as they carried in the firewood. The lads took turns waiting with Yseult to

watch the cart.

Once they finished, Lonán asked Éibhir to pass on his thanks and regards to his master.

"I shall," Éibhir said. He led the cart away, bidding the potter a good day.

Lonán waved goodbye and returned inside. The three lads and Yseult followed.

"Pardon me, sir. Lonán?" Ruairí said.

"Aye," he stopped and turned. "How may I help you? Is there something in particular you're looking for?"

"Actually, sir, we came to see you," Ruairí said.

Lonán narrowed his eyes. "Me?"

"Yes, sir," Ruairí said. He took out his grandmother's pendant and held it before him.

Lonán's face lit up as he gazed upon the jewel. "Are you acquainted with Saershe?" The Lady of Green Trees?" he asked.

"She's my grandmother, sir," Ruairí said.

The potter's jaw dropped. "Ruairí isn't it?"

"You—know my name?" Ruairí asked.

"I met you once, laddie. You were only a wee baby," Lonán said. "I can hardly believe how much you've grown. How fares your grandmother?"

"She's well, sir. Thank you. Oh, these here are my friends, brothers Dermot and Brian from Emerin, and Yseult."

Lonán greeted them individually. He shook the brothers' hands then petted Yseult's head.

"Let's go into the hearth chamber, where we may talk in privacy," Lonán said.

"Of course," Ruairí said. "Thank you."

Lonán led them through an open doorway at the

other end of his shop. They were greeted by a comfortable hearth room which strongly reminded Dermot of home, apart from a round bronze shield hanging on the wall. He, Brian, and Ruairí sat down together at a small table. Yseult in turn sat beside Brian. Lonán, however, first walked over to an aged, large chest positioned beneath the shield. He raised the lid slightly. As soon as Dermot asked him if he was all right, the old potter replied yes and shut it.

"I thought something seemed odd what with Éibhir calling you men," Lonán remarked.

Ruairí explained about the fi-fá, and the old man nodded, saying he suspected as much. He asked the boys if they wanted anything to eat or drink.

"What do you have?" Dermot asked.

"Just bread and milk, I'm afraid," he said. "I never was much of a cook, and I have always preferred simple foods."

"That will be fine, thank you," Dermot said.

"Thank you for your hospitality, sir," Ruairí said as the potter poured water into wooden cups and placed bread on wooden plates.

"Not at all," Lonán said, handing them their food before sitting down. "Now, what brings you to Harlíeo? I presume Saershe is someplace nearby."

Ruairí opened up at once, recounting every detail of their plight to him. Lonán did not seem to be alarmed, at least until Ruairí revealed Taranis had returned to Denú. The potter listened throughout, greatly intrigued.

"My Grandma hopes that if we can find Iorwerth and reunite the Dríacht, Maeve and her youngling might not only be safe from harm, but we may have a chance to

defeat Taranis once and for all," Ruairí said.

Lonán thought for quite some time, rubbing his fingers back and forth across his chin.

"I think you should go into the heart of the county of Wykúm," the potter said finally. "In a vast meadow bordering the Forest of Ámhen, one of the most copious forests in all Denú, there is a ring of standing stones near the foot of a solitary knoll. Saershe knows the place, for the Dríacht met there often in ages past. Iorwerth and his apprentice pass that way from time to time, I believe."

Dermot's ears perked. *Iorwerth has an apprentice?*

"Thank you, sir," Ruairí said.

Lonán smiled, and turned and gazed out the window. "Oh my, is it that time already?"

The boys glanced out the window at the fading sun.

"We've got to go," Dermot said.

"Very well then," Lonán said. "But before you go..."

He returned to the chest and opened it. He brought back a set of weapons: a longbow made from yew wood, a quiver filled with arrows, a sword in a leather sheath, and a small battle-axe with a leather guard. The potter laid them out on the table, along with the bronze shield that hung over the hearth.

"How did you come by these?" Brian asked.

"I'd served for a time in the king's army," he explained. "It was so long ago. But I'm sure you lads will need them in days to come, more so than I. Take them, I insist."

No one argued with the potter. Dermot reached for the sword, gripping the sheath. He thought once more of his father's swords, only now he possessed no desire to wield this one like a fabled warrior. He tied the sheath to

his belt, and took the shield. He offered the axe to his brother, who accepted it with trembling hand. Ruairí strapped the quiver tight over his shoulder, and grabbed the bow.

"Farewell," Lonán said, shaking each of their hands.

"Thank you for your kindness, sir," Ruairí said, whose hand the potter shook last.

"There's no need for that," Lonán said. "I wish you the best of fortune, me friends."

As they departed, Dermot thought of the potter. There was something about him, but he couldn't figure out what or why he felt this strange way.

"Are you all right, Dermot?" Ruairí asked.

"Ah, yes, I'm fine," he said. He expected Ruairí to speak again, but he did not.

They tramped through the streets, keeping their weapons concealed beneath their cloaks. They turned the corner and saw the foregate lowering.

Chapter 23

With little time left, they sprinted toward the foregate. Not one amongst them shouted out to the guards to stop lowering the portcullis.

They were too late. The gateway was sealed with a loud clunk. They halted dead in their tracks. By this time, shadows crawled across the dirt court as the sun slid below the horizon. None of the boys took notice. Their eyes, and Yseult's, were fixed on the gate.

Dermot's strength, like his posture, sagged, and his legs grew heavy. He heard Ruairí's long, low sigh and watched in despair as Brian lowered his chin to his chest.

A brief whooshing sound came from behind them. They whirled in alarm, but saw nothing. Yseult snarled, but a noise alarmed the boys. Yseult snarled, but Ruairí hushed her and shooed the brothers away from the square and into a corner. With reluctance, the dog followed.

"What're we going to do?" Brian whispered.

Ruairí took a deep breath. "We have to do our best to remain hidden, while we figure out a way to escape, so we can rejoin my grandmother and Maeve."

Dermot felt a strong sense of purpose manifest within him so acutely he froze. "You're right. We must reach the woodland."

Yseult whined, *I'm with you, always.*

Brian, seeing the older boys' determination, pushed his shoulders back. "So, what do we do? How're we going to get *out o'* here?"

"Ruairí," Dermot said. "Your grandma transfigured into a gryphon. Could it be possible you could change yourself and us into flyers?"

Ruairí shook his head. "I'm sorry."

Brian's eyes widened "Are you serious?"

Shapeshifting is a highly advanced, and dangerous magic," Ruairí explained.

"You haven't mastered it?" Dermot asked.

"I haven't even been taught it yet," Ruairí said.

Dermot pressed his lips together. Brian turned away, huffing.

"I'm sorry, I..." Ruairí said.

"It's all right, it's all right," Dermot said. "But we have to figure something out, and we'll have to do it without magic, like with that baby bird."

"Right," Ruairí looked around. He rubbed his chin with his fingers, deep in thought. "The gate's has already closed. We can either try to scale the wall, or find a way underneath it, like a drain pipe, without being spotted."

"What about a spell like the one Saershe used earlier on us?" Brian asked. "The fee—uh—whatever it's called?"

"Fí-fá," Ruairí said.

"Aye. That's it. That way, we can climb over the wall and be unseen."

"I can't perform a spell that would conflict with one my grandmother's already used. That, too, would be dangerous. Even if I could, Grandma's magic is far more advanced than mine. I couldn't surpass her. Besides, we can't climb down the wall. We need rope."

A thin crescent moon emerged in the deepening blue sky, as did a few gleaming stars. While Brian and Ruairí were talking, Dermot tuned them out, glancing around

the square. To his surprise, he saw Lonán standing on the other side of the square. Nudging Brian, he then caught Ruairí's attention. They went to meet the old man.

"What are you doing here?" Ruairí asked.

"Hello, lads," Lonán said. "I was worried you might not make it back to the gate in time, so I came to make sure you had. I'm glad I did."

"So am I," Brian said.

"We don't have much time," Dermot said, giving Brian a nasty glance. "We must get out of Harlieó and into Fianúa Forest—tonight."

"Yes, of course. Come. Let's get out of sight again." He led them through the darkening, empty streets. Not a soul was to be seen. Everyone was tucked into their homes for the night except the town watchmen and guards. Stopping at the corner of a house, they waited as a pair of watchmen walked past. It reminded Dermot of when he and Brian went looking for Saershe and then returned home, skulking about Emerin.

With care they returned to Lonán's house, following him inside. The potter lit a candle on the table and asked Dermot to hold it while he searched about until he discovered what he wanted. He pulled out two long coils of thick, heavy rope. The boys stared at them, then him.

"Where did you get these?" Dermot asked.

"Where is not important," Lonán said sternly. "What is important is that you get you out of town tonight. I will distract the guards so you can use these to sneak over the wall."

"But what if something should happen to you?" Dermot asked.

"Aye," Brian said. "They will lock you up if…"

"Don't worry about me, me lads," the old man said. "Now let's get going. I know the path to the nearest stairway up the wall."

They followed him, doing their best to walk as silently as possible. The light of the moon as well as torches positioned along the walls lit their way enough to see. In good time they came to a stairway in a darkened corner behind a rundown house.

To Dermot's surprise, it was not guarded. They waited until there were no sentries nearby up on the wall.

"Now," Lonán said. "This is where we'll truly bid farewell. I'll do what I can to buy you as much time as possible."

Ruairí thanked him, "We're indebted to you."

Dermot gazed up at the torches. "If those weren't lit our chances of getting over would be far greater."

"Good thinking, Dermot," Ruairí said.

And idea popped into Dermot's mind. "We may have to use a little magic after all. Your grandmother commanded the winds in her fight against Taranis, Ruairí. Could—I mean, can you summon a wind to blow those torches out?"

"I—I've tried mastering the element of air in the past, yes. But I've never attempted something like this in my life, not in these circumstances. I don't know if I can."

"Could you try, please?" Brian asked.

Ruairí didn't respond.

Dermot put his hand on his shoulder. "You can do it, my friend. I believe in you."

Yseult made another noise so feeble only the boys could hear. *This is a ridiculous plan. But if you're determined to do it, I'm with you.*

Dermot truthfully knew not what to believe, but he felt he had to try. Fortunately, Ruairí smiled and nodded. Stepping forth, he shut his eyes and lifted his arms, whispering beneath his breath. A wind came, not through the town but above it. The soldiers patrolling the wall were not blown off their feet, but the torches were all extinguished at once.

Ruairí relaxed, even as they heard a sentry.

"Well done, Ruairí." Dermot said.

"What happened?" one of the guards shouted.

Another yelled. "We need light! Fetch a fresh torch."

"All right then," whispered Lonán. "Go now, me lads. Hurry!"

They didn't hesitate. With Ruairí leading the way, they charged up the stone steps. Once they reached the top, they paused. Yseult huddled against Dermot legs.

They heard a guard coming their way, but they couldn't see him yet. Ducking down into the shadows, they watched and waited with bated breath. Dermot kept his arms wrapped around Yseult as the guard's footsteps grew louder. Had they been discovered?

The sentry came into view, fully armored and armed. He didn't carry a torch or the means to light one, for he made no attempt to light the torch near him on the wall. His helmet juddered as he swung his head.

To Dermot's relief, the sentry turned around when an owl hooted overhead.

"Argh!" cried a voice—Lonán's voice. The old man cried out repeatedly for aid. The sentry stopped and turned to look down into the town. So did the boys.

"Where's that coming from?" he called.

"O'er there!" another guard shouted. Dermot saw him

standing a few yards away from the first.

The guard nearest them continued moving in the opposite direction. The watch arrived below. One or two of them carried smaller torches whose light wasn't strong enough to illuminate the lads and Yseult. Once the watch was out of earshot, the boys got to work making a crude sling to lower Yseult. She whined a bit, as if begging them not to let her drop but the boys urged her to be quiet. Still she moaned. *Please be careful.*

Slowly Dermot and Ruairí lowered her down with Brian accompanying her on one of the ropes, all the while hearing the commotion on the other side of the wall.

One of the guards shouted, "Go fetch the physician!"

Once they were on the ground, Brian untied Yseult. They waited as Dermot and Ruairí slid down the ropes.

"Use your axe to cut the ropes," Dermot told Brian.

"Wait, look!" Ruairí pointed.

A large, tawny-colored owl with an impressive wingspan appeared, landing atop the wall where the rope was tied. The boys paused, spellbound at the bird.

"I've often heard owls, but I've never seen one this close before," Dermot whispered, gazing at the bird. "I've always wanted to though."

"Shush," Ruairí said. "Look!"

They watched the owl's talons grasped the rope, unraveling it until it fell to the ground in front of them.

The bird flew off, with a long, eerie 'whoooo' echoing in his wake.

"Unbelievable," Dermot murmured.

"Come on," Brian said. "Let's go before we're seen."

"Right." Ruairí picked up the ropes.

"Let's go, girl," Dermot urged Yseult.

The threesome and their canine companion promptly forged ahead toward the darkened woods. Dermot felt a moment's a twinge of fear in remembrance of how dark and foreboding the Úaene Forest was the night Taranis destroyed the village, but nevertheless he and the others ran straight into the midst of trees. They hopped repeatedly from behind one tree to another, wary of the sounds of their movement. Daytime creatures had withdrawn into the trees, ground, or undergrowth. Dermot could hear crickets chirruping.

Brian whispered. "Ruairí, how are we..."

"Get down!" Ruairí said.

They dropped to their knees. Yseult lay on her belly, with her mouth to the eart, too. When nothing happened, they raised their heads, peering through bushes.

A mairág stood in the distance brandishing his sword. Two more joined him. Together they searched the area where the lads lay hidden. After a moment, the Mairágh walked away, fading back into the shadows.

"That was close," Dermot whispered.

"Too close." Brian turned and sat down, his head in his hands.

"Let's go," Ruairí said.

They continued on their way, pausing every so often to rest. All the while, Dermot imagined Taranis's mairágs prowling the dark of the forest, ever watchful and alert.

We're the prey. Dermot understood that. He didn't like it, but he understood it. *Hiding in the shadows from the predators...*

"Any sign of them?" Brian whispered.

"No." Dermot shook the thoughts out of his head.

"Shush," Ruairí said. "Look."

The lads fell quiet.

Chapter 24

The greenwood sheltered numerous animals, all of whom appeared like magic. Owls and bats flew overhead. The light of fireflies flickered in the darkness. Millipedes crawled across large, moss-coated rocks. Small serpents and lizards rested so still on the trees it was as if they were one with the bark. Now and then one of them did make a sudden move or noise, startling the boys to step back. Moles vanished as fast as their heads popped out of the earth, resuming their diligent digging. Hedgehogs and rabbits alike remained silent amidst the undergrowth.

To Dermot's bewilderment, he found himself able to distinguish the forest's diverse colors, plant and animal alike, despite the night. Even so, he was far too captivated to dwell on it. For several minutes, Dermot listened to and observed everything around him, his eyes shifting from one creature or plant to another. Even the dog remained quiet and observant of their surroundings.

"What're those animals doing?" Brian asked.

"I think they're trying to tell us something," Dermot said. Gazing up into a large oak tree's gnarled branches, he saw, to his delight, an owl perched amongst the leaves. He knew somehow in his heart this owl was the same one that helped them escape Harlíeo. The bird's head swiveled repeatedly one way then the other, the throat fluttering all the while.

Dermot broadened his focus to listen and observe every animal he could see. There was indeed something deliberate with them all, something sweet and rhythmic.

"It's not just them," Ruairí said. "The trees are whispering to each other and to us."

"What?" Brian whispered.

Dermot's gaze immediately shifted to the trees. A gentle breeze carried enough strength to make every leaf swish and the thinnest of branches sway. Their shadows danced around them. He recalled something Ruairí told him once.

To those who are willing to listen, the trees, even the animals, they speak back.

"He's right," Dermot said. The trees, the creatures, their movements, their voices, all made sense, as if he heard their voices speaking to him. He felt his heart stutter. "They're—they're showing us the way."

"Aye," Ruairí said with a smile.

Dermot's saw Brian's mouth move, but not one word came out.

Yseult barked, running off in that direction. *Come on!*

"Where're you going?" *Dermot shouted.*

Her barking tore him away from his surroundings. Instinctively all three gave chase, not wishing to lose sight of her. Dermot could feel the presence of the animals all around him even if he was too busy running to pay close attention to them.

Losing all sense of time, they scurried between the trees, across uneven land, leaping over giant roots, and fallen logs. In due course, Dermot stopped, only to realize he had lost sight of his friends. His heart felt as if it would implode. A noise made him recoil, pressing his back and

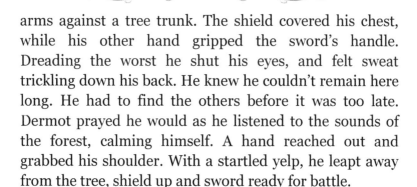

arms against a tree trunk. The shield covered his chest, while his other hand gripped the sword's handle. Dreading the worst he shut his eyes, and felt sweat trickling down his back. He knew he couldn't remain here long. He had to find the others before it was too late. Dermot prayed he would as he listened to the sounds of the forest, calming himself. A hand reached out and grabbed his shoulder. With a startled yelp, he leapt away from the tree, shield up and sword ready for battle.

"Brother, Brother!" Brian said. "It's me."

"Don't do that again!" Dermot said. He took a deep breath to calm himself down.

Brian didn't respond.

"Well, never mind that," Dermot said. "Thank the heavens you're okay."

"Listen," Brian whispered. "Did you hear a frog?"

"Aye," Dermot said as a hoarse croak echoed between the trees, then another. "There must be water close by. Wait. Have you seen Ruairí or Yseult?"

"I thought they were with you!" Brian said.

Dermot shook his head.

A loud bark echoed through the night air, alerting all the Mairágh who scuttled toward the sound. The brothers headed toward it, with Brian panting hardest. Dermot grumbled.

In the distance, they heard Yseult bark again and changed direction, just as a mairág leapt from behind a yew tree, bearing a blade and shield. With a guttural roar, he charged at the boys, first knocking Brian to the ground and then whacking Dermot's sword out of his hand, launching it several feet away. Dermot backed away, his eyes fixed on the mairág.

Howling with a wolf's fury, the mairág swung his sword at Dermot, who protected himself with the shield, frantically looking around for his own sword. He managed to dodge another attack, but tripped over a tree root and fell onto his back. The mairág's sword missed him by inches. It smashed into a nearby tree trunk with a solid thunk.

Dermot kicked the mairág, who wobbled backward. Then, he saw his sword inches from his hand and grabbed it. The mairág struggled, then wrenched his weapon free. When he swung it at Dermot again, he quickly deflected it.

Brian leapt up and rushed in, swinging his axe. The mairág knocked him down again with his sheld. He then turned to Dermot, stating, "Both of you will die!"

"Over here!" Ruairí appeared out of the dark.

Yseult, belly to the ground, snuck in behind the mairág. When she was close enough, she launched herself at him, taking him off his feet. The mairág fell forward with a thud. Ruairí was on him in an instant, banging his helmeted head against the ground.

Roaring, the mairág struggled to get the boy off him.

Suddenly, a blinding white light flashed so brightly for a second or two, they were blinded. When the boys could see again, the mairág lay motionless.

"Thank the heavens you're all right," Ruairí said when he saw Dermot moving around.

"Ruairí," Dermot gasped for breath, "thanks." He and Brian slowly picked up their weapons.

"Come on!" Ruairí urged. "This way, hurry!"

They followed him until they were stopped once more by a blinding white light. Throwing their arms across their

faces, they were again blinded for a few seconds. Thankfully, the light was gone quicker this time.

When it faded, the boys lowered their arms. A small encampment, accompanied by a cozy, warm fire greeted them. With a sigh, Dermot let the fear and tension flow from his body as he saw Saershe standing by the campfire. Maeve rested behind her, alongside one of the ropes. Dermot presumed the other had been cast into the flames.

"Please forgive me," Saershe said. "I should never have put you in this plight."

She held out her arms. Her grandson embraced her at once. The brothers sat down, setting their weapons beside them.

"Thanks for saving us, Ruairí," Dermot said. "And you too, Yseult."

Yseult winked her eye. *You saved me.*

"You're welcome," Ruairí replied. "And thank you for sending those creatures to guide us, Grandma, especially the owl."

Dermot nodded his head in understanding. *I knew it.*

"Of course," Saershe said. "How is Lonán? I hope he is well."

"He is, Grandma," Ruairí said. He told her what the potter suggested.

"Excellent," she said. "We shall begin our journey there in the morning."

"Oh," said Dermot, remembering the egg. "Has..."

A faint noise cut his words short. Everyone glanced downward. The egg lay at Maeve's side. Motionless at first, it started to move. The wobbling hastened to the point where the egg exploded. The boys moved back, their arms protecting their eyes. Cautiously, they lowered them

once all was quiet again.

There, atop the eggshell's fragments, lay a baby male gryphon, almost an exact miniature of Maeve, apart from the brilliant blue eyes. Saershe and the lads smiled. Yseult tilted her head, making a faint noise.

"Congratulations, Maeve," Saershe said. "He's a fine boy."

Dermot approached the youngling. He knelt down and with a smile on his face he gently stretched his hand out. The infant scuffled backward, squawking. Dermot kept his hand extended, but he did not move. Nor did he take his eyes off the newborn.

"It's all right," he whispered, trying to sound like Ruairí. "I won't harm you, little one."

The newborn sought reassurance from his mother. When she nodded, he tottered up to Dermot whose smile widened even more as he stroked the baby gryphon's head. Brian joined him and together they petted and talked to the baby. Saershe viewed them keenly before making eye contact with her grandson. The brothers were too busy with their new friend to notice.

"So what're we going to call him?" Dermot asked.

Maeve squawked. *His name is Ferghus.*

Everyone stopped and looked at her.

Saershe smiled, "A perfect choice."

Maeve squawked again. *Yes.*

"Ferghus," Dermot repeated, smiling.

All eyes turned back to the young gryphon.

Hello, Ferghus squawked. He began bouncing joyfully. Maeve nudged him lovingly with her beak. Yseult alone kept silent, sniffing Ferghus first before licking the side of his face. Ferghus, curious as he was, didn't mind at all. Saershe opened a water skin to wash him. As she prepared to dry him off, the baby gryphon shook his body. Saershe and the lads got a little wet as a result. But they all laughed after Ferghus stopped.

"Come," Saershe said to the boys. "You must be hungry. You've had a trying night. Eat hardy."

They sat down before the fire, opposite her. She took the fresh meat and positioned it above the blazing, crackling flames. She calmly blessed the food, giving thanks to the plants and animals, and praying for their spirits. None enjoyed supper more than Yseult and Maeve. Ferghus alone ate no meat. He drank milk provided by his mother instead.

Chewing his food, Dermot gazed into the flames as they hissed and snapped. It evoked his father's words that fire was a living, breathing being. After he finished eating, he dug his fingers into the earth, then lifted them, watching soil fall. His gaze moved to the roots of an ash tree not far away. Saershe's words about never forgetting deep roots, together with those regarding branching out, rang in his ears. Finally, he recalled his father's emphasis on the importance of family to survive.

Dermot gazed at everybody in the camp one at a time. Once, not long ago, he thought himself lonely, without deep roots. He didn't feel lonely any more. They were his family now, not just Brian. Dermot knew what he needed to do. He thought also of Lonán's courage in helping them escape, and prayed the old man would come to no harm at the hands of Harlíeo's authorities.

His gaze landed on Ferghus last. The young gryphon had drank his fill, and now lay with his eyes half-open, his head resting against his mother's breast as it rose and fell.

Saershe sat beside him. She hummed while stroking his head and neck.

Dermot listened carefully. He recognized the tune as *Beyond the Forest*, and hummed along, thinking only he could hear himself. Saershe looked up at him and smiled. Dermot felt his ears go red, and he stopped. Saershe, smiling still, sang the words:

Beyond the forest this path goes
Where spirits roam wild and free
A seed so deep forthwith grows
On high be the great mighty trees

Ever so deep there is to see
A kingdom for their sacred kind;
Fur and feather, green and grove
There's so much more that ye may find

And something special there's to be,
For when a gentle breeze blows;
'Long by great and mighty trees,
Beyond the forest this path goes.

Dermot's gaze never left Saershe's face throughout the song. He felt a warmth flow within him. Never had he heard anyone sing so beautifully.

Ruairí leaned over and whispered in his ear, "You should hear her play the harp. It's equally spellbinding."

Dermot's emotions were too close to the surface for him to speak, but he acknowledged Ruairí with a nod.

Ferghus fell asleep. Dermot vowed he would protect both him and his mother. He then looked at Maeve, who

nodded, thanking him.

"Is something on your mind, Brian?" Saershe asked. "You seem to be deep in thought."

All eyes turned to him.

"Well, it's just—I've been wondering," Brian said. "Why is Taranis so determined to kill Maeve and Ferghus? I mean, isn't he seeking retribution on all gryphons and dríadórs? What is it about them that he hates so much?"

Chapter 25

For a moment, Saershe didn't speak. She stood while everyone else remained seated. All their eyes remained on her as she took a few steps away from them, looking out into the shadows of the dark woodland. Ferghus continued slumbering, undisturbed. Saershe lowered her head as if gazing down, but Dermot couldn't tell with her back to them.

Saershe folded her hands behind her back, lifting her head again. "When it comes to Ferghus's family, Brian, Taranis does carriy a strong, terrible grudge."

The two brothers gazed at her. Ruairí's eyes fell.

"Ferghus shares his name with his grandfather," Saershe said. "Ferghus the Elder was one of the noblest gryphons I have ever known. He was a good friend, loyal and kind.

"When Taranis betrayed the Dríacht, we sought out the gryphon tribes that dwell within the Denuan Spine. We chose not to do so with the dragons. For all their tremendous strength, they're too susceptible to avarice and power. A fault Taranis himself took advantage of, for he won many of them over to his cause with the promise of riches. Unicorns, though pure at heart, each swear an oath to never shed another animal's blood.

"So, therein lay our decision to seek an alliance with the gryphons, a breed renowned for their valor, strength, and for being noble and honorable at heart. It was

Ferghus the Elder and his beloved mate, powerful leaders among their tribes, who supported the alliance, and succeeded in forging it. Taranis thenceforth swore to wipe out their bloodline. During the war, he slew them both."

Dermot's breath caught and he wondered if his face was as solemn as Brian and Ruairí's.

"However, he didn't succeed in killing their son, Caomh, Maeve's mate and young Ferghus's father, Caomh," Saershe continued.

Yseult and the lads turned toward Maeve and Ferghus. The mother kept her sad eyes on her sleeping son. She blinked back a large tear.

"Caomh and Maeve remained loyal friends to our coven," Saershe said. "But after the deaths of Caomh's parents, the other gryphon leaders sought no more bloodshed upon their kind. Despite Maeve's and Caomh's efforts, not even their own families would support them. So they chose to leave their home in the Denuan Spine. We ourselves wandered from forest to forest, never settling in a single place. 'Twas not long before those of us still alive traveled separate."

"And Caomh?" Dermot asked. "What became of him?"

"Yeah, where is he now?" Brian asked.

A grave look suffused Saershe's face. "Taranis was soon in pursuit. Caomh chose to stand and fight, to give his beloved mate and unborn child a chance to live. He fought for, and lay down his life for them both. His body was never recovered."

Dermot turned once again to the gryphons, sorrow in his eyes. For his part, he felt sad as well. However, he felt an even greater connection to Ferghus. Like him, the

gryphon had lost a beloved father, but Ferghus had never even known his.

"So their family remains symbolic of the alliance between the gryphons and the Dríacht," Dermot raised his chin. "As long as their bloodline endures, so does the chance of the alliance being renewed."

"Precisely," Saershe said. "And Taranis knows it. If he ignites another war upon this kingdom, the Dríacht will need that alliance once more. Taranis will then see we are not divided, and that the Dríacht doesn't stand alone. You understand now, young Ferghus has a great destiny ahead of him. He will be vital in the restoring that alliance. The day will come when he must be ready."

Dermot was left in solemn awe at the story. Not a single sound escaped his lips for a short time, which felt endless in his heart.

"You'll need the gryphon tribes by your side to defeat Taranis," Brian said.

"For their sake as much as the spirits of the wild and ours," said Saershe. "Else everything his father and grandfather fought and died for will have been in vain. You see, my young friends, it's not only sacred Nature whom we dríadórs venerate, but the memory of our ancestors who preceded us, who created the world and families we live in. No doubt you understand"

"Aye," Dermot said.

Brian didn't say anything.

"What is it?" the sorceress asked him.

"Growing up in Emerin," Brian said, "whenever we congregated to remember our ancestors, we spoke of Ma's, but never Da's. Da never spoke of his past, or his ancestors."

Saershe gazed at Dermot, who remained silent. When she asked if anything was wrong, he assured her there wasn't, to which she asked what he was thinking about.

"Da spoke to me of his past once. It was a long time ago. He made me promise not to breathe a word to anyone, not even Ma, or you, Brian."

Brian pushed hair out of his face.

"Why?" Ruairí asked.

Dermot hesitated. "Da preferred to think about us rather than his ancestors. Please, I'd rather not reveal what he said to me, not yet."

Brian looked away into the night, rubbing his fingers together. Saershe sat down amongst the boys again, tending to the fire. Dermot lifted his head, keeping his eyes on Ferghus. His resolve to defend his family had grown stronger, especially regarding Ferghus.

In time, Saershe poured water onto the fire, extinguishing the light yet not the warmth, which lingered for some time. They lay down and drifted off, except Dermot. For a short while, he gazed up through the treetops, marveling at the twinkling stars and crescent moon. Eventually, however, he did surrender to slumber.

The lads awoke one by one the following morning. They found Saershe, already awake, smiling at them as she prepared breakfast. Maeve, also awake, remained lying down, with Ferghus still fast asleep underneath her large wing, with his head pressed against her breast. She gently stroked his head and neck with the top of her beak.

"Good morrow, lads," Saershe greeted, providing food. "Did you all sleep well?"

"I think so," Dermot replied. "Yes."

Ruairí and Brian both said they had also.

"I'm glad to hear it," Saershe said. "Eat up now. You'll need your strength."

Yseult barked. *It's delicious!*

She's already eaten, Dermot thought.

Yseult barked again. *You'll love it!*

Ferghus squawked. Everyone watched the young gryphon stretch his wings and legs. He walked around with difficulty, for he fell to his knees every few minutes.

It's his first morning of life, Dermot thought. *Somehow, I can feel in my bones it will be a great and long life, a life that will be remembered for the ages.*

"You're doing marvelous, little fellow," Dermot encouraged. "Keep it up."

Ferghus looked at Dermot. He squawked again, making Dermot chuckle, even wink his eye. Yseult walked up to the infant and sniffed his cheek. Ferghus remained still, staring at the retriever, who in the end stared back at her.

As Dermot sank his teeth into an apple, his eyes met Yseult's. Brian threw her food. He did the same. She lifted her head, only to lower it slowly, blinking twice.

"You're welcome," Dermot said.

"Who're you talking to?" Brian asked, mystified.

Dermot leaned his head in the retriever's direction. She ate what they gave her along with her own breakfast. *Delicious! I love it!*

"You're welcome," Dermot said.

"Sometimes I still can't help but think how fortunate it was that we found her when we did," Brian said.

"Nay, it not fortune, young Brian," Saershe said, "fate."

None of the boys responded. It wasn't long before

they finished breakfast. Dermot smiled, to which YsoltYseult titled her head at him. *I told you it was delicious.*

Dermot nodded, smiling again.

"We'd best make for Wykúm," Brian said. "We've a long way to go."

"Aye, we will soon," confirmed the sorceress. "But first, we must send word."

"Word?" Dermot asked.

Saershe faced the trees, whistling. There was a pleasant rhythm to her whistle that could have made a song. Birds, to the lads' delight and surprise, were full of song, between the trees' thick, winding branches. Many of them appeared hovering before her, chirping: thrushes, robins, woodpeckers, bluebirds, sparrows, blackbirds, ravens, swallows, and many, many more. Saershe smiled at them all.

The brothers and Ferghus watched in curiosity and admiration. The birds flew away in various directions. Saershe herself, as the gleaming rays of light shone down on her through the leaves, what with the green of her attire and her warmth of heart, she seemed to meld in with the greenwood. Ruairí observed her with a knowing look in his eye.

One by one, the birds flew away, though their songs echoed throughout the leafy green canopy. Saershe lowered her arms and turned to the boys. They couldn't help but half-smile.

"Many were willing to help," she said. "Iorwerth shall know where to meet us."

The boys nodded. Dermot gazed at the last few birds still within view soaring away on their small wings,

singing. He wished them the best of fortune. Then, it was as if he could hear them thanking him from a distance.

Once they had washed their hands and faces in the stream, they packed up their few belongings. Brian and Dermot were delighted to be clean, but it had been Ruairí who took the greatest, yet calmest, pleasure in the cool water kissing his flesh.

"We're almost done, Saershe," Brian said.

"From this point forth, my friends" she said, as she finished combing her hair. "We shall avoid traveling near any settlements, instead remaining within the wild, where we may blend in easier. I know the best wooded paths which will lead us to the ring of stones."

"But, Saershe, what if Taranis scours the wild instead?" Dermot asked. "I mean, won't he be expecting us to do that? All Denuan forests could await the same fate as Úaene. More innocent lives will be in peril."

"What about other towns and villages?" Brian said. "Won't he burn them to the ground like Emerin, to lure us out? Will he burn Harlíeo?"

"I know the risks, my friends," Saershe said. "And I know what is at stake. Those birds you saw, I didn't force any to send word to Iorwerth. Not all of them will go, as there are a great many young birds that need caring for, like Ferghus. But we must survive too if we are to reunite the Dríacht and make a stand for Denú. There are always risks, but if none are even taken, all shall be lost. I believe you truly understand that now."

Dermot and Brian nodded.

"Grandma shall provide safe passage across Denú," Ruairí said. "Nature's forces will protect us all the way, together with her magical instincts."

"Have faith in yourselves," Saershe said, "and in the world of Nature."

Dermot understood the sense in her words. He knew action had to be taken. He still prayed they would endure. Whatever would come to pass, his only certainty was in knowing more than ever they had to remain by one another's side. He turned to look at the young gryphon. Ferghus's head titled as he in turn gazed up at him. Yseult made a faint noise.

"Is there anything else?" Dermot asked.

Chapter 26

Battered and weary, with bloody feet, Pádraig, Granuaile, and their fellow survivors, stopped scurrying about the ruined woods. With no way out in sight for so long, their running became second nature. Fortunately, no murderous black-armored men had been seen since the soldiers of Harlíeo fought them, but neither had a Harlíeo warrior had been spotted.

The day following the night of young Ferghus's birth, they continued as they had done, but many complained they could wander no longer. Pádraig and Granuaile were walking with their hands joined. The smith only realized now how sore his feet truly were.

"Darling," she whispered. "We must to find food and water fast."

"I know, my dear, I know," he replied. "We..."

"Granuaile, Pádraig," a woman interrupted. "What are we to do?"

"Where are we to go?" another asked.

"The smith stopped and raised his hand, stopping everyone else in their tracks.

A weary, wounded soldier from Harlíeo lay ahead. His armor was dented, and his tunic in tatters. Both were smeared with dried blood and soil, like his face. But his tunic's emblem was still recognizable as the yellow hand of Harlieo.

Groaning, the soldier tried to crawl forward. Alas, he

was far too weak to move. A shield lay nearby, as did a sword. Both had been cleaved in two.

Granuaile and her husband rushed forth, turning the soldier onto his back. The smith grasped the man's hand. Granuaile, laying his head on her lap, whispered for him to relax, assuring him he was safe now. She urged the other survivors to maintain their distance from him. They kept staring nonetheless.

"We..." the man stammered. "Those warriors in black—killed—my men—all..."

"You're all right now, sir," Granuaile whispered, trying to ease his grief.

The man grasped Pádraig's hand tighter. "Hear me. My sword and my shield, I wish to die with them. Please. My torque, promise me you will return it to my father in Harlíeo. I beg you. Please."

Pádraig bit his lip at the mention of Harlíeo.

"Please!" the man begged, "Promise me!"

"By the ancient spirits I will," Pádraig swore. Before he could ask him his father's name, the soldier thanked him and took his final breath. Man and wife looked at one another before they, like many others, lowered their heads despite not knowing the man, for they still were in mourning for their fellow villagers. Pádraig somberly removed the soldier's golden neck ring.

One villager alerted the small horde. To their astonishment, they realized the forest's edge lay near.

"Who will help me carry him?" Pádraig asked in regards to the dead man.

"We cannot leave him," Granuaile said.

They, along with four others, carried him with what strength they had left. Two women carried the pieces of

his sword and shield. Everyone slowly made their way to and across the forest's edge.

To their shock, they found themselves back in the village, or rather what remained of it. None of them could tear their eyes away from the charred ruins. A few shed tears, but most were too grieved beyond tears. Those who took a few steps toward the village did so feebly, their knees wobbling. Pádraig and the others carrying the dead soldier gently laid him down.

"Gone," one woman sniffled, "It's all gone. All..."

Most however could not even find words.

"Maybe the food pits still have food in them," another woman said. "Let's go take a look."

Slowly they made their way through the rubble. It was an unsettling task, but they searched as best they could. Though some of the food pits they uncovered had been ransacked, some were not. To the delighted cries of many, especially the children, a little food was found. One woman proclaimed it a miracle as they ate ravenously, until Granuaile yelled at them to stop.

"Please, everyone, listen. We cannot stay here," she said. "We're still in great peril. The longer we linger, that peril woll grow. We must conserve what food we have for the journey ahead of us."

"I'm surprised we haven't seen the wizard since that awful night," Pádraig said. "But Granuaile's right. He's still out there, and so are his minions."

"But what can we do?" one woman asked. "Where can we go? Who would help us?"

"The town of Harlíeo is the nearest settlement," one of the men said, "That's where this soldier and his comrades came from."

"That's where we must go," the same woman said.

"The *town* of Harlíeo?" Pádraig asked.

"Aye," the man nodded. "You promised to return the soldier's torque to his father there, remember?"

Pádraig's eyes dropped. He turned away, looking at the torque in his hand.

"What's the matter, Pádraig?" another man asked, which made everyone else turn their eyes toward the smith.

Pádraig dithered. "It's that, well, I—I never—I..."

Granuaile walked up to her husband, putting her hand on the back of his shoulder.

"Dear husband," she said, putting her hand on his shoulder. "What's wrong?"

"My—my mother," he stuttered.

"Oh, of course," she said, lowering her hand. Forgive me, darling."

He turned and gave her a weak smile. "It's all right, my dear."

"What's the matter?" one woman asked.

Both Granuaile and her husband looked toward the others.

"Leave it," Granuaile said with a stern voice

The smith turned his head in the opposite direction, as if embarrassed. Granuaile on the other hand became unusually somber. The other survivors drew nearer. Granuaile did her best to keep them back, holding up her hands. Her husband turned.

"Maybe it's best to tell the truth," he said without looking at his wife.

"Are you sure?" Granuaile asked.

"I am."

Granuaile didn't argue. She took his hand in hers. The smith turned to the small group. "Most of you may not know, except the few elderly amongst us, that I am not a child of Emerin. My roots are not here."

One of the children asked him where he was from, only to have the woman holding her shush him.

"I was born in the village of Caemoch, further south of Harlíeo. My father was conscripted into the king's army, to help quell a rebellion in the southern province, so I'm told. I was but a small infant. He never came home."

"Was he slain in battle?" one woman asked.

"I don't know," Pádraig said, gazing at his soiled boots. "Sometime after the rebellion was put down, my mother received word he had gone missing. My father was never seen again. My mother told me all their friends in Caemoch eventually came to mourn him as dead. There were some who thought he had deserted, and thus branded him a coward. But my mother, despite the passing of time and no word, always held onto the hope that he would return someday. She often told me he was a brave, kind, and gentle man who loved his family, refusing to even consider that he might have abandoned us.

"We were soon destitute, and made for Harlíeo. Yet we were no better off there than Caemoch. It was never home. Our situation grew much worse. Ma couldn't remarry, since she never knew Da's fate. She eventually fell ill and died, leaving me with nothing. I had to fend for meself. Eventually I had no choice but to leave Harlíeo. That's how I made my way here."

"I remember," Granuaile said. "My mother died

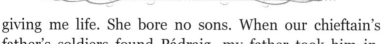

giving me life. She bore no sons. When our chieftain's father's soldiers found Pádraig, my father took him in, and raised him as his own. That is how he came to be my father's apprentice."

"I remember it as if 'twere yesterday," the smith said. "I worked hard. Fate gave me a chance to rebuild my life. I dared not squander it, for my mother's sake."

All the survivors were stunned into silence. Some exchanged wide-eyed glances.

"Please," one of the men said. "If we are to make for Harlíeo, we must do so now."

Many others voiced their agreement, turning and nodding to one another. Pádraig rose to his feet, holding up his free hand. The crowd fell silent. He said, "Aye, we must do so, and warn them of the impending danger."

"But will they even believe us?" one woman asked.

Granuaile spoke with firmness. "If we do nothing, other lives will be lost for sure. If we act, there is still a chance for hope. We must try."

"She's right," Pádraig said. "But before we go anywhere, we must bury this fallen man."

Pádraig and several others dug a grave with their bare hands. They lay the man inside. After placing the pieces of his sword and shield on his chest, they pushed the earth onto the soldier until at last he was interred.

Pádraig, in the absence of their sagart, prayed aloud, "May he find peace as he crosses the gateway into the otherworld. And may the ancient spirits bless him and those he loved and left behind."

There was no time for more ceremony. Though it was with the greatest reluctance, in due course they walked away from their former home, from their whole world.

Heads were bowed, eyes red, and voices silent apart from the whimpering of those children not asleep as they were carried or led along.

Many of the villagers did glimpse back, but not for long. Several others carried what food hadn't been eaten, doing their best to avert their hungry eyes.

"You mustn't blame yourself, my dear," the smith whispered to his wife.

"I should've seen it, Pádraig," she replied. "I knew something was amiss with our sons. Yet I did nothing. I should've done..."

"We can't dwell on that now, darling. Please."

Granuaile sighed, closing her eyes.

"Dermot was an exceptional apprentice," Pádraig said, trying to cheer her up. "Yet I honestly believe he never gave up on his childhood dreams of adventure."

She stared at him. He quickly added, "But of course, I know he never forgot what I told him about family, and myself, nine years ago. Perhaps both are what enabled him grow into the young man he has become."

"Yourself?" she asked. "Do you mean..."

"Aye," he said. "When I spoke with Dermot nine years ago and offered to teach him my trade, I confided my past to him. I think that's what convinced him to accept."

"And you never once feared he would tell anyone, darling?"

"I asked him not to. He gave me his word, and I trusted him. Dermot has always held undying loyalty towards those he cares for."

Granuaile remained silent, appearing for a moment as if in a daze.

"I've been proud of him over these past nine years,"

she finally uttered, "Truly."

"So was I. And Brian too," Pádraig said. "I do love them both very much."

"So do I," smiled Granuaile solemnly, shedding a tear. "When my father was on his deathbed, his last words were of them. He said he knew they were in good, loving hands."

Pádraig was touched. She never told him that before. He kissed her forehead.

Some time elapsed when at last they reached the forest's edge. There, Pádraig and Granuaile stared at each other. Some of the children hid behind the adults, parents or not.

"Should we travel inside Oísein?" one woman asked. "That wizard may not expect to find us back in there."

The younger children shuddered. They covered their ears, pressing their faces against adults' skirts and trousers, clenching their hands even tighter. The adults turned to the smith and his wife. Pádraig and Granuaile looked at one another, then to the others.

"We might be safer from those monsters in there," Pádraig said. "Yet we could as easily lose our way and not reach Harlíeo in time. Besides, that dark wizard may begin hunting us there. To that end, let's take the best of both: travel inside the forest for cover, but make sure not to lose sight of the edge, so we don't get lost. We must be careful when lighting fires, else we could draw the attention of his minions. We must keep near the stream as well for fresh water."

Nobody argued. In sad silence, after drinking stream water with and without their hands, they hiked in the shade within the forest.

"Are you all right, darling?" Granuaile asked her husband. "Are you thinking of Harlíeo?"

He sighed, "Aye. The memories of that place aren't pleasant for me. I'd hoped to put all that behind me. But I gave that soldier my word. I must keep it. I pray nobody there recognizes me, or even remembers me, even if it's been a great many years since."

"Of course, darling; forgive me."

"There's no need to apologize, my love," Pádraig said. "Right now, we must focus on staying alive, and together, that we may find our sons."

"Whatever lies in store, I pray they're all right, wherever they are."

"I do too, my dear," Pádraig said, clasping her hand. "We *will* find them. I promise you."

"I know, my darling, I know. But they are still in trouble for lying to us."

"Yes, dear," he replied, almost chuckling.

Even she came close to a laugh, but rested her head on her husband's shoulder instead. They kept their arms around each other for the rest of the day.

Chapter 27

Maeve squawked impatiently as Saershe examined her wings. Ferghus stood beside her, with Yseult and the boys behind him. They were standing in the middle of a vast meadow swathed in red clover, having left Fianúa Forest a few weeks ago. Ámhen Forest could now at long last be seen in the distance. According to Saershe, the stone circle lay on the forest's other side.

"Well, Maeve, I am pleased to say your wings have fully healed," Saershe said.

Everyone was delighted, none more so than Maeve. Once Saershe removed the bandages, the gryphon stepped ahead, Ferghus watched her with utmost curiosity. She stretched her great wings, and cawing, ascended into the sky.

Her friends down below watched her every move. The boys were deeply impressed, even Ruairí. For indeed, as Dermot knew all too well, she was a powerful flyer.

"Look at that," Saershe said. "Maeve is free. It is that wondrous sense of freedom all winged creatures feel and fully embrace."

Watching her soar, "Dermot wished he could feel as free as she looked.

Maeve called down to Ferghus, enticing him to join her. However, the youngling was a little apprehensive. He barely moved, instead looking to Saershe and the three lads. His mother descended, landing gently before them.

"Don't be afraid, Ferghus," the sorceress smiled. "Flying is something every other gryphon has learned. Even your mother had to practice at your age."

Maeve nodded, squawking with her head high. *Every gryphon born before you learned to fly. Every gryphon to come after you will learn too. You will learn.*

"You can do it, little fella," Ruairí assured Ferghus. "Believe in yourself."

"Aye," Dermot said with a smile. "I believe in you."

Yseult nodded. *I do too.*

"Me, too," Brian said.

To everyone's delight, Ferghus flapped his wings. He didn't get far off the ground. Despite repeated efforts to go higher, he grew tired and panting hard, gave up. Ferghus hung his head in shame. Maeve composed herself well. Dermot sensed that if she felt any disappointment as a gryphon, as a mother she had none.

Dermot leaned down and stroked the gryphon's ear, smiling. "Don't worry. You'll get the hang of it."

The others gave him further encouragement. Maeve nudged him. Saershe meanwhile paused to seek permission to collect red clover from the meadow. When she received it, she produced a small knife with a white handle and curved blade, which she used in collecting the clover.

They were soon on their way again. Ferghus skipped happily around them, squawking endlessly. His behavior delighted his companions. Yseult jumped about, playing with him. Maeve not only let her. She encouraged it.

"Maeve's got her eyes on Ferghus," Brian said as they approached Ámhen. "You know her focus hasn't drifted from him once."

"Can you blame her?" Saershe said. "He's the light of her life. The same can be said of any mother, in relation to those she brings into this world. He's also all she has left of his father."

Yes, Maeve squawked.

Saershe's words for Dermot unfortunately conjured memories of his mother. For every moment of tenderness she had shown him, he recalled tenfold times the two of them arguing, often with bitter words. The lad's face could never hide his emotions, even when he didn't want to. He rubbed his nose with two fingers, and froze.

His boot pressed on something that felt unusual in touch. Puzzled, he lifted his foot and peered down. To his alarm, he saw a dead blackbird. He stepped back, shuddering.

Brian paused, asking Dermot what was wrong. The others stopped as well. Dermot pointed out the carcass to them, his finger shaking.

Ferghus stepped forth. His mother squawked aloud, which Dermot guessed to be a warning to her son to not get close. Dermot felt sorrow flow through him like a river. His eyes never looked away. The worst revelation was to come.

"Goodness gracious," Saershe said. Their attention converged to a stretch of grass between the meadow of red clover and the wizened trees, and to the terrible sight awaiting them. Countless small dead birds lay scattered everywhere.

"What happened here?" Brian asked, his voice conveying his grief.

"I don't know, but something isn't right," Dermot said, maneuvering through the birds' bodies, careful not

to crush any of them under his boots.

"There isn't any visible trace as to why they died," Ruairí said. He bent down to examine a bluebird. "Wait, I recognize a few of them."

"You do?" Dermot asked.

Everyone else's eyes turned toward Ruairí.

"Yes. They were among those sent out with your message, Grandma."

Everyone looked to Saershe. She closed her eyes in deep sorrow. The brothers knew Ruairí had to be right.

"Whatever's taken place here," Saershe said. "I am certain Taranis is to blame. We'd better be more watchful, lest something terrible comes to pass."

One by one, the boys warily navigated the graveyard of birds, crossing into the deep-rooted forest. They halted and turned, realizing Saershe, Yseult, and two gryphons stayed behind. They subsequently rejoined them.

Saershe raised her arm, at which point her green eyes glowed even greener. A patch of earth uprooted on its own beside each feathered cadaver. She gently waved her other hand, and each dead bird rose in the air, before gently descending into the corresponding grave. In the end, tiny mounds of earth marked their individual resting places.

"Tis the least I can do," she said somberly.

Dermot and the other boys nodded. Dermot was on the verge of tears and saw Brian and Ruairí blink back their own.

They all bowed their heads in mourning. When it was time to leave, Saershe said, "Stay alert. Taranis's forces may still be close by."

They continued onward, wearily keeping an eye on their surroundings as they walked ever deeper within the greenwood. White lilies and little shamrocks grew amongst the grass.

"Stunning isn't it?" Ruairí said, trying to cheer the somber mood.

"What?" Dermot asked. He had been keeping an eye out for mairágs, despite thinking how strange it was they hadn't seen one for quite some time.

"How all of these trees have grown strong and tall," Ruairí said. "Every single one of them, and all the others we've seen in Denuan forests have been around for so long, perhaps longer than us. They began life as tiny little seeds, and grew into the wise, ancient beings they are now, home to so many creatures. It's simply enchanting."

"How true," Saershe said, "and they're so full of remembrance. They have witnessed events from long ago, counting generations of wild animals who inhabited them. One cannot begin to imagine all they have seen and beheld. Even now, we are giving them new memories."

"Aye," Dermot said, lowering his eyes. Though he was deeply moved and saw the trees in a way he hadn't before, he still couldn't help but think of Úaene, of that afternoon when Saershe brought him to Maeve, and the horrible fate the forest suffered, and wondered something else. *Why is it that such beauty and goodness always fill me with grief? Can't I ever feel true peace in my heart again, even if for just one more afternoon?*

"Look!" Ruairí pointed. Everyone stopped and turned.

Dermot spotted a moving beicreature, the sigh of which prickled the hairs on the back of his neck, making him forget all his woes and other thoughts.

The creature they beheld running ahead, despite

bearing a striking resemblance to a snow-white steed, was most certainly no horse. He had other features far more affiliated to a goat. The hooves were divided, and a small beard protruded from his chin. Both the tail and mane were thin and silky, like his beard. Yet for all these telltale features, the only one needed to betray this creature's identity was the spiraled horn protruding from the center of his forehead.

"Am I seeing things?" Brian asked.

"Nay, my young friend," Saershe replied. Her face lit up like a midsummer morning sky. "This is no enchantment."

Dermot's jaw dropped. Like Brian, and Ruairí, he was in a daze. The magnificent unicorn sprinted away faster than any charger Dermot ever saw.

Suddenly, a second unicorn dashed down the same direction. A female, as indicated by the lack of a beard. Her large eyes were dark, like the first unicorn.

They disappeared as swiftly as they arrived, which did not diminish the wonder in which the boys were entranced. Dermot recalled from folktales that no horse in all Denú, not even the celebrated royal chargers, could outrun a unicorn.

"Come," Saershe said. The small group progressed into a sunlit glade. From there they browsed the midst of the forest. They watched butterflies hover past. A woodpecker's tapping, far swifter than normal, echoed throughout the trees. Clouds blotted out sun.

"Where could they have gone?" Dermot asked.

"I know not," Saershe said. "But they were running in fear. Oh me, something indeed is terribly wrong. I can feel it. They are nearby."

"Who?" Brian asked. "Who's nearby?"

Before anyone could speak again, a large black arrow whistled through the air, smashing squarely into a tree trunk, inches from Brian's nose, startling everyone.

Dermot spun. "Mairágs!" he yelled.

A band of Taranis's underlings hurtled toward them. The brothers prepared to flee, but Yseult, Maeve, and Ferghus dug their heels into the soil. The retriever and mother gryphon growled. Ruairí and Saershe stood firm as well. Impressed, and ashamed, the brothers took their place beside their friends. Dermot was determined to do his part, ashamed to have thought of running.

Dermot unsheathed his sword and held his shield in front of his chest. Ruairí drew an arrow for his longbow and Brian removed the battle-axe from its guard.

"Ye cannot escape us!" one mairág jeered.

"Our master shall reward us for our efforts!" another said. "First we'll deal with you, and then we'll finish off those unicorns!"

"You shall not harm Maeve, Ferghus, or the unicorns," Saershe said. She thrust her staff forward as if it were a spear. Every mairág spun in midair before tumbling to the ground, their armor clanging.

"Boys," Saershe said. "Take Maeve and Ferghus, and run."

Ruairí's jaw dropped. "But, Grandma..."

"Do as I say!" she said. "Now go!"

"Come on!" Brian urged.

Dermot didn't hesitate, but he turned with reluctance as he, Brian and Ruairi dashed away. Dermot looked back to assure himself the three animals followed. A beam of yellow light froze them in their tracks. An old tree erupted in flames, catching the bush at its base which also burned

hot and fast.

Spreading fast, the fire consumed one wild plant after another, turning them into nothing more than a pile of ash. Still they kept running, while Saershe summoned a powerful gust to combat the flames. Dermot didn't look back, but saw Ruairí turn his head again and again, even though he could no longer see his grandmother.

A mairág sprung out in front of them, and they slid to a stop. Taranis's underling raised his axe as if to strike the boys. Instead, the blade glowed yellow.

Chapter 28

Lightning bolted from the minion's weapon. Yseult and the boys managed to hurdle out of the way in time. Numerous leaves, birds, and other animals plummeted to the ground, singed. Dermot had no time to mourn the dead creatures. Roaring like a dragon, the mairág hurtled after them. Brian threw a rock but missed.

Dermot looked around. His eyes landed on a bough overhead. The next thing he knew, the branch pummeled the mairág to the ground. His armor clattered as his weapon and shield fell from his hands. Dumbfounded, he didn't make a move.

The mairág arose, stepping backward. He held his shield and sword in a defensive pose. Several other mairágs did the same, never giving a sign to attack. The three boys encircled themsclvcs around the gryphons, grasping their respective weapons. Maeve's limbs formed a cage around her young one. Ferghus cawed impatiently, desperate to break free, but he couldn't get out from underneath his mother's belly.

"Now what do we do?" Brian asked.

"I'm not sure," Dermot said. "Why don't they attack?"

"Keep your heads straight," Ruairí urged. "Stay calm. Don't panic. Otherwise, we won't get out of this."

"All right," Dermot said. Had *he* brought that branch down on the mairág? All he did was stare at it, nothing more. Could *he* have somehow caused it to move? *Nay,*

that's impossible.

He saw Ruairí focus his gaze on that branch. In the middle of his bewilderment, Dermot spotted something from the corner of his eye. Looking hard, he could tell a woodland creature lurked in the underbrush.

Meanwhile, Brian's eyes darted in every direction where other creatures might be lurking. Dermont didn't know, but he direly prayed that someone would to come to their aid—anyone.

Without warning, various birds, squirrels, serpents, foxes, ants, and bees, descended on the Mairágh in innumerable numbers, so much so the mairágs were unable to fight back. Next, tree branches came swooshing down, and the mairágs fell to the ground. These wild creatures, now including two gigantic boars and a pack of wolves, remained unharmed.

"Whoa," Ruairí said.

Maeve nudged the boys one at a time. They all looked at her. Her eyes shifted from her son and back up to each of them.

"You want us to protect Ferghus?" Dermot said.

Maeve nodded, and then she charged at the minions herself. She slapped two mairágs with her wing and forced down another with her talons. She tore at the third mairág's throat. Blood stained the grass and his armor. They boys were stunned stiff. So were Yseult and Ferghus.

"They're not finished yet," Ruairí said.

A new legion of mairágs stampeded straight for them. Ruairí repeatedly drew arrows and unleashed them. He proved a most excellent shot. However he only wounded the mairágs, delaying their advance.

"Now's your chance, Maeve!" Dermot shouted. "Take

Ferghus and go. Do it!"

Maeve refused. Ferghus jumped, his wings fluttering relentlessly. Unfortunately, no matter how hard the young gryphon leaped up and down or beat his wings, he could not stay in the air. By then, the mairágs were drawing nearer.

"Oh it's no use!" Brian said. "We can't force Ferghus to learn to fly in a minute!"

"Brian, we..." Dermot said.

A blinding white light threw the area in stark reflief. The boys threw their arms up to shield their eyes. They could hear the Mairágh howling as if wounded. When the light finally dimmed, out of the corner of his eye Dermot could see the unicorns again. Startled, they watched as those beautiful creatures produced an aura of light around their bodies, focusing their greatest intensity against the Mairágh.

"Unbelievable!" Brian whispered.

"Move!" Dermot said, "Now's our chance! Maeve, take Ferghus like you did me the day we met. Fly away! Go!"

She squawked back at him. *I'm not leaving you to die! We stay together! Don't argue!*

More creatures joined in the melee. Amidst leaves and flower petals floating on the breeze, Dermot blinked. For a second he thought he saw faces amongst the leaves and petals.

More mairágs appeared, but a swishing sound attracted everyone's interest. For the first time since they started running, the boys beheld Saershe. She spread out her arms, summoning winds directed against the Mairágh. None amongst them could withstand them and thereby assail the

sorceress. However, a couple of them moved to assault the boys again. They braced themselves.

Another blast of wind sent those same mairágs flying through the air, smashing into trees. Weakened, every mairág fled. The lads whirled to stare at Saershe, with not one scratch on her skin or clothing. Then, the clouds broke. The sun reemerged. Light flooded through the lush boughs. Ruairí, Maeve, and Ferghus gazed at the brothers. Saershe trekked up to them. They faced her, sheathing their weapons. None of them could find the right words to say.

Saershe examined each of their faces and limbs. "Are you all right?"

"Aye, I believe so," Dermot said. "Maeve and Ferghus were brilliant."

Yseult barked. Ferghus squawked. Saershe gazed deeply into Maeve's eyes.

"I'm impressed, Ferghus," Ruairí said. "You're holding up surprisingly well with all this traveling."

"What do you mean?" Brian asked.

He explained, "Young gryphons are normally born in mountain dens, which they don't leave 'til they're at least a little older."

Saershe meanwhile observed their surroundings to ensure there would be no further destruction. She examined every animal and tree, rubbing her fingers through leaf, fur and feather, and stroking her palms across bark. Those animals that died she buried like the birds in the meadow. All the while, her companions, save Ruairí, who assisted her, watched her with absolute focus.

Dermot was greatly absorbed, even as he, Brian, and Ruairí each drank water from the skin Saershe provided.

She also summoned water from a nearby pond to wash the wildlife and be sure no more fires might ignite.

"Are they all right?" Dermot asked.

She stood and faced the boys. "They are indeed. These trees and animals shall continue to endure. I am profoundly grateful that you all are all right too."

"Thank you," Dermot replied.

Nodding, Saershe turned back to the birds and other forest creatures who lingered. She whistled again. The birds whistled back. She walked up them, kneeling before them. She slowly waved her hand as if she were petting them. Dermot had no doubt she was speaking in the old language.

Then, as the creatures departed, she conferred with the trees. A breeze rattled their branches and rustled their leaves. That same breeze carried their voices away. When Saershe rejoined the lads, Dermot asked if word had been sent again to Iorwerth. Saershe smiled, complimenting him on his intuition.

"Forgive me, Saershe," Brian said. "But aren't those creatures in the same peril as the others were? The birds we found dead, I mean."

"We are all in danger against Taranis's forces," Saershe replied. And you needn't apologize. Your concern for their lives touches me."

"But, is it right to place them in the same peril given that the others were killed?"

"I told you, Brian, none traveled who aren't fully aware of the risks, nor were any ordered to go. I asked each to consider if their families needed looking after. They are our allies too, and they all know what we are up against. Did you not think risks must be taken in order to

defeat evil? You saw how passionately Maeve fought those mairágs, and you yourselves defended her and Ferghus. She would willingly sacrifice her life for her child, as I would for my grandson, for all of you."

Dermot was touched.

Saershe continued, "Remember, we are a part of Nature, remember. Like all trees, wild plants, and animals we owe our lives to this world. Every creature must eat to survive, including us. Every species therefore keeps one another in balance and harmony, but not eradicating any. That balance would be disrupted were even one's numbers too many or too few. You have seen how Taranis cares naught for life, only his own power. He will burn everything."

At that moment, a shimmering light greeted them. A female unicorn emerged a short distance from where they stood, her stride through the lilies ever so graceful, followed by a male. Dermot knew at once they were the same two they had encountered earlier.

Saershe walked up to the unicorns. She stroked both their necks. "It's been far too long, my dear friends."

The unicorns bobbed their heads and neighed.

Saershe turned to the others. "Everyone, permit me to introduce Olwen, matriarch of the Denuan unicorns, and her mate, Aengus."

The boys, Yseult, and the gryphons bowed their heads simultaneously as Saershe introduced each of them to the unicorns.

"It's a pleasure to meet you," Dermot said.

Olwen bowed her head in return, as did Aengus. She neighed. *The pleasure is ours.*

Saershe whispered into theeach unicorn's ears, both of which twitched. First Olwen nodded and neighed.

Aengus then did the same. Dermot wondered what Saershe had said to them.

Saershe turned back to the boys. "They have agreed to take us to the ring of stones."

"I thought you said unicorns took no sides in war," Brian said.

"They have taken vows to never shed blood," corrected Saershe. "But that doesn't mean they are unwilling to help their friends."

Olwen neighed. *There are ways to defend goodness without fighting.*

"So that's what the mairágs meant," Dermot said. "They were here to kill the unicorns, because they are the Dríacht's allies too."

"They must've killed those birds too!" Brian said.

Aengus nodded, making a gentle noise. *We must go. We have a long way to travel.*

"Come, lads," Saershe said.

The brothers hesitated. The sorceress stopped and gazed at them, eventually remarking, "Ah, of course. You two have never ridden before, have you?"

"No," Dermot was first to admit.

"Well then, this shall be new experience for you," she smiled.

"What?" Brian gasped. "Are—you sure we're even up to it, Saershe?"

She smiled. "You can't do something well without trying it first. Trial and error precede success. There are always new things to learn in life."

Dermot was speechless. He looked to Ruairí, recalling he once said his grandmother told him something similar. Ruairí only smiled.

Without any further words, Saershe mounted Olwen, who along with Aengus had knelt down. Ruairí joined his grandmother. The brothers struggled to maintain balance once they sat on Aengus's back. Brian wrapped his arms around Dermot's waist the same way Ruairí did with his grandmother. Dermot kept his hands braced on Aengus's shoulders. Saershe somehow didn't have to. Yseult held her head high with confidence. Maeve held hers high too, with Ferghus trying to imitate his mother.

"Comfortable?" Saershe asked the brothers.

"Aye," Dermot said uneasily. "I think so."

"I hope you're sure about this, Saershe," Brian said.

"We don't even have saddles," Dermot said.

Aengus snorted. The hairs on Dermot's head prickled.

"Unicorns never wear saddles," Saershe said. "Dríadórs have always been able to ride them as such. Worry not, my friends. With patience, determination, and continued practice, I have faith it shall become natural to you both."

Dermot nodded slightly. He apologized to the unicorns, assuring them he meant no offense. Olwen whinnied in acceptance, and so did Aengus.

"This is going to be fascinating," Ruairí grinned. "I've never done this before either."

Brian shook his head with a crooked smile. So did Dermot, who stifled a chuckle.

Aengus neighed with insistence. *Let's get moving.*

"I couldn't agree more," Saershe said.

Together they forged ahead. The brothers almost fell off when Aengus started, shouting in chorus, "Whoa!!!"

Fortunately they managed to stay on, albeit rather nervous. Saershe and Ruairí in contrast laughed heartily. Ferghus and Yseult ran behind them. Maeve soared high.

Chapter 29

As the sun was setting, Lonán made his way amongst the graves. The potter approached one that had eroded considerably. He had always been able to find his way back since the first time he came to this burial ground. He could have found his way if blind. The old man got down on his knees, hanging his head. A small tear came into his eye, trickling down his cheek.

"Please forgive me," he whispered, sniffling as his hand reached out to the earth before him. "I should've been there for you. I failed you both. I pray you are at peace together in the otherworld, and that someday we will all be reunited there in eternal happiness. But, if we aren't, please try to understand that I never abandoned you. I never wanted this for us."

Lonán wept incessantly. He couldn't help himself. Finally, drying his eyes, he stood and gazed at the evening sky. Clouds were aglow in vibrant yellow and orange. Unfortunately, he couldn't bring himself to smile. He didn't bother looking to the fields surrounding the town, or the few other people who were there.

"May the Dríacht and those young boys be guided by the spirits down the path to victory, that this land shall know peace," he whispered beneath his breath before making his way back.

He observed tired farmers passing through Harlíeo's foregate, returning home. Two guards stood tall and

proud bearing halberds on opposite sides of the entrance. Lonán entered in town with a slight pain in the back of his throat. He knew he wouldn't sleep well tonight, as he had not since he last saw those he loved most.

Lonán made his way through the streets, looking on the market square. Quietly, he watched merchants and other farmers pack their goods. A few, keen on making a few last deals, dawdled despite the fact that the square was no longer bustling. Though he faced them, in truth the old potter saw them not, for his mind was elsewhere. He had not forgotten those dark days long ago, the last time dragons had been seen in the land, or how, almost to his amusement, he chanced upon the Dríacht.

"Master Lonán," a familiar voice said.

The potter, having gone even deeper into thought regarding the distant past, halted to see Éibhir passing by him. He said, "Ah, good evening, my friend. Are you returning home?"

"No, not yet," the boy said, holding up an empty bucket. "I've got to collect water from the well first. Are you all right, sir?"

"Why do you ask?"

"Beg pardon, sir, but you don't seem quite yourself anymore, not since the night you had that incident. You know, the day those three men..."

"Rubbish, Éibhir," Lonán said. "I recovered quickly. For my old age, the physician and guards disregarded it."

"All right," the lad faltered, rubbing his hand on his leg.

"Thank you. Oh, me lad, I suggest you keep your eyes open."

"Open for what, Master Lonán?" Éibhir asked. "Is

something wrong?"

The potter paused, having had a slight headache beforehand that now became a blinding one. "Please, trust me. You need to be ready in case something horrible happens."

"What do you mean? I don't understand."

"Don't question me, lad. I wish I could tell you more, and maybe I will later. For now, please take my word."

"All right, I just wish..."

"Not now, my young friend. Please try to sleep well, if you can."

They bid each other good night and parted. Lonán eventually returned home, but before going inside he stopped and gazed to the heavens. In the distance, a thick blanket of darkening gray clouds was moving through, cloaking the sunset's glorious colors.

"Something wicked is brewing," Lonán he muttered. It was not only the clouds he was thinking of. Ever since the lads came to Harlíeo, he knew that Taranis would make his move soon, and had been weary ever since. What pained him most was that he knew not how he could warn the people of Harlíeo of the impending danger so they would believe him. He had been battling with this question ever since Ruairí and those brothers came through his door.

He wished now he had told young Éibhir more, but he had been petrified by fear that the lad would tell others. No matter whether Éibhir believed him or not, as an elderly man, whom the guards believed almost died while out alone at night, he would be taken for a delusional old fool. For who amongst them would believe the word of an old common man, especially when there had been no

other news from Emerin? The southern dragons had not attacked Denú for years as far as Harlíeo knew.

On the other hand, he understood if he did nothing, there would be no chance for Harlíeo or other Denuan lives to prepare for the worst. He had to do something. The old soldier would not retire for the night just yet.

**

"What's that?" a guard said, cocking his head.

"What?" a second asked.

"O'er there. You see that?"

"Good heavens, what is this?"

The two sentinels patrolling Harlíeo's walls found themselves taken aback by a throng looming larger in the distance. A small crowd of people, tattered, broken and bleeding, emerged from the wooded border, stopping at the lake to wash and have a long drink.

It became apparent to the guards these people were bound for the town. Most of them waved their arms weakly in Harlíeo's direction upon seeing it. The sentries often expected the soldiers sent out to Emerin to return over the past few days, but none had been seen since they'd left.

"Come!" the first sentry called to the other guards patrolling the wall. They all stopped and looked. Only a few came to his side.

From the refugees' position, the sight of Harlíeo was a welcome relief, a miracle renewing hope in their hearts. Some of them openly stared, whereas others blinked rapidly. Those who did wave poured all their strength into their arms, which sapped their voices. Therefore none of them called toward the guards, however much they wanted to.

Pádraig, in spite of a desire to remain still for a short while, further encouraged them over the moaning and whimpering of the children. "We're almost there! We've made it! Just a little ways to go! Don't give up!"

At long last they came up near the closed portcullis. Seeing the guards watching from above, Pádraig held up his hand and they all stopped. Some dropped on their knees, and a few children lay on their backs. The smith and his wife remained on their feet, walking closer to the giant foregate.

"Halt! Who goes there?" yelled one of the sentries.

"We are weary refugees, in need of your protection!" Pádraig said. "Please, let us in! We mean you no harm! As you can see, we are not armed! We seek food and shelter!"

Pádraig held out his arm toward the women carrying tired children, some passed out by now, a great many more crying. The guards observed them, but not one said a word. Only one or two whispered into another's ear. They didn't move from where they stood.

"The land is in peril!" cried Granuaile, clasping her hands so tight they turned white. "If you don't help us, more lives will be lost!"

The sentries gave no immediate response but instead traded glances. Pádraig was not surprised, but still terribly frightened.

"Please!" he said. "There are children out here!"

Granuaile grabbed his shoulder, whispering, "Pádraig, the torque!"

"Of course," he said. He reached into his pocket and held up the torque.

"What is that?" the first sentry asked.

"This belonged to one of your own!" Pádraig said. "His last request was that we return it here to his father!"

At last, one of the guards shouted, "Open the gate!"

The same guard who spoke to Pádraig gazed at another sentry, who with a single nod of his head raced off toward the castle's keep. Pádraig assumed it was to relay the tidings.

They gathered in the town square. Most plopped onto their knees or sat down. Some even lay on their backs. Several townsfolk appeared, staring incredulously, but no one said a word.

Lonán walked the fastest of all. He felt his stomach harden. *Mercy of the heavens! These must be survivors from Emerin! Oh my goodness. Wait, could the brothers' family be among them? I must find out. They need to know the lads are alive.*

Soldiers stormed into the square, fully armored and carrying spears. Quietly the potter stopped in his tracks and stepped back while the soldiers circled the newcomers, aiming their spearheads directly at them. No one could escape without confronting their sharp iron. The refugees were far too tired to react defensively, except for Granuaile.

"What are you doing?" she asked.

"Silence, woman!" barked one of the soldiers, a captain Pádraig guessed by his garb. "Now then, whereabouts are you lot from?"

"Emerin, just beyond the Forest of Úaene, sir," Pádraig said, putting his hand on his wife's shoulder.

Several refugees' faces sagged further, but Granuaile's reddened. The soldiers slightly lowered their weapons. Lonán

felt his heart skip a beat.

"Why have you come here?" another guard demanded.

"Because our home has been destroyed," Pádraig said, "by a dragon."

Silence swept over the square. Though the soldiers were as stunned as the townsfolk, they made every effort to hide it.

"A dragon?" the captain said.

"The dragon scorched everything," Pádraig said in a sharp tone, for he saw the guard was not convinced. "An evil wizard has imprisoned our chieftain and killed many others. His name is Taranis, and he took everything we had from us—everything. We barely escaped with our lives, and knew this to be the closest settlement."

"We've been meandering for days now, scavenging up whatever we could find, trying to find our way here to warn you," Granuaile said. "Some of us nearly perished from hunger and exhaustion!"

"Am I to take your word on this?" the captain snapped. "Is his lordship? No dragon has been sighted from our walls, nor any smoke beyond the forest."

"We're not lying, sir," Pádraig said. "By my mother's good name I swear, tis true."

"Did Harlíeo not send soldiers to Emerin?" Granuaile asked. "We encountered them. The wizard's forces slaughtered them all! You saw the torque my husband showed you."

"Let me see it," the guard said.

Pádraig handed the torque over. The captain ordered his subordinate to keep order in the square while he left with it. It was then that Lonán found his legs again.

"Stay back there," a soldier ordered, pointing his weapon at Lonán.

The potter made eye contact with the smith and his wife. "Do you..."

"Don't speak, old man!" the same guard thundered.

"Sir, I must speak with..."

"Stay back, you fool!" the soldier threatened more harshly. "And keep your tongue silent, else you shall be bound in irons!"

Granuaile furrowed her brow. Before she or the potter could say another word, the captain returned. It had been half an hour, but felt much longer. Anger could be seen written plainly across the captain's face. He announced, "That torque was a gift from his lordship, the Earl of Harlíeo, to his only son and heir."

Pádraig went cold. Was the warrior they buried really an earl's son?

The captain continued, "By his lordship's order, you are to be held within these walls for questioning tomorrow, so the truth may be determined."

Granuaile stepped forward. The nearest soldier drew his sword, but her husband stepped in front of her. He threw his hands up, stating, "Please, pardon my wife."

The guard put his weapon to the smith's throat.

"Away with you lot!" the captain said, "Now!"

Chapter 30

Pádraig spoke up. "I do not wish to protest, sir, but please. You can see many of us can't go another step. I beg you to see to reason."

"Sir, this isn't hospitable..." Lonán said. Other townsfolk, he could tell by the look in their eyes were as upset as he was.

"Stay out of this, Lonán," the captain said, glaring at the old man. "Return home before you fall ill again."

"You will need all the help..."

"Enough!" the captain thundered, slapping Lonán's face. Many refugees and townsfolk gasped, but the captain took no notice. Instead, he turned back to the refugees.

"The hour grows late," he said. "Eventide is upon us. Tomorrow, another envoy shall be sent to Emerin to learn the truth. Tonight, you lot shall remain under heavy guard in the castle."

"May we please at least have some food?" Pádraig asked.

"His lordship has arranged for that," the captain said, "On his advisors' counsel."

Many refugees smiled and sighed. Pádraig thanked the captain, but said nothing more.

As the refugees were led away, Lonán attempted to speak to them again, but guards kept him back. He chose not to protest. He knew no good would come of it.

Defeated, all the old man could do was watch and still

wonder if the brothers' family was among them. He never guessed they might be same man and woman whose eyes met his again as they walked off.

Returning home, Lonán paced about, before bringing together another sword and shield from his army service. However, his sense of foreboding was strong. He left the weapons on the table and glanced out the window. Thick gray clouds still steadily moved overhead, blotting out the sky. His eyes never left those darkening clouds slowly passing overhead.

**

The refugees' delight in rediscovering the tastes of fresh bread, meat, and vegetables that night overshadowed any discomfort at being kept under lock and key in a large room near the castle's great hall, until they realized they had to spend the night without blankets.

Granuaile pounded on the door asking for them, but after several minutes with no response, she gave up at her husband's urging.

"They do not treat underlings with kindness," he told her. "They never have."

They nevertheless slept sounder than they had in all the nights they'd spent wandering. All it took was a single loud, crashing noise hours later to jolt them awake.

"DRAGON!" one voice outside yelled. Several shrieks soon followed.

At first, none of the refugees knew what to do. Then, Pádraig found his voice and rushed toward the window.

"Harlíeo's being attacked!" he shouted. "Get up! Save

the children! Hurry!"

Everyone complied. They dashed for the doors, which of course were locked. They banged on them begging to be freed. Pádraig found a large table, and together with five other men, they eventually knocked them open.

The guards hadn't left, but they alone could not halt the stampede as the refugees rushed out through the castle. They found little resistance through the hallways for the other guards were scurrying, headed for the battlements.

Pádraig and Granuaile remembered the path they had taken when coming in. Leading the villagers out, they firmly kept them all together.

Once outside, they were greeted by a scene that was all too familiar to them, for it was almost as if they had returned to that dreadful night. Townsfolk scrambled about in absolute panic as soldiers tried to control them and assemble together along the walls. Fire streams plunged like heavy rain, incinerating numerous homes.

"Look!" Pádraig said to his wife.

Sure enough, a large dragon soared above the town. Not the red dragon that burned Emerin, but one with a far more serpentine body, and stone-gray scales. Those eyes, however, blazed the same fiery orange.

The Mairágh breached Harlíeo's walls, storming over them and through the foregate. Slaughtering wayward townsfolk, they brought in a battering ram, as well as catapults, ladders, and gigantic crossbows. They made their way toward the castle. Those who were not slain on the spot either lay wounded or ran about screaming.

"Charge!" a commanding voice roared.

All eyes converged in the direction of that voice,

including the mairágs. All activity momentarily ceased.

Brandishing a spear and shield, the Earl of Harlíeo himself led his troops, both those on foot and horseback, to meet the invaders. All were armored and armed, but only some had had time to apply the traditional blue face paint of Denuan warriors.

The Mairágh resumed their onslaught. Sadly for the refugees, in their panic to avoid being trampled, they became separated from one another. Pádraig did his best to protect his wife, but it didn't take him long to realize they were on their own in this melee. He led her away through the burning town, evading livestock and people as well as falling rubble.

Weapons clashed. Blood was spilt, covering the town square. Amidst the confusion, one mairág spotted Pádraig escorting his wife, presently evading fire and crumbling shards. He charged at them, and they froze in terror.

Then, to their shock, Lonán jumped out to defend them with a sword and shield bearing the emblem of Harlíeo, but to no avail.

A broadsword's pommel came down on him. Though it struck his shield, his age sapped him of his strength, sending him to the ground, groaning. He nevertheless maintained his grip on his weapons.

Shoving Granuaile out of the way, the mairág charged at Pádraig again. The smith curled his fists, attempting to fight back. Unfortunately, the mairág proved quicker and ducked. His blade sliced into Pádraig's left leg. Granuaile, who had fallen alongside Lonán, froze in horror.

Howling, Pádraig found himself seized bu two other mairágs. They dragged him away, as he struggled to break free.

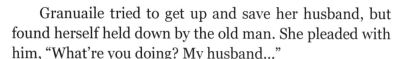

Granuaile tried to get up and save her husband, but found herself held down by the old man. She pleaded with him, "What're you doing? My husband..."

"You're no match for them, my dear," Lonán said. "Please. You won't survive. How could you save your husband if you're dead?"

She struggled to break free, but his grip remained firm. At last giving up, she wept.

Lonán's face saddened, but he couldn't shed tears, until he saw young Éibhir's lifeless body lying not far away, smeared with soil, rubble, and blood, his eyes and mouth wide open.

The potter was wracked with guilt. Startled by a falling timber from a nearby house, he led Granuaile away, his shield protecting them.

The invasion had ended by dawn. Smoldering ruins, along with countless corpses were everywhere. Warriors, some of whom had been forced off their steeds during the fray, stood awestruck with foot soldiers and the townsfolk. The Mairágh had fled, having taking Pádraig, the earl, and several other hostages, townsfolk and soldiers alike, all able-bodied men. No one was in any condition to pursue.

Granuaile shed many tears. Lonán wrapped her in his arms, attempting to comfort her as they sat together in the middle of the town square. She buried her face in his breast, drenching his shirt. He didn't mind, not after what happened to her.

"Please, don't lose hope, my dear," Lonán said. "We cannot foretell how fate will take its course."

Her grief wasn't dissuaded. "You don't know what I've suffered and lost, old man," she sobbed. "What could you

possibly know of it?"

To that, Lonán said, "Why do you think I risked my life to help you and your husband as I did when you came? For the same reason you and he guided your people here. They need you more than ever. We all need each other. As a good friend once posed to me, which is the greater evil: the pain and suffering of one, or of all?"

Granuaile looked up. She wiped her nose with her sleeve, as she managed to hold her tears back. "Forgive me. Your name is Lonán isn't it, good sir?" she asked, sitting upright. "I heard that captain call you that."

"Aye, I'm the town potter."

"My name is Granuaile. Thank you for what you did earlier for me and my husband. It took exceptional courage. Where did you get those weapons?"

"You don't need to ask forgiveness from me, my dear. These are mine. I was a soldier once in the king's army. I faced death in battles long ago. It no longer frightens me, my dear, though it seems my age has hindered me, more so than I believed it would."

"My husband's father was a soldier."

"Your husband is a brave man. I could see that."

"Oh he is, Lonán. He is the bravest man I've ever known, and the kindest. I wouldn't have been able to raise a family without him. Now they're all gone."

Lonán paused, blinking. "I had a family once meself, a wife and son. But I lost them long ago."

"I'm so sorry. What happened?"

Lonán hesitated to answer, but did speak in the end. "It's a long story. There was a time when I might have died, if not for a coven of sorcerers. They saved my life. Ever since then, I've been their ally, for they stand in

Denú's defense. One among them was a kindly sorceress who became a close friend of mine, the same friend I spoke of. Her name is Saershe."

Granuaile froze. "Did you say, Saershe? You mean—not the Lady of Green Trees?"

"Yes. How do you know of her?"

"She saved my life and my husband's life, and those of us refugees who survived Emerin's burning. She fought off that evil wizard. We wouldn't have escaped without her."

"Her grandson came to Harlíeo not long ago. There were two brothers from your village with him."

Granuaile's skin tingled. "B-Brothers you say? What—what were their names, these brothers?"

"Dermot and..."

"...and Brian," she finished, covering her mouth with her hand.

For the first time since arriving in Harlíeo, Granuaile truly smiled.

"Do you know them?" Lonán asked.

Clutching the old man's arm, she shook it violently. "They're *my* sons!"

She felt a flutter in her belly.

"Where are they?" she asked. "Please, Lonán. Tell me everything, whatever it may be."

"In Saershe's company, and under her protection," he said. "Their destination is an ancient ring of standing stones in the county of Wykúm. They were seeking an old associate of Saershe's, a dríadór named Iorwerth, the Dragon's Bane. Their purpose is to reunite the coven of the Dríacht. The lads came to warn me of Taranis's return."

Granuaile's smile receded. She paused, staring into the

old man's face. "Are you saying—you knew about Taranis? You knew this whole time, and did nothing?"

"Who would've believed me?" asked Lonán. "I..."

She sprang to her feet. "If you had spoken up, more lives might have been spared! My Pádraig wouldn't be a prisoner of those monsters!"

Lonán, who had remained seated, felt his blood run cold. "What did you say?"

"Were you not listening to me, old man? Are you going deaf?"

"No, no, I mean, his name. Tell me. What is your husband's name?"

"Pádraig, but what does that have to do with anything?"

Lonán looked away, a fine sheen of sweat covering his upper lip.

"What?" Granuaile eye's flared. "Speak!"

"My—my son," he whispered. "I had a son. His name—was Pádraig."

Granuaile didn't respond.

"Was your husband born in Emerin?" Lonán asked. "Or did he come from my village, Caemoch?"

Granuaile's eyes widened. She stepped back, pointing at him. Her hand trembled, as did her voice. "You—you..."

Chapter 31

Olwen and Aengus made good time through Ámhen over the next several days, even if they didn't run as fast as they could, so Yseult and Ferghus could keep up with them. The old trees and dense bushes compelled them further to maintain a careful pace. Still, more ground was covered in a day than walking. Periodically they stopped for a short rest or water, as they did at present alongside a shallow stream bank where Saershe accumulated fresh wild mint.

Yseult drank a lot of water, far more than the unicorns. The lads and Saershe dismounted. Dermot felt somewhat shaky in his legs, but managed to stay on his feet. He noticed Ruairí, standing tall and taking in a deep breath. Then he saw Brian hanging his head. Maeve descended.

"Please, try to relax, little brother," Dermot said to no avail. Even he struggled to calm down. They hadn't seen any mairágs lately, but he still wondered when they would appear next.

"It's not easy. Not after what we've been through."

I knew he'd say something like that, Dermot thought.

"Why not try something Grandma taught me for whenever I feel stressed," Ruairí said. "Let's lean against this oak together. We shut our eyes, and stretch our back and arms, taking deep breaths. We don't speak, or think. Just listen to the sounds and silence of the forest."

"I agree," Saershe said, glancing up at the trees with her usual wide smile. "It will do you all good."

Ruairí spread out his arms, with his back against the trunk. Dermot and Brian did the same. Initially, Brian appeared no less anxious. He opened his mouth and eyes as if to say something, but Ruairí placed his forefinger against his lips and shook his head.

Dermot blinked and averted his attention back to Brian, who kept silent.

They shut their eyes. Gradually, to his astonishment Dermot did indeed calm down. When he opened his eyes a little, he noticed Brian was calmer as well. He closed his eyes again and breathed deep. He listened to the forest as Ruairí said, and in his deep breaths, he could smell the woodland's many aromas.

Dermot sensed not only harmony within but far and wide. A comforting, profound yet enigmatic impression emanated from the earth, coursing throughout his body akin to trees during their growth and development, taking deep root. He wondered if the others were feeling the same sensation. A mild breeze stirred the leaves above them, swaying even the thinnest of the branches.

Somehow, Dermot found himself connected to that tree on which he leaned, receiving images in his mind of the tree's growth. Once again he felt that strange, warm sensation he couldn't fully explain, but welcomed all the same. The tension within him vanished. Opening his eyes partway, he thought he vaguely perceived far more wildlife than he viewed amidst the greenwood. Making no sudden moves, he shut his eyes again, swiftly opening them, half-wondering if he merely dreamt it. Then he picked up a distinctive sound.

"You hear a buzzing noise?" he asked the others.

"O'er there," Ruairí said, pointing to his left.

Sure enough, situated inside a hollowed area within an oak's trunk, aloft near the branches, bees bristled outside a hive. The brothers jumped up and backed away. Saershe approached. She hummed so beautifully the buzzing dwindled. To Dermot's surprise, not one bee made an attempt to sting her, even as they hovered about her face.

From one of the bundles, Saershe retrieved a small ceramic flask, whereupon she returned to the hive and collected fresh honey. Several bees returned to the hive afterwards. Others flew away in search of flowers. Saershe topped off the flask then faced the brothers.

"I have welcomed many an insect into my garden, my friends," she said. "I have watched them float o'er those plants I sowed and tended with great care. One cannot interrelate with Nature unless all her children are treated with the utmost respect, including insects. Like so many people, I have seen you recoil from some of them as if you were soldiers facing an enemy without weapons or armor. I had hoped you would release yourselves, and bloom out to all of them."

Saershe hummed again, holding out her hand. There landed a bee from the hive. Out of nowhere, a small spider descended from an iridescent, semi-invisible thread onto her hand next to the bee.

"Please extend your fingers," she said.

Both brothers hesitated. Nevertheless, they did as she asked.

"You lads approached a young bird within Oísein with relative ease," Saershe said. "Why should these creatures

be any different? But perhaps it'll be easier if we begin with different insects."

Dermot attempted to speak, but Saershe hummed again, extending her other hand. A cricket with a powerful voice leapt off a tree onto it, as a large brilliant blue butterfly appeared and fluttered down beside the cricket.

Saershe lowered her hand, allowing the cricket to hop onto Brian's finger, while the butterfly landed on Dermot's. Both the boys and these insects remained very still, although the cricket chirped and every now and then the butterfly's wings fluttered.

With a nod from Saershe, the butterfly took flight and the cricket hopped away. The butterfly however remained a moment, bringing a smile to everyone's face by landing on Yseult's nose. The retriever didn't bark. She remained still, looking at her new friend. When the butterfly flew up and away, Yseult sneezed.

Now Saershe extended her other hand near Brian's. The spider crawled over his hand, as the bee landed on Dermot's. Once again, there was a brief moment of silence and profound stillness. Neither insect moved. Both brothers again remained still. Dermot did his best to stay relaxed, breathing in and out deeply. Then the bee moved a little around on his finger, but didn't sting him.

"Very well," Saershe finally whispered.

Brian raised his finger so the spider trotted back to the web, gilded with sunlight.

The bee flew away from Dermot, returning into the hive's depths. A warm, relaxing feeling engulfed him. He couldn't help but smile. "That wasn't too bad."

"Aye," Brian said. "Not at all."

"Well done," Ruairí said with a chuckle, gently patting

their backs one at a time. Dermot almost laughed.

"So long as you give them no reason to fear you, nor make any sudden moves that'll scare them," Saershe said, "all o' these creature, not merely bees and spiders, shall pose no threat whatsoever toward you. Respect their territory and their space. Try speaking to those that do come near you. Often they're merely curious. You shan't feel so tense. The same goes with every other wild animal. Never forget: there are worse things to fear than insects."

The lads nodded, at which point Saershe decided it was time for them to leave. They remounted the unicorns. Maeve spread her wings.

"I can hardly believe how much ground you have covered since we met," Dermot said to the unicorns. "You're much faster than I ever imagined."

Olwen and Aengus whinnied simultaneously. *Never underestimate anyone, young one.*

"Well, 'twas fortunate we crossed their path," Ruairí said. "Then again, like you always say, Grandma, in Nature as in all things, fate intervenes."

"Indeed," Saershe replied. With that, they were off again, and Maeve ascended.

Before long, Ámhen's borderline beckoned, speckled with sunshine. Brian pointed it out immediately. "Look! We're almost there!"

They didn't have to wait long. A wave of bright light deluged them. The unicorns ceased running. The lads shut their eyes momentarily. Reopening them, the awaiting sight captured their interest. They stared in awe at what lay ahead.

In the distance, there was a ring of huge, and uneven, standing stones. Some were more lopsided than others,

where a few had fallen on their sides. Beyond them, the ruins of a castle stood on a small knoll. Its windblown stone walls were set with thick ivy and missing large pieces. A single tower, its top long gone, loomed over the walls. A tall, knotted alder tree grew near the foregate. The castle's wooden doors had long since rotted away. The portcullis was still there, albeit dreadfully rusted.

"Is this the sole ring of stones in Denú, Saershe?" Dermot asked.

"No," she said. "There are many scattered throughout the land. These standing stones were a central gathering site for dríadórs when magic thrived. They have withstood time, even conflicts."

"Conflicts?" Brian asked. "Do you mean the war Taranis waged against the Dríacht?"

Saershe nodded.

"And—those ruins on the knoll?" Brian asked.

"They are the remnants of a once-glorious stronghold of Denuan kings, before the seat of royalty was moved permanently into the central province of Raiph."

Dermot sensed an air of reflective sadness in her voice. Then it dawned on him: now that they'd arrived, what if Iorwerth never did?

"Let's go," Saershe said. They made their way down to the standing stones. Finally nearing them, they dismounted. Saershe thanked Olwen and Aengus for bringing them here. The two mystical creatures bowed their heads. The companions watched them both dash away at full speed, far faster than any horse Dermot had ever seen.

"Where are they going?" Brian asked.

"To rejoin their fellow unicorns," Saershe said. "The

Mairágh, remember, were trying to kill them when we crossed paths. Olwen and Aengus need to make sure the others of their tribe are all right, including their beloved daughter, Vannora."

"I see," Dermot said. "I pray they'll be safe."

"Come, boys," Saershe said.

Slowly they made their way to the standing stones, with the sorceress leading them. Finally reaching the circle, they came to a standstill.

Brian leaned his head back in awe. Dermot however strolled from one stone to another, running his fingertips across each. Some smaller, eroded boulders lay dispersed, entrenched in the earth amongst grass, weeds, and clover. Ruairí also meandered around the stones, touching every single one of them. Yseult sat beside Brian.

Dermot looked up at the ruined fortress. Drawn by curiosity, he advanced towards it. He halted near the foot of the knoll. The others noticed and came up beside him.

"Shall we?" Saershe asked.

Slowly they hiked uphill, stopping at a wide, empty ditch that was too deep to cross.

"Did the air grow a little cooler?" Dermot asked.

"I feel it too." Brian rubbed his arms together.

Everyone glanced upward. Swirling dark clouds loomed overhead. The sky became much more foreboding as a grayish hue replaced the blue.

"Looks like it's going to pour," Dermot said.

"Aye," Ruairí agreed.

"Look! Over there!" Brian gasped, pointing to the edge of the ditch.

They hurried over. Much to their dismay, they came upon an all-too familiar sight: several dead birds sprawled

out across the hillside.

"Dear me," said Saershe, clutching her heart.

"I think we've got company," Brian pointed again.

Everyone's eyes followed his finger. A small legion of the Mairágh was in the field, headed their way. Red clover withered as Taranis's minions passed through them.

Chapter 32

Ruairí readied his longbow. Saershe stood in front of the group and raised her arms, her staff in one hand, uttering an incantation in the old language. Dermot wished he knew what she was doing, but had learned not to question her whenever she cast a spell.

Without warning, Taranis's troops dropped their weapons. They beat their chests, roaring in the manner of infuriated beasts.

"What're they doing?" Dermot asked.

He didn't have to wait long to find out. Twisting and groaning, each mairág fell on all fours. Their armor burst off their bodies and turned into black powder. Instead of human skin, what was revealed was black fur and feathers. Some of them opened their mouths wide, revealing sharp fangs or tusks. All of their eyes glowed bright yellow.

"They're shape-shifting!" Dermot said.

"I don't believe it!" Brian said.

Indeed, a few of the mairágs took on either the form of a bear, wild boar, or wolf. Most, however, became crows or insects and took flight. All of them expressed unbridled ferocity. The bird-mairágs unleashed a terrible caw all at once. Dermot then realized something else. The clouds had darkened further, and were rolling even closer together. He recognized what Saershe was doing when he saw her staring at the sky.

"Here they come!" Brian said.

The mairágs on the ground charged. Their winged allies descended rapidly.

Rainfall, as directed by Saershe, poured down. It soaked the side of the hill, yet did not touch the castle ruins or Ámhen. Somehow, the undeterred mairágs withstood it surprisingly well in their altered forms. Ruairí shot arrows straight ahead and upward, hitting his mark each time but inflicting little damage.

Saershe ascended off the ground, her robes and hair fluttering, with the latter losing petals and leaves. She rapidly grew in size, sprouting wings, fur, feathers, and her nails elongated into claws. She had transfigured into a gryphon once more. Together she and Maeve together fought off the mairágs, keeping most of them at bay. Alas, they couldn't prevent a few from slipping toward the lads. The winged hordes swooped down.

"Brace yourselves!" Ruairí yelled.

Dermot raised his shield above his head. He and Brian fended the aggressors off by waving their weapons, whacking them in midflight. They, Ruairí, and Yseult all stepped backwards in the process. Yseult took one step too far and tumbled into the empty ditch, wailing as she fell.

"Yseult!" Ruairí cried. He and the brothers jumped in after her.

"Get off her, you fiends!" Dermot screamed. He beat crows-mairágs away from her. She bore talon marks stained crimson.

Dermot raised his shield to prevent them all from being pricked and bitten. They ran the length of the empty ditch, but were pursued. There was nowhere to hide.

Returning to the front, they halted and ducked as Saershe and Maeve dived in, driving a number of them away.

"Everyone all right?" Ruairí asked.

"I think so," Brian said. "Are you?"

"Look!" Dermot said.

It was not more mairágs, but the supple alder bending downward. Some of the branches were within reach. The lads each grabbed hold of one. Yseult stood on her hind legs, grasping Dermot's trousers with her teeth. They were then lifted out of the ditch. Once their toes touched the top, they let go. The alder whipped upright, barely missing Brian's face. Yseult released Dermot.

Unfortunately, once again the flying hosts nosedived at them. Saershe had no time to cast a countercharm. The frays was so overwhelming that Dermot lost his footing. He hit the ground hard before rolling downhill.

Finally stopping, he looked up. To his distress he discovered his brother and Yseult in midair, furiously struggling to break free from the grasps of crow-mairágs' talons. The insect-mairágs meanwhile plagued the two, attacking their flesh and forcing them to recoil. Yseult barked furiously. Brian struggled to break free, shouting at his captors to let him go.

Dermot tried to chase after them, but Ruairí suddenly appeared, grabbing him. He pointed, "Wait. Look."

Maeve and Saershe charged. Ferghus, trailed them with crow-mairágs on his tail, cawing. *No! You won't take them away!*

The earthbound mairágs pursued him as well, and they were fast. Ferghus exchanged frantic caws with his mother. Dermot could feel the urgency in Maeve's caws for Ferghus to fly, and Ferghus assuring her he was doing

his best, like voices echoing from within his heart.

"Careful, Ferghus!" Dermot shouted. *Please, somebody help Brian! Please!*

Ferghus paid no heed. He repeatedly failed to get off the ground. But he didn't give up. Then, at last, he was up! It took a little more effort, but he managed to gain control, and flew in a straight line, higher and higher. Elated at first, Ferghus quickly raced to join his mother, with the winged mairágs still chasing him. Although concerned for his friend, Dermot smiled at the sight of Ferghus soaring.

The gryphons lunged for the transfigured mairágs again. Caught by surprise, they let go of Brian and Yseult. They plummeted, hitting the ground feet first. Dermot felt his heart skip a beat, relieved they were free. This time he called to his brother that he was coming. Then, he felt a frosty impression hanging in the air. His ears picked up faint whistling from behind, coupled with ruffling leaves.

Ruairí shouted, "Look out!"

Dermot turned to see one of the wolf-mairágs charging at him. He held his shield in front of his body, but was unable to prevent the fiend from pouncing on him. Luckily, he managed to hold off the beast's drooling snout by keeping the shield between his assailant's front legs, and under its throat. He tried hacking his sword at the beast's back, but failed. Claws got around his shield, scratching him between his breast and shoulder.

Dermot growled as crimson blood spurted over him. He didn't lose his grip, though he could feel his strength slowly seeping away.

Much to Dermot's relief, Ruairí appeared, sinking an arrow into the beast's eye. At that, the mairág staggered away, wailing. Ruairí helped Dermot to his feet, and they ran to meet Brian and Yseult, who were limping toward them.

Dermot and Brian made eye contact while Yseult sniffed Ruairí, who petted her head and examined her injuries. Out of a newfound impulse, the brothers hugged each other tight, before abruptly realizing for first time in their lives they had willingly, truly embraced one another as brothers, and relished the moment. They stepped back, still smiling. Dermot turned to the dog, kneeling down to her. She sniffed his hands then licked his face, making him laugh.

"Oh dear," Ruairí said. "We've got more company."

They saw the other groundling mairágs charge uphill, led by a particularly huge boar-mairág whose mouth was wide open. Dermot gripped his shield and sword tighter. Ruairí fired arrows, which delayed their advance. He whispered to the brothers, "Remember, try to remain calm. We can get through this."

Saershe's gryphon wings beat the air. She attacked the swarms overhead alongside Maeve. Swooping down, she next made wolves and boars tumble to the ground. Instantly, she turned and sent the wounded wolf-mairág, still staggering in pain, hurtling into the air. Arrows passed close around her, but she continued the assault.

She battled the legions on the ground while Maeve attacked those in the air.

Suddenly, Olwen and Aengus appeared out of nowhere. Their bodies produced a vivid, silvery light that repelled Taranis's followers.

Dermot couldn't help but be bemused. *Fate intervenes.*

The skies cleared as the insect and crow-mairágs flew away. Those on the ground were pursued by unicorns, whose brilliance diminished as the mairágs scrambled for safety. Maeve and Ferghus chased the beasts while Dermot and his companions watched with satisfaction.

Rainwater intermixed with blood. The gryphons landed gently beside their friends. Once her feet touched the earth the sorceress resumed her true form.

With a single gesture from Saershe's hand, Maeve lowered her back, squawking once. Saershe, herself practically unhurt herself, hastily loaded the boys onto Maeve's back as the gryphon grabbed Yseult in her talons. Saershe then climbed onto the mother gryphon. Ferghus squawked in protest that he'd carried no one before, but his mother silenced him with a stern look.

To gain momentum, Maeve and Ferghus ran a short distance before leaping into the air. They soared over the castle's battlements, and landed in the courtyard.

Saershe led them beneath a great stone arch into a corridor not far away, where she tended everyone's wounds. Whispering incantations in the old language, she slowly waved her hand across their injuries. Her palm emanated a brilliant blue light. Both gryphons painfully stretched their wings. A few bloodstained feathers fell.

She wiped blood not washed away by the rain off everybody one at a time. They watched her pound wild mint flowers and mix them with honey, while red clovers were steeped in a tiny copper kettle. She conjured fire that flared vigorously, causing the water to bubble instantly.

Once the red clover tea was ready, Saershe poured it into three wooden cups and added thick honey.

"Why honey?" Dermot asked.

"It will taste much better," she said, handing the cups to him and the other boys the cups.

"Oh." Dermot nodded, and drank. Indeed, he tasted delicious honey.

"I can feel it working," Brian said.

"Me, too," Dermot said. "What's this red clover tea for, Saershe?"

"Red clover tea purifies the blood," she said.

"You were incredible, Ruairí," Brian said. "Where did you learn to shoot so well?"

"Grandma taught me."

Brian turned to Saershe. "Really?"

"Don't be so surprised," she said with a smile. "Did you honestlty think men alone fought the Dríacht's battles? When I was younger, I was a shield-maiden for our people. I've fought alongside Iorwerth and many other dríadórs against Taranis and other foes. We trained and fought together, man and woman. Two of our coven's chief principles are equality and respect."

If only there was more respect in more peoples' hearts in this kingdom, Dermot thought, remembering her fight with Taranis back home. *It would be a better, happier place.*

He faced Ferghus, grinning. "You flew. Well done."

Ferghus squawked. Maeve nudged the side of his head, her voice resembling a cat's purr.

Sometime later, the rain outside the fortress stopped. They set up camp as they had done every night since their journey commenced. The boys first removed their cloaks and rolled them up to serve as pillows. They laid them out with blankets in a straight line under the arch. Their bundles were piled nearby. They did their best not to

strain the injuries they'd incurred.

In the greenwood, they looked for food for supper. Ruairí also asked the brothers to look for twigs, brush, and large rocks. So they searched around, bringing what they found to Ruairí. After he was certain they had enough, they returned to the castle while the gryphons continued hunting.

Ruairí used his hands to loosen a patch of soil at the heart of the encampment. He arranged the stones in a small circle. The brothers placed the twigs and brush within it. Ruairí reached into his satchel and took out a small knife and stone. He repeatedly struck the blade on the rock. A spark was produced and flew down, catching the tinder. Ruairí blew on it several times.

The fire ignited, but meekly, providing little light and less warmth. Ruairí waved his hands side to side above the fire, whispering. Gradually, the flames gained strength, brilliance, and heat. Their warmth seeped deep into their flesh, relaxing their muscles.

Maeve returned, carrying fresh meat in her beak, tossing it near the brothers. Once, her actions would have startled them, but now they barely looked up. The meat was fresh and ready for cooking. It was impossible for Dermot to determine what kind of animal it may have been. Saershe prepared the meat above the flames, saying a blessing for the meal and a prayer for those lives lost.

As Dermot watched her, his memory traced back to those times he fought with his mother again, and the hours spent in the forge with his father.

"I grew so used to our life in Emerin, more than I ever realized," he acknowledged to his brother, gazing at the passing, rolling clouds. "It isn't the same, having been apart from it for so long."

"I miss them dearly," Brian said. "I miss it all."

"I know, brother. Me too."

They still needed to locate Iorwerth, but Dermot wondered how they were going to do that.

Chapter 33

Under a blanket of murky black clouds, the Ashland was alive with activity, the sight stunning Pádraig the moment he set his eyes on it. Roaring flames and clashes of iron echoed throughout the dreary smog-laden land. The dense sooty air and stifling heat seemed to have no effect on the fully-armored mairágs, even those busy feeding the fires inside forges, assembling iron weapons and war machines.

The mairágs dragged Pádraig, the Earl of Harlíeo, and their other prisoners past the forges. Pádraig repeatedly glanced left and right, seeing war machines and humongous fires devouring chopped pieces of tree trunks. Grit from the fires brushed against the smith's face, and he choked on soot. Many mairágs gazed at the prisoners as they passed, albeit briefly. Pádraig was still limping from his leg injury, although it had been bandaged by his captors.

The smith could not help but worry. *Mercy of the heavens, what have we gotten ourselves into? What is to become of us, of the kingdom?*

He looked up. A lofty stone fortress loomed over the entire valley from the mountains in the distance. It was barely visible against the mountains and the sky. Pádraig had only spotted it by chance. It appeared to have been erected from dark stone. Its walls were high, and there were many towers. One of them stood higher than the

rest. His heart sank as he grasped the situation they were in.

He glanced back in the direction they'd come, only to see the higher southeastern mountain range that was part of the Black Mountains separating Ashland from Denú.

He absorbed everything he saw, but his mind was in a whirl from everything that was happening to him. He and the other hostages had been forced to march to the sounds of wooden cartwheels turning night and day. For the mairágs had not only taken hostages. They plundered Harlíeo of many necessities, from wood and tools to practically the castle's entire armory.

The memory of those hostages far too exhausted to continue distressed him, for those poor souls were slaughtered on the spot. Nevertheless, he knew he couldn't give up, not while his wife and boys still lived.

The most frightening moment came on a foggy night in an empty field. When they stopped, Pádraig and the others fell to their knees, more horrified than ever when not one, but three dragons landed before them. Four or five prisoners fainted on the spot. One of the mairágs approached these dragons and said, "We must get this lot beyond the Great Sleeping Dragon and into the Ashland at once."

The dragon nearest him snorted. From the red scales, Pádraig presumed this to be the same one who incinerated Emerin. The mairág continued as if he could understand the creature. "Don't worry. We have a few fainted-hearted souls here, still fresh and warm."

Pádraig could only watch as those most exhausted and nearest death were given to the dragons as fodder. A few of them screamed, only to be silenced in seconds.

Those who were already dead were simply abandoned to the elements.

The living, including Pádraig, turned their heads in disgust at the sound of bones crunching under the dragon's teeth.

Another mairág said, "Our master cares not for the faint-hearted. The weak are useless to his cause."

"Lord Emerin?" Pádraig asked, recognizing his chieftain's voice.

"Shut your mouth!" the mairág snarled, slapping him in the face. "You'll speak when spoken to!"

"Lord Emerin, I demand a..." the earl began.

"Be silent! And that goes for all of you!" the former chieftain said. "Do you understand?"

"How dare you speak to me in such a manner!" the Earl of Harlíeo said. "Do you know who I am?"

Fast as a striking snake, Lord Emerin held a dagger to the earl's throat. He said, "You are one of his highness, the Dark Prince's prisoners, and a particularly fussy one. That's who you are. You're worth more alive than dead, but every time you protest, you will be taking another step closer to a slow death. Do I make myself clear?"

The earl didn't speak. Lord Emerin turned to Pádraig. "Well, well, fancy seeing you here, smith. You escaped us at Emerin, only to be ensnared once more at Harlíeo. I must say that's a truly tragic tale."

Pádraig said nothing. Lord Emerin asked, "What's the matter? Has your tongue been cut from your mouth?"

"I have nothing to say to you," Pádraig said, stiffening his spine.

"Wise to keep silent, smith, and you will keep your life at least a little longer than this lot."

Lord Harlíeo's eyes turned cold, but he still didn't speak. He and the smith exchanged brief looks. What followed defied belief and enhanced fear beyond its heights for Pádraig. Before the smith realized what was happening, he was on the ground. Before sinking into blackness, he saw the mairágs clouting another prisoner about the head. Only once did he briefly regain consciousness, viewing the world upside down as he was carried by chains from the dragon's claws over the mountain. The next thing he remembered was waking up in a mountain pass. The mairágs subsequently led the prisoners down into the heart of the Ashland.

"Keep moving, you lousy scum," Lord Emerin said.

Pádraig gazed up at the cloudy sky, where he could barely make out the silhouettes of the two dragons.

Meanwhile, another mairág approached the column. They all stopped when he stood face to face with the former chieftain.

"Are these the prisoners from Harlíeo?"

Pádraig recognized his voice too. It was the sheriff.

"Aye, and look who we have here!" Lord Emerin pointed to Pádraig. "I'm sure our prince will want to know about this."

"I shall inform him at once," the sheriff replied. "Secure this lot now."

"Of course," Lord Emerin said with a vicious hiss. He turned to the other mairágs. "Take this rabble to the dungeons until our prince decides what's to be done with them."

Pádraig looked up at the castle a second time, where he noticed a dim silhouette observing the action below. Pádraig didn't have to guess that figure's identity. His

limp worsened. At one point he nearly stumbled, had not the mairág clutching his arm wrenched him back up, asking him if he wanted to die. The smith didn't respond.

"Wise again," the mairág said.

With a huff, Pádraig turned his head away. He had been reminded of what befell the chieftain of Emerin at the hands of Taranis, by the mairág's words of the faint-hearted. He chose not to speak of it. He had no desire to appear weak or cowardly. Above those feelings, he knew speaking of it would only dishearten the others.

We must stay alive, he thought. *We must stay strong until we can escape.*

They were led into a giant cave. Some of the prisoners might have stopped dead in their tracks if they were not dragged inside. The cave became a winding, narrow tunnel barely lit by the torches of their captors. As they descended deeper and deeper, Pádraig wondered how far down they would go.

He did not have to wait long to find out. They stood before a great pit deep within the mountain, dark and dank with doorways blocked off by iron gates. The pit itself had been divided into tiny cells, all in good condition, with stone walls and barred tops. One by one, the prisoners were thrown into empty cells, each even smaller than Emerin's lock-up. There was scarcely room for them to move around.

As soon as each prisoner was confined, the mairágs left. Pádraig sat down. Lord Emerin whispered to him from the next cell through a tiny barred window, "Why you, smith?"

"What do you mean, milord?"

"Why would their master want to know about you?"

Pondering for a moment, Pádraig spoke. "He has an enemy, a sorceress called the Lady of Green Trees, whom he fought back in Emerin. My two sons are with her."

"I see," was the nobleman's only reply.

"Where exactly are we?" asked one of the prisoners.

"We must be in the Ashland. That mairág mentioned we were to be taken beyond the Great Sleeping Dragon," Pádraig said. "It's an ancient name for some of the Black Mountains, specifically those which mark Denú's southern provincial border."

"The Black Mountains?" another prisoner asked.

"Aye," the smith said. "From the Denuan side, at a distance they resemble an enormous dragon lying in slumber. Such a name is befitting, since those mountains are home to the dragons, just as the gryphons roosted in the eastern Emerald Mountains in the east. The Ashland is a valley enclosed within the Black Mountains."

"You seem to be well versed in our kingdom's lore, smith," the earl said.

"My elder son was fascinated by it. I can remember him recounting all the stories he listened to as a little boy during the festivals about the Sleeping Dragon, and the vast treasure hoard purported to be within it: precious jewels hewn from the rock, together with endless deep rivers of gold, silver, and copper, not to mention riches plundered from Denú."

"No southern Denuan has dared venture near the Sleeping Dragon for years," Lord Harlíeo said, "For fear of incurring the dragons' wrath.

"It's a similar story with the Emerald Mountains, Pádraig said. "Gryphon roosts, known as eyries, are rumored to contain precious emeralds. That's how their

territory earned its name. Mining still occurs for iron and salt, but never anywhere close to the roosts."

"Gryphon roosts are known as eyries. It is rumored they contain precious emeralds," Pádraig said. "That's how their territory came to be named for that gem."

"Why are we even talking about creatures and tales?" Lord Harlíeo asked.

"To keep our hearts hopeful and minds sane by remembering what we love and cherish," Pádraig said.

"Perhaps it's better to perish here than wait for whatever fate this wizard, whoever he is, has in store for us," a prisoner murmured.

His name is Taranis, Pádraig thought. He kept that to himself, thinking of his wife and children, praying they were all right. He wished he knew where they were, yet was glad not to. As much as he wanted to hold and hug them again, he feared what might become of them.

**

Taranis gazed out over his industrious military forces from his castle, his hands pressed against the terrace railing. His pride swelled.

"Splendid," he said. "Soon we'll be ready."

Presently, the wizard saw an unwelcome scene. Flocks of crows, accompanied by swarms of insects, dived down into Ashland. In due course, the mairágs reverted to their true forms.

Taranis pounded his fist. "Intolerable! I grant them the gift of shape-shifting, yet they still can't stop my enemies. Must I fight the Dríacht myself?"

He knew he couldn't grant them the form of the

dragon. He had to maintain his superiority in dark magic.

Taranis turned from the terrace back into his private quarters, his inky garments sweeping behind him. A throne room dominated the steeple, so dim the candles and fire in the hearth carved from the walls barely illuminated it. Between the throne and hearth was a massive, polished black crystal globe resting on a dull, gold rostrum fashioned to resemble a dragon encircling it.

Around a giant simmering pewter cauldron before the fire, there stood four women. Three were old crones with wrinkled skin. The first wore an aged black robe and skull cap from which her ears protruded through slits. A pallid gray overlaid her entire right eye.

The second, slightly taller, but more wrinkled, was arrayed in a brown robe and a white, soiled shawl. She held up her hands, both of which bore four fingers instead of five, which they always had. The third was a midget compared to the others. She had to stand on a large stool in order to stir the brew. An extensive splotch of purple skin could be seen on her forehead above her left eyebrow. She, too, wore a black skull cap, but lacking in ear slits. Her robe was an ashen gray.

The fourth was taller than the others, but not quite Taranis's height. She looked nothing at all like her sisters. Her copper hair was long and flowing, her flesh smooth and clean. Nevertheless, her smoldering eyes and seductive leer betrayed her malevolent spirit. She wore a black robe embroidered with a dull gold. She placed her arms around the first two, who stood on either side of her, placing her hands on their respective shoulders.

"Sisters," Taranis said. His eyes instantly targeted the fourth. Hers gaze alone met his, and the grin she cast was

twice as alluring. The other sisters looked at one another, bobbing and turning their heads.

"My skin's all a-twitch," Myf, the first witch cackled.

"It's the Dark Prince himself," Oona, the second witch said.

"Aye, the Dark Prince himself," Myf repeated.

The fourth witch, seing Taranis, trudged up to the wizard, and curtsied. "My prince."

"Rise, Neasa," Taranis said, a lustful look in his eye.

"My sisters and I be almost ready, milord," she said, her voice smooth and alluring.

"Most excellent," Taranis said. "I must know."

"Patience, sire," Neasa said. "Come."

Chapter 34

Neasa and Taranis joined her sisters around the cauldron. The murky, bubbling brew boiled, into which Myf tossed a wide variety of ingredients, humming as she did so. The midget witch, Eigyr, stirred the potion, murmuring beneath her breath. Oona and Neasa fed the fire with wind from bellows and wood.

A low, deep hum from the four witches filled the air. Taranis held his hand above the bubbling cauldron and uttered an incantation in the old language:

Burn splendid fire, the great force thou art,
With such a prowess, hungry a hateful heart,
O fearsome flame roaring with not a shame
Here from rage craft glorious success!

Myf beamed. "Our concoction is complete, my prince, through flame, wind, and lightning."

"Yes, yes!" Eigyr clapped.

"Excellent," Taranis whispered, "Most excellent."

The brew produced a sharp-smelling smoke. He breathed it in. The sisters meanwhile hummed the same rhythm over and over, with Eigyr pounding on a small drum. Taranis staggered, kept erect by Neasa and Myf.

The witches' hum changed to a low-pitched guttural sound as they guided him to the black globe. The wizard stared into the crystal, watching as a violet fog surfaced.

He uttered aloud the following in a deep voice not his own:

When the tree and beast next convoke
'Twill be by the great standing stones,
Dawn go thence scorch fiery cloak,
Forest of Ámhen blood and bone,
Great Mother lost to cavernous deep,
Those who held her shalt ever weep!

Taranis shook his head, standing without need of the sisters' support. He stepped a few paces away from them.

"What have you seen, great prince?" Myf asked.

"I saw the young gryphon, Ferghus," he whispered, "He has the eyes of his father and grandfather, always a distinction of their male line."

"What else did you see?" asked Oona.

"I beheld dragon fire and death."

Neasa kissed his cheek. "The dark spirit has spoken. Your victory beckons, my prince."

"Indeed," Taranis said. "Tomorrow the gryphons shall have witnessed their last rising sun. I took the father and the grandfather. I will take the child and his mother. I must see what condition they are in."

Taranis gazed into the crystal again, thinking of his enemies. The violet fog faded to reveal Saershe and her allies. They were within the grounds of a ruined castle he knew well. Saershe tended to their injuries from the fight.

"I'd rather not discuss it," Dermot said. *"Those fiends were absolutely brutal."*

Huffing, Brian crossed his arms.

"You must remember," Saershe said. *"Those weren't*

real wild animals, but Taranis's mairágs transfigured into their likenesses. Nature isn't evil, my friends, nor is any true wild creature."

Brian opened his mouth, only to close it again. Dermot watched as Saershe tended to Maeve and Ferghus, humming to the younger one.

"You should never foster attachments to what you could lose, Dermot," the wizard said with a snicker. "It will beget misery and woe. Someday you'll catch yourself wishing you had never met them."

Neasa almost divulged her annoyance at Taranis's words, but once the crones praised his wisdom, she composed herself with another devilish grin.

"To love is to be strong, I was told," Taranis snorted. "Yet opening the heart renders it vulnerable."

"You must let loose your anger, sire," Myf advised. "Now is the time to act. If the Mairágh cannot defeat the Lady of Green Trees with shape-shifting, then you must show them what true power means. Show them their leader is capable of doing what he expects of them."

Instantly, Taranis was on his feet. He hissed, "You are right. Sending mairágs to prowl the forests accomplished nothing. They merely silenced messenger birds and other wild animals. They didn't slay one unicorn either. Ah, yes. It was a mistake to not unleash Lúg's fury at the outset. He will scorch the dawn."

"Yes!" Eigyr said. "Yes, yes, yes!"

Taranis glared at her. She ceased bouncing, confused.

"I would advise you to keep that dwarf silent," he said to the one-eyed sister, who bowed her head. A loud knock on the door prompted Taranis to yell, "Enter!"

The sheriff entered the chamber. He pressed his fist

to his heart then held his arm straight out, saying, "Greetings my noble prince!"

"Well, what tidings do you bring?" Taranis asked.

"Milord, Harlíeo has fallen as swiftly as Emerin. The hostages and supplies have arrived."

"Excellent. Where are the hostages now?"

"We've thrown them into the dungeons, sire. There are two two amongst them you should know of; the Earl of Harlíeo, and the smith."

"What smith?"

"He's the father of the two brothers from Emerin."

Taranis paused, as did the sisters. He asked, "Are you certain? You must be certain."

The sheriff nodded. "I saw him meself, sire. It would appear Lord Emerin is more competent than I presumed."

"My prince," Myf interrupted, "There's something 'bout the Emerin smith you need to know as well."

"What do you mean?" Taranis said. "Speak!"

He leaned down so she could whisper in his ear.

His eyes glowed. "Can this be true?"

"Aye, sire," she replied.

He smiled in delight.

**

Harlíeo's stone foundations had stood firm, but the walls and homes were in ruins. The wisps of black smoke were not yet gone, curling up to the sky. The dead had been buried outside of town. Presently, Lonán gazed at Granuaile, who stood a short distance away.

Arms crossed, her lips formed a slight frown, yet her

eyes bore her grief. She thought of her husband, of when he and she were prisoners of Taranis. She remembered with a chill the wizard's words to her right before his battle with the Lady of Green Trees.

Worry not, my dear. Once your beloved husband is one of mine, I shall have him dispose of you personally.

Her husband was lost to her. She didn't doubt it. Her sons were lost too, gone where she didn't know. For the first time in her life, she was alone. Everything she treasured was gone, and she wasn't sure what to expect. Were her sons still alive, remote as the chance seemed? The future looked bleak, and she began to wonder at this point whether anything mattered anymore.

"You're not alone," Lonán said, walking up to her.

After a moment, she said, "And what would you know about that, potter?"

"Do you believe I don't feel as you do? I am still in utter disbelief that *my* son is still alive after all these years. I saw him, and I didn't know. If only you knew..."

"You know nothing of what you've done. Now go away."

Lonán raced after as she turned and walked away. He pleaded, "Please let me explain. You have to know. You have to understand why. Please, daughter..."

"Don't you dare call me that!" she shouted as she stopped and turned to him. "You have no right. Now leave me alone. I want nothing to do with you!" Once again she turned away from him, never looking back.

He stood where he was, a low moan coming from deep within. "My son—my son has been alive all this time. I didn't look for him. I should have persisted. Why did I give up?"

A trumpet sounded. Granuaile stopped short. The few remaining of the Earl's council and soldiers, including the flustered captain of the guard, called the survivors together. The crowd converged before them like a flock of sheep to their shepherd.

The captain addressed them. "In the absence of his lordship the Earl, we have gathered to determine what is to be done. It is apparent with the town and surrounding fields devastated, we can no longer remain here."

Cries erupted. "Where are we supposed to go? How are we going to eat? What are we going to do?"

Granuaile remained silent. Her lip twitched. If only they had listened earlier.

The captain spoke again. "It is therefore our decision that we must appeal to his grace, the Duke of Núinna."

The crowd remained silent to this proclamation.

"We have already sent out riders to report our situation to him. Take only what provisions you need. Personal treasures must be left behind. We leave tomorrow morning. We will travel to the nearest village of Caemoch, and then on to Núinna."

Whispering amongst themselves, they asked each other if it would be safe, would the dragons return, and if there was honestly any hope of survival.

Granuaile stood silent as the crowd swirled around her. She hung her head. Would she ever have a family again? Would she ever have a home once more? Was anyone to be trusted?

She turned and saw Lonán standing nearby, enough for her to overhear him.

"Caemoch, my home. I haven't been there since I left my wife and son for war. My son—my son."

**

Taranis descended a dank, winding narrow staircase carved into the rock, leading the way for the sisters. The path was so narrow they had no choice but to walk single file. The deeper they went, the darker it became, until the torch Taranis held was the only source of light and it was so weak they had to feel their way down the treacherous steps. Deeper in the tunnel, the air grew stale and smelled of ash. The jagged, gritty walls shone as if greased.

They emerged into a tremendous, fiery cave. Razor-sharp stalactites covered the ceiling. In the dim firelight, a large, dark shadow contorted on the wall. The pounding of rock was loud in the confined space as a creature of massive proportions thumped his tail back and forth, taking out huge chunks of rock. Eigyr and Neasa covered their ears as the beast continued to growl.

"Leave us," Taranis ordered the women.

Myf, Oona, and Eigyr walked back to the dark tunnel. Neasa lingered, for Taranis placed his hand on her waist. Although they had noticed, her sisters pretended not to.

"Meet me in my chambers later tonight, where your feminine charms may cultivate themselves," he whispered in her ear.

"As you command, my prince." She curtsied, turned and walked away. Taranis watched until she was gone.

"Excellent," he whispered, turning to the creature. "Most excellent. Everything is falling into place. Saershe Greentrees, Iorwerth Dragonsbane, Brothers of Emerin, soon you will all come to me."

The creature rumbled louder. As the roar died away, a

tremondous spout of flame rose toward the ceiling, illuminating the entire cave in orange light.

Chapter 35

Morning arrived, bringing warmth to the old fortress and bathing the surrounding landscape in brilliant gold. Dermot woke to birds flying overhead, cheerfully saluting the new day with their voices. Ruairí, Yseult, and Ferghus were already up, but that did not surprise him. He knew Ruairí to be an early riser like his grandmother.

Ferghus nudged Dermot on the cheek, squawking to him a good morning. Yseult, after sniffing Dermot's hand, let out a soft but fierce yawn.

"Morrow all," he greeted.

Ferghus squawked as he rubbed his eyes.

Ruairí, sketching in his leather-bound book, grinned. By then, Brian had awakened as well. Yseult proceeded to sniff him in the face. He couldn't help laughing as he pushed her nose out of the way.

"All right, all right, girl, I'm glad to see you too!"

The two older boys chuckled. Ruairí, having finished his newest sketch, flipped through his journal's pages, reflecting on older ones.

"May I take a look?" Dermot asked.

"Be my guest," Ruairí said, handing him the book.

Dermot couldn't flip through the pages without gazing long at every single sketch, plant and animal alike, in all their outstanding detail and design.

"You like them?" Ruairí asked.

"They're marvelous!" Dermot said.

Brian agreed after leaning his head and seeing a few for himself.

"Grandma tells me I inherited my talent from my mother," Ruairí said. "So how are you two feeling this morning?"

"My legs are still numb from all this walking," Brian said. "Other than that, I'm fine."

Mine too, thought Dermot, but he said nothing of it.

"Dermot?" Ruairí asked. "Are you all right?"

"Oh," he said. "I'm fine. Your grandmother's remedies are quite the charm. I'm already feeling—well—better."

Dermot grabbed his shoulder, groaning. Brian could not help but grin. He remarked as Dermot handed Ruairí the book back, "I take it you slept well then."

"As a matter of fact, I had a rather curious dream last night. I..."

"Pardon me, I almost forgot," Ruairí interrupted. "There's someone you have to meet."

Movement to their left drew their gaze. A young girl with a roundish face stood there. She was about the same age as Ruairí and Dermot, perhaps a little younger. Waves of raven black hair fell past her shoulders onto the brown cloak she wore. The hem of her dress was not long enough to hide her boots, which were similar to the lads'. She gazed at them with penetrating gray eyes. In her hand she held a hiking stave.

The brothers took a step back.

"Who are you?" Brian asked. "How'd you get here?"

Dermot meanwhile glanced at Yseult and Ferghus, who remained oddly calm.

"Forgive me if I frightened you. Allow me to introduce

myself," she said. "I'm Ciara, apprentice of Iorwerth. It's pleasure to meet you all."

"What?" Dermot asked.

"They arrived late last night," Ruairí said.

"How can we know you're telling the truth, Ciara?" Brian asked.

"They were here with Grandma when I awoke," Ruairí explained.

Dermot was stunned. "Does that mean...?"

"Yes," Ruairí replied. He proceeded to introduce the brothers to Ciara.

"Hang on," Brian said. "Where are they? Saershe, Maeve, and Iorwerth. I mean. If..."

"The ring of stones," Ciara said.

They walked out the castle gateway together. Outside, they looked over endless meadows adjoining Ámhen covered in red clover. Then they they beheld another sight.

Concentrating, Dermot's vision enhanced like magic. Below, amidst those windswept standing stones he saw Maeve and Saershe with somebody he did not recognize, but knew had to be Iorwerth.

Ferghus stretched his back low, squawking. *Are you all ready?*

Dermot was surprised, but one by one they climbed on the young gryphon's back. Despite having ridden unicorns, a slight chill settled over Dermot when he mounted. The young gryphon on the other hand beamed with wide eyes. He stretched his wings and leaped into the air, carrying them with relative ease.

Ferghus flew down to the stones, landing beside his mother with a whoop. She squawked at him to be silent.

Saershe and Iorweth came to meet them. The brothers' eyes were fixed on the sorcerer. Yseult and Ferghus on the other hand seemed completely at ease, tilting their heads back.

Iorwerth was a graybeard with long hair, though not the length of Saershe's. He wore a brown tabard and traveling cloak over a tan-colored robe, in addition to a pair of thick brown leather gloves. A large, beautiful hawk's feather adorned his round, wide-brimmed brown hat. Wooden beads, assorted feathers, tiny animal bones, and teeth comprised the necklace dangling from his neck. His eyes were a quiet, soft grayish-blue. They conveyed experience, wisdom, perhaps even grief.

"Good morrow, lads," Saershe said. "I have no doubt you know who this is."

"Aye," Dermot said.

"It's a pleasure to meet you, brothers." Iorwerth slowly bowed his head, speaking in a voice filled with warmth and familiarity. "Saershe speaks highly of you both. I'm glad to finally meet you."

"And you, sir," Dermot said.

"I awoke early," Saershe said, "shortly before Iorwerth arrived with Ciara. I had no desire to disturb your sleep, so we came to the standing stones to talk. I'm sorry if you were alarmed."

"It's all right," Dermot said.

Smiling, Iorwerth removed his gloves to take a drink from the water skin slung around his shoulder. His right wrist bore a golden bracelet featuring a polished yellowish-brown stone. He wore on his left forefinger a simple gold ring, similar to the one Saershe wore.

Iorwerth offered water to Ferghus and then Yseult,

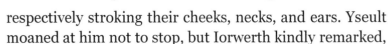

respectively stroking their cheeks, necks, and ears. Yseult moaned at him not to stop, but Iorwerth kindly remarked, "Don't you worry, my furry friend. You'll get more."

Iorwerth put his gloves back on after kissing her head. Resting against his arm was a tall, ashen staff with a pattern engraved into it that reminded Dermot of a bird's feathers. It was capped by a pair of carved outspread wings flanking a large colorless stone.

"Now, there's someone else you children must meet," Iorwerth said. He extended his arm out, calling, "Keane!"

A magnificent falcon swooped from the sky, perching on Iorwerth's hand. The second and third fingers of the sorcerer's other hand reached up and stroked the bird's thick, beautiful feathers. The head, wings, and back were dark in color, while the belly, throat, and legs were grayish specked with black. Ciara walked up to the falcon and stroked his belly with two fingers. He looked at her with his head at a slight angle. Dermot eyed them both curiously.

"My dearest and cleverest friend," Iorwerth said. "We've been through much together, Keane and I."

Keane screeched, greeting them. Dermot asked Iorwerth if he could pet him. He nodded. Keane screeched in agreement. Dermot knew he meant yes. Dermot walked up to the falcon, followed by Brian and Ruairí. They took turns and stroked Keane's belly with their fingertips.

"How did you find us?" Brian asked.

"Olwen and Aengus alerted us after the skirmish," Ciara said. "Iorwerth helped them and Saershe drive away the mairágs who attacked you back to the Ashland."

"So you're aware of everything, then?" Dermot said.

"Saershe has informed me of all that's happened,"

Iorwerth said. "I'm truly sorry for you and Brian. By heart and hand, I promise we dríadós will do all we can to vanquish Taranis. We must continue onward before his forces return."

"First," Saershe said, "you must all take sustenance. We cannot travel while starving."

They ate a breakfast comprised from fruit and vegetables Saershe had procured from the forest earlier. Maeve and Ferghus hunted for more meat for the oncoming journey. After eating, they returned to the castle to retrieve their belongings. Most of that morning and into the early afternoon, they kept close to Ámhen's border. Clouds swirled and blotted out the sunshine every so often. Presently, they paused to rest.

"So, um, Ciara," Dermot said, "How long have you been Iorwerth's apprentice?"

"Since I was a little girl," she said. "Iorwerth is like a father to me. Like the wind we've roved across all Denú, moving from one place to another. There's always a new path to tread and a new adventure with it!"

"What about your parents?" Brian asked.

Her face turned grave. "They were were slain by Taranis's hand, like Ruairí's and yours. Yes, Ruairí told me."

Dermot and Brian were the first to apologize.

"It's fine, honest," Ciara said.

"We're all in this together," Iorwerth said. "Now we need to figure out how we are going to confront Taranis when he makes his move."

"Shouldn't we march to the Ashland, Iorwerth?" Ciara asked. "Meet him head on?"

"That would be too risky, what with all his mairágs.

We barely survived each encounter before," Brian said.

"And there's the dragons," Ruairí said. "We don't have the strength to match his forces yet."

"Indeed. Unfortunately," Iorwerth said. "We have to wait and see what course Taranis takes. What we can do is ensure the safety of as many lives as possible."

"Where are we going?" Dermot asked.

Iorwerth held up his hand, telling them all to be quiet. "I sense something ill in the wind."

"So do I," Saershe said.

"What? What is it?" Brian asked.

They gazed upward, following Iorwerth's lead. The entire sky was covered with dark gray clouds. The sound of large, strong wings flapping reached them. Iorwerth pointed his finger. A dark, vague speck slowly emerged from within the clouds ahead.

Dermot squinted. Then his eyes grew wider. "Oh no, please tell me this isn't happening!"

"It's happening," Brian said.

A dragon, with a wingspan three times as long as Maeve's, flew overhead. Black scales covered the body. Sharp iron-gray spikes lined the spine from head to tail. The tail itself was long and suitably muscular, as were all four limbs. The eyes were the same color as those of the red dragon that burned Emerin, likewise bearing a similar, evil gleam.

"That's the largest dragon I've ever seen," Ruairí said.

"I know him," Iorwerth said. "It's Lúg. He was the first dragon to embrace Taranis's cause."

"If he wants a fight, I say let's give him one," Ciara said, gripping her stave like a shillelagh.

Both gryphons squawked in agreement.

"Mind your boldness, Ciara," Iorwerth said. "That goes for you gryphons too, particularly you, Maeve."

The young gryphon and his mother both grumbled as a loud caw sounded overhead.

Chapter 36

Keane was but a dot in the sky compared to the dragon. He barely evaded the river of fire Lúg unleashed. The fire, fortunately, didn't reach Ámhen's treetops, so nothing was scorched.

"Saershe, get them to safety," Iorwerth ordered.

Saershe grabbed his wrist. "I am not leaving you to fight alone. I am a dríadór, same as you. We stand together, always."

The boy's kept their eyes on the hovering dragon, drawing their weapons. Dermot's heart beat heavily against his ribcage. Although a little shaky he gripped his sword and shield tight.

"Heads up!" he cried.

It was too late. Lúg let loose a gushing, fiery river. Those trees nearest where they stood went up in roaring flames. Dodging at the last second, the group managed to avoid the fire that in a matter of seconds. It reduced the tree to smoldering cinders. Dermot rushed behind a large tree, his legs shaking. He put his hand to his head, willing the dizziness away.

With a loud cry, Lúg swung his tail, obliterating dozens of trees. Branches split, and were swept up by the wind from the tremendous force of the dragon's tail, peppered the group as they dodged and tried to evade the debris raining down on them.

Dermot quickly threw his shield over his and Brian's

heads to protect them as much as he could.

Badly shaken, they looked up when the debris ceased falling. They saw Lúg turning around in midair. He was a large, and had been flying so fast he had to turn around to attack them again.

"Keane, fly!" Iorwerth ordered. Soaring into the air, he didn't go far from his friends on the ground.

Iorwerth extended his arms, incanting in the old language. Slowly he levitated off the ground as a bluish light glowed from him, distracting Lúg. His eyes shone a sparkly blue as he sprouted silvery-blue reptilian wings and a scaly body of armor. He let loose an ear-splitting roar, causing his friends to cover their ears.

Observing both Lúg and the socrcerer, Dermot understood what Iorwerth was doing. It was a challenge, a duel from one dragon to another, one, at least in dragon form. Lúg roared out in acceptance. Iorwerth swooped under Lúg, who tried to seize him. Iorwerth was faster if not an equal in speed to Lúg if not faster.

Saershe meanwhile raised her arms and changed an an incantation in the old language, with Ruairí translating for the brothers.

Element of water,
Power of healing,
I summon thee.
Flowing through earth
From the sea cometh forth,
And quench the seed
By which may sprout!
Element of water,
Power of healing,

I summon thee!

Just as in Úaene, summoned water from the nearby stream flew and doused the flames, saving the lives of many forest animals running for their lives.

Saershe urged Dermot and the others away.

Keane flew around the dragons, screeching at Lúg as if to distract him so his master could strike. Maeve grumbled and tore at the earth with her talons, wanting to join the fight in the sky. Dermot sensed her stubborn courage. He knew she would never flee.

She squawked at her son, *You stay here.*

"Maeve, no!" Saershe yelled. But there was no stopping her, nor was there any way to prevent Ferghus from disobeying his mother and soaring after her.

"What're you thinking?" Dermot cried. "Come back!"

"Ferghus!" Saershe shouted.

"They're doing what they think is right," Ciara said. "They cannot be blamed for it."

Dermot gave her a half-agreeing, half-irritated glance. He saw Saershe frown at her, but Ciara didn't seem to care. Dermot suspected she would have reacted differently were it Iorwerth. Nevertheless he thought to himself he would likely do the same if he were in the gryphons' position.

Lúg breathed fire at Maeve and Ferghus, who managed to dodge the blaze, but by a hair and feather. Dermot sighed with relief.

It was short-lived. Iorwerth and Lúg grabbed one another in midair, biting and clawing at one another. Dark blood and scales fell, for only the teeth and claws of a dragon were capable of penetrating their hides.

However, Dermot noticed Maeve was attempting to strike Lúg's eyes.

"Come on, Iorwerth!" Ciara said. "Get him! You teach that dragon a lesson!"

"I don't know how much longer he can keep Lúg away," Dermot said. "What if he's slain?"

"He is the Dragon's Bane," Ruairí said, despite a small tremble in his voice. "He must know what he's doing."

For a moment, Dermot wondered how Saershe and Iorwerth acquired their respective monikers. It made him think back to his childhood fantasies and playtime with friends, during which he had bestowed on himself the title of "Oakenheart" for he had envisioned himself a great warrior with a heart of solid oak. However his attention quickly revered to the matter at hand.

"We've got to do something to help them!" Brian said. "Saershe, what can we do?"

"You head for the safety of the greenwood," she said. "I will join the others."

Before anyone could argue, the sorceress soared, glowing blue as she gained altitude. As she took on the form of a gryphon, the others did as she commanded.

They ran through the trees. To Dermot the greenwood became a veritable maze of obstacles. Breathing heavier by the minute, he charged bravely on. He wasn't sure how much further he could run at this pace. Despite his legs tiring, he still charged bravely on, knowing his life depended on it.

His memory flashed back to Emerin as it was consumed in the fiery bloodbath of that other dragon. Even as he ran, he glanced around but saw no woodland creatures, nor could he see the dragon whenever he looked up. He forced himself to repeat Saershe's words about being brave in difficulties over and over in his mind, for being almost out of breath he couldn't even whisper them.

Fear surrounded him on all sides; the distinctive flight of creatures he couldn't see, yet he felt their panic as he ran.

A humongous fire ball crashed beside them. With a yell, Dermot dove to the right. As more fire balls bombarded them, he veered back and forth through the forest, not knowing or caring where he wound up as long as they outran the danger around them. He darted left and right, drawing up short when another fire ball exploded in his path, igniting the trees.

As Lúg and Iorwerth fought, Lúg's tail smashed not only the trees in flames but those that had not been set afire. A heavy, thick branch snapped from its base, landing on Dermot and Brian. The impact inflicted more shock than pain.

Roaring, Lúg continued to fend off his opponents. Soon, he soared higher, and they followed. Distracted as he was, he no further waste to the forest below. The dríadórs and gryphons certainly had an advantage in numbers, but Lúg's strength, speed, and hard scales kept the clash at a stalemate.

On the ground, Dermot and Brian struggled harder to push the large, heavy branch off them. They had been awarded more time with the battle continuing overhead, but Dermot couldn't know how much longer it would be. Lúg, he suspected would not be distracted long.

"Come on!" Dermot begged. "Push, Brian!"

"I'm pushing! I'm pushing!" Brian said.

Together, the brothers pushed with what little strength they had left, and were making headway. Much to Dermot's relief, Ruairi, Yseult, and several forest dwellers came to their aid.

They pushed and pulled and lifted until at last the brothers were free, albeit battered and bruised.

The sound of Keane's voice attracted their attention. He circled them, squawking. *This way!*

"Come on!" Brian said.

They followed the falcon through the trees as he ducked under and flew through branches and around tree trunks. Repeatedly Dermot glanced up to catch a fleeting glimpse of the sky battle between flashes of light and shadows. He was surprised the dragon was kept at bay.

Hurry up! Keane screeched.

"Where are we going, Keane?" Dermot shouted. "Running isn't going to help them!"

The falcon cawed. *I know! I'm working on it!*

He's working on it? Dermot asked himself.

"Oh no, look!" Brian said.

Lúg, at last, managed to evade his foes. He unleashed another wave of fire straight down into Amhen.

Dermot stopped, watching the flames that didn't spread. Instead, they swirled, rising higher and forming a column of flame. It was terrifying in both size and heat. Dermot could feel the heat from a mile away. Everyone, human and animal alike, stared at the flames.

"What in the high king's name is that?" Brian asked.

"A fire whirl," Ciara said. "It's a cyclone of flame."

Dermot's throat ached from the scorching heat. "Listen! Do you hear that? It's like a distant voice in the air!"

Yseult barked. *It's the Dark Prince!*

"He's conjuring the fire whirl out of Lúg's breath," Ruairí said.

"What do we do?" Brian asked.

"Run!" Ruairí yelled.

With a quick, terrified look at each other, they spun and ran. As the fire whirl gained strength, it also grew faster and wider. Trees, ferns, bushes, grass, various creatures, and even giant rocks were swallowed up. The earth, in its wake, had been butchered, scorched black.

"This isn't working!" Brian said.

Keane, still leading the way, screeched again. *We can still lose the fire whirl! We've got to keep away long enough for Iorwerth and the others to come!*

"Why don't we split up?" Brian asked.

"No!" Dermot said. "Ma would never forgive me!"

Yseult growled again. *I'm not leaving either.*

"Nor are we," Ciara spoke for herself and Ruairí.

"Together to the end," Ruairí said.

The heat grew more intense and Dermot was sure he could feel it licking at his backside. Abruptly, sharp talons clutched at his shoulders. Dermot found himself ascending into the air away from the flames. A few seconds later, he realized Yseult had also been rescued.

Ferghus squawked at them to hold on. Dermot, after waving his arms, managed to cling tightly to the young gryphon. Ferghus cawed as he struggled, but managed somehow, to climb up onto his back. Yseult remained in his claws. Dermot hoped the dog was all right as he heard her moan several times. Relief washed over him when he saw Brian, Ruairí, and Ciara astride Maeve.

Ferghus had no difficulty bearing their weight, but their own exhaustion and the anxiety coursing through their veins caused them to slip repeatedly.

Ferghus snarled. *Quit being so ridiculous! You're going to get us all killed!*

"Thanks Ferghus," Dermot said. "You're a hero, like your mother."

Ferghus soared higher over the half-devastated greenwood, screeching every few minutes. He turned his head so Dermot caught a glimpse of his eye. *You humans ought to be more careful.*

The gryphon squawked, descending with his mother into the open meadow. The fire whirl changed course, thus putting them and out of immediate danger. The lad's hugged each other, the gryphons, and petted Yseult.

Lúg continued to fight off the two dríadórs. He would swing away from one only to be met head on by the other. Events were happening so quickly it proved hard for Dermot to keep trace of which side had the upper hand, but he managed.

As the dríadór hit Lúg broadside, Dermot saw Saershe dart in close. Blood rained down as she stabbed Lúg's eye with her talons. As the large dragon screeched in pain, Iorwerth and Saershe joined together, spinning so fast Dermot couldn't tell where one began and the other ended.

As they spun, swirling clouds formed, growing darker and darker. A torrent of rain spilled from the sky, dousing the fire whirl.

"Look!" Brian shouted. "It's working!"

"Yes!" Dermot said, jumping with joy.

The fire whirl began to abate. The two dríadórs dived

down from the sky, and glowing with a blue light, they resumed their true forms in a matter of seconds. Their blackened and disheveled clothes were evidence of their mighty battle. Ciara and Ruairí ran to them first, hugging Iorwerth and Saershe tight. Dermot and Brian, overcome by emotion, hugged Saershe simultaneously.

The downpour diminished as swiftly as it developed. The three boys and Ciara breathed a sigh of relief that it was finally over and they could relax.

That dream was shattered when Lúg, roaring in pain and fury, plunged toward them. *You will suffer for this! All of you!*

Saershe and Iorwerth instantly raised their staffs. Instead of striking them, Lúg's tail again swept through the forest, leveling trees so thick they came close to burying them.

Ferghus took flight, but Lúg intercepted him. Claws outspread, the dragon aimed for the young gryphon. His mother squawked in warning.

Barely warned in time, Ferghus managed to evade the large dragon. As he spun away, Lúg's claws left a line of thin scratches down his side. Feathers floated in the air. Maeve, roused with anger readily apparent, attacked, going for Lúg's neck. But he shook her off with ease.

"Listen!" shouted Ciara. "There's Taranis's voice again!"

"Look!" Ruairí pointed.

A dense fog was forming near the gryphons. The familiar whoosing sound of arrows set loose cut through the air. They were, Dermot realized, aimed directly at mother and son.

Both gryphons' heard the arrows seconds before they

saw them, and with swift maneuvering, managed to evade them. Unfortunately, it became clear to Dermot they had gone the wrong way.

The Mairágh was back.

"No!!!" Dermot shouted. Yseult barked.

Lúg, using his razor-sharp claws, and with the aid of the Mairágh's arrows, herded the gryphons into the fog.

Dermot hung his head. Keane made a valiant effort to follow them, but wasn't fast enough.

The gryphons and the dragon vanished in the fog. With that, no more arrows came.

Chapter 37

Green had become a scarce color for this part of Ámhen. Clouds of smoke ascended from the blackened wood carcasses. Ruairí, Ciara, and the two brothers plopped down beside one another on a broken log. As Saershe tended their wounds, the foursome gazed at the breaking clouds and fading fog.

Sunlight returned to the land, but none of the young people found any warmth. Their bodies sagged. Dermot couldn't bear to look at the ruined trees.

Saershe gave them each a cup filled with red clover tea she had prepared. Not all of it was for drinking; any leftover she used to dab on their burns. Wherever they bled, she bandaged. She, alongside Iorwerth, focused next on the brave forest-dwelling survivors who came out from the woods in swarms.

Yseult inched up to the boys, her cold black nose nudging them. The retriever's efforts did bring temporary smiles to their faces as they petted and rubbed her ears.

Dermot whispered, "Thank you, girl."

Saershe and Iorwerth whispered quietly to each other before returning to join Dermot and the others.

"I will not have you four wilting like autumn flowers," Saershe said. "Not while I still see strength within your limbs and hearts."

Dermot couldn't contain his emotions. "Maeve and Ferghus are gone. For all we know, Taranis has slain

them. We failed them."

No one spoke, but the sentiment was the same in each face. Tears traced dirt streaks on Brian's face and Ruairí and Ciara buried their faces in their hands.

Iorwerth frowned. "I cannot abide giving up. You don't know we've failed, me boy."

Dermot lifted his head. "You think there's still a chance, Iorwerth?"

"I know there will be none whatsoever if we do nothing, laddie. Only then will we have failed," he said. "Tell me, can Taranis beat your will down so easily?"

"You are all stronger than this," Saershe said. "After all we've been through together; I know you are strong, capable, and brave. I have never doubted any of you once."

"We live, learn, and in the end, must forge ahead," Iorwerth said. "Our choices shall determine what we can attain. What will yours be?"

Dermot lifted his head. Before he could do anything, Ciara jumped up, abandoning her grief temporarily. "Well then, let's go hunt the Mairágh!"

Yseult barked. *Yes! I'm in!*

Dermot stood. He spoke to the elders. "You're right. Maeve and Ferghus are counting on us. They're family."

Brian's eyes widened. He stood by Dermot. "I'm in."

"Count me in," Ruairí said.

"Excellent," Iorwerth said with a smile. He directed their focus to the part of Ámhen miraculously not ruined. "The arrows came from that direction. You can see some afar, sunk in the earth. Beyond that wooded border, we must track them wherever they have gone. If we can find the Mairágh, I'm certain we will find our friends."

The dríadór made a whistling noise. A responding loud whinny caught the group's attention. Dermot knew that whinny.

Olwen, accompanied by Aengus and several other unicorns made their way through the devastated forest. Iorwerth stepped forth to face Olwen, Aengus, and a third unicorn. Iorwerth petted their necks. He said to the boys, "I don't believe you've met Vannora, Aengus and Olwen's daughter."

"It's a pleasure to meet you," Dermot said.

Vannora neighed, conveying the feeling was mutual.

One by one, they each mounted a unicorn. Iorwerth himself sat atop Aengus, and Ruairí upon Olwen.

"All right, let's go!" Ciara shouted.

"Patience, my young novice," Iorwerth said.

Aengus grumbled in agreement.

It was then Dermot realized Saershe remained where she stood.

"Saershe?" he asked. He couldn't say anymore, for he realized the truth.

"Don't be afraid," she said.

"Wait." Brian looked from Dermot to Saershe. "Aren't you coming with us, Saershe?"

"Someone needs to stay behind and help Ámhen's survivors," she said. "They need guidance, care, and hope. Vannora and the other unicorns will also remain and aid me."

Ruairí stared at her. Dermot had never seen him look so fearful.

"Iorwerth and I have discussed the matter," she said.

"What about Maeve and Ferghus?" Dermot asked.

"I have faith in you. I know you can do it," she said.

The corners of her mouth turned up in a smile. She walked to the animals surrounding them. Dermot knew in his heart she was right. He saw a tear in Ruairí's eye, even as his friend nodded.

"Don't worry," Saershe said to her grandson. "We'll meet again."

"We will," he replied.

Olwen angled her head, winking. She then whinnied to those unicorns remaining behind. *My daughter shall lead in our stead here. Look to her as you would me and Aengus. Vannora, be strong, and fair.*

Vannora nodded. *I will, Mother.*

Aengus whinnied. *I know you will do us proud, dear daughter.*

"We mustn't delay," Iorwerth said. "Come, Aengus."

The unicorn and his mate neighed, Olwen far more kindly than Aengus.

Together, they forged ahead, along with half the unicorns. Ruairí kept his eyes on his grandmother as she mingled with the wild creatures until she was no longer in sight. Dermot watched her too, but for not as long.

For some time, they wound their way amidst trees, mostly thick oaks and pines. Although the unicorns did not run as fast as they could, their light-footedness was still enough for them to cover a great distance over time.

"Keep your eyes open," Iorwerth said. "Tales always unfold from the tracks that are left behind. Any whiff no matter how faint might prove essential to finding Maeve and Ferghus. Leave no stone unturned when you are tracking."

"Um, Iorwerth?" Brian asked.

"Yes?" the dríadór replied.

"Well, what if the Mairágh have covered up their tracks somehow? What do we do if we can't find any?"

"There are always tracks to follow," Iorwerth said. "You just need to know where to look. We can still track a dragon in the sky. Like birds or any other winged creatures, dragons prefer to fly in certain directions, often along the same paths. For a dragon such as Lúg, being a mountain-dweller he'll always return there."

"I see," Brian said, nodding his head.

"Saershe and Ruairí told us about your skill as a tracker, Iorwerth," Dermot said. "We heard nothing but the highest praise from her."

"She flatters me still," he said with a grin. "I am never one to boast of meself, nor is she. You can learn so much once you are able to read tracks and trails, me boy.

"Now, given the direction of the arrows, and accounting for the wind and rain, we ought to be coming nearer to where the archers stood."

Dermot gazed about the greenwood, but for reasons he couldn't explain, he didn't feel that sensation, that strange inner warmth he enjoyed during previous experiences within the forests. His heart was instead weighed down with worry for Maeve and Ferghus. He dreaded to think of what could have befallen them by now at the hands of Taranis and that dragon. Then, from the corner of his eye, he saw something.

"Stop!" he shouted. Dermot's pointing finger alerted everyone to what he spotted on the ground ahead.

"Tracks!" Brian said.

"Good eye," Iorwerth nodded with satisfaction.

"Just luck," Dermot said.

"Nay," the dríadór replied.

They dismounted. Brian reached to pet Yseult who was panting heavily. Iorwerth knelt to examine the tracks, with Ciara by his side. They were by now deep within the dense greenwood. Dermot, for a moment, could sense the lingering smell from the rainstorm on his skin. It was a cool, soothing sensation. It made the air thick, which he also felt when he took in a breath.

"We're making good headway," Ciara said.

"Come," Iorwerth beckoned. "What can you tell me from these?"

"Were these left by mairágs?" Dermot asked. "They appear too large to me."

"Why do you say that?"

Unsure if the dríadór was testing him, Dermot looked closer and reached down. "Well, there are leafy bits, sticks, and gravel lying across these tracks. They feel rather loose, and they definitely don't look fresh."

"Correct," Iorwerth said.

His tone made Dermot suspect the dríadór was waiting to hear something else, something specific.

"Could the rain possibly have had something to do with that?" Brian asked.

"Very intuitive," Iorwerth replied. "With age, wind, and rain, tracks enlarge. They can eventually look like something else, or having been made much later than they were."

"So what does it mean?" Dermot asked.

"No doubt humans left them," Iorwerth said. "Perhaps the rain washed in this leafy material, weathering the tracks in the process."

"Let's follow them, and see where the trail leads," Dermot said.

Iorwerth agreed. They remounted, keeping the footprints in sight. In time they indeed became more human. Once again, the group stopped and dismounted.

"What do you see, Iorwerth?" Brian asked.

The dríadór examined a number of the footprints, even stepping in some, as if mimicking their makers. "Observe these footprints, unaffected by the rain. Here, you can see many clumped tight together. Here is where they are deepest. They stood together. Given how sunken they are, their weight must've been heavy, as if clad in armor."

Iorwerth put his dominant foot out in front. "This is the spot where the arrows were fired, up through that opening in the treetops."

"Then what happened?" Dermot asked.

Iorwerth pointed. "You see there, several of them atop others, but further apart than when they were in line. The heels aren't sunk as deep as the toes. They must've been running..."

He looked up at the sky. "...towards the southeast."

"Look!" Dermot said, picking up a large feather, one of many. He handed it to the dríadór, who examined it. He declared it to be a gryphon's.

"Yseult, my friend," Iorwerth said, "come here."

She trotted to the wizard. He took the feather and held it to her nose, stating, "Saershe told me she has seen you sniff Maeve and Ferghus many times over. You must know both their scents. Is this feather from one of them?"

She sniffed it and barked enthusiastically. *Yes!*

The wizard then asked first if it was Maeve's feather. She shook her head. *It's Ferghus's.*

"Thank you. Good girl." Iorwerth petted her

adoringly. He stuffed the feather into a cloth pouch hanging next to an elegant, black-handled double-edged dagger on his brown leather belt.

"We must be on the right path!" Brian said.

"Make haste," Iorwerth said, his voice stern.

"They may yet be alive." Brian said.

"Could this be a trap?" Dermot asked.

The graybeard stared at him, then to everyone. "Indeed. Taranis undoubtedly will keep them alive, if not unharmed, to use them as bait for us. Either way, we must be ready to risk our lives for theirs, and be ready for whatever lies at the path's end. We cannot abandon our friends to darkness, Dermot. Were it us, they would do the same."

Once remounted, their pace quickened. Dermot was uneasy. He kept remembering that dream he had prior to meeting Iorwerth, which burned in his mind by Saershe's praise for him, and Iorwerth's words of darkness. A strange thing—it didn't feel like a dream at all, but rather a memory of the day he first met Saershe and Ruairí, right after she made him fall asleep and they laid him down on the bed where she healed him.

"Couldn't we have shown him the way, Grandma? If not, why not?" Ruairí asked.

Saershe looked at him, her eyes stern. "We can't take that chance at this time. You know that. He must make this decision himself. I pray he does choose to return, for if I'm right, it would spell tragedy if left in darkness. I shall aid him of course, but neither of us can choose for him. For now, we shall keep watch. Do not seek him out."

Dermot didn't know what to think. It also felt as if he was on a path created for him, yet he had chosen it himself.

Chapter 38

Emerin's former chieftain watched over the prisoners in the bowels of the Dark Prince's fortress with three other guards. Pádraig watched his fellow captives huddled in the pit, starved and bruised from torture at the Mairágh's hands. He could see the Earl of Harlíeo motionless in the cell beside him, likewise bruised. Finally, he couldn't stand the silence any longer.

"Friends," he whispered as low as he could, keeping one eye on the guards.

"Are you mad!" another captive said. "You know what they said! Subject to torture…"

"We can't lose hope!" Pádraig said. "My wife is still out there somewhere, and so are me two sons! I have something worth living for, something to fight for until the final breath leaves my body, no matter what tortures they inflict on me."

"You may not wish to live after what they do to you!" the same captive warned.

Lord Harlíeo lifted his face. "You have sons, smith?"

"Yes. We dwelt in Emerin. I built a life for my family there. Every day I was grateful to have them, to have all that made up our home. There was a time when…"

"When what?"

"When I thought I had nothing, when I thought I had lost what was precious to me," Pádraig said. "Then I found Granuaile, a home, and a purpose. Next Dermot

came into this world, and Brian followed. 'Twas then I knew I had a family again. Oh, the memories I have of those years."

"I see," the earl said. "You're one of the refugees aren't you? You're the man who returned my son's torque."

"Yes. It was his final request, milord. He spoke of his love for you before he died. We buried him with what dignity we could."

"I thank you for that."

"You're most welcome, milord. I barely knew him, but in that moment, I could see he was a brave and honorable man. I'm sure he did you much honor."

The earl struggled to hold back tears. His voice maintained his nobleman's pride. "He did."

"Then don't let his death be in vain, milord," Pádraig insisted. "Fight on in his memory, for his honor. Remain strong. The memory of who my wife and two sons are what preserves my strength."

"Oi!" one of the guards shouted. "What're you lot conversing about down there?"

Voices fell silent, even the smith's.

Lord Emerin knelt down, his visor set on the smith. "So, it's you again, Pádraig."

For a moment, the smith's blood ran cold. In all the time he had been in his chieftain's presence, never had he referred to anyone by name in Emerin, even his own guard. But he didn't let it show.

"I see that defiant look in your eye, smith," the chieftain snarled. "I'm told your son bore the same look when my prince first met him. You amass secrets too, don't you?"

Pádraig blinked. He had taken Lord Emerin, or rather his mairág-self, as a simple brute who took orders from Taranis.

Lord Emerin started, "Well, let us..."

"Halt!"

The smith knew that voice all too well. It was the sheriff, who entered the dungeon along with two other mairágs.

The chieftain stood. "What brings you here?"

"The Dark Prince wishes to see the smith from Emerin," the sheriff said.

Every captive's eyes darted between the mairág and Padraig.

"As his highness commands," the chieftain said. He opened the smith's cell and dragged him out.

Pádraig knew his fellow prisoners were watching.

"Why do you think he wants to see him?" one said.

"Could it have to do with his sons?" someone else suggested.

"Silence!" the chieftain yelled.

No further words were spoken within the dungeon. The mairágs gathered around Pádraig. In the next instant, manacles were secured around his wrists. With a mairág on either side, he was dragged out and down that dark, dank tunnel, still limping.

"I heard what was spoken, smith," the sheriff hissed.

Pádraig didn't respond.

"What's the matter, my friend? Your tongue hasn't been cut out yet has it?"

"Why should I speak to you, traitor?"

Pádraig had cracked, and he knew it. As he was pushed up through the winding tunnel, the sheriff said,

"You are a remarkable man. I know not what my great prince has in store for you as to his plans for Denú, but the time will come where you will serve under me as I serve him, benefitted by my willingness."

We'll see, Pádraig thought. Fear nonetheless dominated his mind with every single step taken. He had been a prisoner before, but had learned to hide his fear from them. Otherwise, he knew his captors would never cease tormenting him.

**

The four witches were congregated with Taranis in his throne room.

"Everything is proceeding as planned, milord," Myf said with delight.

"Aye," Neasa said. "Your greatest adversaries will be at your mercy, my prince."

"Most excellent," Taranis said. "Now with but portions of the tapestry of truth…"

A loud knocking on the door attracted their attention.

"Enter!" Taranis bellowed, at which the sheriff complied.

"Have you brought him?" Taranis asked.

He bowed his head. Yes, your highness."

Taranis waved his hand, and the rest entered.

"On his knees!" the sheriff shouted.

Pádraig was forced into the center of the room by the other two mairágs, who hurled him onto the cold hard floor. Having landed on his belly, with his cheek pressed against the floor, the smith was then pulled up onto his knees.

"Welcome to Magh-Tuira, Pádraig," Taranis said. "My

modest foothold."

"Spare me the gloating," Pádraig said.

Taranis laughed. "Indeed you have a defiant strength within you. Dermot is his father's son, is he not?"

The sisters snickered.

"Leave my family out of this," the smith growled.

"That's not possible," Taranis said. "How little you see the important role your sons have to play in this feud, like those with whom they travel."

"If you're hoping to learn from me where that sorceress has taken them, you'll get nothing. I don't know where they have gone."

"Ah, you know the art of interrogation well, despite the years long past. Oh yes, I know your story. I could extract any truth from you if I wanted to right now. But this isn't an interrogation. I know you haven't seen them since Emerin's destruction. This is your induction into a higher calling, where you will be a great player in a new age for our homeland."

The smith's legs weakened. He felt lightheaded. What courage still lingered he plucked up. "Don't think for a moment I will assist your cause."

"You eluded me once," the dark wizard said, his voice smooth. "That shan't be repeated."

"You can do what you wish with me," Pádraig said, "but I refuse to serve you."

"Oh, you ignorant fool!" Taranis circled the smith. "I *will* do what I wish with you. You shall serve me for that is what fate's planned for you. It is your destiny to be first of my newest legions of troops: the Scáithír, greater in strength and endurance than the Mairágh."

The sheriff rocked back, but caught himself. Taranis

pretended not to notice.

"Never!!!" Pádraig's voice filled the near-empty room.

Taranis leaned in so his eyes were but a few inches from Pádraig's. "Smith, if I had my way, I'd lash your hide 'til it bled dry. Consider it merciful you'll be spared any further agonizing torture. On the other hand, were I in your position, I'd want, I'd *beg*, for death."

"If I were you," Pádraig said, "I'd wish I hadn't taken this man prisoner, for it will be an action that you will greatly regret someday."

The witches hooted, and Eigyr bounced again, yelping, "Yes!" only to be restrained by Myf.

"Your courage is admirable," Taranis said, "Which is precisely why I *will* harness it to my cause to demolish the Dríacht. They never saw my importance as they did their own. But they will know mine soon enough."

Pádraig said no more. He had nothing to say.

"By the way, brave fool," Taranis said, "how did your father receive you?"

Puzzled, Pádraig said, "What do you mean? My father vanished long ago when I was but a wee baby. He was never seen again. I never even knew him."

"Once again, how little you know," the wizard said. "How little you know what your father did. Would you like to know the truth? Yes, I can feel it in your bones. Don't you want to know why he never came home to you and your mother?"

Pádraig's heart hammered against his chest so hard he thought it would burst.

"Your host," Taranis said, "the old potter, Lonán. He is your father."

Pádraig froze. "What! How's that possible?!"

Taranis gestured his head. The witches dragged Pádraig before the dark crystal, his eyes almost touching the polished surface. Another violet cloud developed within it. Once it parted he could see his wife with Lonán amid Harlíeo's ruins. His face lit up as images of them emerged and vanished in the cloud.

"Are you saying—you knew? You knew this whole time, and did nothing?"

"Who would've believe me? I..."

"If you'd spoken up, more lives might have been spared! My Pádraig wouldn't be a prisoner of those monsters!"

"What did you say?"

"Were you not listening to me, old man? Are you going deaf now?"

"No, no, I mean, his name. Tell me. What's you're your husband's name?"

"Pádraig, but what does that have to do with anything? What? Speak?"

"My—my son. I had a son. His name—was Pádraig. Was your husband born in Emerin? Or did he come—from Caemoch?"

"You—you..."

The smith saw his wife walk away from the old man, who did nothing to stop her. No more visions manifested thereafter. Pádraig's heart slowed, but he was still confused.

There was a gleam in Taranis's eye as he bent down. He whispered into the smith's ear. "Now you know. You father was not only alive all this time, he was close to you, and he never came back. What did he care for you? He left your mother to die alone, and for you to live alone. But

you didn't. Out of nothing you made a life for yourself. You never needed his help. He worked instead for those who will mislead your sons. They will use Dermot and Brian as they have used your father, for their own purposes.

"Order must be maintained. Did not your wife's father instill that in her? It is time to take action, to take your revenge on those who abandoned you, who ridiculed you. As a child you were thought worthless. But I know you weren't. You endured. You always wanted revenge, didn't you? Now you have your chance to prove to all your capacity—your power."

Pádraig winced. He couldn't breathe. He couldn't understand it, but something was happening within him, within his head. Thoughts of dread and hopelessness were being eclipsed by something else: rage, a rage like none he ever felt. Memories flashed inside his mind with every word pronounced by the wizard's mouth, memories of those soldiers in Harlíeo who hunted him as a youth, who dragged him away from his mother the day she breathed her last, of feeling all alone, grieving for her.

Pádraig felt the veins in his head tighten. He fought his hardest, but he could not quench that fiery anger. His wheezing grew into gasps of pain. It was as if he was being imprisoned within the darkest corners of his own head by his unbridled rage, which gave way to new thoughts.

They mistreated me. They mistreated Dermot. Why have I never made them pay? I should've stood up and fought back! They thought me weak? Lies! I'll show them all! I will have vengeance!

Taranis stretched out his hands with the palms facing up. He shut his eyes and uttered an incantation familiar to

Pádraig:

Shadows so dark
Escape no free will
Shadows so dark
Spreading to every heart

From Taranis's palms sprouted black smog, encircling Pádraig. The smith caved in. Yet when he did, he felt stronger than he had in a long time.

Once the smog faded, Pádraig stood, his leg healed. The other mairágs, except the sheriff, dressed and armed him. He was now clad as they were, except his tunic bore orange edges and a crest: an orange inverted pentacle crest.

Shoulders back, Pádraig brandished his sword like a torch. He pledged, "To the Dríacht's fall, my prince. You shall restore order and might to the kingdom."

Taranis smiled. The sheriff clenched his fist.

Chapter 39

Running faster, the unicorns continued on their journey with Iorwerth and the lads. They never seemed to tire. Even so, Iorwerth decided they needed a short rest to regain their strength. Once they halted, their riders dismounted. The boys grumbled while stretching their legs. Yseult panted heavily.

"We shouldn't rest too long," Dermot said. "The longer we delay, the more Maeve and Ferghus's lives are at risk."

Aengus snorted. *You must learn patience, Dermot. Do you expect to succeed by rushing into things?*

Olwen nudged her mate with her nose, motioning toward Dermot. *Please, dear. Be nice.*

Aengus cocked his head, snorting softly.

Dermot meanwhile pondered once more over this memory, if it was indeed such, of Saershe and Ruairí in Úaene. What did Saershe fear would be left in darkness had he not returned to her? Had she been aiding him as she said, and if so, to what purpose? He remembered then something she told him long ago.

I have grown very fond of you. I see something deep within you, something good which I sense your brother shares.

"Dermot?" Ruairí asked.

"What is it?"

"Is something wrong? I said your time twice."

"Oh, nothing," Dermot was quick to reply. "Sorry."

Ruairí gritted his teeth. Dermot narrowed his eyes. He suspected Ruairí was hiding something, as Saershe had done once.

"Come, eat," Iorwerth said. "We shan't save Maeve and Ferghus on empty stomachs."

"Oh, thank goodness. I'm famished," Brian said.

Iorwerth handed them fruit, wild berries, mushrooms, nuts, and other green foods which he said Saershe had collected for their journey, including a couple apples that had ripened early. Yseult barked, pleading for some herself. They complied.

Quietly and hungrily they ate, finding the food delicious and the water from the water-skins refreshing. Bits of food fell out of Brian's fingers, but he didn't bother picking them up. Some sparrows and woodcocks hopped toward their boots. The lads watched these birds pick up several crumbs then disappear again amid the dense undergrowth. The unicorns both feasted on thick grass.

"We had sparrows lodging in our roof," Brian said.

"Sparrows are more capable of getting into tight places compared to other birds," Iorwerth said, "in order that they do not draw attention from predators. They seize opportunities as they come, knowing nothing's too small to be of no use. Woodcocks nest on the ground. They, too, know to blend in, by means of their mottled feather patterns."

Dermot finished off an apple. Thinking the apple core would rot back into the earth, he tossed it off to one side, where a mouse appeared, sniffing it excitedly. A rat joined him, demonstrating an identical tendency.

"They're attracted to that?" Dermot asked.

The mouse looked up at him, whiskers twitching.

Think twice before you throw anything away.

Dermot remembered what Iorwerth just said about sparrows. Needless to say, he felt a twinge of guilt. Yseult licked his hand, making him grin.

"Rats infested our cottage," Brian said, "Always stealing our food, hiding in the loft, in every nook and cranny."

"Rats and mice are some of the most resourceful and adaptable of creatures around," Iorwerth said. "Excellent climbers, they can live anyplace, and make use of whatever's on hand. Frogs likewise know how to survive, spending time on land and in the water."

"I think we're being watched. Somewhere over there," Brian said. He crept closer to get a better look, wrapping himself in his cloak. Iorwerth warned him to be careful. His brother, along with Ruairí and Ciara, watched in anticipation. Dermot could feel his tension level rising. Out of nowhere a female red fox sprang, leaping so close Brian stumbled backward. Ruairí and Dermot helped him to his feet. Yseult sprang up ready to pursue but Aengus raced in front. He stared at her. *Don't think you can ever outrun a unicorn, Yseult.*

She tried to get around him, but he and Olwen blocked her path. Without warning, Ciara pounced on Yseult, forcing her to the ground. The dog growled.

"That fox hasn't attacked any chickens, girl!" grumbled Ciara. "And we can't squander our time! Think of Maeve and Ferghus! I beg of you!"

Dermot and Brian pulled Ciara off the dog. Iorwerth whispered in Yseult's ear. She sneezed, but calmed down.

Iorwerth thanked Aengus for stopping her. He said to Ciara, "You're quite right. Still, a dog cannot be blamed

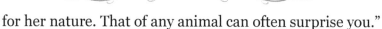

for her nature. That of any animal can often surprise you."

Yseult barked.

"What do you mean, Iorwerth?" Dermot asked, despite his growing awareness.

"From wild animals," he said, "both predator and prey, ye will learn valuable lessons and principles that may serve to guide your own life, even in our present mission to rescue our friends. You have already learnt from sparrows and rats. The fox is quick and clever, able to elude threats and seize opportunities. The stag is ever watchful, always minding his surroundings, always alert, prepared for potential danger. The rabbit imparts love and fertility into her young, akin to any mother. The frog demonstrates cleansing, healing oneself with tranquil thoughts, such as when they return to the water from time on land. The turtle, whose lifespan exceeds many other animals, is a creature of wisdom and endurance against constant cycling changes."

As he spoke, the dríadór held out his hand toward those particular animals he referenced who were nearby. Dermot was surprised each time by their presence, and from the look in Brian's eyes, he knew he was too. Ciara bent down to observe some ants and Ruairí joined her. At that moment, an apple fell from a branch above them. Before any of them could claim it, the ants beat them to the fruit, crawling all over it.

"Look at them," Ciara said, "busy as can be, like those honeybees up there."

The bees left their hive deep in the apple tree's trunk, buzzing toward wildflowers abloom below. Ladybugs preferred the leaves.

"They're working together, it looks like," Dermot said.

"All equal."

"True," Iorwerth affirmed, "To such insects, equality is vital. Even in the smallest, darkest places they can subsist. They do their part for one and all. Beehives and anthills alike depend on cooperation for survival. That goes for all of us."

Yseult moaned as he spoke, but Iorwerth stroked her cheek, assuring her while looking at the boys. "All creatures great and small live and learn, even humans. Blaming and resenting one another will do nothing to help our friends."

Yseult licked his hand affectionately. Ciara pointed out a gray squirrel, grasping an acorn in his teeth. He furiously dug deep in the earth, whereupon he buried the plump acorn before immediately racing back up an oak tree. Yseult bent her neck down, watching silently.

"Spirited little fellow," Dermot said, "and quite frisky, I must say."

"Saving for midwinter, no doubt," Brian said.

"And not all sacred seeds buried will be eaten," Iorwerth said. "From some shall sprout new trees, another way which wild beings affect each other here within the woodland."

Dermot recalled Saershe speaking of squirrels saving uneaten acorns for wintertime. That gray squirrel took one long look at them each from overhead. *Best to save, should there be tough times ahead you can't foresee.*

The entire group faced Iorwerth, who gave them a wide grin. "Like I told you, by observing wild animals, no matter if great or small, their lifestyles, speech, behavior, and unique traits, altogether demonstrate much on how we ourselves ought to lead our own lives. Heed

whatsoever wildlife shows or communicates during your future.

"Saershe could tell you the same regarding green beings. They, too, impart meaningful, moral lessons of life. Consider the grass we walk on; always growing together, never alone, and durable so creatures' feet don't harm them. Hence, we can value the efforts of durability and teamwork, akin to any creature living in a group, or pack, like the wolves."

**

Pádraig, the scáithir, observed the boys with his master through the wizard's crystal.

"Most excellent," Taranis said. "Lúg has done his task well, though I would have expected more from Iorwerth in his hunt."

"I'm ready to play my role as the mighty dragon did his, sire," the scáithír avowed.

"Lúg is the mightiest of Denuan dragons," Taranis said. "Long ago, our paths crossed within the legendary treasure hoard of the Great Sleeping Dragon. Possessed by greed, fiercely he and his kind guarded those riches for years. Their hearts proved rather easy to manipulate, with the promise of keeping and enriching the treasure. You know how easy a task that is."

"Nothing can threaten magic as potent as yours, my noble prince. Why is Lúg not still there, safeguarding that treasure hoard?"

"I control numerous dragons. They take turns defending it and killing my foes. Thus their strength and fury never wane. None of them shall succumb to sloth, the

inevitable fate of guarding wealth day and night, and doing nothing else. Nor shall their covetous hearts lead them to self-obliteration, squabbling over gold."

"That is brilliant, my liege."

"Indeed. Now listen to me carefully. Inside an undistinguished foothill, not a great mountain you understand, there reside empty caverns where despair may reach significant depths. To that end, the first purpose I have in mind for you must be accomplished, and accomplished well."

The scáithír's interest peaked. He leaned in close while his master murmured in his ear. The sheriff stood by the wall, watching with a tight grip on his sword.

When the wizard finished, both he and Pádraig pulled their heads back and stared at each other. Taranis asked, "Do you understand?"

"I do, sire."

Taranis turned to the sheriff. "I have received word that Granuaile and Lonán are among the refugees bound for Núinna. You know your orders."

**

Dermot and his friends continued on their way until late in the afternoon. When they stopped again for a rest, Ruairí approached Dermot.

"Um, Dermot," he managed to utter, "There's something I think..."

"Look!" Brian said. "Over there!"

They had stumbled upon more distinct impressions in the earthen trail.

"These tracks you can tell have changed gradually,"

Iorwerth said, "Animal tracks replace men's there—wolves' tracks."

"The Mairágh have transfigured into wolves in the past," Dermot said, thinking of the foray at the standing stones.

"How can you be sure they're wolf tracks, Iorwerth?" Brian asked. "I mean, they do resemble a canine's paws, but they could be anything..."

"They're not as rounded in front, around the claws, like a fox. You can see how they're clumped together. Well, that indicates a pack, or a legion of the Mairágh in wolf form."

"But they could still be real wolves," Ruairí said.

Iorwerth stopped. "Look."

Chapter 40

Everyone beheld a rocky outcrop encircled by broad oak trees, where a wolf pack huddled together, with pups all around them. Most licked their lips or paws. The group was aghast by the blood staining the gray fur of every wolf. Not one amongst the pack made a move beyond turning their heads. Ruairí, Ciara, and Iorwerth led the way as they came up to them.

Dermot could sense innocence and a good, loving hearts in these wolves. In each friendly, yet saddened gaze, he felt he saw Yseult, or rather that innocence he always saw when gazing into her eyes. The retriever, who was presently beside the unicorns, sniffed the air again, her nose up high in a different direction.

"What is it, girl?" Dermot asked as she walked away from Olwen and Aengus. Many amongst the wolves fixed their eyes on her, their ears lowering defensively.

Yseult's legs stiffened. Ciara took a firm step in front of her. Keane screeched, reprimanding the dog. *Don't even think about it!*

Yseult eyed Keane, growling. *I'm not going to run off!*

Ciara stepped back. The whole group turned to see what had roused Yseult. Gazing back at them from the underbrush was another wolf pup, not seriously injured, but far younger than the other pups. All heads and ears from the pack perked, but one she-wolf stood up. The pup made his way clumsily toward her. She sniffed and licked

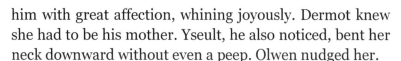
him with great affection, whining joyously. Dermot knew she had to be his mother. Yseult, he also noticed, bent her neck downward without even a peep. Olwen nudged her.

Ciara took a step closer. "It's all right, little fella. We're of the Dríacht. We mean you no harm."

The pup cradled himself behind his mother's leg. The she-wolf lowered her ears again.

"Truly," Dermot said calmly. "We are friends. You needn't be afraid."

The pup peeked out from behind his mother. He eyed them with as much curiosity as the sparrows and squirrels had earlier, with that youthful vigor Ferghus had shown shortly after his birth.

The young wolf took a step toward Dermot, and then stopped. He howled once, appearing curious and energetic, albeit hurt. Dermot knelt down, extending his hand to pet the pup. He withdrew it, watching the mother wolf as her ears perked. There was a musky scent about her, but Dermot didn't mind. She and the pup both sniffed him.

She bowed her head. *You may.*

"Thank you," Dermot whispered. The pup finally crept close to him, raising his head into Dermot's fingers. He wasn't sure what to do next.

Ruairí, Ciara, and Brian came alongside. The pup sniffed each of them. One at a time, they rubbed the pup's ears, their thumbs moving in circles. The pup smiled, as they did. Dermot leaned in so close his nose almost touched that of the pup. The pup immediately licked his face, making him and the others laugh.

Dermot sensed strength of heart and a playful spirit within the pup. Then, gazing deeper into the little one's

eyes as he had with Ferghus after he was born, Dermot suddenly felt a strong wave of heart-wrenching emotions take hold of him.

First, confusion flooded through him. In his mind, he was running for his life, as he had from the fire whirl. In an instant he was filled with terror as if he were seeing those closest to his heart suffering. He felt the wolves' pain and grief. It proved too much for him. He rubbed his hand across his forehead.

The pup barked. *They attacked us, as wolves.*

Dermot looked again into the wolf pup's eyes. This time, he somehow leaerned the pup's name.

"It's nice to meet you, Fáelán," Dermot said.

Fáelán angled his head slightly. Dermot saw Ruairí gaze deep into Fáelán's eyes. For a moment, he thought he saw the blue of his friend's eyes glow.

Olwen joined them. Yseult and Aengus edged closer. Standing beside Ruairí, Olwen gazed down into Fáelán's eyes. Her head lowered so her nose's tip reached the pup's, which sniffed her in response.

Ruairí stood up, looking at Iorwerth. "The Mairágh have come this way."

"But why would they harm these wolves?" Brian asked.

"For their amusement," Dermot said.

"More than that," Iorwerth curled his lip. "If not to delay us reaching the gryphons, the answer is to taunt us, to lure us out into the open. Taranis's mind is so twisted he doesn't care what he does to make us—the Dríacht—suffer. You know he likes to torture before killing."

"Aye, but why does he hate you so much, Iorwerth?" Dermot asked. "Why did he betray the Dríacht?"

Iorwerth grew still. "Tell me, have you ever felt unappreciated? Held back?"

Brian looked at Dermot, who lowered his eyes.

"Torin believed himself to be special," Iorwerth said. "His ambition clouded his heart and mind. He taunted others, mistreated them. He thought himself, as a dríadór, superior to Nature and other beings, not a caretaker of wildlife, their equal in spirit. He failed to understand that magic and power, are a responsibility to others. Torin's pride and selfishness gave birth to Taranis."

Dermot nodded.

Iorwerth stated, "Don't misplace your own minds, or hearts. If anguish begets rage, you will not think straight, and be easier for him to kill. Don't misjudge me, my friends. To feel, and to grieve, proves your capacity to love and care. Tis what makes you a fellow living being unto all others. Nevertheless, if you do not control your emotions, they will control you. Sometimes it is best to hide them so not to hurt those you love. But be sure never to bury them too deep for long, for they will wither away. Then you will become no different than your enemy."

"I see," Dermot said, unsettled.

"Focus on our mission, my friend," Iorwerth said. "But remember always who we are doing this for, and why we are in this together."

Because we are family, and we love each other, thought Dermot, feeling as he did the night of Ferghus's birth. Yseult made a noise, begging Fáelán to approach her. He didn't recoil like his mother, but Dermot assured her Yseult wouldn't harm her pup. The she-wolf consented despite the looks from her male pack members.

Yseult came up to Fáelán and nudged his head with

her cold, wet nose. Dermot looked down and smiled, petting her cheek. Fáelán kept his head high. Dermot then gazed into the pup's and his mother's eyes again, even deeper than before.

"Strength, cunning, courage, and loyalty in order to survive," Dermot said, "whether predator or prey."

Iorwerth, who had been tending to and intermingling with the older wolves, smiled. They all licked his face, which Dermot realized was their way of saying hello.

Then, Iorwerth's head jerked up. He gazed around with a raised eyebrow.

"Listen," the wizard said, standing.

"What is it?" Brian asked.

"Shush." Iorwerth shook his hand to still Brian's questions.

Everyone fell silent. Dermot heard nothing except songs from birds. Almost immediately, he spied swallows, sparrows, bluebirds, pigeons, robins, blackbirds, and many other birds settle atop the leafy boughs. Some birds like woodcocks, appeared on the ground. Iorwerth's hand gestures were no longer needed to keep Yseult at bay, and she behaved well. Presently, a splendid raven landed on a nearby branch, cawing louder than the other birds.

"Birds possess a dialect all their own," Iorwerth said. "Diverse, colorful calls and songs are used for various purposes. Listen to them. Are their voices not beautiful? You can learn a great deal about their fascinating culture, not to mention your own surroundings. Birds are exceptional mentors."

"Their songs are beautiful." Ruairí smiled.

"I only hear loud chirps and caws," Dermot said.

"Fret not, me lad," the dríadór said. "It took me years

'til I understood their language."

Iorwerth listened acutely, whistling back to the birds, almost as if he were whistling a song. He fascinated Dermot with the way his whistling resembled the birds' voices. More of them came flying overhead. Squirrels even appeared.

"What're they saying?" Dermot asked. The graybeard strongly reminded him of Saershe, only more eccentric.

"It's an alarm call, forewarning danger."

"Danger?" Brian said. "What danger?"

"Not so loud," the dríadór said softly, listening to the birds anew. One wren in particular voiced more forcefully than the others. Keane swooped down, screeching. Iorwerth extended his arm. Keane landed on the wizard's thick glove, still screeching.

"What is it?" Ciara asked.

"Several large, black-coated predators are traveling east as we speak," Iorwerth said. "Their pace has quickened. The Mairágh must know we are on their trail."

"Have you seen them, Keane?" Brian asked.

The falcon squawked once, *Aye.*

Iorwerth whistled a new song to the birds, raising his arms. Many whistled back before they flew away. He turned to the wolves. "Don't worry. Aid is on the way."

Dermot wondered if he was referring to Saershe, but his mind was too preoccupied with Maeve and Ferghus to think beyond that assumption.

The group prepared to leave, walking toward the unicorns. Dermot stopped, catching one more glimpse of Fáelán, who gave him a parting bark. *Good luck.*

Dermot nodded in thanks. *I hope we meet again soon.*

Fáelán angled his head. His ear twitched. *I do too.*

Yseult barked, compelling Dermot to come. He noticed she looked back at the pup, catching Fáelán off guard with a tiny wink. Dermot, surprised as well, smiled.

Iorwerth maintained an open sense of awareness as they rode east. Ardently he listened, observed, and smelled about the greenwood. Then, he had the unicorns stop so he might examine a couple pine trees with broken boughs.

"These needles were recently disturbed," he finally said. "See here. Needles are strewn about and there are deep scratches in this trunk, as if a large creature with talons tumbled down through these trees. Look there. Tell me what you see."

"These tracks appear fairly fresh," Dermot said, kneeling alongside the others.

"Different kinds too," Ruairí added.

"From what I can tell," Ciara said, "they include those of wolves and boars."

"They're not in straight lines either," Iorwerth noted. "They've scuffled and scattered, as if a struggle had ensued. Wolves' paw prints aren't as close together as when walking. Hence the prints are further apart. Their heels aren't sunk in as deep as we've previously seen. They started running again."

"Not the boars," Brian said, "they're still roughly the same."

"A boar's legs aren't as long as other creatures, so their tracks are closer together," Ciara said. "What's more, there's a giant impression on the grass, they ran over."

"You can tell a large creature lay here, with no indication he or she got up. Yet that creature is no longer here," Iorwerth said. "Perhaps Lúg seized his prey."

"Astounding," Brian said. "I never imagined that tracks could tell so much."

"There're opportunities every day to discover something new within Nature," Iorwerth said, echoing Saershe's words. "You never outgrow them. Keane, like any falcon or hawk, is capable of seeing from afar. Soaring o'er the trees, he may soar o'er barriers. Though they are predator and prey, wolves and deer alike value utmost loyalty to their group. They stick together with each member contributing his or her part, akin to ants and bees, as would any true family. Wolves are excellent pathfinders, notably wise, and nurturing."

"O'er here! I found something!" Ruairí shouted.

The group hurried toward him. He first plucked transparent reddish-brown hairs from a bush. Next, he brandished a long black arrow, like the ones used by mairágs. A few crimson droplets were on the arrowhead.

"Good eye," Iorwerth said. He took the hairs, holding them to Yseult's nose.

He did not have to ask. She sniffed them meticulously, and wailed, confirming they were the gryphons'.

"If this blood is Maeve's or Ferghus's..." Ruairí said.

Keane cawed, abruptly swerving his head. *The sun is setting!*

"Yseult," Iorwerth said, "see if you can track their scent. It's getting late. Darkness will obscure our vision. We must follow your nose."

She barked, promising she would. She licked Iorwerth's hand, making him chuckle. Right away she sniffed the soil, grass, and tracks as intently as she had those hairs. Yseult's eye briefly met Dermot's. *No whiff*

must be left ignored. Why else do you think I'm always sniffing everything, and looking around?

Another valuable lesson, Dermot thought, remembering Iorwerth's words earlier.

Yseult looked up. She barked then dashed off. The others promptly sprinted after her. Before long, she stopped. Together they beheld where the trail took them.

Chapter 41

Yseult had led them to a cave. Twilight descended as blue skies deepened into a deep shade of violet. A single star was visible, only to vanish behind the clouds. With the setting sun behind them, the trees on the horizon became nothing more than dim silhouettes. The heavens continued to darken, giving rise to a starless, moonless sky. With the night air growing cooler, the crickets' chirruping faded with the light.

"A cave in the middle of a forest?" Dermot asked.

"It resembles an open mouth." Brian looked away. Dermot saw him shiver.

"You're right," Ruairí said.

The jewel atop Iorwerth's staff glowed, providing better light. They stared into the black emptiness of the cave's interior.

"Something doesn't feel right," Iorwerth said

"What do you mean?" Brian asked. "Yseult traced their scent here, and we've followed the tracks too."

The retriever stared at Dermot, yawning. *I wasn't wrong.*

"I know, girl." Brian patted the dog's head.

Iorwerth replied, "I don't doubt Yseult's nose, me lad. The blood suggests as much, as do the stray feathers and hairs. Impressions in the dirt indicate a large creature lay here, maybe even thrown from the sky, and was subsequently dragged inside that cave. No dragon save a

young one could enter here, but a gryphon certainly can."

"Yet?" Brian asked.

"Yet it seems too perfect, too easy."

"So does that mean it's was a trap? Or a false trail?" Dermot said.

"I have never doubted that Taranis would set a trap for us." Iorwerth turned to look at Dermot. "He's drawing us in. I have a feeling in my bones something else is afoot. What I cannot say."

"So what do we do?" Brian asked.

"We walk in, of course," Ciara said. Everyone looked at her as she stiffened her spine.

"We must venture inward," Iorwerth said. He glanced at Ciara sternly. "But *I* will lead the way. Everybody stay close behind me. Understand?"

Dermot and Brian exchanged nervous glances. Dermot feared what he might find inside. He knew he had no choice but to go forward. If Maeve and Fergus were in there, they had to rescue them. But before they stepped into the cave, they turned to the unicorns.

"We are deeply indebted to you both," Dermot said." Thank you for everything."

Olwen bowed her head, followed by the others. *Think nothing of it.*

Dermot ran a hand under his nose, and then wiped a tear from his cheek. "I—I hate to say farewell."

This isn't farewell. Be careful, Olwen said. *Seek our aid should you ever need it.*

Be not tempted by evil, Aengus said, *else you shall be lost like Torin.*

"Thank you," Iorwerth whispered.

The unicorns turned and walked away.

"All right," Iorwerth said. "Let's go. Yseult and Keane, you two stay here, keep watch, and stay out of sight."

The two of them nodded, with Keane flying to the high branches of a nearby tree.

One by one, they entered the cave. Dermot gazed at it's ceiling while passing beneath it.

Slowly they crept through the dark. Iorwerth tapped his staff into the earth. The top glowed bright enough for them to see giant bats that squeaked as they swarmed everywhere. Unlike the sorcerer, the boys dropped to their knees, afraid the bats would attack. Instead, the bats flew over their heads and out the cave entrance. With relief, they got back on their feet.

"Have no fear," Iorwerth said. "The light merely startled them. Be on your guard. Many villainous forces adore taking advantage of humankind's fear of the dark. Therefore, one must always be cautious, ready for whatever lurks ahead."

"Right," Dermot said.

"The night isn't anything to be afraid of," Iorwerth said. "Nocturnal creatures learn to embrace it, and use it."

"Oh, how I wish Grandma was here," Ruairí whispered.

"Me too," Dermot said.

"Every bird must leave the nest." Iorwerth said. "No, the time hasn't come yet, but a day shall come when you will spread your wings."

The further in they went, the more the air became rank. Dermot wondered if the others were finding it as difficult to breathe as he was. The walls and floor of the cave were slippery, whether from water or bat guano he didn't know. It smelled so bad he finally put a hand over

his nose.

Dermot paused. Something was different. As he carefully took another step, he realized the cave floor was sloping down.

"Wait," he whispered. When the others stopped, he wasn't sure what to say next. He finally pointed it out to them, and said, "I don't like this. We don't even know how far we have to go underground."

"You're right," Ruairí said.

"What is this place?" Brian asked.

"It could be a tunnel linked to caverns within the mountains," Iorwerth said. "In the Great Sleeping Dragon there are some that extend fathoms deep into the earth and were used by dragons for transporting plunder. Or, it may be one of those subterranean lairs the ancient races of Denú used as burial grounds. They believed them to be gateways to the otherworld."

Dermot remembered hearing at festivals that gryphon's nests, or eyries were reputed to contain the emeralds from their mountainous habitat. A dragon's hoard, in contrast, or so the tales claimed, included treasures of gold and silver to precious stones of every color. Even so, both dwellings were sought by those hungry for wealth as much as glory.

"We must keep going," Ciara said.

Iorwerth agreed. "Steady on."

A moment later, the sorcerer held up his hand, and they stopped. At the path's end a short distance away, a vivid reddish-orange light flickered off the rocks. The hairs on Dermot's neck stood on end like a hedgehog's quills. A loud caw reverberated throughout the tunnel.

"It's Ferghus," Dermot said. There was no mistaking

that caw. He knew Ferghus's voice all too well.

"You're right," Brian said. "He sounds as though he's in agony."

"I smell smoke," Ruairí said. "A fire's burning."

"I smell it too," Ciara said.

"I fear the worst," Iorwerth murmured.

"Mercy of the heavens, what do we do?" Brian asked.

"Quiet!" the sorcerer said. "Let me devise a plan."

They heard another caw, this time accompanied by rattling chains.

"Oh no! Maeve!" Brian said.

Dermot's heart thudded so painfully, for a second he was sure it would burst out of his chest. "We've got to save them before they're killed!"

"What can we do?" Brian asked. "It's not like we can walk inside."

"Why not?" Ciara asked.

Why not, indeed? Dermot wondered as he watched Brian's jaw drop as though walking into trouble was a new concept. He turned to Iorweth as the sorcerer gave a curt nod, which surprised him.

"I couldn't agree with Ciara more," he said.

"Steady," he cautioned. "Stick together."

Cautiously, they crept nearer to the light. No one made a sound as they realized they had stumbled on a subterranean cavern. Once inside, Iorweth beckoned to the others. He slipped behind a large boulder, while the others crowded in around him.

Dermot couldn't believe how large the cavern was. He wondered how many fathoms deep within the earth it was. Peering around the boulder, Dermot saw firelight flickering against the rock. Hearing Ferghus's caw again,

he grasped his sword and shield tighter. One inky, wraithlike individual came into view, standing center stage on a patch of elevated ground that was surrounded by large boulders. He jerked backward, pressing his spine against the cold stone.

"Taranis," Dermot said.

The dark wizard's voice echoed throughout the cavern. "Good evening, my friends. You needn't hide. I know you're there, thanks to Dermot. Come out, wherever you are."

Brian frowned at Dermot. He stared back at his brother, wanting to apologize and insist he couldn't help himself, but no words escaped his mouth.

Iorwerth stepped out first, with the others on his heels. To their horror, they saw Maeve and Ferghus, restrained by large chains, battered and awash in dried blood. The Mairágh stood guard around the gryphons, holding torches and carrying weapons. Both Maeve and Ferghus, Dermot could tell, had been tortured with water, and plucked of their feathers and fur.

Mother and son cawed. *What're you doing? Are you insane? Get out of here! Run!*

Not without you, Dermot thought.

"Here we are, as you wanted," Iorwerth said.

"Yes, welcome," Taranis sneered. "Ah, Brian and Dermot, there's someone I want you two to meet."

The wizard snapped his fingers. Beside him they saw a mairág, unlike any other they had ever confronted. His attire was far more elaborate than the other mairágs present. This one's voice echoed off the rocks: "Brilliant, my noble prince! The time has arrived to annihilate your greatest adversaries!"

Dermot couldn't believe his ears. "No!"

"It can't be!" Brian wailed.

"Da?" Dermot said.

"Your father is no more, boy," Pádraig said. "I am the first of the Scáithír, a new standard of the Mairágh, with grander prowess!"

"How can this have happened?" Brian asked.

"Taranis must've chosen to spare your father's life when he captured him," Iorwerth whispered. "It was only a matter of time then."

"No!" Brian said.

"He's cast a spell o'er you, Da!" Dermot said, "Please, let us help you!"

"Silence!" Taranis's voice echoed throughout the cavern.

For a moment, they were shocked into silence.

"Weren't you intending to regale us, Dark Prince?" Iorwerth asked. "To explain to us how this meeting came to be?"

Is that a good idea, enticing him? Dermot wondered.

"Ah yes, of course," Taranis said. "My original plan was for Lúg to chase this foolhardy young gryphon and his mother to the Ashland, while my men created a false trail for you to follow. After they encountered that wolf pack, however, I knew your tracking skills wouldn't fail. I decided then to give you lot a chance to watch these gryphons die, before joining them in the otherword."

The wizard waved his hand through the air. At his once the scáithír and mairágs brandished their weapons, as more of them jumped out from behind scattered boulders.

"Well done, Iorwerth." Taranis boasted. "I learned my

lesson, to lure in prey with bait they cannot resist. The end has come for you. I only regret Saershe isn't here to share it."

"Indeed you've learned your lessons. You should know then Torin, if hunters truly want to trap prey, they must catch them off guard," Iorwerth said.

The dríadór thrust his staff upward. A bolt of lightning flashed from its top, scarring the rock for several feet. The Mairágh were knocked off their feet as a second bolt broke the chains restraining Maeve and Ferghus.

Before the blinding light disappeared, Iorwerth shouted at the gryphons to get away. Weak and weary, both managed to spread their wings. Dermot's heart soared as they took to the air. They flew so close over his head he had to duck.

"Kill them!" Taranis roared.

"Back to the forest!" Iorwerth said.

They darted out of the cavern and into the tunnel, moving as fast as the slippery floor would allow. Dermot heard the mairágs close behind with Taranis yelling, "Seize them!"

The journey upward was more arduous. Dermot's heartbeat accelerated. Gasping for breath, he dared not stop. Ciara and Iorwerth kept the Mairágh at bay as the boys ran for their lives.

Fresh air from the world above helped Dermot's breathing somewhat, but he was still gasping as he finally stumbled out of the cave.

Once outside, they panicked, scattering like sheep with a wolf on their heels. Dermot found he was alone. Terrified to the bone, he had no idea where the others went. Nor did he see Yseult or Keane.

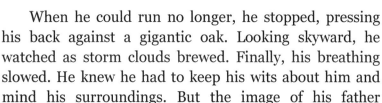

When he could run no longer, he stopped, pressing his back against a gigantic oak. Looking skyward, he watched as storm clouds brewed. Finally, his breathing slowed. He knew he had to keep his wits about him and mind his surroundings. But the image of his father standing beside Taranis came back to him. In spite of his determination to be strong and brave, tears gave way. He cried, "Oh, Da! What have you become?"

Hearing a noise, he fell silent. He sensed a presence behind a nearby tree. He slipped away in the opposite direction, his gut telling him the presence was not friend but foe. He had known for some time how it felt to be hunted, and he felt it now. Cautiously, he crept from tree to tree, watching always for the enemy. Rounding the trunk of a giant oak, he bumped into somebody.

Chapter 42

Dermot yelped, scuttling backward. Both he and the other person reached for their weapons. Upon recognizing each other, they breathed hard, lowered their weapons, and hugged one another tight.

"Thank goodness," Dermot said, "Are you all right?"

"Aye," Brian said.

"Have you seen any o' the others?"

Brian shook his head. They wandered carefully about the woods, seeing no sign of anyone.

"What are we going to do?" Brian asked.

"Shush."

Looking up, Dermot saw two owls, one with rather long ear tufts, the other with short ones, watching from different branches of the same tree. Both birds flew away, silent and calm.

"Iorwerth said owls and other nocturnal creatures use the night to their advantage," Dermot said. "We'd best follow their example. Let's heed the lessons of the animals. We can adapt and survive."

Brian nodded. "Let's do this. Let's show them what we can do."

"We were hunted. Now we'll hunt, together."

They drew their weapons. A rustling in the woods sent them behind the bushes, dropping to their knees. Dermot whispered, "A hunter can hide, waiting for prey."

Brian shushed him as mairágs emerged from the

shadows, brandishing their weapons, and hacking their way through the undergrowth. Both brothers did their best to keep calm, despite their hearts pounding.

Two familiar caws penetrated the dark midst. To his delight, Dermot saw Maeve and Ferghus swoop down. Ruairi, Ciara, and Iorwerth joined them as more mairágs emerged between the trees. Yseult and Keane arrived next. Two mairágs came near the brothers, one bearing an axe, the other a sword. Dermot and Brian attacked, but unfortunately the mairágs were not caught off guard. Other mairágs rushed forward, but were met with a volley of arrows. Ruairí fired the arrows as fast as he could. "Need help?"

"We have it under control!" Dermot said.

"Do you?" Ciara whacked a mairág with her stave.

The fighting continued, filling the night air with clangs and groans. A mairág knocked Dermot's shield from his hand. Without taking his eyes off his opponent, he reached down and grabbed a handful of small stones. The mairág lunged. Dermot tossed the stones into his face as hard as he could. The mairág ducked and Dermot managed to retrieve his shield.

He knew if he didn't stop this mairág, more would join him and he was afraid for his brother and friends. With a wild yell, he charged, his sword slashing and cutting. Backing up, the mairág stumbled and Dermot ran him through. With a grunt, the minion slumped to the ground, his blood staining the forest floor.

Dermot turned to be met by another. This one had a sword as well. He countered the mairág's every move. Dermot remembered his father's face as he last saw him in Emerin, which gave him the strength he needed to

overpower the mairág, and that man joined his companion in death.

Taking a deep breath, Dermot turned to check on his friends, but stopped in mid-turn as a loud voice yelled, "Halt!"

Fear clawed its way up Dermot's chest as Taranis emerged, brandishing a large, black spear in one hand, his staff in the other. Instantly, the forest became deathly silent. No one moved.

Iorwerth stepped out in front, confronting Taranis. The two chanted incantations in the old language, waving their arms and staffs as they ascended into the air. They invoked wind, lightning and water, the latter of which flew in rivers like serpentine dragons, all sending the mairágs off their feet or sending them into the air.

Keane and Yseult suddenly appeared, calling Dermot and his companions away. They complied as the gryphons fended off the mairágs, receiving more blows due to their weakened state. One arrow struck Ferghus's wing and he crashed into a large branch, splitting it as he tumbled to the ground.

Snarling, Taranis turned sharply away from Iorwerth, diving towards Ferghus with intent to slay him. Iorwerth followed with the intent to stop him, but Taranis evaded the beams of lightening from his opponent's staff.

Maeve caught sight of Taranis and managed to separate him from her son, landing in between them just in time. Ferghus simultaneously went straight to the brothers' aid, knocking any mairágs that got in his way to the ground. But Maeve didn't move.

A loud case filled the air. In that moment, all activity stopped. In horror, they watched as Taranis's spear struck

Maeve near her heart. Her wings furled back and she fell toward earth, her face and claws digging up the ground as she slid to a stop. Maeve screeched with all the force in her soul. It was not out of fury, but agony.

In that moment, all activity stopped. All eyes watched as the mother gryphon wobbled, and then fell on her side.

"Maeve!" Dermot screamed.

Her breaths grew heavier as her friends attempted to rush to her side. Only Ferghus and Yseult made it. Ferghus's beak nudged his mother's cheek as he moaned. She lowered her head slightly. One tear slid down her face and fell on her young son's head. The side of her belly facing skyward rose and sank with each passing, shortening breath. Unfortunately, more mairágs emerged, flinging a giant net over Ferghus. Yseult was taken up by two mairágs, while others seized the rest of the group.

"Maeve!" Dermot yelled, struggling to free himself. His captor's forced him to drop his weapons and he shuddered at the sight of Maeve's wound, gushing blood.

The mother gryphon made a last attempt to communicate with her son. *Don't be afraid for me, my boy. Oh, my dearest, darling boy. Your father would be so proud. Now fight on! You're a fighter. Fight!*

With a heart-broken squawk, he pulled hard against the four mairágs struggling to hold him back. They hacked at his body, spilling blood and feathers.

At each terrified and painful screech, Dermot's anger grew. Yseult, too, was being torturously injured, her mournful wails adding to Dermot's rage.

Maeve screeched for her son.

Dermot cried out, as did Brian and Ciara, "No! Stop it! Leave them alone! No!"

Iorwerth repeatedly tried to reach their side. Taranis stood in his way with his black magic, forcing him to continue the duel. The scáithír walked up to Maeve and stood over her, the tip of his blade pointed at her.

"Da, no, please!" Brian begged.

"Da, stop!" Dermot shouted. "This isn't who you are! You don't know what you're doing!"

It was no use. He plunged his blade into her side. Maeve exhaled slowly. Then, she lay still. The light in her eyes faded. No one moved.

M – Ma?

Ferghus's feeble squawk pierced Dermot's heart. He couldn't believe his eyes. Time halted. Yseult and Ferghus raised their heads, their anguished voices lifted on the breeze. Everyone wept.

The young gryphon squawked. *Don't leave me, Ma! Please don't leave me!*

Taranis, in the chaos, landed in front of his followers and prisoners. Iorwerth charged down, facing him and Pádraig, with Keane alongside. Other mairágs held their blades to the prisoners' throats.

"You fiend!" Ciara yelled. She cringed as one mairág's the iron blade dug deep into her skin.

Taranis ignored her as he cackled. "Iorwerth, you know if you harm me, they die. If you try to save them, you die. You see, it's futile. Give yourself up, they will be spared."

"You shan't keep your word," Iorwerth. "You never have. I lost Maeve. I won't lose them."

"Maeve has joined her beloved Caomh in the otherworld," Taranis said. "She always wanted it. She never wanted her child."

Liar! Ferghus screamed.

Taranis's cold cackle sent chills down Dermot's spine. "Save your breath, Ferghus," the wizard said. "No, Iorwerth, I won't keep my word. I'm the greater practitioner of magic here. No matter what, I triumph."

Ferghus gazed at all his friends. *Shall we, for Ma, together?*

They looked at him, then at each other.

Together, thought Dermot. He could feel the same idea in the others. He listened to the forest as his breath deepened. Once again a strange sensation suffused his soul. This time it gave rise to courage, a will strengthened. He sensed he would get through this, in spite of the odds.

If Saershe sees something in me, let it ignite, he thought. *I pray what she sees does mean something.*

Throwing his head back, Dermot roared. After a second of stunned silence, the others joined in. At the sound of their voices, branches on the nearby trees moved in a swift arc. They swept down, tossing mairágs every which way. Yseult was freed. She leapt toward Ferghus and tore at the net with her teeth. With assistance from the other animals, they tore the net away. Keane, owls, bats, and many more creatures, both groundlings and fowl, joined the fray, fending off the Mairágh.

Taranis failed to stop them, due to his fighting Iorwerth, who despite his age, proved a formidable adversary.

"Stop them!" Taranis shouted to his minions. "Kill them!"

Dermot and his friends charged straight in. Each of them fought a mairág, and despite their fury, kept their cool and easily dodged their opponents' weapons. Then,

the four found themselves back to back, surrounded.

Undaunted, Ciara said, "To the end."

The three boys echoed her words.

They raised their weapons. Together with Ferghus they roared in even greater fury. Without warning, a blinding green light flooded the area. To Dermot, it was a startling sight, but his energy didn't dwindle. It grew stronger. Winds hastened, crackling leaves.

The mairágs fled, or at least the ones who hadn't been swept off their feet. Taranis bellowed, "No! Come back you cowards!"

In the wizard's attempt to rally his forces, Iorwerth seized the opportunity. A powerful blue light emanated from his staff, smashing into Taranis's back. The wizard roared.

Dermot, at last, felt himself weaken. His body could take no more. He was horrified as to what might happen if he didn't fight on, but it was no use. Both legs faltered, and he sank to the ground as blackness claimed him.

**

Birds' songs and rustling leaves woke Dermot. Blinking, he looked around. His first thoughts were of the battle. Where'd the others go? Brian? Who'd won? Then, he remembered Maeve. Oh no, what about Ferghus?

He looked around. Not far away lay Brian, just waking as well. On closer inspection, Dermot realized they had slept inside a modest cave. He straightened his back, albeit painfully. Helping Brian to his feet, they walked into the light. The cave was situated beneath a large earthen mound with grass, ivy, and moss covering

the dome. Everywhere else they looked, they were surrounded by greenwood.

The sensation they were not alone crept up the nape of Dermot's neck, and his mouth went dry. When would they ever find peace again? He just wanted to enjoy the warm sunlight warm on his skin and to think of nothing but how good it felt. Unable to resist, he looked over his shoulder, then poked Brian in the ribs with his elbow.

Ruairí and Ciara raced up to them, throwing their arms around the brothers. Yseult and Ferghus followed, although more slowly as they were still weak from the beatings they had received. Someone had bandaged their injuries with poultices. Yseult licked the brother's hands. All were heavily bandaged.

Dermot's voice caught in his throat, "Saershe."

"Good morrow, brothers," she greeted. "Welcome to Glascoil Forest."

"Glascoil?" Brian asked. "Whereabouts is that?"

"The county of Denaloin," she replied, "In Crandáir."

Dermot was startled. *We're—we're in the Western Province? So—so far from home...*

Not far away, a wolf's howl caught their attention and looking around, they saw the same pack of wolves they'd met before. Each wolf's ears perked. Their tongues were hanging out as they panted. Each appeared to be smiling. Dermot recognized the pup he'd befriended in Ámhen. He called to him, waving.

Fáelán playfully barked twice. *Dermot! Dermot! Yay!*

The pup came running toward them. Before Dermot or anyone else could approach him, Yseult beat them to the young wolf. Fáelán showed no sign of fear. Yseult lowered her head, sniffing his head and ears. He rubbed

his cheek against her leg and the dog licked his brow.

"I think you've grown since we last met, little fella," Dermot said.

"How have you two been faring since last night?" Iorwerth asked as Keane landed on an oak branch nearby.

Iorwerth's voice startled him as he hadn't heard the man approach.

Dermot slowly stood. No one spoke for a moment, until Brian muttered Maeve's name. Ferghus sniffled.

"You're not to blame," Saershe said. "None of us are."

"We failed her," Dermot said with a catch in his voice.

Ferghus wept as though he'd never stop. Ciara rubbed his neck.

"Nay," Iorwerth said. "She sacrificed her life to save Ferghus. Tis an act any mother would make for her child. Any one of you would have done the same for her, or any of us. We can't wallow in mourning forever. Maeve wouldn't want that. Certainly not for you, Ferghus. You are her greatest legacy. She would want us to keep on fighting so that we may live to see a more peaceful world. She made her choice. Respect her for it. Remember who she was in life. Honor her memory by fighting. Do you understand?"

"It reminds me of something Grandma once told me," Ruairí said, "about my parents."

"What's that?" Dermot asked.

"So long as she and I love them, and remember them for whom they were in life, as long as we loved one another, they will always be alive. They will always be with us, and within us, keeping us strong."

"Indeed." Saershe raised her chin. Her face lit up with a knowing smile. Ferghus raised his too.

Dermot nodded. It was good advice, but could he use it when it came to his own father? Although his father wasn't dead, he was essentially dead to him and his brother in the current state he was in. By continuing the fight, would it be possible his father could come back to them?

Ferghus nudged Ruairí. With a tear in his eye, Ruairí touched the gryphon's forehead with his own. "Your mother loved you, Ferghus. She was proud of you."

Ferghus squawked. *I know, Ruairí, I know.*

"Forget not your deep roots," Dermot said.

Saershe smiled. "Iorwerth told me what has become of your father. Dermot, Brian, I am so sorry."

Dermot lowered his head. Then he looked up again. "Can we save him? There must be a way to free him."

"None whom Taranis has enslaved has ever been freed," Iorwerth said. "But that certainly doesn't mean it is impossible. We have tried, and we shall keep trying."

"I hope so," Brian said, looking at Dermot. "We can't lose Da."

"You two are capable of far more than you realize," Saershe said. "You are here for a reason."

"What do you mean?" Brian asked.

"Remember the day when you first met Olwen and Aengus? The forest's inhabitants fought alongside you, against the Mairágh. Only a dríadór could have summoned them."

"Aye, 'twas you," Brian said.

Saershe shook her head. "Nay, it was not me."

"It wasn't?" Brian asked.

"No."

"Wait," Brian said, "what're you saying, Saershe? If it

wasn't you, who elsecould it have possibly been?"

Saershe asked, "Brothers, don't you understand how it is you can feel the emotions plants and animals alike communicate to you; why you survived last night?"

Everyone fell silent.

Before Saershe could answer, Dermot stated calmly, "Because we're the same as you, aren't we?"

Brian jerked his head to face his brother, his eyes widening.

"Yes," Saershe nodded. "You are both dríadórs."

Chapter 43

Keane screeched loudly, even for a falcon. Brian blinked rapidly. Struggling, he managed to speak. "Ho—how did you know, Dermot?"

"I didn't. I suspected," he replied. He related his memories of Saershe, and the various forests, finishing despite a shred of disbelief still lingering in him. "Perhaps I did know, longer than I thought. I don't know."

Saershe smiled. "Every day since we met, you impress me, Dermot."

"Are—are you sure?" Brian asked.

"You both have approached wild animals with relative ease several times," Saershe said. "The day I brought you to meet Maeve, Dermot, I already suspected you possessed the great gift, the spiritual connection. She claimed so when you asked her to let you go. The way you reacted, I could feel it. I felt it again when Brian joined us."

Those memories resurfaced in Dermot's mind, making more sense than ever.

"I informed those creatures the night of Ferghus's birth you'd come. But you—on your own—understood they guided you along the right path. That day we crossed Olwen and Aengus's path, I knew for sure."

Brian's jaw dropped. "So we—Dermot and I—*we* summoned those beings, and conjured the light?"

"I saw the green in your eyes glow," Saershe said.

Dermot recalled Ruairí's eyes glowing blue while interacting with Fáelán. He gazed back at the wolf pup, who smiled.

"Saershe told me the morning we first met," Iorwerth said. "Your abilities became readily apparent to me as I watched you interact with Fáelán and his pack, and again during last night's battle. You four together unleashed your full potency."

Dermot looked at Fáelán again. The pup angled his head. One corner of Dermot's mouth turned up in a half-smile.

"Why didn't you tell us before, Saershe?" Brian asked.

"We had to be certain," she said. "Moreover, I felt it best to wait 'til the time was right. Perhaps I was wrong."

Dermot stared at Ruairí and Ciara. "Did you know?"

"Aye," Ruairi said. "I wanted to tell you, but Grandma forbade me from opening my mouth. Please forgive me."

Dermot, realized Ruairí did try to tell him once. He put his hand on his shoulder. "There is nothing to forgive, my friend."

Ruairí smiled. Brian looked to Ciara, who threw up her hands. "Don't look at me. I didn't know until this morning."

"But why us?" Brian asked. "I mean, Saershe, how can me and Dermot be dríadórs?"

"It remains a mystery what makes anyone a dríadór, my friend," she said. "It does run in many bloodlines, yes. Yet for others, it simply manifests after an extensive period spent amongst wildlife within their mystical realms, especially the forests. It has always been apparent to us that no dríadór has chosen this path. Rather, it selects us."

"Let us take a stroll together through Glascoil, and you shall see," Iorwerth said. "Let us put to rest any doubt you're still carrying about your destiny."

The sorcerer guided them through the greenwood's midst, with Saershe alongside. He turned his head left and right repeatedly, akin to a great owl perched atop a tree branch on the lookout for prey. However, scarcely any animals were to be found at present amidst these broad, tall trees. Dermot did spy a spider's iridescent web, which intrigued him, until it vanished in the sunlight. He wondered if it might be an omen of some kind. Fáelán's pack followed close behind.

"Opening yourself to Nature shall never bear fruit if you as a dríadór are not fully open," Saershe explained when they stopped. "Now, each of you imagine yourself as a great tree. Stand absolutely still, firmly rooted. Absorb from the earth, air, wind, and water. Let your roots descend deep. Raise your branches so you may take in the golden sunlight. Breathe deep. Feel love within your heart. Be aware and open, like I have seen you do so many times. Become one with the greenwood."

"Indeed," Iorwerth said, "Dispel all thoughts and feelings regarding trouble and woe. Let Nature's spiritual forces flow within you. You'll know in your hearts the truth. Instill peace and goodwill into your souls."

"The greenwood must accept you," Saershe finished.

The elder mystics extended their arms. The youths followed suit. Gradually, Dermot became aware of the breeze whistling through the leaves. As his awareness continued to open, he could hear a veritable ensemble of birdsongs and feel the sun's warmth penetrate his flesh. His breathing relaxed. Once again, he felt that soothing

sensation course through his veins. Only this time, it was not at all strange. It felt natural, and right.

Dermot connected to the earth by deep roots, and this feeling came from the trees, the fresh air, and the earth beneath his feet. His eyes locked on the trees. He sensed great love and wisdom, while examining the distinctive patterns in their bark, branches, and lush leaves he'd never noticed before.

The forest teemed with life. The animals appeared out of the green, for they had been there all along. The birds chirped from both the ground and treetops, as did the crickets. Grasshoppers raised their voices, filling the forest air. Woodpeckers scuttled up tree trunks, pounding on the thick bark. Several deer young and old stood together in the shade. In a small pond not too far away, croaking frogs jumped in and out of the quiet water, where fish, newts, and turtles swam. Dermot stood very still, watching everything.

Atop ample moss-covered rocks, millipedes and caterpillars crawled. Serpents slithered so smoothly that even when they weren't resting, they seemed almost one with the trees. Lizards were the stillest of all. A few darted like arrows, but they didn't startle Dermot. Whatever was flourishing inside him, it kept him at ease. Butterflies, together with other winged insects, hovered all around him. Moles popped their heads out from the earth, while badgers scurried about.

An all-encompassing harmony prevailed. The group remained serene, lowering their arms slowly.

"Remain calm," Saershe said, "and move about everyone. Go on."

As Dermot did so, his magical connection to the earth

and greenwood remained strong. More and more, he could tell what he felt was indeed magic.

He, Brian, Ciara, and Ruairí walked around slowly, observing the woodland creatures. Most bore colors which helped them blend in with the forest's subtle brown and green tones. Their eyes all imparted the same message. *Welcome.*

Happiness engulfed Dermot, and he sensed the others were just as happy, and not merely from the looks on their faces. Brian appeared the most surprised of all, but still happy. Nevertheless Dermot resolved to stay at a safe distance from the creatures.

Ruairí sat down on an old moss-covered log. He reached into his satchel that he had brought, and retrieved his journal. A little brown rabbit watched him sketch the various trees and creatures.

Dermot gazed as much at the trees as the creatures. He gently stroked his hand across their bark while observing those lush leaves and winding branches, through which sunlight trickled. He smiled all the while, especially as even more forest creatures came into view. This deep magic was growing stronger with every one of his senses.

"Remarkable," Ruairí whispered, composing a sketch of the rabbit, his fingers black with charcoal.

"Over here," Ciara called.

Gazing back at them through the underbrush was a female red fox bearing a strong resemblance to the fox they saw during their search for the gryphons. Then, Dermot knew it was her as he looked into her eyes. Greater astonishment came in the form of the baby fox she carried in her mouth.

"More bees," Brian said.

Sure enough, they buzzed busily outside a hive in an ash's tree trunk. They traveled from one flower to another, nuzzling amidst every collection of multicolored petals. Saershe hummed exquisitely, calming them. She looked to the brothers, dipping her head.

Dermot watched as Brian held out his arm, offering the bees a place to land. He copied his brother's movements. Not one stung them. After a few minutes, the bees flew away. A faint but distinct brilliant blue light glowed from it. He turned to Brian. His own palm also glowed blue. Their smiles widened in amazement.

Dermot felt content, and secure. When the bees flew away, Iorwerth collected fresh honey from the hive. Dermot circled to see all the other creatures again, not to mention the ancient, knowingly wise, leafy trees.

"Incredible," he said.

"Aye," Brian said.

"You see now," Saershe said. "You *are* dríadórs."

Dermot didn't have to answer. *It's true.*

Brian's face appeared graver, but Dermot could tell he knew it too.

"You have observed Nature's magic and miracles," Saershe said. "Now that you both know who you are, together with Ruairí and Ciara, you shall observe much more. Plant and animal alike has a spirit, the same as you and me."

"Spirit," Iorwerth said, "is shared by all living beings. It is the great element of Nature. Each of you have felt it within your heart, all around you, from every wild animal and plant, to the leaves and bark of trees, and above to the clouds and stars. You heard it within the wind, the flow of

water, clashes of thunder, crackling flames, birdcalls and songs, the cry of the wolf, frog, owl and cricket. Spirit binds Nature together, wildlife and the elements. You have interacted with and learned from your surroundings. You have embarked on this journey so as to become one with Nature."

"One with Nature?" Dermot asked curiously.

"Aye," Iorwerth said. "These cherished moments spent within these mystical greenwoods, 'twas meant to inspire you, to forge spiritual wisdom and character, to further your deep connection to Nature. And we shall continue to guide you along this path. You shall learn to control the magic you've felt. In time, you shall summon the elements, and learn our inherent ability to shape-shift into animals."

"This balance and harmony maintains the world we all share," Saershe stated in an uplifting tone. "Tis a greater, deeper magic connecting us, but Taranis seeks to dominate it, to destroy us and our coven's legacy to conquer Denú. If he succeeds, he will cover this world in darkness. We must work together to vanquish him. It is our sacred duty. Our magic is to be meant to protect, never to destroy, or to be used for gain."

"I know," Brian said. "I'm just afraid. I feel so alone."

"Fear cannot be evaded," Saershe said.

"You mean like change?" Dermot asked.

"Aye, but it's nothing to be ashamed of. We all feel fear, and we always shall. But we cannot let it define our lives. Doing so prevents us from ever moving forward. If you run, you will never stop. You must accept you feel fear in order to grow stronger. Only when you acknowledge and face what you fear may you overcome it.

"You're strong, Brian. I can feel it inside of you. Dermot, you have a heart of solid oak, and a noble spirit too. Do not let it burn. Your wills are great. In the face of the fire whirl, in facing death itself, you stayed together. Last night, none of you succumbed to fear. You showed true courage. You are not alone."

Dermot instantly remembered his self-given childhood moniker of Oakenheart. He couldn't help but feel a strange sense of irony.

Ferghus squawked, nudging the brothers. *I am eternally grateful to have you all in my life. You are all my family.*

"And you are family," Brian said, "all of you."

Dermot nodded in agreement. Ferghus cawed.

"Furthermore," Saershe said, "We aren't alone in this fight. There are a few other dríadórs beside us."

"There *are*?" Dermot asked. His jaw dropped.

"Aye," Iorwerth said. "Dispersed throughout Denú, they watch over the provinces' landscapes and wildlife. Word has been sent to them. Saershe and I will oversee your training; our coven's next generation.

"Tomorrow night when the moon cycles full, you four shall take the Sacred Oath of Nature's Mystery, as every dríadór has done before you. It shall be conducted within the Grove of Three Woods. Now, come and take nourishment. A wholesome breakfast has been prepared for you. Yseult, if you're ready for your bath and grooming..."

Yseult barked delightedly. They all walked off together. Iorwerth noticed Dermot's eyes focused on his boots.

"Is something troubling you, me lad?" he asked.

"Well, it's—I've done so many things I wish I had never done," Dermot said. "I can't stop thinking about them. I feel so ashamed."

"Would you care to hear my advice?" Iorwerth asked.

Dermot nodded, sniffling. He hated that he was in tears in front of Brian, who walked beside him, listening in on the conversation.

Iorwerth placed his hand on Dermot's shoulder. "Learn from the past, and dwell in the here and now, so you may create a brighter future. Past actions cannot be undone. If you keep mulling over them, you will end up repeating them, and you can never move on. If you learn from your mistakes, you may thereby grow stronger."

Dermot nodded. Brian touched his arm, which made him smile. He no longer felt embarrassed or ashamed.

Yseult barked, alerting their attention. Then Keane whistled. The pair imparted the same message: *Yes.*

**

Granuaile was tired of walking. She did her best to make sure no one could see her discontent, keeping her chin high. She always had since childhood. Her father was a stern man, and she was in every way her father's daughter. She thought of him for the first time in years. Her memory harkened back to her childhood, and his lessons. She worked hard and survived. She knew to be tough, but know her place.

She didn't know what to do. Then, she gave in, fell to her knees and wept. Through tears she muttered, "My babies, my love!"

Those nearest her stopped and stared. They asked if

she was all right and offered to help her up, but she refused, shaking them off and standing on her own. She growled at them to leave her be. She then saw Lonán looking like a wilted flower. She wondered if anyone he knew from Caemoch might still be there, along with anything more he was guilty of.

She looked away as he whispered, "Oh, my son. Please forgive me!"

Chapter 44

Ciara, Dermot, Brian, and Ruairí, faced a thick oak, one of three wizened trees that towered over the rest. The other two were a thorn and ash tree respectively, rooted on opposite sides from where the novices stood.

Dermot thought back to earlier that eve in a much more open, shamrock-laden glade, when, in a cloudless sky, innumerable twinkling stars appeared. He had volunteered to personally light Maeve's funeral pyre. It proved a difficult and painful task. Nevertheless, he managed, but not before kissing her forehead and whispering, "Find peace, my friend. We will watch over him. I swear."

The companionship stood together, watching the flames claim her. The smoke rose high into the sky to the sounds of owls and bats. Yseult, Fáelán, and the wolves howled. Keane screeched. As Ferghus wept, Brian stroked his neck. Iorwerth and Saershe chanted a prayer together in the ancient language: "May her soul be released from pain and strife, and be welcomed among her ancestors with great honor in the otherworld. No matter how darksome these days become, let her name and deeds be remembered always with reverence."

Shirtless (except for Ciara, who wore a plain dress) and barefoot, the novices stood together in a line. They had walked steadily through the dark forest toward this glade, where their elders were waiting. The light of the

stars, moon, and fireflies guided them, as did the trees and animals. The scenery reminded Dermot of the night Ferghus was born. Though dark, it was a pleasant dark, one that brought on that same strange, warm feeling of comfort when they stepped into the grove.

Fresh soil formed a spiral at the center, bedecked with flower petals and seeds. Northward rested a fledgling tree beside the great oak, amidst freshly churned earth, decorated with herbs. To the east, surrounded with feathers of all sizes and colors, incense produced a white, sweet-smelling smoke. A fire blazed within a rock circle in the south. On the westward side, a small spring's clear placid water poured into a small pool, gleaming in the moonlight.

Yseult, Ferghus, and Keane watched together from beneath the ash tree. Ferghus and Yseult had accompanied them on their walk to this spot. Keane had gone ahead of them with Iorwerth. The forest-dwellers appeared also to bear witness, even if they were not nocturnal. Their presence, too, contributed to the courage within Dermot.

Saershe and Iorwerth wore vestments white as new-fallen snow, with leafy green sashes over their left shoulders, and crowns fashioned from various wildflowers. He had his black-handled dagger in his belt, while she held in her hands a small silver chalice. They stood beside one another in front of the great oak tree.

Saershe spoke. "Welcome, candidates. Will you freely and willingly take the Sacred Oath of Nature's Mystery, and pledge yourselves to the Dríacht?"

Individually they said yes. With that, the novices walked slowly into the grassy center. They stopped and

faced one another around the spiral. Each of them stood between two of the cardinal directions. They got down on their knees with their hands joined.

All six chanted together:

O Sacred Nature,
Thy great mystery, creatures of the wild,
All which is green and grows, may you hear me
As the wind blows and the clear waters flow.
Here upon this sacred ground,
The mystical greenwood a mighty kingdom
Where thy great magic doth abound;
A path has begun. Wheresoever it may lead me,
May it bring the teachings of Nature's wonders!
Her secrets and magic!
Her mystery and mysteries,
That art everywhere and everything...

Breaking hands, the novices arose. Once standing, they incanted on their own:

Be rooted deep in the earth!
Grounded sturdy as any tree,
That strength is built on strong roots.

Fully aware, the mind calm and clear,
As the soothing wind is fresh and crisp,
That my wisdom might soar, upon great wings!

That flame of courage and will within,
Burn steadily bright, in facing any trial,
That always thence to find the light!

A heart pure, loving, kind, and true!
To all beings, as the waters flow, swirl, and spring,
To drink always to life and prosperity!

    The novices remained still as their elders prepared for
the final rite. Saershe filled the chalice with water from
the pool and brought it to them. They drank, passing the
chalice until it came back to Saershe.

    Finally, Iorwerth held out his dagger. The novices
each extended one hand, pressing their fingertips upon
the side of the blade. They finished chanting:

By the power of the sacred spirits therein,
To every animal, tree and plant, every blade of grass,
Every drop of water, every pebble in the soil and stream,
May Nature's mystic forces, the great gift of life,
Bequeath unto me her hallowed blessing,
For inspiration to unearth my full potency!

To be one with Nature, a solemn vow,
Never to disrupt her sacred balance and harmony,
Blessed be every being who roams a spirit free.
Absorb much as to grow upon this path.
Seeking within the spirit all around,
For I am avowed of the Dríacht!

    The breeze which blew made the leaves whistle and
the branches rattle. The chirrup and croak of cricket and
frog, the owl's hoot, wolf's bay, and many a lively
birdsong, echoed amongst the trees. Those creatures who

did not voice their approval expressed as much nevertheless with their bodies, including the foxes and deer. The unicorns reared on their hind legs.

Dermot himself felt more alive than he had been lately. Ever since earlier that evening, he'd felt as ready as he ever would be.

**

Taranis seethed with fury, pacing in the presence of the sisters and scáithír. "Ruairí, Ciara, and the brothers, have taken the Sacred Oath. There is no turning back for them. They are one with Nature, and the Dríacht. They are dríadórs now, confound it! More dríadórs! And Ferghus! His cursed bloodline endures! I should have foreseen Iorwerth's trickery!"

Neasa said, "Defeat hasn't marked you yet, my prince. It is time to strike back."

"Aye," Myf agreed. "They know not your strength, sire. The dragons are ready. *You* are ready."

"We await your command, sire," the scáithír said.

Taranis stopped, turned and walked up to them. "You're right. I *am* ready. Those creatures have waited far too long to wreak true destruction. You! Prepare to release them."

"As you wish, your highness," Pádraig bowed his head. "What about Granuaile and Lonán?"

"Worry not. We will deal with them soon enough."

The scáithír saluted the wizard with his fist to his left breast. Taranis smirked at the entire group. "The time for hiding in shadows has ended at last. War is coming to Denú."

The sisters grinned.

**

Dermot and Brian had gone strolling together less than a few hours before their initiation ceremony would begin. They stopped beside the stream's edge not far from the cave, listening to the trees, crickets, frogs, and few birds who had not yet returned to their nests.

"Lovely," Brian said. "Saershe says it's a good omen, a red evening sky."

"I know. It's a belief held by those of the sea," Dermot said. His face fell. Remembrances of his parents and recent events overcame him again, and he sighed.

Together they peered down into the placid stream water. Dermot barely recognized the reflections gazing back at them. He stroked his chin, now covered with stubble.

"You just reminded me of my dream," Dermot said.

"You mean the one you had back home?" Brian said, rubbing his neck. "Please, let's not talk about it."

"No, not that dream. I mean the one I had last night."

Brian paused. "Oh?"

"Yes. In it, I was walking alone at night. By the sea perhaps, I don't know, whereupon I encountered this maiden. She was around my age maybe. I distinctly remember her long, flaming red hair.

"Anyway, she gave me a strange smile. She said my name, but I didn't recognize her. I asked her who she was. Then, she sprinted away. I chased her, begging her to tell me her name. And that's where the dream ended."

Dermot noticed his brother grinning. He grinned

back, shaking his head. "I'm never going to hear the end of this, am I, Brian?"

"Maybe," Brian said.

They both laughed. Brian's face however soon turned grave and Dermot asked what was troubling him.

"Do you think we'll ever see Da again?" Brian asked. "I mean, as he used to be?"

Dermot paused. "I can't guarantee anything, little brother. We've got a long road of trials ahead of us. Who can say where they will lead? But, I suppose so long as we stick together, retain an open mind, and adapt, like Iorwerth said, we can endure, and rescue our father."

"Now you're sounding more like him."

"Aye." Dermot chuckled again, "I guess I am."

The boys stopped and looked into each other's eyes, saying not a word. Spontaneously, they hugged one another. It was a true, brotherly hug. It may have lasted only a few seconds or maybe several. Dermot didn't know nor care. He knew somehow that Brian felt the same way.

"Come on," Dermot said. He put his arm around Brian, patting his shoulder. The younger lad sniffled.

"You know, I think you'd enjoy climbing trees. Perhaps I'll teach you," Dermot said.

Brian choked back a bark of laughter, shaking Dermot's arm away. Soon, they were both laughing.

The two brothers walked slowly onward.

END OF BOOK I

Pronunciation Guide

People

Aengus	*AYNG-guhs*
Brian	*BRIE-in*
Caomh	*KEEV*
Ciara	*KEER-uh*
Dermot	*DUR-muht*
Éibhir	*EE-vur*
Eigyr	*EYE-jur*
Fáelán	*FIE-lahn*
Ferghus	*FUR-guhs*
Granuaile	*GRAHN-yoo-wayl*
Haf	*HAHV*
Iorwerth	*YAWR-wehrth*
Keane	*KEEN*
Lonán	*LOH-nahn*
Lúg	*LOOG*
Maeve	*MAYV*
Myf	*MIHF*
Neasa	*NEH-suh*
Olwen	*OL-wen*
Oona	*OOH-nuh*
Pádraig	*PAH-drig*
Ruairí	*ROR-ee*
Saershe	*SAIR-shuh*
Taranis	*TAIR-ahn-is*
Torin	*TOR-in*
Vannora	*vah-NOR-uh*
Yseult	*IS-olt*

Places

Ámhen	*AW-wen*
Caemoch	*KAY-mawk*
Crandáir	*CRAN-dar*
Denaloin	*DEH-nuh-lawn*
Denuan	*DEH-noo-in*
Denú	*DEH-noo*
Emerin	*EH-mur-in*
Fianúa	*fee-AN-oo-uh*
Glascoil	*GLAS-cawl*
Harlíeo	*HAR-lee-oh*
Llyrean	*LEER-ee-in*
Magh-Tuira	*MAHGH-TUR-uh*
Núinna	*NOO-ih-nuh*
Oísein	*ee-SHEN*
Raiph	*RAYF*
Úaene	*oo-AYN*
Wykúm	*WIE-koom*

Others

Blackwort	*BLAK-wort*
Dríacht	*DREE-ahkt*
Dríadór	*DREE-uh-DOR*
Eyrie	*AIR-ee*
Fí-fá	*FEE-fah*
Gryphon	*GRIH-fin*
Knitbone	*KNIT-bohn*
Mairág	*MAHR-ahg*
Mairágh	*MAHR-ahgh*

Rosin	*ROH-sheen*
Sagart	*SAH-gurt*
Saínchí	*SAH-nuh-CHEE*
Scáithír	*SKAH-theer*
Shillelagh	*Shih-LAY-lee*
Wortcunning	*WORT-kuhn-ing*
Woundwort	*WOOND-wort*

About the Author

Andrew McDowell has known he wanted to be a writer since he was a teenager. His novel *Mystical Greenwood* was inspired by his love of fantasy and the environment. He has also written poetry and creative non-fiction. To learn more about him and his work, visit his website at https://andrewmcdowellauthor.com/

CPSIA information can be obtained
at www.ICGtesting.com
Printed in the USA
BVHW03s0950220218
508839BV00001BA/1/P